FRAGMENTS OF GRACE

A MEDIEVAL ROMANCE NOVEL
PREQUEL TO THE DRAGONBLADE TRILOGY

BY KATHRYN LE VEQUE

KATHRYN LE VEQUE NOVELS

Contemporary Romance:

Kathlyn Trent/Marcus Burton Series:
Valley of the Shadow
The Eden Factor
Canyon of the Sphinx

The American Heroes Series:
Resurrection
Fires of Autumn
Evenshade

Sea of Dreams
Purgatory

Other Contemporary Romance:
Lady of Heaven
Darkling, I Listen

Multi-author Collections/Anthologies:
With Dreams Only of You (USA Today bestseller)
Sirens of the Northern Seas (Viking romance)

Note: All Kathryn's novels are designed to be read as stand-alones, although many have cross-over characters or cross-over family groups. Novels that are grouped together have related characters or family groups.

Series are clearly marked. All series contain the same characters or family groups except the American Heroes Series, which is an anthology with unrelated characters.

There is NO particular chronological order for any of the novels because they can all be read as stand-alones, even the series.

For more information, find it in **A Reader's Guide to the Medieval World of Le Veque.**

TABLE OF CONTENTS

CHAPTER ONE

Pendragon Castle, Cumbria
Year of Our Lord 1291 A.D.

"**K**EIR, YOU MUST not!"

A big knight with bloody, well-used armor was standing in his way, blocking him from proceeding up the stairs. They were narrow, steep steps that Keir knew extremely well, considering this was his castle. Right now, his closest friend stood between him and what was at the top of the steps. Keir St. Héver was so far gone with anguish and panic that he lashed out a massive fist, striking the knight in the jaw and sending him in to the wall. Keir tried to shove his way past the man but the knight wouldn't budge. He grabbed Keir as he attempted to push past.

"Nay," the knight breathed, his cornflower blue eyes intense. "Keir, please no. You must not…."

Keir roared with frustration, shoving past, scrambling up the stairs now on his hands and knees because Michael of Pembury would not let him go. Michael held on to Keir's legs, trying to keep the man from seeing what was at the top of the stairs. But Keir would not be stopped – he kicked at Michael, his closest friend, a man who was only trying to protect him.

God help him, Keir knew that. He knew that Michael was only trying to spare him. But he had to see for himself what Michael had seen, what a few of his soldiers had seen, when they had finally retaken Keir's castle and went in search of his young family. His wife and two small children had been in the castle when it had been breached by an envious and vicious neighbor. The man had waited until Keir had taken more than half his army on a mission to a neighboring fiefdom before acting on his jealousy.

Word had reached Keir of the betrayal and he had made haste to return to Pendragon Castle, his garrison, only to discover the castle in a state of chaos. Smoke hung in the air from the burnt portcullis, a twisted charred wreck as a tide of enemy soldiers flooded the bailey and the keep. Keir and his men had fought their way into the bailey, realizing that the remaining men he had left behind were dead or dying, having been murdered and burned by the invaders. The keep, too, was filled with the enemy, looting it of everything Keir had worked so hard to accumulate.

But the loss of possessions didn't bother him. It was his family he was concerned with, his wife Madeleine and their two small children, daughter Frances and son Merritt. He had left them here, buttoned up in Pendragon's solid keep, protected until his return. But those plans had horrifically turned on him and as he ran for the keep, it was all he could do to keep his panic in check. He knew that if his emotions consumed him, he would be no good to his family. He had to save them.

Pembury had made it into the keep before Keir did, racing up the narrow spiral stairs that could be so treacherous, until he reached the top floor where the family's chambers were. He was horrified to see both chambers had been breached, twisted wreckage of doors, and further horrified to see what lay inside. He had stared at the sight, hardly believing what he was seeing, before heading back down the stairs to head Keir off. He didn't want the man to see what he had. No man should see such visions of hell.

But Keir would not be stopped. He was crawling up the stairs now because Pembury was hanging on to his legs, refusing to let him go any further. Keir kicked at Michael, struggling to dislodge him, losing the battle to his panic in the process. He began to sob heavily as he clawed his way up the stairs. Hanging on to his legs, Michael released sobs of his own. The pain was too great for them both. What Michael had seen,

Keir had already surmised. He knew what was up there.

Keir was a powerful man, unnaturally powerful as he dug his gloved fingers into the stone, one step at a time, struggling up the stairs even as Michael tried to stop him. He could see the landing now and two open chamber doors, the smell of smoke and death filling his nostrils. He could hardly see through his tears or breathe through his sobs, but he had to see what Michael was trying so hard to prevent him from seeing. *Just one more step… and one more….*

Keir was nearly to the top of his hard-fought climb when he paused long enough to kick Michael in the face and send the man reeling off him. Scrambling to his feet, Keir managed to stagger to the top of the steps, thrusting himself inside the master's chambers, his ice-blue eyes searching for his wife and children. It was a relatively small chamber so it wasn't difficult to assess the situation of the entire room in an instant. And then, he saw it, lurking through the smoke like a macabre vision from the darkest depths of a nightmare. The sight sent him back to his knees again.

He just sat there on his knees, weeping pitifully at the horror before him. The strongest man in Cumbria, a man with a reputation for might and fairness and intelligence, was reduced to sobbing rubble. Keir St. Héver stared at the body of his wife as she lay crumpled against the wall, smoldering in the corner with the body of a small child. Keir fell forward, ending up on his hands and knees, crawling towards the smoking ruins of the people he had loved best in the world. The heavy, oily smell of burning flesh filled the chamber.

He fell forward onto his belly, reaching out a hand to grasp Madeleine's foot. He was sobbing so heavily that he ended up vomiting, spewing the contents of his stomach across the wooden floor. The bed behind him had been half-burned as had a portion of the floor, now black with soot and char. Whoever had killed his wife and child had tried to burn down the room as well. Keir pushed himself up and went to his wife, trying to take her in his arms but she was stiff and smoking. He remembered her as sweet and soft. Anguish overwhelmed him.

Madeleine's face had been untouched by the flames but her lovely dark hair had been singed off. He tried to hold her, to tell her how sorry he was and how much he loved her, but his grief swamped him and he could not speak. He could only cry. It was then that he took a closer look at the little body wrapped up in Madeleine's lap. Little Frances was fused to her mother's flesh.

As Keir sat on the floor with the corpses in his arms, Pembury reached the top of the steps and stood in the doorway, watching the unbearable scene. He was devastated at the sight, feeling Keir's pain down to his very bones, but as he watched the display, it began to occur to him that one of the children was missing. If Keir's other child was still alive somewhere, Michael was going to find him. With renewed vigor, Pembury fled the room in search.

He hunted well into the day and on into the night, but there was no sign of Keir's two year old son. Eventually, Michael returned to the chamber in the keep, that chamber of horrors, where Keir was still sitting with his dead wife and daughter in his arms. He had stopped weeping and now sat against the wall like a statue with the two of them clutched up against him. It was a pathetic and harrowing sight. It took Michael, two other knights and three soldiers to pry Keir away from his family. Even then, Keir went mad. Michael and another knight, Sir Lucan de Velt, were forced to restrain Keir so he would not hurt himself. The man was bent on suicide, lost to a world of grief that no one could fathom.

After that, something was dead in the man, something that had died the moment his wife and daughter had. The only thing that kept him going was the fact that his son had not yet been found. Somehow, some way, Merritt St. HÉver was out there. He was convinced the boy had survived, an inherent belief that fed his heart and soul and mind. He knew his son was alive, waiting for his father to come for him.

The question remained… where was he?

CHAPTER TWO

Three years later, September 1294 A.D.
The siege of Exelby Castle

"YOU HAVE YOUR orders, St. Héver," an older, much muddied warrior snapped at Keir. "Get moving."

Keir's jaw ticked but it was difficult to see beneath his wet and dirty hauberk. He said nothing in response, knowing his liege knew how he felt but disregarding his feelings completely. They had a job to do.

It had been raining heavily for three days, turning the ground in and around Exelby Castle into a quagmire of putrid muck. The army from Aysgarth Castle, seat of Baron Coverdale, was well acquainted with the mud and its detriment to a successful siege. The baron's powerful army could not move their five big siege engines into position because the mud was so thick, so the archers had taken to shooting heavily oiled projectiles over the wall in the hopes that they would burn long enough in the heavy rain to do some damage. This madness had gone on for two long days.

Keir had charge of the portcullis and the great iron and wooden grate had been heavily bombarded by flame, followed by the battering ram to twist the heated iron. Keir was methodical and skilled in his approach and made sure to keep the enemy soldiers on the battlements above the gate out of range by regular barrages from the archers. Over the course of the two days, wild wind and driving rain, Keir and his men were able to bend the portcullis enough so that two men at a time could squeeze through, and that was exactly what Baron Coverdale had in mind.

By dawn of the third day, the castle was finally breached. Now,

Coverdale was shouting orders to Keir who was extremely reluctant to do as he was told. But Baron Coverdale, Lord Byron de Tiegh, was in no mood for disobedient knights. He was ready to be finished with this obligatory support of Exelby and return home to a warm fire and his young wife with her big, warm breasts.

"Take Pembury and de Velt with you," Coverdale barked again, scratching at his dirty, wet scalp before pulling his hauberk back on. "Get inside and get those women or Lord de Geld will lose his entire family. Of all people, surely you can understand what it means to face the loss of one's family, St. Héver."

It was a tactless remark, one that had Keir's unusually cool temper rising. He felt disgusted and sick. Coverdale was a good commander but an insensitive man. Frustrated but driven by his sense of duty, Keir stormed off with Pembury and de Velt following, marching across the muck, puddles of urine and rivers of blood, until he came within range of the gatehouse. Keir's men were already gathered there, all one hundred and nine of them, awaiting direction from their liege.

Keir reached his men, standing beneath a pair of denuded oak trees, and bellowed orders to them, courtesy of Coverdale. They were to breach the keep and find Lord de Geld's wife and two daughters. De Geld was the lord of Exelby, his castle having been attacked and overrun in nearly the same situation that Pendragon had been those years ago. A neighboring war lord, covetous of de Geld's very rich castle and lands, had waited until the old man was away on business before laying siege and conquering. Coverdale, an old friend of de Geld's, had been tasked with regaining the fortress.

Infuriated and exhausted, St. Héver was the first man through the twisted wreckage of the portcullis. He was immediately set upon by defenders but Keir had the advantage of tremendous size, strength and height. He was moderately tall, but the sheer breadth and circumference of his arms and chest made him a man above men. As he plowed his way through the gatehouse, he used his sword and fists to drive away attackers. Pembury and de Velt were right behind him, powerful and skilled men in their own right.

Miraculously, they made it through the gate house without injury. Considering those who held the castle were using the murder holes in the gatehouse entry to their advantage, it was something of a feat. Bursting into the cluttered and muddy bailey, which was oddly empty, Keir directed more than half of his men to take the walls while he took another twenty men with him and headed towards the keep.

They fought their way through enemy soldiers, having suddenly appeared from the interior of the keep. The soldiers came rushing down at them from the keep entry, down the narrow wooden retractable stairs that were half-burned, and Keir found himself slugging men in the face and throwing them over the railing.

Because the stairs were so precarious, they could only mount them in single file and Keir was at the head, taking the brunt of the warriors coming at them. At one point, an enemy soldier managed to send him off-balance and he gripped the railing, almost falling fifteen or so feet down to the muddy bailey, but he managed to hold on to the broken railing even in the wet rain that was making everything dangerously slippery. Pembury, a mountain of a man with enormous fists, pushed forward and took the lead, throwing men aside with his colossal strength. De Velt pulled Keir away from the edge and steadied him and the three knights, along with their men-at-arms, continued up the stairs and eventually into the keep.

As Keir slugged men with his big fists and fought off broadswords that were flying at him, he let his rage and frustration get the better of him. He didn't want to be here in the midst of this stupid skirmish and he certainly didn't want to be tasked with rescuing women. He didn't want to rescue anyone. He wanted to get out of this mess and return to Pendragon and resume his patrols for Coverdale. A siege is the last thing he wanted to participate in, much less be charged with. As he plowed his way into the keep and met with more violent resistance, he could only think one thing.

Damn Coverdale, he hissed to himself. *Damn the man to hell.*

ᏟᏃ

SHE WAS WAITING for them.

Braced in the large bedchamber at the top of Exelby's towering keep, she was waiting with an enormous piece of wood in her hands, the only weapon they could find in the room. It was her parents' chamber, a luxurious place with fine silks, furniture and under normal circumstances, a warm fire, but this day saw the chamber something of a gloomy and fearful place.

Chloë de Geld could hear men on the other side of the chamber door. They had been attempting to open it for the better part of two days but the panel was made from heavy oak reinforced with strips of iron, bolted together so that it formed a sort of net. The enemy had tried to burn away part of the door but it was so dense and old that it simply smoldered and glowed, falling away piece by piece and filling the chamber with a thin layer of smoke that hung near the ceiling. Yet even when the door burned away, the strips of iron would hold fast and would not allow the door to be opened. At least, that was the theory. Up until today, the theory had never been tested.

So Chloë stood against the wall near the door, club held at the ready and struggling to keep her sister calm. Cassandra was the skittish sort, like their father, whereas Chloë was calm and composed, like their mother. Even now, Lady Blanche de Geld sat in the corner and worked her needle and thread against an elaborately embroidered piece of linen, as cool as a lazy cat on a warm summer day.

Chloë stood near the door, preparing to beat to death anyone who entered the chamber and wondering if her mother even understood what was happening. There was calm composure and then there was pure apathy. Chloë had to shake her head at her mother, wondering which one it really was.

The door panel suddenly shook heavily, as if something had been thrown against it. Chloë and Cassandra shrieked with fear while their mother barely looked up from her needlework. The door rattled again and a huge chunk of it fell away, revealing those on both sides of the door. Gloved fingers began to poke through the iron grate, moving for the lock, and Chloë began clubbing the fingers with wild abandon.

Someone on the opposite side of the door grunted with pain as his fingers were smacked. He tried to thrust his fingers through again and Chloë bashed his fingers furiously.

"Nay!" she shrieked, punctuating each word with a smack from the club. "Nay, nay, *nay!*"

"Lady!" the knight on the other side of the door roared. "Cease! I am here to rescue you!"

Chloë didn't believe him for a moment. More fingers were coming through the grate and she smashed at them as if killing ugly spiders on the wall. *Smack, smack, smack!*

"Nay!" she barked. "Go away!"

As Chloë bashed at the grate with her club, convinced that she was the only thing that stood between her family and complete obliteration, Keir was tired of getting his fingers smashed so he shoved de Velt forward.

"Open the door," he growled.

Lucan looked at him as if he were mad. "Nay, *you* open the door. I do not want my fingers broken."

Frustrated, Keir grabbed him by the neck as Pembury charged at the door, shoving them both out of the way. He grabbed at the iron grate and got his fingers smashed for his trouble. He drew his hands back, shaking out his bashed fingers.

"Foolish wench," he yelled at Chloë. "That bloody well hurt."

On the other side of the blackened iron, Chloë was unrepentant. "Touch this door again and I will pound your fingers into dust."

Michael stared at her in disbelief; he could see a portion of her face through the grate and long, shimmering sheets of deep red hair. One big brown eye was gazing back at him.

"Do you not understand that we are trying to save you?" he asked, incredulous.

On the opposite side of the door, Chloë shook her head, gripping the club with white knuckles. "You are attempting to coerce me into opening this door," she spat. "I am not so idiotic that I would believe you."

"But it is true."

"Liar!"

Michael put his hands on his hips, looking to Keir. "Well?" he lifted a frustrated hand at the half-demolished door. "What do you want to do?"

Keir's frustration was driven beyond endurance. He was struggling to accomplish an unwanted assignment and meeting with great resistance. It would have been extremely easy to walk away and tell Coverdale that the women were beyond recovery. But he gave it one last try. He'd come this far. Moreover, he wasn't accustomed to failure and to walk away would mean surrender. He moved to the grate, shoving Michael aside.

"Listen to me and listen well," he growled to the brown eye staring back at him. "My name is Keir St. Héver and I have been battling to free Exelby for the better part of two days. We have chased off, killed or captured most of the fools who invaded your castle and the last thing I need is a foolish wench resisting my efforts to help her. I can just as easily walk away and leave you here to rot if that is your wish."

"Walk away, then! We do not need or want your help!"

Keir clenched his teeth, struggling with his temper. "You are behaving most ungratefully towards men who have risked their lives to save you."

As Keir spoke, Lucan moved up on his right side and, with stealth, reached for the iron grate. As Keir held the frightened lady's attention, Lucan managed to get his fingers through the grate with great care and carefully lift the bolt. Keir was barely finished with what he had to say when Lucan suddenly threw his big shoulder into the door and the panel popped open.

Cassandra screamed as Chloë began swinging the club with all her might. She caught Lucan on the back of the head, sending the man to the ground.

Keir charged in and made a swipe for the weapon, but Chloë was fast and she darted out of his range, jumping on the fluffy bed in the middle of the chamber and swinging the club with all her might. Keir put up an arm to deflect the blow but she still managed to clip not only his elbow but his head.

Furious, Keir grabbed the club from her hand and tossed it away, hitting Pembury in the process. As Michael grunted from the blow to his chest, Keir leapt onto the bed as Chloë tried to jump to the floor. He caught her around the waist, a wisp of a woman with a head full of intense red hair that tumbled to her knees. The straight, silky strands were over them both as he lost his balance and fell back onto the straw-stuffed bed. In fact, there was hair in his mouth and all over his face as he struggled to get hold of Chloë as she fought for her life.

"Lady," he grunted as she twisted and fought. "Cease your struggles. I swear that you will come to no harm. We serve Lord Coverdale and have come to rescue you."

Chloë was in a world of panic. The knight that had her was easily three times her size and she managed to turn in his arms, throwing a hand up into the open faceplate of his visor. Hit in the face by her fist, Keir did nothing more than grunt. He tried to stand up with the snarling wildcat in his grip but he ended up tripping on her surcoat and they both fell to the floor.

Keir fell on top of Chloë, who ended up on her back. It was a hard fall that momentarily stunned her. Moreover, Keir was an enormous man and his full weight came down on her, armor and all. Suddenly, they were in a very intimate position and when Chloë regained her senses, she went mad, beating at his head and shoulders with her little fists.

"Get off me!" she howled. "You foul beast, get *off!*"

Keir was trying to capture the fifty slapping hands that were flying at his face from all directions. He managed to capture one only to be struck by another. Chloë began gouging at his eyes and he closed them both, pressing his face into her chest as he grabbed for that one final hand in the darkness. Beneath him, the lady's body was soft and supple, but he wasn't thinking about that. He was thinking about trying not to go blind from her frantic fingers.

"Cease!" he finally roared as he captured the last errant hand. He pinned her arms on either side of her slender body, daring to open his eyes and gaze down into her hair-covered face. "Did you not understand me? We are here to rescue you. We are not here to harm you in any way but from the way you are fighting, it will more than likely be me who ends up injured."

Chloë wasn't ready to surrender to the strange knight with the smooth, deep voice. "Get *off*," she commanded.

"Not until you stop fighting me. I have no desire to be maimed by a foolish girl."

"I am not foolish," she grunted as she tried to dislodge him.

He watched her face contort with effort. "You are indeed foolish when you fight against someone who is attempting to help you."

She looked at him, baring her straight white teeth. "I do not know you. You could be lying for all I know, an enemy with the devil's tongue."

"Yet I am not," he said as he cocked an eyebrow at her. "I told you who I am – I am Keir St. Héver, a much decorated warrior who has served Edward Longshanks in the wars in Wales. I am an honorable knight from a long line of honorable knights and your refusal to believe my word is a direct insult. I do not lie and I certainly would not lie to a lady. In any case, you are trapped by a man who is a good deal larger and stronger than you are so if I were you, I would no longer resist. It is futile."

Chloë's struggle ground to a halt and she gazed up at Keir with baleful eyes. He could only see two big brown orbs through the mess of long red hair that was all over them both. Keir could see the turmoil in the brown depths, swirling like a maelstrom, but in that same thought, it occurred to him that they were the most beautiful eyes he had ever seen. The thought startled him.

"Do you understand what I have told you?" he asked again, somewhat less hostile, wondering why he was so mesmerized by those eyes.

Chloë nodded unsteadily. "Are you going to strike me again?" he asked.

She shook her head. Keir immediately let go of her arms and, out of necessity, began pulling strands of long red hair out of his mail so he could stand up and not pull hair from her scalp. Chloë watched him with some fear as he pushed himself off of her. Then he took her by the wrist and pulled her to her feet.

Now that the atmosphere was somewhat calmer and the women realized that the enemy had not captured them after two days of hell, Chloë seemed rather weak and unsteady. It was as if the fight had taken everything out of her. She slumped against the wall, exhaling heavily as she pushed her hair from her face and tried to smooth it down. The long, luxurious red hair was her pride and joy, something she was almost as well known for in the shire as her beauty. To those in West Yorkshire, Chloë de Geld's radiance was the stuff of legends.

It was something that had not escaped Keir's notice, try as he might. He was still frustrated, angry and exhausted, but somewhere in the mix, he realized that he had interest in the lady's fine looks. Rescuing a hag would have been a duty but rescuing an angel was something entirely different. He should have had the same opinion for either, but the truth was most men would prefer to associate with a lovely young lady to an old haggard one. It was beastly but true.

The lady in front of him was average in height but slender in build, with large soft breasts that he had felt against him when he had fallen on top of her. Even through the mail and layers of tunics, he had felt them. Her skin was pale, like cream, and she had a perfectly formed face with porcelain skin and full pink lips. But the eyes that gazed back at him had his attention, a shade of brown that was as deep and brilliant as a gemstone. They were big and beautiful. Keir watched the woman as she struggled to recover her composure.

"What is your name?" he finally asked.

She looked up at him. "I am the Lady Chloë de Geld," she murmured in a sweet, silky voice. "My father is Anton de Geld, Baron Kirklington. This is my mother, the Lady Blanche, and my sister, the Lady Cassandra."

Chloë. It was all Keir heard. The rest sounded like mumble after that – *I am the Lady Chloë blah, blah, blah.* He snapped his fingers at Pembury and de Velt, indicating that each man take a lady in hand, and the two of them rushed to see who would be the one to escort the Lady Cassandra, a pretty blond with her sister's big brown eyes. Michael was a shade faster than Lucan, collecting the lady by the elbow and sneering at Lucan over the top of her head.

Truth was, Pembury was a massive man of great power and even Lucan de Velt, a man of considering strength and skill himself, would not voluntarily tangle with him. So he grudgingly took charge of the mother, an older woman who had sat in the corner doing her needlework while a battle raged on around her. During the entire time Chloë and Keir had scuffled, the woman hadn't moved.

Quietly, Lucan helped the old woman to stand, even helped her with her sewing, which he found a rather ridiculous hobby in the midst of a battle, and followed Pembury from the chamber. He even smacked the man in the back of the head when no one was looking.

With everyone gone and the noise from the fighting faded into nothingness, the chamber was suddenly very still. Chloë was still leaning against the wall, feeling weak and weary as Keir moved to the door, adjusting the helm on his head that she had so furiously smacked. As he fumbled with the hauberk beneath it, adjusting it, he turned to Chloë.

"Come along, my lady," he said quietly.

She looked up from where she had been staring the floor. "Where are you taking us?"

"That is for Lord Coverdale and your father to decide."

She sighed faintly and pushed herself up off the wall, looking around the room as if searching for something. "My father was in Darlington when all of this started," she murmured. "Is the castle badly damaged?"

Keir finished fiddling with his mail. "Badly enough," he told her. "It is not safe as it stands."

She looked at him and he noted the sad brown eyes. They were such lovely eyes, he thought, but just as quickly jolted himself from that line of thought. He'd thought it once before and that was forgivable, a natural reaction. But to think it twice was unnerving. It was too shocking and painful to even consider. He hadn't thought on a lovely woman since....

"Who attacked us?" Chloë asked.

Keir realized he was struggling not to feel something soft or compassionate for the woman. It was purely based on her beauty, he knew that, but he was feeling something warm nonetheless. He was furious at himself, sick to his stomach, realizing he was weak and foolish to think such things. It was ridiculous. Taking a deep breath, he labored to shake off both the foolishness and fatigue.

"They came from Sandhutton," he told her. "We believe Ingilby is involved."

Chloë's big brown eyes widened. "Baron Ingilby from Ripon?"

"The same."

Her pretty, shapely mouth popped open in both outrage and surprise. Then she closed her mouth and turned away, returning with distraction to her search of the room. Keir stood by the door, watching her, as she came across what she had apparently been searching for.

She shook out the cloak that had been wedged in behind her mother's sewing chair, silently moving for the door as she swung it around her slender shoulders. Keir didn't touch her as he preceded her from the room; not an elbow to take or an arm to hold. He was afraid of what would happen to his exhaustion-fed thoughts if he touched her again.

Just as they were passing through the doorway, past the twisted charred wreckage of the chamber door, Chloë suddenly came to a halt and looked at him.

"Did I hurt your fingers?" she asked.

She seemed rather dull and somber, not at all like the firebrand who had given him a fight moments before. He gazed steadily at her.

"Nay, lady, you did not."

She simply nodded, looking rather contrite. "I am sorry... well, if I hurt you," she turned around and headed towards the stairs. "You must understand that strange and violent men have been attempting to get into the chamber for the better part of two days."

He watched her luscious red head as it began to descend the stairs. "I would imagine you would not have made it easy for them if they had managed to breach the door."

In spite of her fatigue, Chloë smiled faintly. "A piece of wood is no match for a man with a sword."

Keir grunted in disagreement. "You underestimate yourself, lady," he said as they came to the landing on the third floor. "You are a formidable foe. My fingers can attest to that."

Her grin broadened and she turned to look at him. "You still managed to capture me."

Keir's heart beat strangely at the sight of her smile, as beautiful and shapely as the rest of her. He shrugged, fighting down the confusing feelings brewing. "Perhaps," he muttered. "But I almost lost an eye doing it."

That comment made her peer more closely at him, noting his ice blue eyes, so pale they were nearly white. "One of them is rather red," she admitted. "I am sorry if I injured your eyes."

Keir almost took a step back as she leaned in to get a better look at his eyes, a natural reaction when something perfect and awe-inspiring makes its presence known. Already, he was fearful of the woman, one who could stir feelings in his chest without even trying. He didn't want to have anything to do with her but on the other hand, in the few minutes he had known her, she had captured his attention no matter how resistant he was. It was an odd amalgamation of curiosity and fear.

"I am fine," he reiterated.

He directed her towards the next flight of stone spiral stairs, this one leading down to the entry level of the dark and smoky keep. Chloë took the lead once again, followed by Keir who was trying very hard not to look at her or touch her in any way.

"I have not seen you before," she made conversation with him, perhaps out of guilt for having nearly blinded the man. "My father and Lord Coverdale have been allies for years. Lord Coverdale visits often and I thought I had seen all of his knights."

Keir had to pick up the hem of her cloak so he wouldn't step on it. "I am a garrison commander for Coverdale," he told her. "Usually, I am at my post. I do not make Aysgarth Castle my home."

"Where is your post?" she looked at him, an innocent question.

He held up the edge of her cloak as she took the stairs. "Coverdale's garrison in Cumbria."

She nodded in understanding. "I see," she said as they reached the entry level. "Did he recall you to help regain my father's castle?"

Keir let go of the cloak, allowing himself to look her in the face. He could feel his palms start to sweat and his heartbeat pick up again at the sight.

"I was at Aysgarth already when one of your father's men came with the request to bear arms," he told her. "My presence here is purely by chance."

Chloë smiled. "Then we are most fortunate for your assistance, Sir Keir," she said. "I am sorry we had to meet under such strenuous circumstances but it was very nice to make your acquaintance. I hope that you do not hold the first few violent moments of our association against me."

Keir stared at her. She was sweet, intelligent and well spoken, something he found deeply attractive. She had such a sweet little voice, like the tinkle of tiny silver bells, and he swore he could have listened to that voice forever. As he opened his mouth to reply, he heard a roar off to his left and he turned to see a soldier he did not recognize charge from a shadowed alcove, a heavy broadsword leveled.

Keir grabbed Chloë and pulled her away from the door, shoving her back behind him as he unsheathed his sword. He brought the weapon up just as the soldier brought his blade down, and sparks flew as metal upon metal met in the darkness of the entry hall.

He was at a disadvantage with a lady to protect in a small space, but he made the best of it. Lashing out a massive boot, he kicked the man in the legs, sending him backwards, and went on the attack. Keir brought his blade down twice in heavy succession, eventually knocking the weapon from the hands of his weaker opponent. Then he grabbed the man by the head, pointing the tip of his razor-sharp blade at the man's neck.

"Mercy, milord, mercy," the soldier threw up his hands, begging. "Don't kill me!"

Keir was emotionless and professional. Simply from the man's rough pattern of speech, he realized that he wasn't an educated or particularly intelligent warrior. He was simply a servant, doing as he was told. A more experienced man would have given him a better fight. Keir tossed him to the floor and put an enormous boot on the man's neck.

"Who do you serve?" he asked.

The man could barely breathe. "I… I…."

The boot pressure grew stronger. "Answer me or I will end your life now."

The man was struggling. "In…gilby…."

Although they already knew as much, it was confirmation. Keir never took his eyes off his captive.

"What were your orders?"

The man was squirming, his face turning shades of red. "I…. don't…."

Keir put more pressure on the man's neck. "Your orders or you die."

"The… *goddess!*" the man croaked.

Keir cocked his head. "The goddess?" he repeated, confused. "Who is the goddess?"

Out of the shadows, they both heard the response.

"The goddess is me."

CHAPTER THREE

K EIR LOOKED TO the sound of the voice. Chloë was standing near the stairs where Keir had shoved her. She emerged from the shielding darkness, wrapped in the dusty brown cloak and looking rather ill. When she saw that Keir was looking at her, she met his gaze with some reluctance.

"It is me," she repeated softly. "That is what he calls me."

"Who calls you?" Keir asked, confused.

Chloë sighed faintly. "Baron Ingilby," she replied softly. "The man has been demanding my hand for two years but my father will not agree. Ingilby calls me the goddess. I suppose he was tired of the constant rejection and sought to take matters into his own hands."

Keir glanced at the soldier once more before returning his focus to Chloë. "Is that why he attacked Exelby?" he asked. "To get to you?"

Chloë appeared hesitant, remorseful. "It is as likely an answer as any."

"Do you want to marry him?"

She shook her head. "He is vile and arrogant. I want nothing to do with him but he cannot seem to understand that."

Keir held her gaze a moment longer before turning to the soldier and yanking the man to his feet. Keir snarled in his face.

"I will allow you to live to carry a message back to Ingilby," he growled. "You tell Ingilby that he shall never have the Lady Chloë or anything about her. She is beyond his reach and any further attempts to abduct or otherwise harass her will be personally answerable to me. Is that in any way unclear?"

The soldier was frightened, cowering in the face of the big knight.

"Who... who are you, m'lord?"

Keir dragged the man to the entry door and tossed him out. The soldier tumbled halfway down the wet stairs before catching himself. Keir stood on the landing, his ice blue eyes blazing at the man. The rain pounded down, dripping off his blond lashes.

"I am Keir St. Héver," he told him authoritatively. "I am a former captain to King Edward, now Guardian of the Coverdale Barony. I am the man that all men fear. You tell Ingilby that any more attempts against the Lady Chloë and her family, and I will come for him personally with the king's blessing."

The soldier slid down the remainder of the stairs and took off running. Keir watched the man go, noticing that Coverdale had control of the bailey now and there were pockets of prisoners being rounded up by Coverdale men. The bailey was a mess and piles of the dead were already being accumulated. It was still raining so it would be difficult to burn the dead. For now, all they could do was clean up and wait for the weather to clear.

Keir turned away from the savage bailey scene only to find Chloë standing directly behind him. She was so close that he had nearly walked into her. She had pulled the hood of the cloak over her luscious red hair, her big brown eyes moving over the horrific scene below.

The castle was upended, the entire place a mess of men, blood and war. It was a sobering sight. Keir watched her face a moment before reaching out to take her elbow. So much for resolving not to touch her – considering he had just appointed himself her personal protector, there wasn't much point in maintaining a distance from her.

"Come along, my lady," he said quietly.

She planted her feet and grabbed his enormous hand with both of her soft, small ones. Her expression was open and pleading.

"What you told that soldier," she said, lifting her shoulders as if searching for the correct words. "Thank you for your sense of chivalry and duty, but it will more than likely do no good. He has been threatened before."

Keir smiled faintly, wearily. "Perhaps," he said. "But he has not been threatened by me. If the man makes another move against you, I will show up on his doorstep and it will not be pleasant."

Her lovely brow furrowed and she grinned simply because he was. "Although I appreciate your gallantry, you do not need to do that," she told him. "My father has his own men to protect me."

He cocked an eyebrow, his smile fading. "A lot of good they did," he jabbed a finger at the broken bailey. "If Ingilby is truly intent on abducting you, we have seen what the man is capable of. He does not fear your father or those who would provide you with protection."

Chloë looked around the yard, seeing her father's soldiers mingled among the dead. She lowered her gaze, shutting her eyes against the ghastly sight.

"So much waste," she muttered with guilt, letting go of his hand. "Ingilby is bold and arrogant but I did not believe him capable of this. He waited until my father left Exelby with a contingent of men before moving to attack. He waited until we were weak."

Keir didn't say any more, fearful that he might sound too interested in assuming the lady's protection. He'd already said far too much. Part of him was the gallant man who would protect the weaker sex, but part of him wanted to return to Pendragon Castle and away from this beautiful woman who seemed so capable of effortlessly captivating him.

In silence, he continued down the stairs, his arm held out in Chloë's direction as she followed so she could grab hold of something should she slip. The old wooden stairs were soaked with rain, slippery and unsteady.

Keir reached the bottom of the steps and plunged into several inches of deep, dark mud. In his heavy boots, he was well protected, but Chloë stopped at the bottom of the stairs, looking at all of the mud with some chagrin. Keir started to walk away, thinking she would follow, but quickly realizing she had not. He retraced his few steps back to her.

"Is something wrong, my lady?" he asked politely.

Chloë didn't want to be a bother but she also wasn't equipped to walk through the heavy mud. With great reluctance, she lifted up her cloak and stuck out a dainty foot.

"I only have my slippers on," she told him, showing him a small leather shoe. "If you will permit me, I will return to my chamber in the keep to see if my boots are still there. I will…."

He was already moving towards her, bending down to scoop her up into his arms. "The keep is cleaned out of most things," he told her, lifting her slight weight into his powerful arms. "We saw the looting when we fought our way in. I doubt your boots, or any of your other possessions, remain untouched."

Swept into his enormous grasp, Chloë wrapped her arms around his neck for support, gazing into his square-jawed, handsome face. Her heart sank at his words.

"Looting?" she repeated, disheartened. "But everything we own is in the keep – my clothes, my sister's clothes, our plate, our…."

"No longer," he interrupted her quietly. "I suspect Ingilby will take it in punishment for not having obtained a betrothal. He will consider it compensation."

"But I was never, at any time, pledged to the man. Why would he steal from us?"

"This I would not know. But he has."

With nothing more to say to that, Chloë remained silent as Keir carried her off across the great muddy bailey, past the mounds of dead men and the scores of wounded lined up against the wall to provide some protection against the rain.

Keir was passing through the gatehouse, crowded with wounded, when he realized that Chloë had buried her face in the crook of his neck, blocking her sight of the devastation a rejected suitor had caused. He could feel her hot breath against his jaw, her warmth against his chest. It had been years since he'd felt such a thing and he was repulsed and thrilled all at once. The last woman he had held like this had been brutally murdered. Keir still hadn't recovered from it. But Lady Chloë was awakening dormant emotions and it scared him to death.

Against his better judgment, he pulled her tighter.

cg

HE HAD A squarest jaw she had ever seen, set like granite. When he smiled, which had only been once, she'd caught a glimpse of a handsome smile only dreamt of in fantasies of foolish girls with too many thoughts of men on their minds. His lips peeled away in a smile to reveal straight white teeth and big dimples in each cheek. His nose was straight enough, unmarred, and his pale blue eyes were both icy and smoldering at the same time. It was a devastating and captivating combination for the feminine appetite.

As Chloë sat in a large tent with her mother and sister, she could see outside to where her father, the fat graying figure of Lord Coverdale, and several knights, including St. Hével, were gathered. The women had been given as much comfort as possible in a dry place with a scorching stove that burned smoky peat, and big cups of warmed wine. As Chloë sat with her sister and sipped wine, her mother resumed her sewing as if nothing in the world was amiss.

Chloë had been watching the activity outside when St. Hével had removed his helm and peeled back his hauberk, scratching his close-cropped blond hair that was wet with perspiration and rain. She could see the kinky texture, even at a distance. He was a tall man, taller than Coverdale and her father but not as tall as either of his two companions, the other knights that had escorted her mother and sister.

Still, the sheer size of the man was something to behold. The size of his arms, chest and hands were like nothing she had ever seen before and when he had carried her to the encampment, she had felt his power. The sensation had captured her curiosity and her interest.

So she sipped her wine and watched St. Hével as he engaged in deep and sometimes animated discussion with Coverdale and her father. The Coverdale encampment was filling up with soldiers returning from the cleanup of the castle and occasionally, groups of men and prisoners would block her view as she watched St. Hével in the distance. Eventually, her father broke away from the group of men and made his way to the tent where his wife and daughters were.

Anton de Geld was the son of a noble family, having achieved wealth through the breeding and sale of sheep. He wasn't a healthy man but he was bright. He had moments of weakness and foolery. As he entered the tent, Chloë rose from the small three legged stool she had been sitting on and offered it to her father. He took it gratefully.

"What will we do now, Father?" she asked, glancing out into the encampment again and noting that St. Héver was still standing there, his head bare to the falling rain as he listened to whatever Coverdale had to say. Her eyes were riveted to the man. "It seems that you had much to discuss with Lord Coverdale."

Anton ran a hand across his thinning gray hair. "Much indeed," he said. "This was Ingilby's work, Chloë. He came for you."

She could hear anger in her father's tone. "I know," she replied softly.

"This was a bold move, even for him."

"What will we do?"

Anton shrugged as he accepted a cup of warmed wine from Cassandra. "I will remain here to oversee the rebuild," he told her. "But I will send you and your sister and your mother with Coverdale. He has offered to house you and protect you until we can adequately repair Exelby, which may take some time."

Chloë wasn't entirely sure she wanted to leave her home but she understood her father's concerns. Looking at all of the wounded men, traversing across the muddy encampment, fed her sense of guilt. Everything had happened because of her, injury and death alike. She glanced up at the gray skies, feeling as sad and remorseful as the gloom above.

"Perhaps I should simply marry him and be done with it," she muttered. "I cannot stomach the men who have been put in harm's way because of me."

"It was not because of you," Anton could hear the self-pity in her voice. "What Ingilby wants is greater than you. He wants you, me, Exelby… everything. He is a greedy man that does not like to be denied his wishes."

Chloë gazed off across the compound again, her gaze falling on St. Hévér once more. The rain was starting to let up and pieces of blue sky were starting to appear, sending beams of sunlight onto the earth below. One beam fell directly on St. Hévér as he stood there with several of his men in continuing conversation. The sun lit him up, like God shining his holy light upon the man. Her thoughts lingered on him.

"What about Coverdale?" she wanted to know. "Does he realize that if I go to Aysgarth Castle, then his properties shall become Ingilby's target?"

Anton drank deeply of the warmed wine. "Ingilby will not find out where you have gone."

She could see Keir as the man broke out in a smile at something that had been said. In fact, all three of the big knights were laughing. But her eyes were only on Keir.

"Aye, he will," she sighed after a moment, shaking her head with regret. "One of Coverdale's men sent a message back to Ingilby and told the man that if he ever attempted to contact me again, then this knight would personally challenge him."

Anton looked up from his wine, surprised. "Who said this?"

Chloë's eyes were riveted to Keir. In fact, she realized even to think on his name gave her a warm feeling deep in her belly. She'd never known that kind of sensation before and wasn't hard pressed to admit she liked it.

"Keir St. Hévér," she replied.

Her father stood up, moving to where she was standing against the tent opening. "St. Hévér?" he repeated. "I was only just speaking with him. He did not mention such a thing to me."

"Perhaps he has forgotten already."

Anton's gaze moved across the muddy compound as well, spying Coverdale's knights still in a cluster where he had left them. His gaze settled on the enormous knight with the kinky blond hair and a jaw so square it was as if it were hewn from solid marble.

"Do you not recognize his name, Chloë?" he looked at his daughter.

Chloë shook her head. "Should I?"

Anton's gaze moved back to the busy, muddy encampment, lingering on the knights. "Keir St. Hëver is the garrison commander for Pendragon Castle, the gateway from Cumbria to Yorkshire," he told her. "Pendragon guards the Mallerstang dale, a valuable and much coveted pass. Coverdale is wildly wealthy from the tribute he collects from those who use the pass and it is a wealth much envied, especially by the Devils from Hell."

Chloë's brow furrowed. "*Devils* from Hell?"

Anton nodded. "That is what those from Hellbeck Castle are called," he said softly. "Surely you know of them."

Chloë was growing interested in her father's story. "I believe I do," she said. "I have heard of them. If I recall correctly, Lord Stain of Hellbeck Castle is akin to the Northumberland Grays."

Anton wriggled his eyebrows. "He is a disgraced kin. He confiscated Hellbeck Castle years ago through a siege against old Baron Asby and killed the old man, stealing his castle. Three years ago, he tried to confiscate Pendragon in the same fashion but was unsuccessful. St. Hëver's wife and daughter were killed in the siege."

Chloë's expression shifted, morphing in to one of sorrow as her eyes widened in realization. "I remember now," she breathed. "I heard about the siege of Pendragon and the death of the commander's wife. That was St. Hëver?"

Anton nodded slowly. "It was."

Chloë's gaze returned to the distant cluster of knights, her hand to her mouth in a shocked gesture. "God be merciful," she murmured. "The poor man."

Anton remembered the dark stories he had heard of that time from Coverdale. "He was so distraught that he could not even attend their burial," his voice grew quiet. "He was locked in the vault to keep him from killing himself. Then, when he recovered the shards of his sanity, he was useless for months. It was a full year before he could return to Pendragon. Coverdale told him he did not have to resume his post but St. Héver insisted."

Chloë was feeling a good deal of grief for the enormous knight. "I wonder why? I would have never returned to the place, not ever."

Anton's gaze lingered on St. Héver in the distance for a moment longer before turning away. "He would not leave because his young son was missing after the siege and presumably abducted by Stain's men, although they have denied it," Anton said as he reached the stool and sat wearily. "Perhaps he hopes that the lad will find his way home someday."

Chloë pondered that information for a moment before returning her attention to the knights in the distance. St. Héver's was a sad and tragic tale. By the time she turned around, however, the warriors had disbanded and the rain had stopped, the clouds parting to reveal a bright and colorful sunset.

Chloë stood in the open tent flap, watching the activity of the encampment before her gaze moved to the wet, smoldering structure of Exelby. Her family had survived the siege and they had been fortunate. It would have been bad enough to lose her sister or mother, but to have lost her husband or children… nay. She could not imagine what pain St. Héver must have experienced.

Chloë turned away from the tent flap, returning to her family as a servant brought bread and more wine. Even as she sat at her father's feet, listening to his version on how brave he was in the recapture of his castle, her mind kept wandering to the handsome knight with the ice blue eyes. She was coming to feel truly sorry for having bashed his fingers and gouged at his eyes when he had tried to rescue her from the chamber in the keep, but in fairness, she truly hadn't known the man or his intentions. The name hadn't meant anything to her, not until her father mentioned the story behind it. Now, she wished she hadn't been so brutal to the man.

A man who had been struck by the Devils from Hell.

CHAPTER FOUR

"WHO TOLD YOU such things?" Baron Ingilby was screaming. "Who has dared to threaten me?"

The dirty, bloody and exhausted soldier cowered in the great hall of Ripley Castle, a tall and proud bastion nestled in the Ripon dale of Yorkshire. The baron's army was returning from the siege of Exelby Castle, empty-handed and defeated, exhausted like the walking dead, and their liege was not a happy man. He was not a warrior and did not attend battles personally. He had a fairly strong army to do that. But their defeat at Exelby had him raging, and the message returned to him by a cringing soldier had sent him over the edge of fury.

"Keir St. Héver, my lord," the soldier told him, spittle dripping from his lips as he trembled in fear. "He said that you will not have any part of Lady Chloë or you shall answer to him personally."

The veins on Ingilby's temples throbbed. He was an older man with blond hair, graying at the temples, and not unhandsome. He was a man of leisure, pursuing women, fine wines, and high stakes gambling games. In fact, he had met Chloë de Geld quite by chance, on the road traveling south from one of his gambling games while Chloë and her family were traveling north, and was immediately taken with the luscious redhead. He had spent two years trying to negotiate for her hand always to end in refusal. His patience ran thin a week ago and he sent his army to take his bride by force, a plan that was not successful.

To be honest, he didn't think it would be. Exelby was well fortified but he had hoped it would convey the seriousness of his intentions to Anton de Geld. To hear that his army had not been successful did not particularly surprise him but to hear that a threat had been sent his way was.

"Who is Keir St. Hévér?" he demanded. "I have not heard of this lord. Is he an ally of de Geld?"

The soldier wiped at his nose with a dirty hand. "A commander for Lord Coverdale, my lord," the man said. "Lord de Geld called upon his ally to aid during the siege."

Ingilby cocked an eyebrow. "Coverdale was there?"

The soldier nodded. "He was, my lord."

"How do you know it was him?"

"He was not shy in announcing his presence," the soldier replied. "He spent two days expelling your army from Exelby. St. Hévér retook the keep and issued you a warning."

Ingilby was calming after his initial outburst, curiosity over a threat from the mysterious knight catching his attention. The addition of Coverdale also had his attention, for Coverdale was a powerful warlord with three major castles from Cumbria to North Yorkshire. Ingilby had never had dealings with the man before but he knew of his reputation. Everyone in North England did. He was heavily allied with the Earl of Carlisle and the Earl of Cumbria. Something about Coverdale's save of Exelby Castle simply didn't sit right.

"Tell me exactly what St. Hévér said to you," Ingilby commanded his soldier. "Word for word, I would hear it again."

The soldier, weary, took a deep breath as he thought on the big knight's words. "He told me his name, my lord," he said. "He told me that he was a former captain to King Edward and now Guardian of the Coverdale Barony. He said he was the man that all men fear. He told me to tell you that any further attempts against the Lady Chloë and her family and he will come for you personally with the king's blessing."

Ingilby digested the statement. He rubbed at the stubble on his chin and began to pace thoughtfully. "Where was the lady when he told you this?"

"She was under his protection, my lord."

Ingilby lifted an eyebrow, "Hmpf," he snorted. "I would suspect that more than likely, he said it simply to impress her. Perhaps he wants her for himself."

"It is a possibility, my lord. She is a beautiful woman."

Ingilby looked at him, annoyed. "Too beautiful for a knight with a big mouth and bold threats," he growled. "Find out what you can about this knight, this Keir St. Héver. We know he serves Coverdale but he mentioned he used to serve the king. See if you can find someone who knows about him. Find out why he left the king. Find out why he feels brave enough that he may issue a threat to me."

"And then what, my lord?"

Ingilby shrugged lazily, his gaze moving to the windows of his solar that overlooked the bailey. He could see his weary and beaten men returning.

"I will know when I find out more about him," he muttered. "No man stands between me and my wants. St. Héver and Coverdale will learn the hard way."

The soldier fled, leaving Ingilby to his twisted and delusional thoughts. The more he thought on the mysterious and audacious Keir St. Héver, the more obsessed he became.

CB

"I HAD NOT heard that the de Geld daughters were such beauties," Lucan said. "Had I known, I might have considered courting the redhead. I still might."

This morning, after the three straight days of rain, had dawned bright and spectacular. The land was green, the hills bright like emeralds glittering under the sun. The army from Aysgarth Castle was returning home along muddy roads and bright skies, bringing with them three members of the de Geld family.

Keir was at the head of the column, riding his big brown charger with the hairy white legs. Mud splashed up as the horses moved along the road, kicking up rocks and debris left behind by the storm.

Keir had been listening to Lucan ramble on about Chloë and Cassandra de Geld, pitting the pretty blond against the spectacular redhead. When he realized that Pembury growled at him every time he brought up the blond, his attention veered towards the redhead and that's where it had remained for the last half hour. Keir had finally had enough.

"Lucan," he snapped. "Head to the rear of the column and remain. Although I do not believe Ingilby to be in any shape to pursue our army, I will not take any chances. Stay back there and ensure our retreat is clean."

Lucan glanced over his shoulder, along the sea of men behind him. "We saw no sign of them this morning or last night," he said casually. "I do not believe they would be stupid enough to follow us. They would only be beat down again."

Keir's normally fastidious patience was in danger of wavering. He was edgy today and had been since they had left Exelby. He couldn't explain why his belly was quivering other than he had spent all night with thoughts of luxurious red hair on his mind. He'd even dreamed about it and then had awoken to an angel in their midst.

Whatever odd pangs of compassion he had felt for Chloë de Geld yesterday had only grown stronger, stronger still when he saw her that morning as she and her family prepared to ride to Aysgarth. He had therefore positioned himself far away from her at the front of the column and Lucan's questioning of an order had him snappish.

"Go," he barked softly. "Remain there until we reach Aysgarth."

Lucan did as he was told without further debate. As he reined his destrier around, Pembury shouted at him. "Stay away from the women," he barked.

Lucan sneered at the man before charging back along the column. That was as much as he dared do, running away so that Pembury could not follow and clobber him. Although he and Michael were old and good friends, Pembury wasn't beyond taking a swipe at him when his temper had the better of him. Sometimes the fun was in provoking him.

Keir ignored the banter between the knights, focused on the mucky road ahead and thinking that they would be seeing the tall north tower of Aysgarth in the early afternoon if they continued at their current pace. Once arrived and Coverdale settled, Keir intended to travel on to Pendragon and forget all about the Lady Chloë de Geld and her supernatural hold on his thoughts. But even as he fought to put her from his mind, she would come back more strongly than before. It was an effort not to turn around, casually, to inspect the column and find her luscious red head somewhere back in the mix. As he struggled with his thoughts, a dark Spanish Jennet appeared next to him.

Keir glanced over at Lord Byron as the man wrestled with the new stallion that was a bit too much horse for him. The man was exhausted from riding the animal over just the few miles they had traveled, but he would never admit it. The baron's ego was a fragile thing.

"Our pace is well," Byron said, two-handing the reins as the horse fought against him. "We should be home in a few hours."

Keir's visor was up as his ice blue gaze moved over the wet, green morning. "I will be leaving directly for Pendragon," he told his liege. "Is there any business you would have me attend to before I go?"

Byron glanced at the knight, a man he'd known since he had been newly knighted at twenty years of age. Keir was the most capable man he knew, strong, fearless and exceedingly wise, but something in him had died that day Madeleine and little Frances had perished. Keir just wasn't the same man, as if all of the joy in life had left him. There was something vacant and hollow there.

Byron swore the only thing that kept the man going was the fact that his son's body had never been found and he presumed the boy had been captured. He swore that Keir lived every day waiting for news of his son, even after they had spent the full year after the siege of Pendragon scouring the entire north of England looking for the boy. No one had seen him or even heard about him. It was as if he had vanished into thin air.

Even now, as he gazed at Keir and the question hung between them, there was still something dead and vacant in Keir's manner. It made

Byron's answer all the more interesting.

"There is, actually," he replied casually. "First, you will tell me why you sent word back to Ingilby that you would personally confront the man if he tried to make contact again with the Lady Chloë de Geld."

Normally unflappable, Keir struggled not to appear confused or defensive. "It was a threat made in the heat of combat and nothing more," he replied evenly. "I thought perhaps it would force Ingilby to think twice before molesting the woman again or trying to attack her family if he believed another knight was involved, someone of power and rank."

Byron wriggled his eyebrows in agreement. "Perhaps," he replied, "but I fear that all you have succeeded in doing is informing Ingilby that Coverdale is now involved. If he finds out Lady Chloë is no longer at Exelby, he will assume she has gone to Aysgarth. It would be the logical assumption."

Keir looked at him. "Perhaps, my lord," he agreed without remorse. "But Aysgarth can take care of herself. Moreover, I doubt Ingilby would risk conflict with you. Your military might is well known."

Byron pulled back on the reins when his feisty horse acted up. "Even so, her father is worried about her. This entire siege was because of her. He wants her safely tucked away."

"And she will be at Aysgarth."

"She will be better protected at Pendragon."

Keir looked at the man as if he had physically struck him. The normally cool demeanor flared as he stiffened in outrage. The first words on his lips were those of refusal but he knew that he could not speak them; Pendragon was Coverdale's castle and he could do with it as he pleased. If Byron wanted the girl to go to Pendragon because he felt it was safer for her, then Keir would have no say in the matter. The thought of Lady Chloë within walls that had seen so much hell and happiness for Keir left the man reeling with shock.

Byron looked at the knight, seeing the fury on his normally emotionless face, and he merely shook his head.

"It is a perfect place to hide the girl, and her sister as well," he told him. "Moreover, you brought this upon yourself when you volunteered to protect her. Her father demands you keep your word. He is very worried for her."

Keir was close to exploding. His granite jaw ticked furiously and he looked away, struggling not to open his mouth and spill forth the refusal he was feeling with every fiber of his body.

"I should not have said what I did," he hissed.

"Are you going back on your word? I find that astonishing."

Keir faltered. His word was stronger than anyone else's in the north of England and he had made damn sure to cement that careful reputation. He never said anything he did not mean and a vow from St. Hévér was bankable. He had the trust of everyone he had ever met, fought with or served. It was perhaps the strongest part of a strong man, something he did not wish to see damaged even in something as small as this. It was his crutch, his curse, his pride. After several long moments, he sighed heavily.

"I only said that I should not have said it," he clarified. "I did not say that I did not mean it. I said it because the girl was terrified. She had just seen her castle ripped apart and men killed all because a jilted suitor could not stomach her denial. I said it to bring her comfort."

Byron was not oblivious to the things young men said in overwhelming situations. He drew in a deep, thoughtful breath and tried to rein his excitable jennet close to Keir so that he could speak and not be heard by others.

"The Lady Chloë de Geld is one of the most sought-after women in all of England, a beauty without compare, but I do not suppose you noticed that," he glanced at Keir only to note the man facing straight ahead, features like stone. He continued. "Her father is understandably worried about her and he knows you by reputation. He has asked that you hold true to your vow to protect his daughter and I have agreed. Whatever feelings you have in this matter, Keir, put them aside and do the duty you are bred to do. Ingilby is a despicable, corrupt man with an earl for an uncle. Should Ingilby call upon his uncle for support, I worry for my old friend de Geld. He would not be able to hold Ingilby off that being the case and we would be drawn into a nasty conflict. Do I make myself clear, Keir?"

Keir's jaw ticked with displeasure and his big body stiffened, all physical signs of his disapproval of the assignment, yet he kept his mouth shut. Coverdale was correct. He had brought it upon himself when he had vowed to protect the woman. There was nothing more he could say.

"You do, my lord," he replied steadily.

Byron smiled. "Good lad," he said. "Anton will be pleased. Who knows? Perhaps you will come to appreciate the lady with time. She is quite a beauty and of marriageable age and you, my friend, are in need of a wife."

It was all Keir could do not to take the man's head off. As Coverdale reined his skittish stallion around and headed back along the column, Keir ground his teeth so hard in frustration that he ended up biting his lip.

CHAPTER FIVE

"THIS PLACE IS desolation personified," Cassandra hissed. "Look at it – the castle is in the middle of nowhere. We may as well be on the moon!"

Wrapped in the heavy, dusty brown cloak that had been her companion for three long and weary days, Chloë could see the dark stoned edifice of Pendragon Castle in the distance. It had been raining on and off all night and now, a few hours past dawn, the skies were clearing somewhat. The landscape of Cumbria was very green and very wet, and great pools of muddy water dotted the rutted road that led from Aysgarth Castle to Pendragon and points north. Astride a little gray mare, Chloë directed the horse around the puddles, following the enormous chargers up ahead and being followed by about one hundred men-at-arms to the rear.

"You could have stayed with Father and Mother," she told her sister. "You did not have to come with me to the ends of the earth. It is me they are trying to distance from Exelby, not you."

Cassandra lifted an eyebrow at her sister, younger by just over one year. "As if they would send you to a remote castle without a chaperone," she replied, her brown eyes drifting to the trio of knights at the head of their party. "I would not leave you alone with three handsome knights. They will be challenging each other for your affections by tomorrow."

Chloë knew her sister was jesting but she was in no mood for it. Morose, she looked away just as a big black charger whirled around and headed in their direction. The horse kicked up rocks and mud, spraying the women as he came to a halt. The knight flipped up his visor.

"My ladies," Michael's voice was soft, deep. "We will be arriving at Pendragon shortly."

Cassandra lifted a mocking eyebrow at the handsome knight with the cornflower blue eyes. "We can see that."

He ignored the sharp tongue. "Do you have any questions or concerns I might address at this time?" he asked politely.

"Indeed we do," she said almost immediately. "We have no clothing or personal items to speak of, as most of them were confiscated from Exelby and we were not permitted to return to gather what was left. We have been traveling and sleeping in the clothing on our backs for two days. This is a serious problem."

Chloë interrupted her snappish sister. "Cassie, please," she begged softly, turning her radiant beauty to the blue-eyed knight. "You are doing all you can to make us safe and comfortable, and we appreciate your effort. But Father has given us some coinage and, at some point very soon, we should request escort to the nearest town of merchants where we may purchase some basic necessities that were lost in the siege. Would that be possible, my lord?"

Michael had only wanted to speak with the blond sister again, as he'd had little opportunity since their flight from Exelby, but he could see she was in no mood for his company. Her sister, however, was tactful and sweet, not to mention outrageously beautiful. He found himself focused on the redhead.

"That will be Sir Keir's decision, my lady, but I am sure he would graciously comply," he told her, eyeing the blond to see that she was deliberately looking away from him. "I will take the matter up with him."

"If it would not be too much to ask, my lord," Chloë said politely.

Michael shook his head and gave her a weak smile. His gaze kept returning to Cassandra but she refused to look at him. Chloë could see his interest, and her sister's stubbornness, and she fought off a smile. She didn't feel so moody any longer with the delicious opportunity to tease her sister.

"I do not know your name, my lord," she said. "You helped rescue us from our compromised chamber at Exelby."

Michael nodded. "I am Sir Michael of Pembury," he replied. "And you, dear lady, smashed my fingers."

Chloë laughed, a beautiful and captivating gesture. "Only in self-protection, I assure you," she said. "I do hope I did not break anything."

Michael shook his head. "You did not."

"But it bloody well hurt," Chloë put in, repeating his words.

Michael broke out in a smile. He was a very handsome man with his dark hair and bright blue eyes, a rugged and strong beauty about him. He was also the tallest man that Chloë had ever seen; she well remembered the man's sheer size.

"It did," he admitted, "but I have since recovered. You did worse to Keir."

Chloë's gaze moved to the head of the column where Keir and another knight rode in strong silence. She realized that it made her heart flutter simply to look at the man, even though he'd hardly spoken a word to her since rescuing her from the chamber two days before. It seemed that when he came around her, he couldn't get away fast enough. It began to occur to her that he must have an aversion to her, more than likely from the fact that she had nearly broken his fingers and gouged his eyes out upon their initial acquaintance. As realization dawned, her good mood fled.

"I did," she sighed heavily. "I am sure he will never forgive me for it, for which I am truly sorry. In any case, it is nice to make your acquaintance, Sir Michael."

"And yours, my lady."

With a lingering look at Cassandra, who still refused to look at him, Michael spurred his charger back to the front of the column.

The remainder of the trip was uneventful. They arrived at Pendragon, a great square bastion on a fortified hill surrounded by earthworks, a series of tall walls, causeways and a great moated ditch.

It wasn't a particularly large castle but it was very tall, well protected and well-fortified. As they drew upon it, Chloë gazed up at the dark gray stone, stained wet from the storms, thinking of the wife and daughter that St. Héver had lost within these massive walls. She couldn't imagine any army penetrating walls such as these.

The castle was built on a fortified mound with a series of earth-works and ditches, and they crossed great elevated causeways between the moats once they were within the enormous circular wall that surrounded the place. They had to pass between a series of mounds, all designed to make an incoming enemy vulnerable to those protecting the castle.

Finally passing through the portcullised entry, they entered a very small bailey. Living quarters and towers were built into the tall exterior walls, including a very tall box-shaped keep that was built into the southwest corner of the structure. There were wooden stairs every-where, leading up into the towers as well as the keep. Narrow wooden walkways bordered the top of the walls.

As Chloë gazed at the guts of the towering structure, she began to notice scorch marks everywhere – around the keep windows, upon the walls, near the portcullis. Burn marks were heavy and frequent, a reminder perhaps of the terrible siege three years prior. She didn't dare ask St. Héver, who had dismounted his charger and was shouting orders to the men as he made his way back to where the women were still mounted near the portcullis.

As he approached, Chloë couldn't help but notice that he had not made eye contact with her, in any fashion. It convinced her more and more that the man wanted nothing to do with her as a result of their rough beginning and her disappointment was growing. She watched him until he came to stand next to her, still snapping orders to the men around him. Without a word to her, and still speaking to his soldiers, he reached down and pulled her foot from the stirrup. Then he extended his enormous arms and scooped her out of the saddle.

Heart beating loudly against her ribs at his closeness, Chloë wrapped her arms around his big neck as he carried her across the muddy bailey towards the keep. Over her shoulder, she could hear Cassandra's voice and she glanced back to see her sister arguing with Pembury. The big knight was apparently trying to offer his services to help the lady across the foul bailey but Cassandra was being stubborn about it. Chloë suspected it was all for show, for she'd never known her sister to show such attention, good or bad, to any man. Perhaps there was something more going on than Cassandra would admit. Fighting off a grin, Chloë returned her attention to St. Héver and the approaching keep.

The man was so close that she could see the stubble on his face and the pores of his skin. He had thick, dark blond eyelashes, the same dark blond color as his hair and eyebrows, and unnaturally pale blue eyes. He was focused on the keep ahead and still hadn't said a word to her. Once they reached the steps, Keir set her to her feet.

"If you will go up the stairs, there is an entry hall that should have a warm fire blazing," he told her.

Chloë simply nodded and Keir actually met her eye for the first time in two days. When their gazes locked, she felt a shock go through her, something that made her heart race even faster. She wasn't sure if he felt it also but he lowered his gaze quickly, too quickly, and turned back for the bailey. Perhaps he felt it and didn't want to. Chloë reached out and stopped him.

"My lord," she said politely. "May... may I have a word with you?"

Keir paused and exhaled heavily; she could see it. He turned to look at her again, his expression cold and guarded.

"Of course, my lady," he said with strained patience. "How may I be of service?"

Now she had his attention, suddenly self-conscious and the least bit nervous. She pulled the cloak more tightly about her slight figure, thinking on how to phrase what she must say. She could only think of one way to say it – the truth.

"I am sorry that my sister and I are here," she said softly. "Surely the last thing you need at a garrison is two women and I sincerely apologize for the inconvenience. Please know it was not my idea and given the choice, I would happily return to Exelby so as not to be a burden on your good graces."

Keir stared at her, feeling the resurgence of the warm emotions he had experienced two days ago, the ones that had scared the hell out of him. Now they were back with a vengeance as he gazed at her porcelain skin and cold-pinked cheeks framed by that glorious deep red hair. It was at that moment that he noticed she cut her hair rather oddly, as she had a fringe of bangs across her forehead, framing her face and eyes, something that only made her more angelic in his opinion. It was strange but wholly attractive. He was under her spell and slipping fast.

"No need to apologize, my lady," he said, averting his gaze because he was afraid to look at her any longer. "I know it was not your doing. We will do our best to ensure your comfort and protection."

Chloë's heart sank as he averted his eyes, unable to stomach the sight of her. "You do not like me very much, do you?"

Keir's head snapped up, his ice blue eyes riveted to her with surprise. "I... I do not know what you mean, my lady."

She smiled faintly, such a beautiful and delicate gesture. "Aye, you do, but you are too much of a gentle knight to say so," she took a step towards him, her face uplifted to meet his. "I was rude and belligerent when we first met and I realize that you must have come to the conclusion that I am a petulant and terrible woman. I did not mean to offend you when you rescued my sister and me from our chamber, truly. I was simply afraid and reacting in kind. I thought I was defending myself. I hope with time you can forgive me and at least tolerate the sight of me. I should not like to make you uncomfortable and unhappy with my presence within the walls of your very own keep."

Keir stared at her as her words sank in. It began to occur to him how his behavior must be affecting her, the coldness and the sense of self protection that he must be projecting. He could see that she was very concerned for his feelings and it touched him deeply, softening him in a way he had never before been softened. The poor woman had just survived a siege only to be taken from her home and traipsed across miles of bad weather and inhospitable land by a bitter and sullen knight.

Even though she frightened him and he sincerely did not want her at Pendragon, it did not excuse his behavior towards her. Gazing into her deep brown eyes, he sighed faintly.

"Nay, lady," he said softly, reaching out to take her hand. "It is I who should apologize. You have not, at any time, offended me. Please forgive me if I have offended you with my surly behavior. It is not directed at you."

Chloë's heart leapt as he held her hand gently. She grasped his hand and held it tightly. "Are you sure you are not angry with me for attempting to blind you?" she teased softly.

He broke out in a crooked smile. "Nay," he answered. "I could never be angry with you."

"Not even when I am deliberately wicked and stubborn?"

He laughed softly. "I do not believe you have those capabilities, my lady. You look like an angel incarnate and I choose to believe that you are as beautiful on the inside as you are on the outside."

She gave him a devilish expression. "Foolish mortal," she jested. "You shall come to regret that statement."

He laughed again, a liberating experience considering he hadn't laughed like that in three years. Not since Madeleine passed. There had been nothing to laugh at, not until this very moment with this exquisite creature in front of him. He realized that it made his heart light simply to look at her. His ice blue eyes twinkled.

"I do not think so," he told her. "But just so you know, I am not beyond spanking she who needs to be spanked."

Chloë put her hands on her hips in mock outrage. "Did my father give you permission to do that?"

Keir winked at her. "I do not need his permission. You are my ward and if you need to be punished, I will not hesitate to do it."

"Is that so?"

"It is."

She gave him a very doubtful, yet very flirtatious, expression. "We shall see, Sir Keir."

Keir was swept off his feet by her charm. He should have fought it with all his might but he couldn't seem to manage it. Grinning, he pointed up the stairs.

"Perhaps," was all he would say. "Go inside now. It is warm in there. I will join you shortly."

Chloë's eyes were glittering, like brilliant stars against the black expanse of night. "Promise?"

He shouldn't have responded to the flirt. He should have remained professional and steadfast, letting his fear and resistance do the talking for him. But he simply couldn't do it. She was breaking him down and he was letting her. After a moment, he simply nodded his head.

"Promise."

As she smiled and turned up the stairs, he would remember her warm, inviting expression as long as he lived.

C820

THE HALL OF Pendragon, like everything else at the castle, had been built against one of the massive exterior walls. It was reached by an expansive arched stone doorway, well protected with its own iron grate and bolts that led to a flight of squat stone stairs rising up into the hall above. The ground floor held the kitchens and stores and there were two hidden staircases that led from the kitchen to the hall above. It was a big, functional hall that smelled to the rafters of smoke and wet dogs.

After warming themselves by the entry hall fire in the keep as the escort of men and animals disbanded in the bailey, Chloë and Cassandra were directed to the hall by Michael and Lucan where food and drink await them. Michael carefully carried Cassandra across the muddy bailey to the hall entry while Lucan had taken Chloë.

Halfway across the bailey, they ran headlong into Keir, who gruffly ordered Lucan to hand the lady over to him, which he did. Safely tucked into Keir's arms, Chloë smiled at him as they neared the great hall entry. He was back to ignoring her after their earlier conversation, or so she thought until he glanced at her and caught a glimpse of her smile. The stone-faced expression cracked and he gave her a weak grin as he carried her into the hall.

Once inside the darkened door, he set her carefully to her feet and took her hand, leading her up the steps and into the hall beyond. It was a large room, smelly, as Keir took her over to the massive oak feasting table and seated her next to her sister. As he went to sit across from her, Cassandra initiated the conversation.

"If my sister has not yet thanked you for assuming our burden, then please allow me to," she said. "I realize my father all but shoved our protection down your throat and for that, we are sorry. This cannot be an easy thing for you."

Keir eyed the woman as he claimed his seat. "Your sister has indeed thanked me and, as I told her, it is no burden at all. We will do our best to protect you both."

Cassandra smiled at him, a very pretty girl but not nearly the beauty her sister was. "If it is not too much trouble, we are in need of a few necessities for our stay here at Pendragon," she said. "I mentioned the same thing to Sir Michael but I am not sure if he has told you."

The servants set great wooden cups down on the table along with big clay pitchers of wine. Keir picked up one of the pitchers and leaned over the table, pouring a measure into Chloë's cup.

"He did," he replied. "I will do my best to accommodate you. What exactly do you require?"

The women looked at each other. Cassandra was usually the more assertive but Chloë was more tactful. She put her hand on her sister's arm to let her know that she would provide Keir with the answers.

"Since our possessions were taken as spoils of war by Lord Ingilby, we have nothing more than what you see on our backs," Chloë said. "We require… necessities."

"What necessities?"

Cassandra jumped in before Chloë could speak. "Clothing, my lord," she said. "Soap, oils, hairbrushes. We will not live like animals here at the ends of the earth."

She said it rather harshly but she had a point. Chloë looked rather fearfully at Keir, hoping he would not deny their request. Keir's patient gaze remained on Cassandra.

"And I would not expect you to," he said after a moment. "Unfortunately, we are not located near any larger towns that may hold a great variety of things for you to choose from but there is a town not far to the north that has several merchants. We can go there to see if they have what you need."

"And what if they do not?" Cassandra wanted to know. "What do we do?"

Keir shrugged his enormous shoulders. "Then we will go to a town that has what you need."

"May we go tomorrow?"

"Absolutely."

Satisfied, Cassandra turned to her sister with a smile of victory. Chloë merely lifted her eyebrows at her sister's bold manner.

"Thanks to you, Sir Keir," Chloë said sincerely. "We are grateful."

Keir's gaze fell upon her and he smiled, the first time since she had known the man that he hadn't tried to avoid looking at her. Chloë smiled in return, a genuine gesture, as Keir picked up the nearest pitcher and poured her more wine. She accepted it gratefully.

A servant set a heaping trencher of boiled mutton and carrots in front of Keir and he immediately slid it across the table to Chloë. Then he plopped his taut buttocks on the table, took his dagger, and began cutting pieces off for her. Unused to such service, especially from a man who had very nearly ignored her, Chloë timidly accepted the meat as he handed it to her.

"I apologize that we cannot offer more by way of comfort," he told her. "I can supply you with a bath and soap, but I fear it is not the soap a young lady would find pleasurable."

Chloë chewed on the tough mutton. "It does not matter," she assured him. "Anything at this point is most happily accepted."

He began cutting up the boiled carrots. "The keep has four bedchambers so you may share with your sister or you may have your own chamber."

Chloë looked at Cassandra, who was in conversation with Michael. She turned back to Keir.

"I think I would rather have my own," she whispered, pointing discreetly at her sister. "She snores."

Keir grinned, looking at Cassandra as she chatted and Michael smiled. She seemed to have the tall knight smitten. He leaned closer to Chloë and lowered his voice.

"Then I will put you on another floor so you cannot hear her," he said.

Chloë giggled and accepted another piece of meat from the end of his dagger. "And if it would not be too much trouble," she was still whispering. "I should like to bathe first. She will take all night."

Keir shook his head as he cut off another piece of meat. "You are divulging your sister's shocking habits, my lady," he teased softly, casting her a sidelong glance. "Are you so perfect that you do not have any bad habits at all?"

Chloë shrugged and accepted more meat. "If I do, you will never hear them from my lips. Remember that you told me that you choose to believe I am as beautiful inside as I am outside. I will continue to allow you to believe that and smite all who attempt to dissuade you."

He laughed softly. "No one could convince me that you are anything less than perfect, so have no fear."

"Even though I tried to smash your fingers?"

He sighed heavily. "I have already forgotten about that. I wish you would as well."

She nodded in agreement. "I will," her smile faded. "Still, when I close my eyes at night, I hear sounds of battle. It wakes me up."

His smile faded as well. "That will diminish also, in time," he assured her, his gaze moving over her exquisite mane of deep red hair, thinking on perhaps changing the subject. "When you are finished eating, I will order you a bath. I apologize that I do not have any female servants to offer you assistance."

She waved him off. "I bathe alone, although I thank you."

"Is there nothing else I can do for you, my lady?"

Her smile returned and her deep brown eyes glimmered warmly at him. "You have done so much already," she said. "I will never be able to thank you enough for risking yourself for a woman you do not even know."

He gave her a crooked smile, being sucked in by the beautiful brown eyes. "I know enough that she tells scandalous tales about her sister and she is unafraid of a man with a sword."

Chloë giggled and returned to her food, a faint blush to her cheeks that Keir found enchanting.

He let the subject die and the conversation along with it. He continued to cut meat and hand it to her, watching her slender white fingers accept the morsels, his gaze moving over her face and hair as if he could not take his eyes off of her. The truth was that he couldn't. Chloë seemed to captivate him like no one ever had and much to his chagrin, he realized he wasn't resisting as he had been. His sense of self-preservation was fading fast and there wasn't a damn thing he could do about it.

He tried not to hate himself for it.

03

IT WASN'T MUCH by way of comfort but it was all she was offered. Keir had taken Chloë to a rather large chamber that was a dusty, disheveled mess, with two small beds in it, one of them half-burned and crumpled against the wall. Keir had ordered a couple of men to remove the burnt bed but had said little else about the room or its state as he had his men bring in a big, dented copper tub.

A bucket brigade filled the tub with steaming water and Keir provided Chloë with a lumpy, misshapen bar of white soap that smelled heavily of pine. When the tub was full, he left her without a word, shutting the door softly behind him while she stood in the center of the room, wondering why he seemed so cold and withdrawn again. He had been charming and warm in the hall, feeding her until she was full, before escorting her to this room that seemed dark and shadowy, even with a fire blazing brightly in the hearth.

Thoughts lingering on Keir, Chloë had taken her bath and scrubbed herself from the top of her red head to the bottom of her little feet. She didn't have anything to dry off with and she noticed the big wardrobe against the wall, shielded by the shadows of the room, but she didn't feel comfortable opening it, so she used her surcoat to dry her hair and body before the fire. Then she laid the surcoat carefully in front of the dusty hearth to dry it out.

Slipping back into her soft shift, Chloë wrapped up in her cloak and called for the soldiers to remove the tub for her sister, which they silently and efficiently accomplished. When they were gone, she bolted the door and lay down on the small, lumpy bed.

Exhausted, she fell into a heavy sleep, only to awaken when the hearth was burning low and great streams of white moonlight were pouring in through the lancet window. As she rolled over, she caught a glimpse of something at the foot of the bed and in the darkness, her eyes adjusted to the sight of a small girl.

Startled, Chloë sat up and stared at the child. She was no more than four or five years of age, with long pale hair and a very pale face. It took Chloë a moment to realize that she was the same color of the moonlight, standing in the darkness at the end of the bed and staring at Chloë with big, bottomless black eyes. Chloë was positive she was dreaming and she closed her eyes tightly, opening them again to find that the little girl had moved to stand directly next to the bed. Her eyes were big black voids in her pasty face and Chloë pulled the cloak more tightly around her body, feeling an icy chill envelope her.

"G-greetings," she whispered timidly. "Who are you?"

The little girl just stared at her. Then she lifted a wispy arm and pointed towards the door. Apprehensive and confused, Chloë looked to where the little girl was pointing and shook her head. She had no idea what the child meant.

"Do you live here?" she asked softly. "Does your father work here?"

The little girl lowered her bony arm and looked at her again. The chill around Chloë grew colder and she could see her breath fogging in the air. Her skin began to bump up as icy fingers grasped at her. She could feel horror and had no idea why. The little girl looked up at her with her big black eyes, dark circled and grim.

"Me-Me," the child hissed.

Chloë wasn't sure what she meant, nor even who the child was. All she knew was that this pasty, ill-looking child had somehow found her way into the chamber. She reached out to gently take the child's arm but her fingers passed through nothingness. In the next instant, the child vanished.

Chloë fled the chamber in terror.

CHAPTER SIX

I T WAS LATE in the night and the keep of Pendragon was finally
settled in to sleep for the evening. A bright full moon hung over the
landscape, bathing the dark stoned castle in silver light. Upon the
wooden parapets at the top of the walls, Keir stood with Michael and
Lucan, watching the landscape that was so brightly lit. They had been
walking the walls for a couple of hours, watching, making sure Ingilby
hadn't somehow followed them.

Keir had put Chloë in the chamber that had once belonged to his
children. It hadn't been used since. He'd shut the door after that fateful
day and didn't open it again until just a few weeks ago when a nest of
bees had built a hive in the ceiling. It had been a strange experience for
him to enter the chamber where Frances and Merritt had played; toys
had still been scattered on the floor and one of the little beds had been
partially burned by the siege. He had steeled himself to toss the
scattered clothes and toys into the big wardrobe shared by the children,
weeping silent tears when he had held the dress of his daughter that still
had food stains on it. When he smelled it, he could still smell her. It
broke his heart.

But he tossed everything into the wardrobe and slammed the door
as his men smoked the bees out of the chamber. He had only returned
to the chamber this night to admit Chloë, who looked around the
chamber with one half-burned bed with big, apprehensive eyes. But she
did nothing more than thank him, even though the linens were dusty
and the room hadn't been cleaned out since the day of that fateful siege
three years ago. Keir suddenly felt very bad for subjecting her to such
filth and discomfort, and had two of his soldiers carry out the burned

bed as Chloë and Keir stood there and watched. He promised her that the chamber would be thoroughly cleaned in the morning but she had smiled bravely and insisted it was fine as it was.

He knew it was a gracious lie, which made him feel worse. He'd had his men bring up the big copper tub and fill it with hot water, providing Chloë with the only soap he had, a lumpy bar that smelled of pine. All the while, he remembered the big wardrobe in his chamber that still contained his wife's possessions but he couldn't bring himself to open the doors and go through it, not even to provide Chloë with something of comfort. That big, oak wardrobe with the carved doors remained closed, a silent testimony to Keir's agony that he was unwilling to explore. Madeleine's possessions were to remain untouched, like a frozen tribute to her memory. It was all better left untouched.

So Keir had left Chloë with a steaming tub, a lump of smelly soap, and naught much else. The invasion into his children's chamber had him reeling again, grief clawing at him as he lost himself in his duties upon the battlements. He thought he was doing quite well at fighting off the memories until he heard a scream emitting from the keep. Startled, he looked at Michael as if to confirm the man had heard it also when the scream came again, louder. The two of them bolted for the parapet stairs.

Lucan, on the opposite wall, had heard the screaming also. He and several soldiers were flying off of the walls, heading for the keep as Keir and Michael were. Just as they reached the stairs, Chloë came shooting out of the keep as if the Devil himself was chasing her.

She flew down the old wooden stairs, screaming at the top of her lungs. Michael was the closest one to her. He reached out to grab her but she swung her little fists at him, dodging his hands as she continued on her way. Keir was too far away to grab her as she bolted past him, running as fast as she could for the castle entry with her amazing red hair trailing after her like a banner. The portcullis was lowered so she couldn't get away, but that didn't prevent her from trying. She ran at the iron grate and threw herself against it, trying to claw her way out.

Keir, Michael and Lucan raced up behind her but Keir held out a big arm to the men, indicating for them to remain where they were. The lady was panicked out of her mind and he didn't want her spooked by too many men trying to render aid. Carefully, Keir approached her as she struggled to claw her way out of the portcullis.

"My lady?" he asked softly, with concern. "What is the matter?"

Through her haze of terror, Chloë heard him. She stopped clawing, turning to look at the men standing behind her in the moonlit bailey. Her luscious hair was hanging in her face, all over her body, like a giant cloak that hung all the way to her knees. She was clad only in her shift and the heavy cloak, barefoot in the muddy bailey. Her lower legs were covered in muck. When she saw Keir and the blind panic faded, she burst into painful tears.

"I want to leave," she sobbed. "Open this gate. I must get out."

Keir was deeply concerned. He waved the men away as he approached her cautiously. "Why?" he asked softly. "What is the matter?"

With a growl, Chloë turned to the portcullis and started clawing again. Even in the moonlight, Keir could see that she was scraping her fingers and drawing blood. Whatever had happened in the keep, the woman was clearly terrified out of her mind.

"Chloë?" he begged quietly. "What happened?"

Her fingers gradually came to a halt and she wept painfully against the iron. "Please," she begged. "Please open the gate. I want to leave."

Keir turned to Michael and Lucan, still standing several feet behind him. "Into the keep," he hissed. "Check it from top to bottom. See what has her so frightened and for God's sake, make sure her sister is well."

The knights fled as Keir turned back to Chloë. She was shivering, wet and muddy. He went to her, hoping she wouldn't try to gouge his eyes out again in her panic.

"Chloë," he said gently. "What happened, love? Why are you so frightened?"

She turned to him, tears pouring down her sweet face, and slumped against the grate. Keir swept her up into his arms because she was close to collapsing onto the wet ground and she threw her arms around his neck, holding him so tightly that she was cutting off his air. He moved his head around, trying to dislodge the arm that was against his throat so he could breathe.

"A… a girl," she sobbed.

He held her close as he began his trek back towards the keep. "A girl?" he repeated. "What girl?"

Her face was pressed into the crook of his neck. "A… a little girl," she wept. "She was in my chamber."

Keir's brow furrowed. "There was a little girl in your chamber?" he repeated. "That is not possible. There are no little girls at Pendragon."

Chloë's sobbing grew louder. "When I tried to touch her, she vanished."

Keir could only think of one possibility for that. "You must have been dreaming, sweetheart."

Chloë lifted her face from his neck, her eye swimming with tears. She shook her head emphatically, her long red hair in her face. "I was *not* dreaming," she insisted. "I woke up and a little girl was standing by my bed. When I tried to touch her, she vanished."

Keir gazed into her lovely face and all he could think to do was kiss her soft, white cheek to comfort her. It was an impulsive gesture but one he did not regret. The feel of her warm skin against his lips stirred something within him, something he thought was long dead.

"It was a dream," he reiterated softly, hugging her against him as he neared the keep. "Sometimes dreams can seem very real. I have had a few of those myself."

Chloë gazed at him, her mind becoming more lucid and wondering if he wasn't correct, when she noticed how close they were to the keep. The terror quickly returned and she began to struggle.

"Nay," she tried to push herself from his arms. "I am not going back to that chamber. I am not going in there ever again."

He came to a halt. "Easy, lady," he admonished softly. "Do you want to sleep with your sister, then? Perhaps she can chase your fears away."

She shook her head emphatically. Then she burst into tears and lay her head on his shoulder, weeping pitifully. With a heavy sigh, Keir continued on into the keep, feeling her arms tighten around him as they entered the dark, musty entry hall. As he mounted the steep spiral stairs, they came upon Michael and Lucan descending. The knights backed up so that Keir could come up to the third level.

"How is Lady Cassandra?" Keir asked.

Michael nodded. "Sleeping like the dead," he said. "Everything else is secure."

"Did you check Lady Chloë's chamber?"

"We did," he said, eyeing Chloë with her face buried in Keir's neck. "Nothing to report. Is Lady Chloë well?"

Keir lifted his eyebrows. "Bad dream," was all he would say. "I am retiring for the night. Send hot water up to my chamber."

Michael and Lucan watched him go, exchanging puzzled expressions before going about their business. It seemed as if Keir was retiring for the evening with the lady in his arms, but it wasn't up to them to make that judgment.

Up the stairs, Keir reached the level that held the children's chamber as well as his own. He glanced into the children's chamber, seeing that it was dark and vacant. Certainly nothing to become hysterical over. He took Chloë into the master's chamber and quietly shut the door.

She had stopped sobbing by this time, her head on his shoulder as she sniffled faintly. Keir went to set her down on the bed but she balked, holding tightly to his neck until he gently coaxed her into letting go. He set her on the big bed as he proceeded to remove what armor he had on his body.

"When I was a wee lad growing up in Northumberland, I used to have an imaginary big brother," he was making idle chatter as he pulled off his helm and mail hood. "When I was sent away to foster, the older boys would pick on me. I told them that my big brother would get them if they did not leave me alone."

Chloë sat on the bed and sniffled, looking pale and exhausted as she watched him pull off his mail coat. "I did not imagine the girl. She was really there."

He shrugged, not wanting to fight with her when he was attempting to show understanding. "I am not saying you did," he said. "But sometimes, dreams or imaginary friends can seem very real. Mine was very real to me at the time."

Chloë could see where he was leading with this and she didn't want to argue with him, either. She had her opinion and he had his, so she picked up on the next subject. "Were you an only child?"

He shook his head. "Nay," he told her, placing the mail on a rack near the door so the chain could dry out. "I have an older brother, Kurtis. In fact, Kurtis should be arriving at Pendragon in the next few days. He is on an errand for his liege and sent word of his impending visit. I would be pleased to introduce you to him. We also had a sister but she died when she was young."

Chloë watched him fumble with his tunic now that the mail was off. "I had a brother but he died when he was young as well," she replied. "It has only been Cassandra and I. Father hopes to make an advantageous marriage with both of us but he wants to marry Cassandra off first."

"Why?"

"Because she is the eldest," she said. "It would be humiliating for me to be married before her."

"Does she have any prospects?"

Chloë shrugged. "None that she approves of," she said. "Father told her that she could approve of her husband but, so far, she had not approved of anyone because she is smarter than most men. She does not want a husband who cannot match her wit. Moreover, Father wants her to marry someone of rank because of our royal bloodlines, but she wants to marry someone she can tolerate, rank or no. They do not agree but my father will do as she wishes in the end."

Keir's eyebrows lifted. "Royal bloodlines?"

Chloë nodded. "My mother is a daughter of Henry the Third."

Keir was shocked. "Your grandfather was King Henry?"

Again, she nodded as if completely unimpressed. "She is a daughter of the king from his liaison with a woman of minor nobility."

"And your father? Surely he must have bloodlines in him as well."

"He does," she told him. "His father was Viscount Narbonne, a title that passed to his older brother. Along with lands in France, my father owns all of the land from Exelby east to the Pennines, north to Langthorne and south to Ripon. Why do you think Ingilby wants so badly to make a match? He will be an extremely influential and wealthy landowner."

Keir was still lingering on her surprising royal relations that she seemed so casual about. "But Cassandra is older and presumably the heiress," he pointed out. "Why did he not seek her hand?"

Chloë turned up her nose. "Because Cassie does not like him just as I do not," she sniffed. "Father told her she could choose her own groom to make her happy and she will."

Keir wriggled his eyebrows in disapproval. "He should have never given her permission to approve her husband. I can already see she is a woman accustomed to speaking her mind. Not many men will tolerate that trait."

Chloë shrugged, only noticing at that moment that her feet and the entire bottom of her shift were caked with mud. She groaned softly.

"Oh, bother," she gingerly touched the hem of her shift. "Look how dirty I am."

Keir was in the process of untying his tunic as he glanced over at her. "That is why I sent for hot water," he told her. "It should be here momentarily."

Miserable, exhausted, she sat there wrapped up in her cloak, shivering, as Keir proceeded to pull off his tunic and toss it into a corner. Chloë was looking at her hands, glancing up at the man to suddenly notice that he was naked from the waist up. After she got past the shock of seeing his magnificent nude chest, she was very embarrassed.

Startled, she bolted to her feet and scurried to the door.

Keir heard her feet hit the ground, turning just as she reached the chamber door. He called to her.

"Where are you going?"

Chloë paused, her hand on the latch, turning to look at him with a guarded expression. "You... you are dressing, my lord," she explained haltingly. "I should not be here."

He looked down at himself, not quite seeing her problem. "I am not troubled by it. You may stay."

Chloë dared to look at the man's naked chest. He was broad and muscular, with the muscles of his stomach clearly defined. She could see all of them, rippling across his tight belly. His arms were massive, his neck thick. In all, he was a striking example of male perfection, something that made her cheeks flush hot and her hands sweat. She began to think that it was extremely improper for her to be here, alone with him. Confused, embarrassed and titillated, she lowered her gaze and opened the door.

"I cannot," she said as she quit the chamber.

The only other option was the room with the nightmare child. She hadn't taken two steps out of Keir's chamber when she came to a halt, her big brown eyes wide on the dark and shadowed room beyond. As she stood there and gazed into the room as if it were going to jump out and bite her, she could feel a body behind her. Without even looking, she knew it was Keir. She was coming to feel like a fool.

"You must think I am a desperate and skittish creature," she whispered. "Since we have met, I have displayed terrible and extreme behavior. I assure you that I am not usually the skittish or extreme sort and for that, I do apologize."

Keir was standing up against her, feeling her petite warmth against his chest and belly. His gaze was focused in the chamber beyond. He sighed, lifting her red hair with his breath.

"I have known times of desperate and skittish behavior myself," he said softly. "Sometimes circumstances are beyond our control and our mind, our thoughts, act accordingly."

She turned to look at him, his magnificent naked chest right in front of her face. It was difficult to think on anything else, this virile and handsome man she had been attracted to since nearly the moment they met.

"You are kind and understanding," she murmured. "But I think I will make another attempt to sleep in this chamber."

He cocked an eyebrow at her. "Are you sure?" he swept an arm in the direction of the master's chamber. "You may use mine if it will comfort you."

She cocked her head. "Where will you sleep?"

"On the floor."

She shook her head. "Nay," she said firmly. "That would not be proper, nor would it be right. I would be a horrible guest to allow you to sleep on the floor of your own chamber."

Keir hated to admit it, but he felt some disappointment at her statement. She was correct, of course, but he was somehow looking forward to sleeping in the same room with such a glorious creature. It was scandalous and caddish, and he knew it. As a chivalrous man, he backed off.

"As you wish, my lady," he told her. "But do you not wish to wash the mud off your feet first?"

She looked down at her legs and shift, nodding miserably. "This is the only shift I have," she lamented. "I will have to sleep in it wet."

He gazed at her a moment, his mind working. Then he shook his head. "Nay, you will not," he took her hand. "Come with me."

He pulled her back into the bedchamber, noticing her reluctance to follow him. He bade her to sit on the bed, which she did nervously, as he continued on to the massive oak wardrobe that was stuffed over against the shadowed corner. He paused in front of the big doors, lifted a hand to pull them open, and then dropped his hand. His reluctance was evident. Taking a deep breath, he lifted his hand again and pulled the stubborn door open.

Chloë could see him carefully pulling things out, setting them aside, and then delving deeper into the wardrobe. Curious, she watched him rummage around until he drew forth a long, pale, silky garment and ran his hands over it, smelling it, holding hit close to his chest as he reached in and pulled out another heavier garment. He seemed to touch everything with the greatest of reverence and it began to occur to her who the wardrobe belonged to. Everything inside was lovely and feminine.

As she watched him move deeper into the wardrobe, a soldier appeared at the door with a bucket of steaming water. Keir caught sight of the man and beckoned him inside, telling him to set the bucket next to the lady. The soldier did so and fled. Chloë immediately put both feet into the hot water, groaning softly with the comfort of it. She put her hands into the water and began to slough off the mud.

"Here," Keir brought over something in his hand, something small wrapped up in pretty cloth. "You may be able to use this."

Chloë took it from him, carefully unwrapping the item to reveal a creamy white cake of soap. She smelled it, the scent of roses filling her nostrils. Suspecting who the soap had belonged to, given the fact that Keir was so worshipful of the items in the wardrobe, she carefully formulated her words to the man. Given what she knew of his history, she didn't want to upset or offend him.

"Sir Keir," she said softly, carefully re-wrapping the soap. "Truly, you have been most generous. I do not need the soap."

"Use it. It will otherwise go to waste."

She looked at him. "Although I appreciate your generosity, I do not think I should. You should put this back in the wardrobe."

He gazed at her for a moment, moderately confused. "Why would you say that?"

She took a deep breath, trying to be very careful in her approach. "Because… because obviously, the items in the wardrobe mean a good deal to you and I do not want to put my mark on them. I will purchase my own goods on the morrow and leave these well enough alone. They belonged to someone very special and we should leave them as they are."

Keir wasn't sure how to react. She was holding the soap up to him and he took it, looking at it with some confusion, before shrugging his big shoulders.

"I do not think she would mind," he murmured. "In fact, she would have given them to you herself had she been here to do it. She was a very generous woman."

The subject of the mysterious and murdered wife came to light. Having heard of Keir's reaction to his wife's death from her father, Chloë was extremely careful in her response.

"Of course she was," she said softly, with a smile. "And she has very good taste in soap. It is very fine quality."

He was still staring at the soap. Then he looked over his shoulder at the wardrobe, now open with garments hanging from the doors.

"She liked nice things," he admitted. "Her tastes were rather expensive. There is an entire wardrobe of expensive clothing and oils to attest to that."

Chloë's smile grew. "You were a very generous husband to allow her such luxuries," she said. "I am sure your wife was very appreciative. What was her name?"

"Madeleine," he replied without hesitation. "The Lady Madeleine de Gare St. Héver."

"How did you meet her?"

He sat down beside her, still staring at the soap in his hand. "My father and her father served together under the king," he said. "We were pledged at a young age and married quite young."

"And you had children?"

"Two," he was speaking quite casually about it, almost detached. "It took Madeleine years to become pregnant and her first two pregnancies were not successful. Then we had a healthy daughter, Frances, and two years later, a healthy son, Merritt. Frances would have turned seven years old next week."

Chloë could feel his sadness even though he was trying hard to fight it. She felt so sad for the man but she struggled against her emotions, wanting his recollection of his family to be a joyful one and not those wrought with pain. She wondered if he could remember them any other way.

"When I was seven years old, all I wanted was a pony for my birthday," she said with a bit of mischief in her eye. "My father would not get me one because he was afraid I would fall off and injure myself. I would suspect that if Frances wanted a pony, you might give her one. You do not seem to be the type that would deny your child her fondest wish."

He looked at her, seeing the twinkle in her eye, and it eased the grief that was seeping into his veins as he thought of his daughter and her impending birthday. Smiling weakly, he shook his head.

"Nay," he muttered. "She had everything her little heart desired. She was spoiled and sweet."

Chloë laughed softly. "I am sure she was," she said. "And she was very fortunate to have a little brother to keep her company. She must have loved him a great deal."

Keir's grin broadened when he thought of Frances and how Merritt used to follow her around, bringing screams of ire from his sister.

"Merritt would follow her everywhere, never giving her a moment's peace," he admitted. "Frances would try to hide from him but he always found her. Then she would cry because he would not leave her alone. Sometimes he would throw rocks at her to get her attention or pull her hair. It was affectionately done but Frances wanted no part of it. Many times I would have to take Merritt with me on my duties so he would leave his sister alone."

Chloë giggled. "Still, I am positive she could not live without him."

"She could not," he nodded in agreement. "In spite of screaming every time he would come around her, she loved her brother and would call him Me-Me because she could not pronounce Merritt when she was very young. We started calling him that also."

The smile vanished from Chloë's face. *Me-Me.* That was what the little girl had said to her, the pale girl with the long hair that Keir had insisted she dreamt. She suddenly felt very shaken, startled, and unsure how to react. Keir was still sitting there looking at the soap and she removed her feet from the warm water and began drying them off with her cloak, trying to mask her shock. Keir saw what she was doing and he quickly stood up, moving for the wardrobe.

"Here," he pulled two garments off of the wardrobe door and extended them to her. "You will wear these. They are clean and very fine. I paid a good deal of money for them and I am sure Madeleine would not mind if you wore them."

Chloë looked up at him with refusal on her lips but when she saw the soft, clean and fine garments, she couldn't bring herself to refuse. With shaking hands, she reached up to take them.

"My thanks," she murmured.

Her quaking hands had not escaped his notice. His ice blue eyes lingered on her. "What is the matter?"

"What do you mean?"

"Your hands are shaking. Why?"

She couldn't tell him. She was afraid to, afraid he might think she was mad. She made up an excuse, the first thing that came to mind.

"I am… cold," she said, rising on wet feet. "I will retire to my chamber now. Thank you again for your kindness and hospitality. My thanks to Madeleine, too."

He smiled faintly. "Are you sure you are well enough to sleep in that room?"

She nodded, not wanting to delve back into the alternative. As attractive as she found the man, she would not compromise herself in such a fashion, especially with Cassandra around. Her sister would murder her.

"I am," she replied, moving to the door with the precious garments in her hands. "I will take very good care of these."

"I know you will."

He followed her to the door across the hall, making sure she was properly settled. It was the polite thing to do but the glimmer in the ice blue eyes was warmer than it had ever been. When she laid the garments on the small, dusty bed, Keir stood by the door and watched her.

"I will have this room scoured clean tomorrow," he told her. "Perhaps we can find a few female servants in town to come here and work for you and your sister."

She eyed him. "Old, ugly women," she lifted an eyebrow. "I will not be responsible for housing a brothel for lonely soldiers."

He laughed softly. "You sound like… well, it does not matter. Old and ugly they will be."

She wouldn't let him get away so fast. "Who do I sound like?"

He was still grinning as he looked at her. "I was going to say my wife."

"She was right."

With a lingering grin and a sidelong glance suggesting he was coming to warm to her just the slightest, Keir bid her a good eve and shut the door. Chloë stood there a moment, listening to his footfalls fade back into the master chamber and the door shut softly.

Now that she was alone in the quiet and haunted room, she began to feel somewhat lonely for him. It was an odd sensation, knowing she must properly separate herself from him, but on the other hand, she did so enjoy his company. There was something warm, humorous and powerful about the man, qualities she found wildly attractive. Moving to the chamber door, she laid her ear against it, listening for any sound of him.

She had no idea that, in his chamber, Keir was doing the same thing. Ear against the door, he was listening for any sound from the intriguing, spectacularly beautiful woman.

CHAPTER SEVEN

INGILBY COULD SEE Exelby Castle from the rise, a grassy hill covered with oak trees that provided shadowed cover to himself and his soldiers. He was riding with a party of twenty of his men from Ripley Castle and their purpose had been to ride to Exelby to see to its status. Ingilby's scouts were constantly monitoring the castle and its repairs but the baron wanted to see for himself. He had heard that repairs were well under way.

He could see the activity from his vantage point. Exelby Castle wasn't particularly large but it was tall and heavily fortified. Ingilby could see swarms of men on make-shift scaffolding, repairing walls and digging out the moat that was cluttered with debris from the battle. It looked like an army of ants from where he stood, all madly working to repair their shattered home.

Ingilby turned to the man directly to his left, a man who was his closest advisor and battle commander. His name was Alphonse d'Oro and he was from a particularly violent region of *España,* a man with great vision and warring tactics. Exelby had been his battle and although he had failed to reach his objective, he had certain done worthy damage.

"It appears as if they are making progress with the repairs," Ingilby said to him. "Am I to understand that the family is not in residence at this time?"

Alphonse shook his head. He was a dark man with swarthy skin and black eyes, breeding the look of contempt about him.

"Nay, my lord," his accent was very heavy. "As far as we know, they left with Coverdale. They must be at his seat of Aysgarth Castle."

Ingilby digested that information. "Aysgarth is a big castle with a big army," he muttered. "I will not attempt to penetrate it. Rest assured, de Geld will return to Exelby and there will be another day and time for me to gain his daughter. I will not fail a second time."

It was an order to Alphonse, who took it in the spirit for which it was intended. "Indeed, my lord," he replied. "We will not be caught off guard by another army arriving to support de Geld. We will be prepared."

Ingilby cast him a long glance. "You should have already been pre-pared," he said, but Alphonse did not respond. Ingilby's gaze lingered on him before turning back to the castle and continuing. "And Coverdale's knight? What have we found out about the man?"

Alphonse was eager to be off the subject of the failed siege and on to better news. "We sent four men to Exelby posing as masons looking for work," he told him. "That is how we found out that the de Geld family has gone with Coverdale to Aysgarth while their castle is being repaired. We were also able to find out about this Keir St. Héver. Apparently, he is a man with a great reputation. He used to serve the king."

"I already know that," Ingilby snapped impatiently. "What more do we know?"

Alphonse's dark eyes moved to the castle in the distance. "We know that the man is a garrison commander for Pendragon Castle," he told him. "It is common knowledge. He is highly respected. Also, the man lost his family three years ago when Pendragon was compromised during a siege. His wife and daughter were killed but his young son was taken as a prize."

Ingilby looked interested. "Is this so?" he asked. "Who is Cover-dale's enemy that he would lay siege to Pendragon?"

"Hellbeck Castle," Alphonse informed him. "Lord Stain."

"Stain?" Ingilby said with some distain. "I know of him. I have heard he eats raw peacock for supper and bathes in the blood of his enemies. Is it this madman who has St. Héver's son?"

Alphonse nodded. "It is speculated," he replied. "St. Héver spent a year trying to locate his son but has yet to find him. According to the men at Exelby, the man has not given up hope. He continues to search for him."

And it is this man who threatens me, Ingilby thought to himself. *A man who has suffered tragedy is weakened whether or not he realizes it.* Although Ingilby had never met Keir St. Héver, the threat alone regarding Chloë de Geld was an introduction. Now they were adversaries who had never even met. It was a matter of pride now and Ingilby was on Keir's scent.

"Send a missive to Lord Stain and tell him I will make a handsome offer for the son of St. Héver if he still has possession of him," he told Alphonse. Then he laughed. "It would do well for me to hold the boy because the next time we lay siege to Exelby, we can hold off Coverdale's assistance simply by letting them know that I hold St. Héver's long lost son. Do you think St. Héver would do anything stupid if he knows I hold the boy? Of course not. He, and Coverdale, will mark time while I demolish Exelby and take the Goddess for my own. Perhaps I will not even marry the woman. Perhaps I shall simply make her my whore as an example to all who defy my wishes."

He was chuckling lewdly, as was Alphonse. It was always wise to concur with Ingilby in any arena.

"A brilliant plan, my lord," Alphonse agreed.

"See to it personally, Alphonse. Know that I will not tolerate failure."

Alphonse already knew that. He did not plan to fail a second time.

☙

THE BERG OF Kirkby Stephen was more cosmopolitan than Keir had let on. About two hours north of Pendragon, it had a concentrated town center with merchants and vendors lined up in a tight circle around the village square. The day was bright and windy, and when the party from Pendragon arrived with three fully armored knights, two small women and forty men-at-arms, the people from town turned out to inspect the important visitors. The square was soon a very crowded place.

Dressed in the same clothing they had been wearing for four days, Chloë and Cassandra were ready to procure their "necessities". Cassandra was the first one off her palfrey, taking a moment to scope out the circle of stalls before charging into the first shop. Carrying the coinage their father had given them, Chloë followed.

Keir gave orders to his men to spread out around the square and watch the road leading in and out of the town. Lucan stayed in the center of the square, monitoring the activity of the area, as Keir and Michael followed the ladies. They stood outside the door of the merchant stall, listening to Cassandra ask the merchant who the finest seamstress in town was. The man recommended his wife and the negotiations began in earnest.

Keir stood in the doorway, watching Cassandra barter with the merchant as Chloë moved among the piles of fabrics, pulling out luscious dark blues, yellows and greens. She was very calculated and methodical in her fabric hunt and a little boy, the son of the merchant, followed her around and took the fabric that they pulled from the shelves.

Keir found himself watching Chloë like a hawk, her graceful movements and the serious expression on her beautiful face. She had a job to do and she was completing it concisely. He had to admire the sisters for their tactics because before the merchant realized it, he was barely making a profit on the material and had committed his wife to sewing six surcoats by the end of the day.

The man eventually hailed his wife, perhaps in a panic, and the woman appeared with a very old woman in tow, who immediately began measuring Cassandra and Chloë with her gnarled hands. Chloë explained what they wanted, the older women listened carefully, and with that, the commitment had been made. Paying the man half of what they had promised him with the agreement that they would pay the remainder when they returned for the dresses, the ladies quit the shop and moved on to their next target.

Keir and Michael followed them as they walked the streets, inspecting the leather worker's stall as well as the stall of a man who sold all manner of jewelry. Cassandra wanted jewelry but Chloë was more practical and told her sister they needed to buy their "necessities" first before buying things they truly didn't need. Michael stepped in at the disappointed look on Cassandra's face and offered to buy her whatever she wished, which thrilled Cassandra. Chloë just shook her head at her greedy sister and continued on to the next shop with Keir close behind her.

Chloë kept turning around, seeing Keir walking behind her like a massive, silent sentinel. His helm was on, his visor up, and his ice blue eyes were scanning the area for any threats, perceived or otherwise. But when Chloë turned around to look at him, he focused on her instead and she grinned at him.

"You do not have to walk behind me like a servant," she waved her hand at him, motioning him forward. "Please walk beside me."

Keir grunted. "I am afraid to."

Her smiled broadened. "Why?"

"Because you might do to me what you did to that merchant in the shop. I will soon find myself sewing all of your dresses for a mere pittance."

She laughed at him, a glorious gesture that had him captivated. "I will not force you to sew my coats."

"Promise?"

She nodded. "I do," she cast him a long glance over her shoulder. "Now, will you walk with me?"

Fighting off a grin, Keir moved up beside her. He and Chloë exchange a few flirtatious glances, mostly Chloë looking at him as he pretended not to look at her. But he was most definitely looking. As they approached another small stall, he took her hand and gently tucked it into the crook of his elbow.

Chloë held on to him tightly, as if afraid he might try to get away.

He refused to look at her, knowing she was smiling up at him, but he couldn't wipe the grin from his face as he reached down with his other hand and captured the fingers clasped around his elbow. She gripped his fingers tightly and Keir could feel his heart lighten, giddiness filling him as he'd not felt in years. He did look at her, then, only to see that she was still smiling at him. He winked at her. It was the best he could do without making a fool out of himself completely.

Chloë was so swept up in looking at the man that she hadn't realized they were at their destination. Reluctantly, she let him go and began to peruse the small selection of carved wooden boxes that contained oils to soften the skin. The oils were contained in small clay jars nestled in the boxes and she carefully went about smelling them.

She pulled Keir into her inspection and would hold up one jar for him to smell, watch his reaction, and then move on to the next one. He liked the florals and not the spices like cinnamon, clove or thyme, so Chloë purchased four phials of floral oils, three lumpy white bars of Castile soap, two ivory hair combs, and a phial of oil that was supposed to make the hair soft and shiny. The shopkeeper, a small man with rotted teeth, wrapped it all up in roughly woven fabric for her to take with her.

Keir carried the packages as they headed back to find Cassandra. They could see the blond sister and Michael across the square at another merchant shop and they moved in that direction. The wind was picking up, blowing escaped tendrils from Chloë's braided hair across her face as they crossed the muddy square with the well in the center of it.

Women from the village were gathering there with their wash and children to collect water. The well was a gathering place for tasks as well as gossip. Several of the women spied Keir, tall and strong and handsome, and immediately the blouses began to come down and expose white shoulders and smiling, come-hither faces focused on him.

Chloë noticed the female attention on Keir and she slipped her hand into the crook of his elbow, a silent inference of possession. The man didn't belong to her in the least but she wanted every woman in town to think he did. She gazed up at him, smiling, realizing that she wished he did belong to her. She wished it with all her heart. Keir caught her look and winked at her. It was enough of a warm gesture to crush the cluster of hopeful female faces.

Victorious, Chloë was silently laughing at her triumph but more than that, she wondered if Keir might actually find interest in her. He was certainly acting the part and hope bloomed in her heart. As they passed the cluster of hussies, one of Keir's soldiers swiftly approached. The man saluted sharply.

"My lord," he said to Keir. "Riders approach – two knights and about ten men-at-arms. They are riding hard from the north and will very soon be upon us."

Keir was cool. "Colors?"

"None that we could see, my lord."

Keir nodded. "Very well," he grasped Chloë by the hand and began to pull her towards Michael and her sister as the soldier followed along. He snapped orders to the soldier. "Put ten men armed with crossbows into hiding along the north road. I want the rest of them in town with me. Hurry."

The soldier fled. Chloë skipped along next to Keir, feeling some apprehension. "Is something wrong?" she asked.

He shook his head. "Not yet," he told her. "But I would rather be prepared. You and your sister will stay with Michael while I see who approaches."

Michael and Cassandra saw the pair approaching quickly. Chloë was practically running to keep up with Keir's long-legged strides. Michael had seen the soldier speak with Keir, the same man who was now running off, past the women who had tried to attract Keir and disappearing between a pair of stalls to the north. He looked expectantly to Keir as the man approached with his hands full of packages and Chloë on his arm.

"Orders, my lord?" he asked.

Keir handed him the packages. "You will take the women to safety until I know who approaches the town," he told him. "I am told two knights and ten men-at-arms are swift on the approach."

Michael understood. "Aye, my lord," he had the packages in one hand and Cassandra in the other. Chloë was still holding on to Keir and he nodded to her encouraging. "Come along, my lady."

Chloë appeared hesitant. She clutched Keir, looking anxiously to Michael and then back to Keir again. "You are not going to battle, are you?" she asked softly.

He could hear the fear in her voice. The last time unknown knights were sighted in her world, they had attacked her home. Keir smiled at her, patting her hand.

"Nay," he assured her. "But it is prudent to be cautious. I am sure there is nothing to fret over."

"Then let me come with you."

His smile faded. "Nay," he caressed the fingers in his grip. "You will go with Michael to safety."

Chloë didn't want to argue with him but she was apprehensive. Suddenly, a flood of St. Héver men came rushing into the town square and Lucan was in the middle of them, directing the men to take position. Chloë's apprehension grew but Keir watched the activity calmly before turning to her once again. He lifted her hand to his lips and kissed her warm fingers.

"Please," he murmured. "Go with Michael. Everything will be well."

"Promise?"

His smile returned. "I do."

"Keir!" Lucan suddenly called from his position near the well. "They are splitting off."

Keir strained to catch a glimpse of what Lucan was talking about, craning his neck to see up the northern road. "Where?"

Lucan put a hand in the air and motioned in circles. "All around us," he said. "They are moving to the east and west."

Keir didn't have any more time to waste. Kissing Chloë's hand again, he pushed her in Michael's direction as he moved away from her and unsheathed his broadsword. Michael was moving to pull the women into the nearest stall when a charger bearing full armor and a well –armed knight suddenly burst from the alleyway behind them, nearly running Chloë over. She shrieked in fear and bolted off, separating herself from Michael and Cassandra.

Keir wasn't far off; he saw what had happened and he rushed in Chloë's direction, holding his sword leveled at the big and fearsome knight.

"You whoreskin," he spat as he pulled Chloë against him protectively. "I ought to take your head off for nearly trampling her."

The knight just sat there, his helmed head unmoving. Then, he reached up an enormous glove and flipped up the visor. Ice blue eyes glimmered at Keir.

"It is good to see you, too, brother."

Keir growled at the man, shaking his head with frustration. "What in the hell are you doing, Kurt?"

Kurtis St. Héver's icy eyes were glittering with warmth at his younger brother. "Did I frighten you, little girl?"

"You did not. But you nearly ran the lady over."

Kurtis' gaze moved from his brother to the spectacular redhead in his arms. She was a magnificent vision of porcelain skin and perfect features. His expression moved from warm greeting to cool regard.

"My apologies," he said, his voice deep.

Keir still had hold of Chloë against him, realizing that she was trembling. Simply to comfort the shaken woman, he caressed her back soothingly as she pressed fearfully against him.

"This is the Lady Chloë de Geld," he introduced her. "That is her sister, the Lady Cassandra, under Michael's protection. Ladies, this is my brother, Sir Kurtis St. Héver."

Chloë politely acknowledged him, relishing the gentle caress of Keir's hand against her back but not entirely comfortable with it in a public venue. She discreetly moved away from him to recover her composure.

"It is a pleasure to meet you, Sir Kurtis," she said.

Kurtis dipped his head but said nothing. His eyes were the same color as his brother's but they were somehow harder, more intense. He regarded the spectacular woman for a moment before returning his attention to his brother.

"What are you doing here?" he asked. "I thought you would be at Pendragon."

Keir gestured to the women. "We have guests at Pendragon," he said. "It is a long story, but suffice it to say that I am charged with the protection of Lady Chloë and Lady Cassandra for the time being. The ladies wished to do some shopping so here we are."

Kurtis' cold gaze moved back to Chloë and then to Cassandra. "I see," he replied, although he really didn't. He refocused on his brother. "I am returning from Penrith on an errand for Northumberland. I sent a scout ahead about a half hour ago, meant for Pendragon, but he returned to say that he saw you in town."

"So that is why you were riding hard to reach us."

Kurtis nodded. "I wanted to surprise you. Perhaps even rob you if you had purchased anything worth stealing."

Keir just shook his head, grinning, and sheathed his sword. He watched Chloë as she moved a wide berth around Kurtis' menacing charger to reach her sister. She whispered something to Cassandra, who nodded, and the pair moved off into another stall. Michael followed, leaving Keir behind with his brother.

Kurtis dismounted his charger and removed his helm, scratching his white-blond hair beneath. He was a big man like his brother, shorter than Keir by a few inches, with a steely demeanor about him. He had a shadow of his brother's good looks but not his pleasing personality. But there was no one in Northern England better with a sword and Kurtis had seen many battles against the Scots to cement his powerful reputation. His post with the Earl of Northumberland was a prestigious one. He eyed his younger brother as he fidgeted with his hauberk, his helm.

"You are looking well," he commented. "Old, but well."

Keir gave him a crooked grin. In spite of everything, he was very glad to see his brother. He slapped the man on a broad shoulder.

"And you are every inch the idiot I remember," he replied. "How is Northumberland treating you?"

Kurtis nodded. "Well enough," he replied. "I am now Captain of the Guard so I cannot complain."

Keir was impressed. "Congratulations," he said. "I hope you choke on it."

For the first time, stone-faced Kurtis cracked a smile. "I fear I already have," he muttered. "Speaking of choking, what are those women really doing at Pendragon?"

Keir folded his big arms across his chest, shifting on his legs. "We attended a siege at Exelby Castle several days ago, defending those women and their family from an onslaught by Baron Ingilby," he told him. "Ingilby wants to marry Lady Chloë but she wants nothing to do with him, so her father has asked that I take charge of both women and hide them at Pendragon until the situation settles down. Exelby is in ruins and they have nowhere else to go."

Kurtis listened intently. "John Ingilby?"

"The same."

"The man is Northumberland's kin."

"I know."

Kurtis scratched his chin with some agitation. "You are hiding the man's betrothed from him? What if he comes to Northumberland to seek support to regain her? I will...."

Keir waved him off. "She is not, nor was she ever, betrothed to him," he clarified. "Ingilby simply cannot accept her refusal and resorted to laying siege to Exelby in the hopes of capturing a bride."

Kurtis wasn't comfortable with the situation; that was clear. He spied the women in the distance, rifling through the goods of a merchant stall, and finally shook his head.

"She is not your burden," he told his brother. "You should have nothing to do with this."

Keir nodded. "I agree, but Coverdale gave me an order and I must comply. Exelby is an ally."

"Does Ingilby know you have her?"

"He does not, at least at the moment."

Kurtis grunted. "When he finds out, he will come for her. I hope you are prepared for a siege."

"I am always prepared."

"I know you are, but this would be a waste of men and material. She does not belong at Pendragon."

"Then you go and tell Coverdale. Let us see if he will listen to you."

It was a sarcastic remark, one that Kurtis lifted an eyebrow at. He could see there was no simple answer to the situation so he shook his head again, eyeing the women in the distance. After several moments of deliberation, he sighed heavily.

"This cannot be good for you," he finally said, his tone considerably softer. "Having a woman at Pendragon… it simply cannot be good for you."

Keir knew what he meant and he averted his gaze, not wanting to delve into that touchy subject. "I am fine," he insisted quietly. "Lady Chloë and her sister have been a delight."

Kurtis looked at him. "Truthfully?" he wasn't sure he believed him. "For the man I have known over the past three years does not react well to the presence of women."

Keir's manner was growing increasingly defensive. "I appreciate your concern, but I assure you that all is well."

Kurtis wouldn't back down. He fixed on his brother. "I did not imagine your arm around her when I rode up," he snapped softly. "What are you thinking, Keir? That perhaps you want another wife? I will protest that decision until the day I die because I know, for a fact, that you could not stand to lose another. I watched you go through hell after Maddie's death and it nearly destroyed me as well. It was me who chained you to the walls of the vault so you would not kill yourself and me who sat with you day after day, making sure you had food and water, taking care of you because you were incapable of taking care of yourself. Get those women out of Pendragon, brother; get them out before they are the death of you."

Keir laughed bitterly. "So you think to box me up and keep me in solitude for the rest of my life? Why am I not allowed to reclaim the happiness I once knew?"

Kurtis looked at him as if he were mad. "Are you actually considering it?"

Keir threw up his hands. "I do not know," he insisted, his hands coming to rest on his brother's wide shoulders. "I appreciate your concern and loyalty, Kurt, I truly do and I love you for it. But you worry overly. I am fine."

The last few words were punctuated with a slap to Kurtis' cheek. Keir smiled at his brother and removed his hands from his shoulders, his gaze finding Chloë and Cassandra as they moved to another stall with tall, broad Michael following. Kurtis, at a genuine loss for words, turned to see what had his brother so captivated. As he noted at the onset, the redhead was a lovely little thing, as was her blond sister. Kurtis had always preferred blonds and his eye naturally went to Cassandra. He finally grunted and looked away.

"Are they both unattached?" he asked.

Keir nodded. "Cassandra is the older sibling," he told him. "Their father will not marry off Chloë until Cassandra is married."

"Chloë is the redhead?"

"Aye."

Kurtis stared at the woman, nodding his head after a moment. "She is magnificent, no doubt," he admitted. "I have seen many women in my lifetime but never one of such radiant beauty. No wonder Ingilby wants her."

Keir gave him a crooked grin. "True enough, but I need her sister out of the way before I can court her. Will you do this for me, brother?"

Kurtis' stone-like expression fractured into a sneer. "Never," he snapped, turning back to his horse. "Find someone else to do your dirty work."

Keir bit off his laughter. "Cassandra is a beautiful woman. Very intelligent also. She would make a fine prize."

Kurtis reached his horse and prepared to mount. "Go away and leave me alone."

Keir was starting to laugh. "You need a wife so you will not be so bitter and surly all of the time," he told him. "You have the charm of driftwood, Kurt. A woman will do wonders for you."

Kurtis mounted, fixing his brother in the eye as he settled himself in the saddle. "Like a woman did for you? No, thank you. I do not want any part of that."

Keir's laughter faded but his smile remained. "Do not let yourself be fooled," he insisted softly. "The years I was married to Madeleine were the best years of my life."

Kurtis leaned forward on the saddle, his icy blue eyes intense. "Would you say that losing your wife and children in the end was well worth those wonderful years?"

"So you would rather live your life a miserable man, safe from the threat of love?"

"I would rather not lose something I so desperately loved that it took the life right out of me like it did you."

Keir's smile faded completely and the pale blue eyes dulled. After a moment, he simply turned and walked away. With a heavy heart, Kurtis watched him go. Perhaps he had said too much but, in his opinion, Keir needed to be reminded of what a woman could do to a man's soul. Infatuation could do much to cloud memories. He simply didn't want to see his brother hurt again.

He knew, for a fact, the man would not survive.

CHAPTER EIGHT

THE BRIGHT SILVER moonlight streamed in through the lancet window, softly illuminating the chamber where Keir's children had once slept. A fire burned low in the hearth, crackling, as Chloë slept warm, clean and cozy in a new sleeping shift and freshened bed linens.

Chloë and Cassandra had spent most of their money in town, coming away in early evening with twelve new surcoats between them, shifts, pantalets, and all manner of combs, scarves, hose, oils, creams and soaps. They nearly bought everything the merchants carried, including a giant trunk made from cedar wood that one of the fabric merchants used to store his goods. Keir had purchased the trunk since the ladies didn't have anything to carry their new things with. Since they hadn't brought a wagon, the men-at-arms took turns lugging it.

Better still, they were able to secure two women servants in town, older spinsters who were willing to work at Pendragon with the promise of good wages. They were old and ugly, as Chloë had insisted, but they cooked and cleaned like angels.

The evening meal was delayed due to their late return from the town but the two older women managed to pull together a plain but plentiful feast of mutton, beans, peas and big hunks of brown bread and butter. While the knights and ladies ate, they had moved into the two chambers that Chloë and Cassandra were assigned and scrubbed the daylights out of anything with a surface. Places that hadn't been cleaned since Madeleine's death were now shiny and new again, properly cleaned for proper ladies.

But it was a process that took time and it was close to midnight by the time Chloë and her sister went to bed. The rooms were swept and scrubbed, the linens marginally cleaned with the promise of washing on the morrow, so the women bid the men in the hall good eve and proceeded to bed. They were both exhausted. Dressing in a rough-finished sleeping shift with a heavier robe of rabbit-lined linen, Chloë had fallen into a deep, sweet sleep almost immediately.

Now, in the dead of night, the moonlight was very bright and somewhere, an owl hooted into the darkness. Chloë was dreaming of bread custard her mother used to make, with raisins and nuts, dreaming that she was eating it as it snowed inside the hall at Exelby. It was very cold and she shivered, pulling the covers more closely around her.

But warm dreams of bread custard faded as she awoke, groggy and half-asleep, to realize that it was freezing inside the chamber. She looked to the fire, seeing that it was still glowing, but her breath was hanging in the air. There was mist upon the wind and the hair on the back of her neck began to stand up. Suddenly, Chloë wasn't so groggy any more. She was scared.

Terror filled her and her heart began to pound against her ribs. Eyes open, she dared not move as her eyes darted about, searching for the source of her terror. She could feel it somewhere, knowing it was lingering close by but too frightened to move. She wanted to scream but couldn't. As her eyes searched the darkness, a small, ghostly shape suddenly emerged from the wall near the hearth. It passed right through the stone and moved, shapeless and shiftless, near the bed.

Terrified, Chloë sat bolt upright in bed as the specter of a little girl took shape. Gradually, she could see every detail of the child, from her long pale hair to her piercing black eyes. The child was shades of gray so she couldn't discern any color, but she did think that the shape of the child's jaw was familiar. She had a very square jaw just like....

"Frances?" Chloë asked timidly "Is it you?"

The little girl stared at her with her dark-circled black eyes. Then she pointed in the general direction of the big wardrobe, the wall. "Me-Me," she hissed.

Chloë was frightened but somehow, she felt as if the child were coming to her for answers or assistance. She wasn't sure which. But this was the second night in a row that the phantom had appeared to her and she instinctively wanted to help. If this was true and she wasn't dreaming, then Keir's little daughter's soul was not at rest and the thought was heartbreaking. The child needed, or wanted, something desperately enough to remain behind when she should have gone straight to heaven. The clue was in the asking.

"Me-Me," she repeated, whispering. "Are you looking for Merritt? I do not know where he is."

The wraith was still pointing at the wall. "Me-Me," she murmured again.

Chloë nodded, feeling a little braver. "Aye, Frances, I know about Me-Me," she whispered. "But I do not know where he is. Are you looking for him?"

The specter continued to stare at her, growing oddly paler by the moment. "Me-Me."

Chloë looked to the wall where the child was pointing. She couldn't see anything there in the shadows other than the door, the wall and the wardrobe. Feeling increasingly sad and frustrated in her desire to help, she shook her head at the specter.

"Me-Me is not here, sweetheart," she said gently. "We do not know where he is, I am sorry. Do… do *you* know where he is, perhaps?"

The phantom was beginning to undulate now, shape-shifting. "With thee…," she murmured, "now I sleep."

With that, a huge icy wind suddenly arose, enveloping her, swirling over her and Chloë screamed in fear as the specter suddenly howled an unearthly roar and ballooned to titanic proportions, dissolving into mist and shadow. Chloë covered her eyes, terrified, as the phantom blew through her, lifting her hair like a wild wind. But in that contact between the spirit world and the world of the living, Chloë felt the overwhelming emotions of sadness, fear and pain. She could feel distress and terror on a level she had never before experienced. It filled every inch of her and she gasped as the sensation swirled through her body.

She tried to stagger to her feet but ended up falling to the floor. As swiftly as the wind rose, it was abruptly gone, leaving horrific grief and sorrow in its wake. When it was vanished and all was suddenly still, Chloë found herself on her knees in shock.

Mouth hanging open and hair askew, she found herself staring at her shaking hands as if hardly believing what had happened. Her heart was pounding so hard she was sure it would pound right out of her chest and in the midst of it all she could smell a distinctive scent. It was something between dirt and roses, a warm, pervasive scent. Smelling her hands, it was strong. Sniffing her arms, and then her robe, she realized it was all over her.

The smell was everywhere, the scent of a little girl lost. She burst into tears, sobbing into her hands as if her heart were broken. She fell forward, onto the newly swept floor, weeping pitifully. Outside her chamber door, she began to hear sounds as someone called her name and tried to lift the latch. But the door was bolted and she heard someone shout her name again.

It was Keir. There was no mistaking his strong, booming voice. Chloë struggled off the floor, picking herself up and staggering to the door. She threw the bolt and yanked open the oak panel, sobbing deeply. Before Keir could ask her what the trouble was, she shoved her hands in his face.

"Smell!" she wept, pushing her hands into his nose even as he reached out to steady her. "Do you smell her? She was here. *She was here!*"

Keir had heard her screaming from downstairs. He had raced up the stairs only to find a locked bolt and the sounds of weeping from the other side. Chloë was pale and frantic, pushing her hands into his face, and he had no choice but to do as she commanded. He smelled her hands. Then his eyes widened.

"What…?" he smelled again, deeply. "God's Blood, what *is* that?"

Chloë was struggling to calm herself but she wasn't doing a very good job. She lifted her robe to his face, pushing it into his nose.

"Do you smell her?" she asked, tears and mucus pouring down her face. "Do you smell Frances?"

Keir's face paled as he smelled deeply of her robe, her arm, her shift, anything she would lift up to him. He began to tremble.

"I smell…," he muttered hoarsely.

"It is her," she cut him off, putting her hands on his nose again. "She was here. She asked for Me-Me and then she went right through me. Keir, she went *through* me. Do you smell her?"

Shaken, Keir began to tear up because he could indeed smell his daughter on the woman's hands. He didn't know how or why, but he could. He hadn't smelled that wonderful smell in three long years and it was enough to choke him up. Kurtis was standing beside him, bewildered and mildly outraged, but Keir grabbed her hands and shoved them into his brother's face.

"It is her," he insisted quietly. "It is Frances. Do you smell her?"

Kurtis smelled flowers and something earthy, along with the warm smell of human flesh. He looked at his brother, wondering how to tell the man that he was following a crazy woman's fantasy. He sighed heavily.

"Keir, get hold of yourself," he told his brother. "You smell the soap we purchased this afternoon and nothing more."

Chloë looked at Kurtis, the voice of dissention, and suddenly realized how idiotic she must appear. Keir understood but Kurtis did not. Even Cassandra, awakened by her sister's screams, was standing next to her and looking at her as if she had lost her mind. Chloë was normally an intensely private person and the attention, as she came to her senses, was not something she was willing to insist upon. She didn't want to make Keir look like an idiot because she knew, as she gazed into his shaken face, that he would believe her. Perhaps he missed his family so badly that he would believe anything.

Lowering her hands, Chloë turned back for the bedchamber but Keir grabbed her. "Hold, lady," he murmured. "Where are you going?"

She looked at the three curious faces gazing back at her as she labored to recover her composure. "I… it must have been a dream," she said, backing into the room. "Keir, I am sorry. I have had dreams since I was here and I did not mean to… I apologize for making a mockery of your child. I did not mean to but the… the dreams are very vivid."

Keir had his hands on her, not wanting her to get away. "You have not made a mockery of anything." He lifted her hands, smelling them again. His pale blue eyes glowed. "I smell her. This is my daughter."

Chloë could see over his shoulder that Kurtis' expression was darkening by the second. Fearful of the man's reaction, or perhaps how he would view his brother, she shook her head. "Nay," she insisted. "I… I apologize. I had a nightmare, 'tis all. You only smell soap."

Keir's brow furrowed in disbelief, perhaps some anguish, as Kurtis grasped him by the arm. "You heard her," he said quietly though firmly. "It was simply a figment of her imagination. Let her go back to bed."

"Are you saying my sister is mad?" Cassandra chimed in, her fire focused on Kurtis. "My sister is as levelheaded and sensible as any woman who has walked this earth. If she said a little girl came to her, then she did. She would not lie and she is not insane."

Kurtis looked at the woman, a very pretty spitfire of a woman, and his square jaw ticked impatiently.

"I did not call her mad," he pointed out. "I merely said she imagined it and now she has my brother imagining it as well."

Cassandra would not let him go so easily. "How do you know what is truth and what is not?" she fired back. "It is possible that my sister dreamt of Keir's daughter."

Kurtis wasn't going to fight with the lovely blond, although he wasn't particularly fond of outspoken women. This one was certainly outspoken. He grasped his brother by the arms and tried to turn him back to the stairs.

"Come along," he instructed quietly. "Let the women return to bed."

Keir wouldn't go with his brother, shrugging him off. "Take Lady

Cassandra back to her chamber," he told him. "I will stay with Chloë awhile."

Kurtis didn't like that idea at all. He shook his head. "Keir...."

But Keir cut him off, lifting his eyebrows for emphasis. "Go," he told his brother kindly, firmly. "Please, Kurt. I will see you on the morrow."

Jaw ticking, Kurtis did as he was told although he made it very clear that he was unhappy about it. He had noticed from the onset that afternoon that the lovely and luscious Lady Chloë had some kind of hold over his brother, something he had never seen before. His brother was obviously enraptured with the woman and Kurtis didn't think it was healthy for him in the least.

Even now, she spoke of crazy dreams involving Keir's children and the man believed her. But Kurtis knew his brother well enough to know that all the arguing in the world could not dissuade him. If Keir wanted to stay with the woman, then he would. Frustrated, Kurtis reached out to politely take Cassandra's arm but she balked.

"I can find my own chamber, thank you," she snapped, looking at her sister with a softened expression. "Are you sure you are well, sweetheart?"

Chloë nodded. "I am," she said. "I am sorry to have awoken you."

"Why not sleep in my chamber with me? You might sleep better."

Chloë shook her head. "I cannot sleep with you and you know it. Your snoring keeps me awake. But I thank you for the offer."

Cassandra appeared defensive as well as embarrassed. "I do *not* snore," she insisted, purely for the benefit of the knights. She frowned at her ungracious sister. "If you change your mind, you know where I am."

Chloë smiled at her sister, not oblivious to the fact that she had embarrassed her, as the woman moved down the stairs. Kurtis silently followed.

When the landing was still and quiet but for the two of them, Chloë turned to Keir. Her smile faded and her brown eyes grew serious as she gazed up at him.

"She *did* come to me, twice," she whispered. "You said I was dreaming the first time. Now, do you believe me? Can you really smell her on me?"

Keir's eyes were riveted to her. Reaching out an enormous hand, he fingered her hair, the luxurious red strands that fell in a great thick mane to her knees. He brought a handful of hair to his nose, inhaling deeply.

"I can," he murmured.

Chloë felt the heat from his gaze, thrilling and unnerving her. She was not particularly accustomed to men and their charms, as her father had focused most suitors on Cassandra while he hid her well away.

The problem was that when men saw Chloë, they forgot about all else, including Cassandra. The younger sister with the glorious red hair had been the true de Geld prize as legend of her beauty spread. Chloë had therefore had little exposure to the ways of men but with Keir, everything seemed to flow on instinct. It was as if the two of them were gradually becoming symbiotic.

He was still holding her hair when she turned away and went into her chamber. Keir followed, his eyes darting around the dark chamber, sniffing the air to see if he could smell the same scent that was on Chloë. But there was nothing in the air other than smoke and the scent of cold, damp stone, so he moved to the hearth and threw a few hunks of peat on it, stoking it. By the time he turned to Chloë, she was sitting on the bed.

She was watching him feed the fire, the firelight flickering off her glorious hair. Keir stood up, looking at her expectantly, waiting for her to speak. It was apparent that she was wrought with much on her mind. He could just tell by her expression.

"May I ask you a question, my lord?" she asked softly.

He nodded faintly. "Please," he said, "you will call me Keir."

"Keir," she whispered. "Will you... will you please tell me what happened to your children? Why is this little girl appearing to me and asking for her brother?"

He drew in a long, thoughtful breath, lowering himself onto the bed beside her. He was pensive, calm, his elbows resting on his knees as he clasped his big hands.

"I had been away for a few days when I received word from a panicked soldier that Pendragon was under siege," he said softly. "I had the bulk of my army with me, almost eight hundred men, so I knew the castle was undermanned. However, Pendragon is so fortified with moats, walls and causeways that I was not particularly concerned. At least, I was not particularly concerned until I returned home and found the castle breached."

Chloë could see that speaking of it was painful. She reached out to comfort him, laying her hand over his clasped fingers. He took her hand and held it tightly, warmly, between his two big palms before continuing.

"I did not know the keep had been breached until we managed to fight our way into the bailey," he told her. "Then I saw smoke and fire everywhere, pouring from the windows of the keep. Knowing my wife and children were inside, I made all due haste to reach the keep and almost got myself killed in the process. Michael somehow made it into the keep before me and found my wife and daughter. He begged me not to go to them but I refused. I think I even hit him in the face at some point. I found them… Madeleine and Frances were in the master's chamber and the attackers had burned what they had not looted, including my wife and daughter."

Chloë's eyes widened. "She was… burned?"

He nodded weakly, gazing at his hands as they held her small, soft one. "Mostly," he whispered. "We buried Madeleine and Frances together."

"And Merritt?"

He lifted his shoulders, struggling against the horrific memories of his wife and daughter's deaths. He had never spoken of them, not to anyone, but Chloë had somehow eased him enough to discuss it. It was as if telling her brought him a certain amount of consolation, odd as it was. Somehow, he just didn't feel the pain he used to, the stabbing grief that ate at him. As he looked into her beautiful eyes, he could see comfort and kindness there. It helped him a great deal.

"We never found him," he muttered. "We searched this castle from top to bottom but he was never found. I thought perhaps Lord Stain, the man who destroyed my castle and killed my wife and daughter, had somehow taken him to ransom but that was not the case. Coverdale spent months negotiating with the man and was convinced he did not have my son. So I have spent three years looking for him, searching, making contacts and hoping somehow I would discover his whereabouts, but no one could help me. It is as if he has simply vanished."

Although Chloë had already heard the gist of the story from her father, to hear it from Keir's lips was truly agonizing. She felt a great deal of pity for the man. She slipped from the bed to the floor at his feet, clutching both of his hands as she gazed up at him.

"God bless you for the horror you have endured," she declared earnestly. "I cannot imagine your suffering. I cannot imagine what it would be like to lose my entire family."

He gazed into her sweet face, the most beautiful he had ever seen. Aye, it was true. Madeleine had been beautiful in a sweet sort of way, but Chloë's beauty was the stuff of legends. She was magnificent, in every way. Ingilby called her *the goddess* and he was absolutely right. The name suited her perfectly. Keir cupped her face with a big hand and bent down, kissing her sweetly on the cheek.

"If God is merciful, you will never have to," he muttered, his lips still against her face. "But I thank you for your words of comfort. It has done my heart good to come to know you, Chloë de Geld. You remind me that there is still kindness and beauty in the world. It is something I had forgotten."

She could feel him breathing against her cheek and her heart began to race. "I have come to see you as a good and true man, Keir St. Héver. Perhaps God will take pity on you and bless you someday with greater riches than you have ever known. You have earned it."

Keir's lips were still against her cheek, his nose inhaling the scent of her skin, of that magnificent red hair. The hand that cupped her cheek began to caress it, feeling her silken flesh against his fingers. It had been years since he'd tasted a woman and the feel of her, the scent of her, was overwhelming him. His other hand came up, cupping her entire head between his two enormous hands as his lips began to move along her jaw line.

Chloë felt his hot, gentle kisses and her body began to tremble. His touch had an intoxicating effect on her and she could feel herself collapsing, surrendering, as his mouth moved across her chin. He was close to her lips but he didn't kiss her mouth, instead continuing across her jaw to the other cheek. It was erotic, gentle and wholly passionate as his kisses gained strength and moved across one eye and then the other. Chloë shivered, gasped, feeling every kiss like a thousand pinpricks of light, filling her and illuminating her, waiting for the magic moment when he would claim her mouth.

Keir was moving in that direction and the taste of her, the feel of her, dissolved his control. She was warm and sweet and delicious, better and more than he had ever tasted in his life. He didn't realize until he touched her how starved he was for her. He slanted his mouth hungrily over her lips, his hands moving into her hair, holding her head against him as his mouth ravaged hers.

In his grip, Chloë whimpered softly at the delight of his touch, her first experience with a man and his magic, and she was not disappointed. In fact, she was wildly aroused by it. The beautiful, sheltered and proper young woman was coming out of her shell. It felt like the most natural of things, his lips against hers, his hands in her hair. She knew she could learn to love it. Her arms wound up around his neck and she pulled him close.

Keir felt her respond to him and it fed his lust. He removed his hands from her hair and wrapped his big arms around her body, pulling her up against him. His tongue licked at her lips, begging for admittance, and she timidly opened her mouth because he was. He invaded her with his tongue, tasting her sweetness and losing himself completely. He'd spent so much of his time fighting his feelings for the woman that now the dam had burst and everything was gushing forward.

Chloë held on to him tightly as he flipped her onto her back, laying her on the mattress and covering her with his enormous body. His mouth was a wicked thing, sucking every thought from her head as he tasted her passionately. His arms, massive strong things, were around her but she could feel his hands moving, caressing her, exploring her back and her torso.

She was enjoying his closeness, her first foray into the world of passion, when his hand began to move across her belly, up towards her breasts. She could feel it getting closer and closer, finally stroking the underside of her right breast. As exciting and titillating as it was, she also knew it wasn't proper. She did not want to be groped by the man, no matter how attracted she was to him. When he moved to enclose her breast in his palm, she put up a hand and stopped him.

"Nay," she breathed, tearing her mouth away from his. "Please… you must not."

Keir had been far gone with passion, only aware of his strong reaction to Chloë and her sweet body. But as she spoke, stopping his onslaught, he came to his senses enough to realize he was moving for intimate places. He further realized that he fully intended to bed the woman. There was no question in his mind. But as he pulled back and gazed into her gorgeous, somewhat fearful face, his ardor cooled.

"Forgive me," he whispered. "I should not have taken such liberties but… Chloë, I cannot explain what I feel for you, only that I do. I have not felt anything in three years, not since I found the smoldering body of my wife and child and swore I would never feel anything again. But the first time I saw you, even as you were gouging at my eyes and fighting me, something inside me reawakened."

Chloë listened, wide-eyed. "You… you *feel* something for me?"

He nodded, pushing himself off of her and refusing to look at her. He sat on the edge of the bed, looking rather stiff and ill. Chloë sat up next to him, studying his powerful profile.

"What do you feel?" she whispered.

He shook his head, hanging it. "I do not know," he muttered. "I can only tell you that it is soft and warm, and it consumes me. It is like nothing I have ever felt before and it scares me to death."

Bewildered, Chloë sat next to him, trying to decipher his feelings as well as her own. She had feelings, too. It was not fair for him to be the only one forced into a confession.

"I have lived a very protected and privileged existence," she murmured. "Although Cassandra dreams of marrying a man she loves, I have never had such dreams. My parents exist in marriage but do not love one another. Love or emotion does not enter into their bargain, as it was arranged by their parents. My father explained to me many a time that marriage is a contract and nothing more, and that is how I understand it. But you... you have changed that perspective for me. What a wonderful thing it must be to be married to someone you adore."

He did look at her then, his gaze moving over her spectacular face. He shook his head in wonder.

"Do you have any concept of how beautiful you are?" he breathed. "You are like an angel descended from Heaven, the most perfect woman God has ever created delivered right into our midst. You said Ingilby calls you the goddess and, God's Beard, the man is completely right in his assessment. You are a goddess beyond my wildest dreams."

She smiled faintly, a soft blush mottling her cheeks. "You flatter me, my lord."

He shook his head emphatically. "It is not idle praise, I swear it. I mean every word. Every man that looks upon you thinks the same thing but I have been given the honor of coming to know you beyond your physical beauty and I will tell you again that you are the most beautiful woman I have ever seen, inside and out. The man who marries you will be the most fortunate man in England, with God as my witness."

Her smile grew, thinking he was leading up to something very hopeful. "Would it be bold of me to ask if it is your intention to be that fortunate man?"

He stared at her, looking rather staggered by her question. He rose from the bed, pacing towards the lancet window as he ran his fingers through his cropped hair. There was nervousness to his movements. When he finally turned to look at her, there was great sorrow in his eyes.

"I do not know," he said hoarsely. "I truthfully do not know if it can be me. All I know is that my feelings for you are very powerful but I do not know if I am strong enough to manage them."

Her smile faded as she watched his tense body language. "What does that mean?"

"It means that no matter what I feel for you, I do not know if there can be anything between us," he said, shaking his head and averting his gaze. "I should not have kissed you but I could not help myself. You are overwhelmingly sweet, Chloë. Perhaps... perhaps I simply wanted to taste you. Perhaps I wanted to satisfy my curiosity. Perhaps I wanted to know what I could never have."

She was crushed, starting to tear up. "Why can you never have me?"

He looked sharply at her, seeing that she was growing upset. He silently cursed himself for his tactless words as he made his way back over to her. He was a truthful man but not always diplomatic. He went to his knees before her, his big hands on her arms.

"Chloë, love, listen to me," he begged softly. "My wife and I loved each other. I had a glorious life with her and my children. When she died, something in me died also, but the past few days with you have seen a resurgence of those warm, wonderful feelings I once knew, even greater than I ever experienced with Madeleine. It is true that I loved the woman but when I look at you... God, I know I could love you so much that it would rip my heart and body and soul to pieces to even be away from you for a single minute. You already consume me as

Madeleine never did, not ever. I cannot stomach to think of you with another man yet it scares me to death to think of you with me. You would consume everything about me, Chloë. You would become my all for living. But the fear of losing you as I lost my wife and children terrifies me more than you can possibly comprehend. I survived the loss of Madeleine and my children and by God's good grace stand here before you a sane man. But if something were to happen to you... I would explode into a million pieces of heartbreak. There would be no recovery. My fear of that has the better of me right now."

Chloë stared at him, fat tears rolling down her porcelain cheeks. Her lower lip trembled and Keir clucked softly, sympathetically, and gently wiped the tears away. He pulled her into his arms, kissing her cheeks gently.

"Do not cry, love," he whispered as she sobbed softly against him. "Please do not cry. I cannot bear it."

Chloë sobbed deeply and threw her arms around his neck, holding him fast. "I want to go home," she wept.

He held her tightly, rocking her gently in the darkness of the night. "Your home is destroyed, sweetheart," he said. "You must stay here for now."

She shook her head, suddenly pulling away from him. Her glorious hair was snagged on his mail and he tried to pull it out even as she stood up, ripping strands from her head.

"Then send me to Aysgarth," she sobbed. "I cannot stay here with you. I cannot be with you... around you every day and know there is no hope between us. I was so happy to come here with you because I had hoped... oh, they were such foolish hopes but hopes nonetheless. I hoped I could make you want me, that perhaps we could be happy together. All I have known in my life are insufferable fools and old men who want to marry me but you are everything I could ever dream of and more. I see something in you that I want very much."

Keir watched her, feeling heartbroken and shaken. "As I see in you," he insisted softly. "Perhaps... you must give me time to understand this fear and reconcile it. Perhaps in time...."

She shook her head, turning away from him angrily. "I will return to Aysgarth tomorrow and marry Ingilby and be done with it," she wept furiously. "You are the only man I have ever felt anything for, Keir, but if you do not want me, then I must leave here and never look back. I cannot stay."

Keir stiffened at the mention of Ingilby. He was on her in three big strides, grabbing her by the arms and spinning her around to face him.

"Listen to me and listen well," he growled. "You are not going to marry Ingilby, not ever. Do you understand me?"

She struggled to break free from his grip. "You cannot dictate whom I shall marry," she snapped. "At least Ingilby wants me."

He wouldn't let her get away. "I never said that I did not want you," he shook her gently in the hope she would focus on him and stop struggling. "I want you in the worst way but I am scared to death. I simply do not know what to do. If you cannot understand that, I am not sure how I can explain it any better."

She ripped her arms free of his grasp and stumbled away from him, turning her back to him. "Go away," she wept, feeling weak and sorrowful more than angry. She buried her face in her hands. "Get out and leave me alone."

Keir stood there, watching her heaving shoulders and feeling as bad as he could possibly feel. He didn't want to leave her, not like this, but he suspected they had moved past the point of rational conversation for now. She was upset and exhausted, and he was confused as hell. But he just couldn't let her go.

Slowly, silently, he walked up behind her. He didn't want to put his hands on her and risk another physical struggle so he bent down, slowly, and gently shoved his face into the left side of her head. Chloë weakly tried to move her head away from him but she didn't go far; Keir pressed his face against her hair, his nose inhaling her sweet, musky fragrance.

"Please do not hate me," he murmured. "I want to love you, Chloë,

I swear it. I just need… time…."

She burst into a new round of sobs, tears streaming down her face. Keir threw his arms around her and she didn't resist. He rocked her gently, feeling the sobs wrack her body, wishing he hadn't upset her so. But he had been truthful.

After several minutes of holding her close, he swept her into his arms and carried her back to the bed, laying her softly upon the mattress. He pulled the covers up over her, tucked her in tightly, and then lay next to her on top of the coverlet. Putting his big arms around her, he pulled her close against his chest and buried his face in the back of her head.

Chloë didn't resist. More tears ensued as she reckoned it would be the closest she was able to get to the man, right here, right now, in this little bed in the spooky, shadowed chamber. She would take what she could get, if even for a stolen moment. Her hand came up, reaching up to touch his cheek as he buried himself in her head. He kissed her hand repeatedly, his big fingers coming up to intertwine in her small, soft fingers. He hand her hand to his lips, holding her tightly in the darkness, until she fell asleep.

Keir stayed awake all night. He didn't want to miss a minute of having the woman in his arms. He wondered if he held her long enough, if his fear would go away.

Unfortunately, it only grew worse.

CHAPTER NINE

I T WAS RAINING heavily this night as Alphonse and four of his men left Hellbeck Castle and made their way east, following the narrow road that wound through the dark and cloudy Pennine dales and on into North Yorkshire. From there, they would cut south to Ripon. Truth was, Alphonse wasn't so sure he wanted to reach Ripley any time soon, at least until he figured out what he was going to tell Ingilby. At the moment, he was at a loss what to tell the man and his apprehension was growing. Stain did not have the boy.

Alphonse had spent three days at Hellbeck, trying to negotiate the sale of the boy with a truly insane man, one who would talk to the moldy green walls and try to burn his fingers in the great yellow licks of a blazing fire. Everyone at Hellbeck was mad as far as he was concerned and Stain would never give him a direct answer as to where St. Héver's boy was. It had made for an odd and somewhat harrowing visit.

Alphonse had therefore sent his men searching as he kept the crazy old fool occupied and his men had come back empty handed. It was only by chance, and a greedy servant who demanded payment in exchange for information, that Alphonse learned Stain did not have the boy. He never did. And with that, Alphonse and his men gladly left the dark, turbulent castle of Hellbeck.

Now it was a matter of dealing with Ingilby. The man would consider Alphonse's trip to Hellbeck a failure if a boy was not produced and he was less than eager to return to Ripley. It was then that Alphonse began to realize that he needed to find a replacement child, something that Ingilby could present as St. Héver's son. It didn't matter if it was not the correct child – all that mattered was that they had a child, any child. St. Héver and Coverdale would not know the child was not St. Héver's son until everything was said and done with, and Ingilby had Lady Chloë. So Alphonse went on the hunt for his mission objective.

They traveled by night through the pass and emerged into North Yorkshire by morning. It was still raining heavily when the rode into the small village of Bowes on the edge of the mountains and took shelter in the only tavern in town.

Alphonse had discussed his idea with his men, all Spaniards who were loyal to him, and the five of them set out to capture a boy under the age of five years. All they knew was that St. Héver's son had been very young when he had been captured so it was the best they could do. But the boy came in the gift of the tavern keeper's son, a five year old with white hair and big brown eyes. He helped his father tend the tavern and when Alphonse caught sight of the child sweeping the floor, he knew he had his target.

The operation worked well enough. As morning dawned, three of Alphonse's men got the horses ready while Alphonse and another man lay in wait for the child. Around the nooning hour when the clouds began to clear and the sun emerged to dry up the oversaturated earth, the little boy went to the well to gather water and was set upon by Alphonse. Hand over the child's mouth, he slipped to the waiting horses and tore off into the town with his stolen property. The tavern keeper and his wife would never know what happened to their bright, helpful son.

The child showed a good deal of strength and kicked and screamed over the thundering miles of road as Alphonse and his men sped southward. Alphonse finally had enough of the boy and tied him up, throwing him into a sack and tying that sack onto his saddle. When the horse raced off again, the sack bounced against the side of the horse and the child eventually quieted. Alphonse didn't stop to check on the boy's welfare until they were well clear of Bowes. The boy was bruised and scared, and a little sick, but unharmed.

The sight of the child fed Alphonse's courage. Giving the boy a piece of hard bread crust, he tied him back up in the sack again, listened to him cry, and continued on his trek to Ripley Castle.

⚜

Seven days later
Pendragon Castle

THE RAIN THAT had saturated the countryside for the better part of the last two months had subsided over the past several days and the sun had emerged, gaining strength as the wet spring months morphed into drying summer months.

The land was still vibrantly green with a gentle breeze caressing the fields. The bailey of Pendragon had dried up and Keir had his soldiers fill in the great holes created by the rain so that the bailey was now a smoother crossing. The ward covered a relatively small area and he didn't need men falling in holes and breaking legs, so it was more of a necessity than an aesthetic repair.

Since the weather had been so agreeable for the past few days, Chloë and Cassandra had made it a daily ritual to break their fast and then go outside to walk among the enormous earthworks and causeways of Pendragon's layout. They would walk and talk until finally finding a place to sit. The two old and ugly female servants followed them around carrying small stools and sewing. When Chloë and Cassandra would find just the right spot, the serving women would lay out a blanket and the stools.

Today was no exception. The temperature was warm enough that Cassandra actually fanned herself as she sat in the sun, working on a small piece of embroidery. They had picked up the thread and fabric when they had visited town earlier in the week, a little kit containing colored silk thread, needles and thimbles. Chloë had her hands on an enormous ball of yarn of very fine lamb's wool, gold in color, and she was knitting furiously with two small ivory knitting needles. She had a talent at knitting, something she had learned when she was young, and the long robe she was making was already taking shape.

The knitting kept her mind off of Keir. Since their admission to each other nearly a week before, she had kept a distance from him. Her feelings for the man were growing stronger by the day and she was terrified that he was going to break her heart with his fear and confusion, so she thought it best to stay away from him. She could see the disappointment in his face when they took their evening meals with everyone in the great hall but he made no move to get closer to her. It was as if he understood her distance, protecting herself, just as he was protecting himself. It had made for long and painful days and nights for them both.

On this lovely day, Chloë sat on her little stool in the sun, focusing on her fingers and trying not to think of the massive knight with the piercing blue eyes. Cassandra lay on her belly on the blanket, carefully stitching a hummingbird. No less than four soldiers were assigned to watch over them, standing a respectful distance away even as the Michael watched them from the gatehouse and Keir watched them from the castle. Cassandra was rattling on about something but Chloë wasn't paying attention. Finally, she heard her sister sigh.

"You have not heard a word I have said, have you?" Cassandra sat up and looked at her sister. "What is wrong with you? You have been like this all week."

Chloë looked up from her knitting. "Like what?"

Cassandra wriggled her arched eyebrows. "Quiet and morose," she said. "What is the matter with you?"

Chloë shook her head. "I do not know what you mean," she said, refocusing on her knitting. "There is nothing wrong with me."

Cassandra gazed at her sister, not believing her for a moment. After a slight pause, she sighed sympathetically. "Sweetheart, have you spoken with him since…?"

"Nay," Chloë cut her off. "I do not want to speak to him and you are forbidden to speak his name. Please, Cassie. I cannot bear it."

"But you…."

"Cassie," Chloë snapped softly, her brown eyes sad and irritated as she looked at her sister. "You know what my issue is so why do you ask such foolish questions? Do not ask me again, please. I am not so fortunate that I have two men vying for my hand."

Cassandra fought off a smile, the same smile that came about every time she thought of Michael of Pembury and Kurtis St. Héver. Not to diminish her sister's misery, but she was quite happy at the moment, happier than she had ever been. She had the attention of two fine knights and was enjoying it immensely. She gazed off towards the gatehouse where she knew Michael was watching her.

"Michael is a sweet and considerate man," she said dreamily, rolling on to her stomach again, "but there is something about Kurtis that I find very attractive."

Chloë was focused on her task. "Kurtis barely speaks," she said. "What on earth to you find attractive about him?"

Cassandra's smile grew. "It is not how much he speaks but what he says when he does," she said. "He is very intelligent and he has a very funny sense of humor. He makes me laugh with his dry comments. You should see the way he baits Michael."

Chloë looked up at her, then. "I *have* seen it," she said, a reluctant smile playing on her lips. "I was in the hall when Michael drank from the cup that had the rim lined with soot. The man walked around with a foolish black smile drawn on his face for nearly an hour before Keir took pity on him and told him why everyone was laughing at him. I thought he was going to kill Kurtis."

Cassandra rolled onto her back, giggling as she gazed up at the blue sky above. "It *was* rather funny."

"It was dastardly."

"You laughed."

"I did not say that it was not funny – it was. But it was also dastard-ly."

Cassandra continued to giggle and Chloë finally broke down into soft laughter. Over the past several days, Michael and Kurtis had entered into a contest for Cassandra's attention and it was quite hilarious at times. Kurtis would put soot on the rim of Michael's cup and Michael would put saffron in the water Kurtis shaved with, turning the man's face yellow. Michael was extremely tall and extremely big, but Kurtis was built of pure muscle, making a physical confrontation at some point both a frightful and interesting prospect. Keir had managed to head the two off of each other but they all knew, at some point, an explosion was inevitable.

Cassandra was the only one who delighted in the possibility. She rolled onto her side, propping her head up on her hand, her gaze now on the castle looming behind them. The tall gray walls were foreboding as she looked at the battlements, seeing men moving along the parapets. One man in particular seemed rooted to one spot, right at the corner of the walls with the best view of where the ladies were.

Cassandra didn't have to see the details of the man's face to know it was Keir. She had seen the way Keir looked at her sister and she knew the man felt for Chloë as Chloë felt for him. She also suspected he was hurting just as her sister was, if not worse. The expression on his face every night at sup when Chloë would not speak to him told the tale.

"If Keir were to pledge for your hand, would you accept?" Cassandra asked softly.

Chloë faltered in her knitting. "Cassie….," she groaned.

"It is a reasonable question, sweetheart," Cassandra insisted. "Is he simply an infatuation with you or do you believe you could happily spend your life with the man?"

Chloë missed another stitch and, frustrated, she plopped her hands and the knitting into her lap. "Have you ever known me to have an infatuation?"

"Nay."

"Then you ask a foolish question."

"Are you in love with him?"

Chloë had enough. Bolting from her stool, she set her knitting down and began to walk away from her sister, across the rolling green earthworks with the rows and rows of spikes hammered into the sides to repel invaders. Cassandra called to her sister as she walked away.

"Where are you going?" she demanded.

Chloë waved an irritated hand at her. "Nowhere," she snapped. "Just…leave me alone. I do not want to speak right now."

Cassandra kept her mouth shut and Chloë kept walking. She wandered across the enormous earthworks, looking over the surrounding landscape from her elevated position. It was a beautiful view and she struggled to clear her mind. Above her, clouds skittered across the sky as the gentle breeze blew and it would have been a lovely day entirely had she not been so saddened. It began to occur to her that she would remain saddened as long as she stayed at Pendragon, caged with a man who could not decide whether or not he wanted her. More and more, she knew she had to leave for her own sanity. She had to leave and forget about Keir St. Héver entirely.

As she wandered to the northeastern portion of the earthwork ring surrounding Pendragon, she began to hear great activity at the gatehouse. She could hear men shouting and a flurry of movement on the wall walk that flanked the gatehouse. Shielding her eyes from the sun, she could see a man on a horse in the distance and Keir's soldiers surrounding the man as he entered the gatehouse. It meant nothing to her, as riders came and went from Pendragon on a regular basis, so she returned her attention to the River Eden which ran directly to the east of the castle.

The gently flowing waters were partially hidden by a grove of trees along the banks. Chloë moved down one of the causeways carved in between the earthworks and the moat, hearing grass moving behind her and glancing over her shoulder to see two soldiers following her at a respectful distance. She made a face, thinking she would like to be without guard dogs on her walk. She wondered if the men reported back to Keir every little thing she did and said. She wondered if he even cared.

She came to a halt on a rise in the causeway, watching the river flow and thinking on Keir. He was all she thought of, day and night, reliving their kiss over and over, feeling shattered that she would never know that kind of passion again. She was dismayed thinking she would not grow old by his side, bearing his children and sharing a love that was rare and precious. Maybe she was a fool; she certainly felt like one. It was enough to bring tears to her eyes that she angrily chased away.

She had no idea how long she stood there, gazing out over the river. The breeze blew her hair gently and with time, she was able to clear her mind a bit. As she was watching a big branch flow down the river, a voice came from behind her.

"My lady?"

Startled, she turned to see Keir standing a few feet behind her. She had never heard him approach. Instantly on guard, she turned back to the river as her eyes welled up with tears.

"I do not wish to speak with you, Keir," she struggled not to weep as the sight of him had her rattled. "Please go away."

She heard him sigh heavily. "Please, Chloë," he murmured. "I need to speak with you."

She shook her head, lowering it as tears popped from her eyes and streamed down her cheeks.

"There is nothing more you can say to me," she whispered. "Please go, Keir… I cannot bear seeing you."

Instead of leaving, he moved up behind her. She could feel the warmth of his body behind her and she audibly gasped, moving away from the man, so very fearful of his touch. She couldn't even look at him, weeping softly into her hand.

Keir stood there, watching her with a breaking heart. "Chloë," he breathed. "I have a message from your father."

Her head came up then, the watery brown eyes focusing on him. The tears stopped flowing somewhat. "What… what does he say?" she sniffed.

He stared deeply into her eyes, mesmerized, feeling his heart shattering into a million pieces. He'd spent the past seven days wrestling with his feelings for her, knowing more by the day that he was in love with the woman and absolutely terrified to embrace it. But the more he saw her, the more she refused to speak to him as she closed herself up in her own little world, the more he knew that he could not live without her.

Perhaps he was fearful of loving someone again, but as he had told his brother, he was entitled to know happiness once more. Seven days of wrestling with that thought had seen him come to the conclusion that he would again embrace the responsibility of a woman he loved deeply, of a woman he could not stand to be away from for more than a minute. He would embrace the feeling of adoration again, stronger than he had ever known it, and he would try not to be afraid of losing it.

As he gazed into her beautiful eyes, he could only feel surrender in his heart. His fist slapped dully against his thigh as he dropped his hand in defeat.

"Chloë," he murmured. "I cannot do this any longer. I cannot go through each day not speaking to you. It is killing me."

She was back to tears again. "Then I must leave," she wept softly. "I cannot stay here because it brings me too much sorrow also. Will you please send me back to Aysgarth?"

He shook his head. "Nay," he murmured hoarsely. "I will not send you back because I am going to marry you."

Chloë's eyes widened and the tears stopped. She whirled to Keir, her mouth hanging open with surprise. She simply couldn't believe what she was hearing after days of agony. For a moment, she thought she might have dreamed it.

"What… what did you say?" she gasped.

He smiled weakly. "I love you," he whispered. "With all of my heart and soul, I do. I am sorry if I hurt you with my fears. It was terrible and wrong of me and I pray you can forgive me. Please say you will."

Chloë stared at him, shocked. But her shock soon turned to realization, then realization to joy, and a smile spread over her face that outshined the sun. She just stood there and smiled, her eyes brimming with happy tears. All of the anguish from the past several days seemed to evaporate at that very moment.

"There is nothing to forgive," she breathed. "I know you had many things to overcome."

"But surely you are angry with me. You would not even look at me, not for all of the days since that night we last spoke."

"It was self-protection, I assure you. I did not trust myself to look at you or speak to you and not break down. It was not because I was angry with you."

"Are you sure?"

"I am."

"Promise?"

"I promise."

His smile grew and he opened his arms to her. "Then come to me," he commanded quietly. "It has been far too long since I last held you in my arms and I cannot go another moment without you."

She ran at him, leaping into his arms. Keir caught her, holding her so tightly that the feel of her, the smell of her, brought tears to his eyes. He buried his face in all of that wonderful red hair, knowing his life was going to change from this point on but not caring. After the hell of the past three years, he didn't think he'd ever feel such joy again. After several moments of happily hugging her, he set her on her feet and took her face between his two enormous hands.

"Listen to me and listen well," he whispered, watching her glistening eyes. "I told you once that I knew I could love you so much that it would rip my heart and body and soul to pieces to even be away from you for a single minute. Already this past week has seen my heart and soul and body ripped to shreds for want of you. I am turning myself over to you completely, Chloë. I am yours as surely as the sun is a part of the sky. I am not a great nobleman who can provide you with titles and wealth, but I swear to you that I will love you until you die. Say that you will be my wife and make me the happiest man in the world."

She reached up and stroked his cheeks with her thumbs, watching him kiss her fingers as she came near his lips. Boldly, she kissed his mouth, not surprised when he wound his arms around her and kissed her deeply.

"I will be your wife," she murmured against his seeking lips. "I love you, Keir. I belong to you and only you."

"Swear it," he breathed.

"I do," she declared, a two-part sentence because he was kissing her so furiously. "You have my heart forever."

He smiled even though he was kissing her. She began to giggle and then he began to giggle, and soon he was spinning her around in happy circles, listening to her joyful laughter. It echoed off the walls of Pendragon, rippled along the earthwork and causeways. Again, there was joy at Pendragon, something that could be heard as well as seen. Keir stopped spinning her long enough to kiss her again.

"I love you," he proclaimed.

"And I love you," she responded breathlessly. "But we have a problem."

His brow furrowed even though his smile remained. "What is that?"

She lifted a well-shaped eyebrow. "Cassandra," she said as if he needed reminding. "I cannot get married before she does. It would be humiliating for her."

Keir's smile faded and his lips pressed into a flat, irritated line. "She has my brother and Pembury chasing after her," he pointed out. "She will not remain unmarried for long."

Chloë shook her head. "Even so, you must do something to hurry them along," she told him. "I want a summer wedding and I cannot do that if my sister is torn between two suitors. I believe your brother has the upper hand in this duel so you must do something to hurry him along."

He nodded patiently, like a man does when his wife is nagging. It was the happiest nagging he could remember and he welcomed it.

"I will do my best, love," he told her. "Do not forget that I want us to be married soon as well. Every day I cannot call you my wife is like torture."

She smiled at him and touched his cheek. "You are so sweet," she crooned, watching him kiss her hand. "I anxiously wait to call you my husband. No word on this earth will have greater meaning to me than that."

His smile was back and he pulled her into his arms again, holding her close against him. Chloë's head was against his chest, hearing his heart beating strongly in her left ear. One strong hand was in her hair, cradling her head, while the other was against her back.

"What did my father have to say?" Chloë asked, snuggled against him, wildly content. "You will have to speak with him very soon about our marriage. In fact, I think we should go to Aysgarth tomorrow."

He was enjoying the feel of her against him. "*We?*" he repeated.

She lifted her head from his chest, gazing up at him. "Do you think I will let you go without me?"

"Probably not."

She grinned. "Then we shall go on the morrow after you have had the opportunity to convince your brother that he must marry my sister."

He scowled at her, though it was gently done. "I only have until tomorrow to convince Kurt to marry your sister?"

"Aye."

He released her from his embrace and took her hand. He began to pull her back up the hill with him. There was urgency in his movements.

"Where are we going?" she wanted to know.

He helped her climb to the top of the wet and slippery earthwork. "To find my brother, for Christ's sake," he told her, feigning annoyance. "I only have eighteen hours to talk the man into a decision that will change his life. I had better hurry up."

She held her skirts up with one hand while holding him with the other as they began to move across the giant earthwork mound. "What of Michael? He will be terribly disappointed."

Keir spied Cassandra in the distance, lying on her stomach on the blanket that had been spread out across the grass. She was eating a green apple but when she spied Keir and Chloë, hand in hand, she suddenly sat up and waved at them. Keir lifted a hand and waved back.

"Sweetheart," he turned casually to Chloë, "while I am doing my part to convince my brother he must marry, perhaps you should speak with your sister and tell her that she must focus on Kurtis. It would help his confidence immensely to know that Pembury is no longer competition."

Chloë eyed her sister in the distance, who was now standing up and brushing off her coat. "I will tell her what she needs to do," she said confidently. "But I warn you, she is enjoying having two men chase after her."

"And they are enjoying the chase, at least for the most part. But I fear the next time my brother puts soot on Michael's cup, there is going to be a brawl of epic proportions."

Chloë giggled. "It *was* rather funny to see him walk around with that foolish black smile on his face."

Keir fought off a grin. "It was humiliating."

They were descending down the slope towards Cassandra, who was now walking over to greet them. Chloë shifted her grip on Keir and took his arm, pulling him closer against her. She was so thrilled to have the man in her possession, with everything well between them that she never wanted to let him go.

"You never did tell me what my father said, by the way," she said softly, gazing up at him with her big brown eyes. "What was contained in his missive?"

Keir wriggled his eyebrows as Cassandra drew near. "He sends his love to you and thanks to me," he replied. "He wishes you and your sister good health, hopes to see you soon, and assures you that Exelby is well on its way to being repaired. God only knows what the man will think about what went on at Pendragon when Kurtis and I ride to

Aysgarth to ask for the hands of you and your sister."

Chloë giggled. "My father wishes for us to marry well," she looked up at him, feigning an imperious demeanor. "Are you wealthy, my lord?"

Keir snorted. "Not if I have a wife who spends my money on silks, oils, soaps and jewelry."

Her mouth opened in outrage. "I did not buy any jewelry!"

He looked over, winking at her. "I will take care of that when I place a magnificent wedding ring on your finger so that all men will know you belong to me."

Her smile returned just as Cassandra came upon them. The blond sister looked between the pair, a knowing smile on her face. She had watched them approach from the east side of the castle, hand in hand, and had felt a great deal of relief for her sister.

"May I assume, then, that all is well now?" she asked leadingly.

Chloë smiled coyly, her gaze moving between Keir and Cassandra. "Well enough," she told her sister, letting go of Keir and moving to her sister. "You and I must have a conversation, Cassie."

Keir watched her go, pulling her sister back towards their blanket with the knitting and stools spread upon it. His gaze drank in the graceful fall of that magnificent hair, the gentle slope of her torso and luscious figure. All of the fear he felt at opening himself up to her, of giving away his heart again, fled as he watched her speak with Cassandra. He knew he had made the correct decision and he could not have been happier about it. But he had work to do and very little time to do it if he was going to meet Chloë's deadline.

"I will see you later, sweetheart," he called to her. "Do not be out here too much longer. The hour is growing late."

Chloë and Cassandra looked to him, Chloë with a sweet smile on her face and Cassandra with an expression of mild amusement. Cassandra's amusement grew when he blew Chloë a kiss and headed back towards the castle. The man was fairly giddy. As he walked away, he could hear the sisters' tittering and whispering, voices growing louder but not agitated. It was clear that Chloë was telling her sister the joyful news and Cassandra was reacting in kind.

Keir held the same satisfied grin all the way back to the castle.

CHAPTER TEN

PEMBURY DID NOT go down without a fight. Literally.

It all started innocently enough. Keir, Lucan, Michael, Kurtis and one of Kurtis' knights from Northumberland, a muscular warrior with a bushy red mustache named Ranulf Kluge, were in the great hall at suppertime, imbibing of the heady red wine that Keir had shipped from Manchester, and speaking of trivial things.

The mood was light, the warm fire burning in the hearth, as one of the serving women began to bring out trenchers of freshly baked bread. Dogs followed the woman, sniffing and begging. The men pulled at the bread, laughing as they shared stories of battles, and women, long past.

Kurtis was in a surprisingly good mood. Usually a silent and dour man, he was actually smiling and laughing along with the others until Michael brought up Cassandra. That was all Kurtis needed to hear for his smile to vanish.

"Wipe her from your mind, Pembury," he said steadily, regarding the cup in his hand. "She will soon be Lady St. Héver and out of your reach."

Michael sighed heavily, his smile fading. "How many times do I have to tell you this? I am more handsome than you are and set to inherit a barony. You have nothing to offer the woman, St. Héver. You would do well to concede defeat so we can remain friends."

Kurtis' pale blue eyes were icy. "At least I would remain true to her. The same cannot be said for you."

The verbal blows were coming low and swift. Michael's humor left him completely. "What do you mean by that?"

Kurtis didn't back down. He had a bulldoggish manner that had served him well as a battle commander. He would keep coming and coming or die trying.

"I seem to remember hearing of a young lady in Carlisle that you abandoned after stealing her virtue," he said casually. "I heard that you left her for another pretty girl, of more noble breeding, because she was better connected."

Michael was outraged. "Who told you that?"

Kurtis was as cool as ice. "De Velt," he said, throwing Lucan to the wolves. "He said that the young lady in Carlisle bore your bastard."

Michael turned furious eyes to Lucan, who immediately went on the defensive. He threw his hands up in surrender.

"I never...!" he sputtered.

"You told him that?" Michael roared.

Lucan stood up from the table, backing away from the enraged Michael. "We were speaking of many things, Michael," he insisted, then pointed accusingly to Kurtis. "St. Héver bedded the sister of a Northumberland enemy so he could glean information from the woman. When she found out she had been used, she killed herself!"

Kurtis was on his feet, posturing furiously as Michael turned his venom back on Kurtis.

"You pretend to be so pious and pure," Michael hissed. "See how the mighty have fallen into the pool of dirty dealings just like the rest of us."

Keir was on his feet, moving between his brother and Michael. "Sit down!" he barked, looking at Lucan threateningly. "Another word from you and I will gut you myself. Keep your damnable mouth shut."

Lucan threw up his hands again and backed away, watching Michael and Kurtis circle each other like hungry wolves. Keir stood in the middle of them with his arms outstretched to prevent them from rushing each other.

"Listen to me, both of you," he growled. "I will not tolerate this foolery. Since when do women come between you two? You have known each other since you were squires. Neither one of you is perfect so put the unsavory accusations aside and reclaim your cups. That is not a request."

Michael, glaring daggers at Kurtis, started to obey but Kurtis wouldn't move. He stood there and glowered at Michael, the man who was indeed set to inherit a barony and was, in fact, gloriously handsome.

Perhaps if Kurtis was to think on it, there was some jealousy there. Kurtis, a rather quiet and serious man, wasn't one to show interest in a woman but for some reason, Cassandra had his full focus. She was bossy and strong willed, but she was also very humorous and sweet. He liked that.

With uncharacteristic frustration, he moved back to the table with his brother right behind him. Sitting heavily, he poured himself a full measure of wine.

"You can have any woman you want, Pembury," he muttered. "I, in fact, cannot. If I told you I was in love with Lady Cassandra, would you leave her alone?"

Michael lifted an eyebrow. "Are you?"

"Possibly."

Michael shook his head. "That is not good enough. Either you are or you are not. Playing on my sympathies will only infuriate me."

Kurtis began to stiffen again. "I do not care if it infuriates you. Why can you not be a chivalrous man about this and understand this is not another one of your conquests? I am serious about Cassandra and I am positive you are simply looking for your next sexual victory. Are there not enough blue-eyed Pembury bastards in Yorkshire already?"

Michael flew over the table with a cocked fist but Kurtis was ready. He clobbered Michael in the face, sending the man spinning off the table. Keir was up, jumping into the fracas as Lucan and Ranulf dove in to separate the combatants. Fists were flying in all directions as Chloë and Cassandra entered the hall.

Eyes wide at the chaos, the women froze with shock the moment they entered the hall. Men were rolling around on the ground, throwing punches, and it was difficult to see who was fighting whom. There were toppled benches and toppled containers of wine, bleeding the expensive red liquid onto the floor. The dogs were barking at the commotion as Michael picked up Kurtis and literally tossed the man over the feasting table. Kurtis flew into the bench, breaking it with his bulk, and Cassandra screamed.

"Kurtis!" she cried.

The brawl came to a grinding halt as the men turned to look at the women standing in the arched doorway. Keir was on his knees, standing up when he saw Chloë, and making his way over to her. She looked at him in shock, noting the blood trickling from his nose.

"What is going on in here?" she demanded softly, lifting a finger to wipe away the blood. "You are bleeding."

He ran his fingers over the smudge she had made, sighing heavily. "A disagreement," he said vaguely.

Cassandra ran to Kurtis, who was picking himself up from the shattered bench. She raced around the table in time to grab the man's arm to try and help him up.

"Kurtis," she gasped. "Are you well?"

Kurtis was dazed. He braced himself against the table so he wouldn't fall down again. "I am fine," he told her. "Nothing to worry over."

Cassandra was deeply distressed. She noted that the red skin around his right eye was already showing signs of bruising and she stroked his blond hair soothingly before turning furious eyes to Michael.

"Why did you throw him like that?" she demanded.

Michael could already see that he was at a disadvantage. His nose was bleeding and he had a couple of loose teeth. He would have liked to have had some female comfort but he could see that was not going to happen unless he could calm Cassandra down and woo her away from Kurtis.

"A fight between men, my lady," he replied steadily. Then he lifted his hands wearily. "It happens all of the time. It is nothing to concern yourself with."

Cassandra was raging. She returned her attention to Kurtis, who was pretending he was worse than he was. He could see the tides of favor rolling in his direction and he intended to take full advantage of it. He put a hand to his hand.

"I think...," he feigned a groan, "that I should lie down. My head is swimming."

Cassandra put one arm around his massive shoulders. "I will help you," she said gently. "Where is your bedchamber?"

Kurtis was feigning injury to the point of disbelief. "In the keep," he grunted. "Your assistance would be most... appreciated, my lady."

Cassandra had a good grip on him as she helped him from the hall, casting a vicious glare at Michael as they went.

"You are despicable," she hissed. "Horrible, terrible and despicable!"

Michael didn't react other than to shoot Kurtis a dubious expression. The man was acting like an invalid all for the benefit of the lady, which put Michael at a terrible disadvantage in the battle for her affections. Cassandra caught Michael's disbelieving glare and she jabbed a finger at him.

"I saw that, Pembury," she snapped. "You are positively hateful. I hope I never see you again, you wicked man!"

Kurtis stopped moaning long enough to glance back over his shoulder, noting Pembury's expression of defeat. When Michael caught his gaze, he sneered victoriously before returning to his moaning routine. As Michael shook his head and turned back for the table, Chloë went to her sister and the wounded knight.

"Are you all right, Sir Kurtis?" she asked anxiously.

Kurtis nodded, one big arm around Cassandra as she helped him to the door. "I shall be fine with your sister's expert tending."

He grunted and groaned his way to the door as Cassandra carefully helped him. Even Keir thought it was an overdramatic performance at best but he didn't let on. He smiled at Chloë when she turned her attention to him and reached out to take her hand as she seemed genuinely concerned for his brother.

"I hope he is all right," she said earnestly.

Keir tucked her hand into the crook of his elbow, patting her soft fingers. "He will be fine."

"Are you sure? Maybe I should go help my sister."

He held on to her. "He will be fine. No need to attend your sister."

"But if she…?"

He turned to her swiftly and lowered his voice. "If you want my brother to offer for her hand by tomorrow, then you will leave them alone."

She looked at him with big eyes, her mouth forming an "O" as she realized what he was saying. Then her eyebrows drew together. "Is he feigning injury simply to gain her sympathy?" she hissed.

Keir chuckled and shook his head, turning to the knights as they reached the table. The smile left his face as he looked at the men around him.

"I trust we will have more civilized dinner entertainment with Lady Chloë at the table?" he asked Michael.

Michael was feeling defeated and depressed. He nodded his head, noticing that Chloë was shooting him daggers with her glare also. He rolled his eyes as he regained his seat; it would seem he was destined to lose in all areas tonight.

Sitting heavily, Michael grabbed a pitcher of wine and poured himself a sloppy cup. Frustrated and a little jealous when he saw how cozy Keir and Chloë were, he ended up leaving the hall and getting quite drunk in his chamber.

As it turned out, one of the serving women Chloë had hired from town was apparently not too old or too ugly for Michael's drunken taste. In a pitch-dark room, he could imagine his bed mate was Cassandra.

CHAPTER ELEVEN

AYSGARTH CASTLE WAS a busy place at any given time, even busier with the party from Pendragon that had unexpectedly arrived in the late afternoon. Now, as the sun set and the skies were turning shades of purple and dark blue, the enormous pale-stoned fortress took on an eerie glow. Torches flamed on the battlements, in the bailey, and in the great hall. There was fire and light everywhere, reaching deep into the night sky.

Pendragon's party consisted of Keir, Kurtis, Chloë, Cassandra, Lucan, Ranulf and twenty soldiers armed to the teeth. Michael had been left behind at Pendragon, mostly because of the hard feelings that existed between him and Kurtis and also because Keir needed the man to assume command of the fortress while he was gone.

Moreover, Keir wouldn't put it past Michael to continue to try and woo Cassandra from his brother, and Keir didn't need battling knights all the way to Aysgarth. After the incident in the great hall, Michael was out for blood. Sullen, defeated, Michael had remained behind.

It was increasingly apparently, however, that Cassandra would not be wooed away from Kurtis regardless of Michael's determination. The morning after the brawl between Kurtis and Michael, Cassandra and Kurtis were intently focused on one another, even to the point where Chloë was giggling happily every time she saw her sister and the knight together, which was constantly.

Cassandra seemed to have found a man who was handsome, intelligent, and apparently didn't mind that she was the bossy sort. Kurtis, big and silent, simply seemed to acquiesce to her in spite of the fact he'd never liked outspoken women. With Cassandra, it was different.

So they had left the next day for Aysgarth, meeting Chloë's dead-line, to discuss marital contracts with Anton de Geld. It had taken nearly six hours to reach Aysgarth, the mighty bastion of Coverdale. Chloë had started off on a small gray palfrey, as had Cassandra, but halfway into the ride, both ladies ended up with their respective knights. Chloë rode with Keir, finally truly happy for the first time in her life, looking forward to a life with the man she loved. It all seemed like a dream, one that she was quite willing to experience. She never knew she could be so full of joy.

Once they reached Aysgarth, the women disappeared inside with several female servants. The knights disbanded the escort, Lucan and Ranulf retreating to the bunkhouse while Keir and Kurtis headed into the enormous keep. Lord Coverdale and Anton had not yet returned from grouse hunting so Keir and Kurtis retired to the solar to wait out their return and possibly discuss the strategies of a marriage proposal. With time on their hands to wait now, anxiety, an unfamiliar emotion, seemed to be creeping upon them.

"I have never done this before," Kurtis said in a low voice. "It did not occur to me until this moment that I would be apprehensive. Since you have already done this once, perhaps you can offer some advice."

Keir looked at his brother, noting the man's upper lip was sweating, which was highly unusual because Kurtis was the consummately cool man in any situation. He fought off a grin.

"The only advice I can give you is to be forthright and honest," he told him. "I have a feeling de Geld will accept nothing less."

Kurtis sighed faintly and began to remove his gloves. He'd been standing, stiffly formal, for over an hour, but his hands were sweating so badly that he had to remove his gauntlets to let his palms dry off.

"I want to tell you something," he said after a moment, his voice soft.

Keir looked over at him from where he was standing near the lancet window overlooking the glowing bailey. "What is that?"

Kurtis met his brother's gaze. He seemed to be having trouble finding the correct words. "I said many things to you last week when I arrived, things that I should not have said," he lifted his big shoulders. "I said them out of concern, brother, and nothing else."

Keir pushed himself away from the window and moved to the fine pewter pitcher of wine. Coverdale's solar was lavish and he had his choice of several types of alcohol. He selected a heavy port and poured himself a cup.

"What things?" he asked.

Kurtis looked somewhat uncomfortable. "I told you to remove the women from Pendragon," he said. "I told you to forget about Lady Chloë. I should not have said that."

Keir looked up from his cup, his pale blue eyes glittering. "I know you said it out of concern. You do not have to apologize."

Kurtis shook his head. "You do not understand," he said. "When I said those things to you, I was remembering the brother who could not function after the death of his wife. I was terrified for you to go through that hell again. I was looking at it from a safe standpoint."

"Safe?"

Kurtis nodded. "There is mental safety in remaining alone. The introduction of a woman you care for threatens that safety because it is too easy to lose control. You are the strongest man I know, Keir. To see you crumble… it was a shattering experience, something I never want to see again. And it is something I never want to personally experience."

Keir made his way to his brother, casually, cup in hand. "Are you telling me that you will not allow yourself to care for Cassandra?" he cocked a disapproving eyebrow. "It is apparent that she cares for you a great deal, Kurt. If you are not intending to permit yourself to become attached to the woman, then…."

Kurtis held up a hand, interrupting him. "'Tis not that at all," he assured him, meeting his eye. Then he shook his head as if truly baffled. "When I first met Cassandra, I was physically attracted to her. She is a beautiful woman. But the courting, the competition with Pembury… it started out as a game but it ended in something quite different."

"Different how?"

Kurtis shrugged. "After last night, I think… I think I love the woman and it scares me to death."

A smile spread across Keir's face and he clapped his brother on the shoulder affectionately. "Do not let it frighten you," he said quietly. "Let it be your strength. You can move mountains with such strength."

Kurtis looked at his brother, grinning reluctantly when he saw the expression on his face. "I am sorry I tried to discourage you from Chloë," he muttered. "I can see in everything about you how much she is coming to mean to you. You were correct; you have the right to find happiness again. I only came to understand that once I realized I was feeling something for Cassandra."

Keir wriggled his eyebrows in agreement and squeezed his brother's shoulder before dropping his hand. There wasn't much more he could say to that. As he turned around to pour himself more wine, the door to the solar opened.

Chloë and Cassandra entered along with an older woman that Keir immediately recognized as Lady Blanche. The woman was formal, proper and austere with a hint of her younger daughter's beauty. Keir winked at Chloë as he went to greet her mother cordially.

"Lady Blanche," he said. "It is good to see you again under better circumstances."

The Lady Blanche de Geld, formerly Princess Blanche of Rochedale, eleventh child of Henry the Third, was cool as she beheld Keir's handsome face. He studied her in return. Due to the chaos surrounding her rescue from Exelby, he'd never truly had the chance to speak with or otherwise interact with the woman. He could see that she had Chloë's big brown eyes and her hair was blond, like Cassandra's. She had fine features and skin that was surprisingly smooth for her age.

"Sir Keir," she greeted him evenly, her sharp eyes still looking him over. "My daughters tell me that you have been a gracious host. You have our gratitude for acting protector to my daughters."

Keir was modest. "It was my pleasure, my lady," he replied. "They are charming guests."

The older woman grunted faintly, perhaps with irony. "Charming enough that I understand you wish to offer for Chloë's hand," she said, her eyes finding Kurtis standing several feet away. "And this must be your brother. Well? Come here, young man. Do not stand in the shadows where I cannot see you."

Kurtis immediately moved to stand next to his brother, feeling his nerves return. The older women with the intense brown eyes had him anxious all over again.

"My lady," he greeted calmly enough. "I am Sir Kurtis St. Héver, Captain of the Guard for Yves de Vesci, the Earl of Northumberland."

Blanche cocked an eyebrow. "You are his chief commander?"

"Aye, my lady. I command his three thousand-man army."

"What is your lineage?"

Kurtis felt as if the interrogation was already underway. There was something in the woman's manner that intimidated him far more than any father could have. He wanted to make a good impression because he sincerely wanted to marry the woman's daughter, and he could feel the sweat popping out on his upper lip again.

"My grandfather served King Henry the Third and Prince Edward honorably at the Battle of Evesham," he replied. "He was part of the successful plot to free Prince Edward from Simon de Montfort's captivity and upon Henry's restoration of the throne, my grandfather was given the commission Baron Glasbury, a title my father inherited. I will inherit it from him upon his death."

Blanche was critical in her assessment. "Are you propertied?"

"I will inherit Afontawe Castle in the Welsh Marches upon my father's death, my lady. It is a wealthy castle with tribute from the roads and passes leading from Hereford and Leominster into Wales."

Blanche's critical eye began to ease somewhat. "And your family, knight? What of your blood lines?"

Kurtis didn't miss a step. "We are Breton, my lady, descended from

Saint Héver of Brittany. We can trace our family line back more than four hundred years."

The knight's quick, forthright answers had Blanche's resistance fading. He was concise and formal in his delivery, something she appreciated. He seemed a little stiff, also, but she nodded faintly at the information, digested it, before turning to her eldest daughter.

"This is the man you wish to marry?" she asked.

Cassandra nodded, her eager eyes on the woman. "Aye, Mother," she replied. "Kurtis is a good man. He will make a fine husband."

Blanche lifted an eyebrow at her daughter. Although she had been vocal of her disapproval of her husband's decision to allow the girls to select their own husbands, secretly, she envied her daughters. She had wanted to select her own husband as well but her parents would not hear of it. Royal blood was not something to be treated lightly. With that in mind, she returned her focus to Kurtis.

"You realize that my father was King Henry, do you not?" she asked.

Kurtis looked startled. His gaze moved between Blanche and Cassandra, terrified that it was something he should have known and feeling rather peeved that no one had bothered to tell him. He said a swift prayer that his marriage proposal, based on that information, would not be doomed before he had a chance to present it.

"Nay, my lady, I did not know," he said honestly.

Blanche peered at him somewhat imperiously. "You are asking to marry a niece of our king."

Kurtis swallowed hard. "I will hold title and property and will provide for her well," he replied evenly. "And I swear to you that the woman will never want for love or loyalty."

As Cassandra beamed radiantly, Lady Blanche appeared dismissive. "Love or loyalty does not a marriage make," she sniffed. "You seem to have the necessary lineage, however, and Cassandra seems convinced that you will make an excellent husband."

Kurtis wasn't sure what more he could say. He looked at Cassandra, grinning faintly at her huge smile. As he waited for the next barrage of questions, Blanche abruptly moved on to Keir.

The woman gazed into the face of the man who had her youngest daughter's heart, wondering what, other than his handsome looks, had her daughter so captivated. She cocked an eyebrow as she scrutinized the big man from head to toe.

"Hmpf," she snorted softly. "He is certainly a comely boy, Chloë. Quite comely."

Chloë walked up beside her mother, winding her hands around the woman's right arm. "Aye, he is," she hugged her mother, her eyes twinkling at Keir, who felt rather like a prize stallion being inspected. "He is smart and sweet and very brave."

Blanche would not be softened by her youngest child, although it was a struggle. Chloë had always had the ability to bend her mother to her will.

"You are the man who saved us from Ingilby," Blanche said.

"Aye, my lady."

"Did you set your sights on my daughter even then?"

It was a blunt question, but he suspected the way the woman had dealt with Kurtis, that she would only respect someone as direct as she was. He shook his head.

"Nay, my lady," he replied. "Lady Chloë spent her time trying to bash my fingers and gouge my eyes out. I could not get a good look at her long enough to know if she could invite my interest. I was too busy defending myself."

Blanche almost smiled. Almost. Instead, she cleared her throat and looked at her red-haired daughter, who was snuggling against her arm. She had never seen Chloë so happy and it was somewhat of a labor to not instantly approve of the tall, handsome knight. For all of her formal manner, inside, she was a mother just like any other and wanted to see her daughters happy.

"I know your lineage thanks to your brother's information, but tell me about your history as your brother has," she nearly demanded.

"Other than garrison commander for Coverdale, what great accomplishments as a knight have you made?"

Keir fixed the woman in the eye. His gaze never left her as he spoke. "I was knighted in twelve hundred and eighty one at the age of twenty years," his voice was low and steady. "I distinguished myself in the wars in Wales against Llewelyn ap Gruffydd, so much so that I was charged with an entire battalion of the king's army at the Battle of Irfon Bridge. Men under my command cornered the last Welsh prince and killed him. I was honored with a battlefield commission of Lord Sedberg, Knight of the Shire, which is how I came into the service of Lord Coverdale. He is Sedberg's liege and the garrison at Pendragon also borders my lands. Serving Coverdale as his garrison commander also serves me well, as I can watch over and administer my own lands from Pendragon. Is there anything else you wish to know, my lady?"

Blanche seemed to like his straightforward manner. Her brown eyes glittered at him as she raked him with her intense gaze once more as if to reaffirm she found something worthy in the man.

"You said you served the king?" she asked.

"Aye, my lady."

"He is my brother."

"I realize that, my lady."

"Would he know you by name?"

"He would, my lady. It was Edward who gave me my battlefield commission."

"Why did you leave his service?"

"Because I married and did not want to spend time away from my wife."

Even Lady Blanche had heard of the fate of Keir's family and she chose not to delve into what would undoubtedly be a painful conversation for the man. She wanted to know about him but she did not want to probe him. She was not cruel. But she wanted to be clear on the prize he was seeking. She turned to Chloë and cupped the woman's chin with her hand, forcing her to look up.

"Sir Keir," Blanche said, her voice firm. "I want you to look at this face. When she was born, I thought she was the most beautiful creature I had ever seen. This is my youngest daughter, the Lady Chloë Louise Isabella de Geld. I named her Chloë because it is a Greek name that means beautiful, lush and verdant. She is all of that and more. You will understand that she can have any man in England for the asking, but she seems to want you."

Keir was fixed on Chloë's magnificent face. "As I want her," he said softly. "Once she stopped trying to gouge my eyes out, I came to discover a witty, warm, intelligent and beautiful woman whom I love deeply. I would kill or die for her a thousand times over. Perhaps you do not believe I am worthy of your daughter, my lady, but I assure you, I will be a better husband to her than anyone else on this earth. I will love her like none other could."

Blanche nodded faintly as if finally approving of what she heard. She peeled her daughter off her arm and handed her over to Keir, who took her hands gently. Blanche was focused on Chloë.

"Are you sure this is what you want, Chloë?" she asked.

Chloë smiled up at Keir. "It is, Mother."

Blanche's gaze lingered on Chloë and Keir before turning her attention to Kurtis and Cassandra, now standing next to one another, arm in arm. Her gaze lingered on her eldest daughter and the knight in her grip, and her manner seemed to relax.

"Cassandra shall inherit the Kirklington barony and Exelby Castle," she said to Kurtis before turning to Keir. "Chloë shall inherit my properties of Rochedale, including lands in Angoulême passed down to me from my grandmother. Now, I will speak to Anton about these marriage contracts. You will all go away now and I shall see you all at supper tonight. Do not be late."

It was the abrupt end of the interview. Chloë ran at her mother and hugged her but Cassandra beat a hasty path from the solar, pulling Kurtis along with her. When Chloë was finished joyfully strangling her mother, she collected Keir and swiftly quit the solar.

Blanche stood in place a moment, going over the past several minutes of conversation. The expressions on her daughters' faces thrilled her, reminding her of a young man she once knew in her youth who gave her the same expression. She thought on the young Frenchman, now long dead, and well-remembered that joy. She was pleased that Cassandra and Chloë had found such joy as well. It was a rare and precious thing.

Sitting in a big oak chair near the hearth, she collected her needlework and began to sew again. Now, she would wait for Anton to return to convince him that his little girls had grown up into lovely women who wished to be wed.

She was sure he would not like it one bit.

CHAPTER TWELVE

T HE EVENING MEAL at Aysgarth later that day was truly a spectacle to behold. The hall itself was an enormous structure with a gallery that encircled it, and two massive hearths on opposite sides of the room that blazed smoke and sparks up to the vaulted ceiling. Torches lined the walls, fixed in big iron sconces, shooting black smoke into the air as they burned hot against the cool night. The great hall was illuminated on a brilliant scale, a warm and smelly place that invited a social atmosphere.

Chloë and Cassandra had brought some of their new clothing from Pendragon and were dressed to the hilt when Keir and Kurtis came to escort them to the meal. Cassandra was resplendent in brilliant blue while Chloë opted for bronze-colored damask that was utterly striking with her coloring. Her dark red hair was pulled off her face with a shell comb, leaving the majority of it to trail down her back all the way to her knees. She looked spectacularly beautiful and Keir couldn't take his eyes off her as he escorted her to the great and fragrant hall.

The room was filled with servants, soldiers, knights and a massive table that was already heavy with food. It smelled strongly of roasted meat and fresh bread. Escorting the ladies to the table, they were introduced to Lady de Tiegh, the baron's new wife, who was a girl of fourteen years of age with long dark hair and big white breasts. She wasn't particularly pretty but she was very sweet. Considering how old the baron was, Chloë and Cassandra were a little shocked to see such a young girl as his wife but they were cordial and kind as Lady de Tiegh seated them around her.

An empty chair sat between Lady de Tiegh and Keir, who had

Chloë on his right. Kurtis and Cassandra sat across the table from them and senior knights, all of whom Keir knew, rounded out the bulk of the feasting table surrounding Lady de Tiegh.

Keir served Chloë himself, making sure she got the best pick of the bread and meat. She seemed to have a sweet tooth and doled out great spoonfuls of milk pudding on her trencher as well as apricots soaked in wine and honey. When Keir would lift an eyebrow at all of the sweets she had on her trencher, she would merely giggle. He would wink at her and return to his own food.

Byron joined the meal when they were well into their food, kissing his wife seductively and stroking her shoulder so that his fingers ended up on the swell of her breast as he took his seat between her and Keir. Cassandra and Chloë exchanged shocked glances at the old man's provocative touch but said nothing, returning to their trenchers and the delicious food.

From the table chatter, they gathered that Lady de Tiegh did not live with Coverdale, but instead, with her mother and father about a half day's ride from Aysgarth. Apparently, they allowed Coverdale to marry their daughter but she was not permitted to actually live with him until she turned fifteen years old, an appropriate age for a wife. It was a bizarre arrangement and Coverdale was going to focus all of his attention on his very young wife until her parents came to squire her away in the morning.

"I cannot help but notice that your mother and father are missing," Keir murmured to Chloë. "Where do you suppose they are?"

Chloë had her mouth full of apricots and she swallowed the bite before answering. "Discussing our future, I am sure," she said quietly. "Mother has given her blessing but now she must convince Father. Remember that he wanted Cassandra and me to marry well. He may not consider knights, as prestigious as they may be, well-to-do."

Keir wriggled his eyebrows. "I have never wanted to be an earl more than I do at this moment."

Chloë put her hand on his knee underneath the table, squeezing it gently. "Even so, I could not love you any more than I do now."

He turned a warm smile in her direction, clasping her hand firmly under the table. "I only meant as it pertains to making me more attractive to your father." He wanted very much to kiss her but refrained from the gesture in such a public venue. "I truly hope your mother is on our side."

Chloë nodded. "She is," she confirmed confidently. "She seemed to like you."

"How could you tell?"

She looked at him in mock outrage. Then she broke down into giggles. "With my mother, it is difficult to know," she agreed. "But she is a good and true woman. She simply controls her emotions better than most."

Keir fondled her fingers underneath the table. "Is she able to influence your father?"

Chloë nodded. "He will do as she asks."

Keir felt some relief at that as he resumed eating his well cooked beef with gusto. He continued to caress Chloë's hand, his fingers moving up her arm, experiencing her silken skin. He found out she was ticklish when he raked his fingers up the inside of her arm near her elbow and she jumped, giggling at his touch. He grinned at her, lifting her hand from underneath the table and kissing it, a bold move against an unmarried and unpledged woman. As she leaned against his arm, snickering at him as she tried to stop him from tickling her again, she noticed Byron and his young wife on the other side of Keir.

Byron had his arm around the girl, fingering the neckline of her surcoat and whispering things that were making the girl blush. Chloë watched the pair for a moment.

"Lord Byron is quite enamored with his wife," she whispered, leaning against Keir. "She is very young."

Keir glanced over at the pair. "She was his ward for years," he leaned against Chloë's head, his lips against her ear. "He married her on her eleventh birthday. He is madly in love with the girl and she seems to feel the same way for him."

Chloë tried not to look shocked. "He is old enough to be her grandfather."

Keir nodded faintly, pulling his face away from her head and moving to claim his cup. But he was still extremely close to her as he offered her his cup to drink from, which she did. He drank after she did, in the same spot, his eyes never leaving hers.

"Perhaps he is," he observed. "But I would rather not speak of Coverdale and his child bride. I would rather speak of us. Should your father give his consent, it is my intention to marry you immediately unless you have any objections."

In spite of the fact that they were surrounded with people and in spite the fact that Chloë was never inclined to approve of public displays of affection, she leaned against Keir, her face an inch from his own. A warm smile spread across her lips and she could feel his hot breath in her face, his lips so close that she could almost taste them. She very much wanted to.

"I have no objections," she whispered. "Where will we be married?"

"Do you have a preference?"

She thought on that. "I was raised at Exelby and our family attended church in Leaming, which is a town nearby. I know the priests there and the parishioners. I am sure my parents would like for me to be married there."

Keir didn't appear too keen on the suggestion. "Exelby was recently compromised and I am concerned that Ingilby is still in the area, especially since he knows you are no longer at Exelby. It is possible that he is looking for you. I am not sure it would be prudent to return to the town. I should not like to have a battle on my wedding day."

She understood although she was disappointed. "Then we shall be married wherever you think is best. I do not care if it is in the middle of a stable, so long as we are married."

His smile grew and he gently stroked her cheek with an index finger, collecting her hand and kissing it reverently. "I do so love you," he whispered.

She watched him kiss her hand, touching his face as his lips drifted over her palm. "And I love you," she replied quietly. "For always, I will love you."

They were so caught up in each other that they were genuinely startled when Kurtis pitched a spoon in their direction, hitting Keir on the shoulder and catching his attention. Keir looked at his brother, prepared to rage, when Kurtis pointed to the entry hall. Both Keir and Chloë looked to see Anton and Blanche approaching.

Chloë immediately sat back in her chair and Keir took his hands off her, both presenting proper behavior as Anton and Blanche approached the table. Cassandra and Kurtis also took their hands off each other, presenting a faux example of prim young adults. Anton kissed Cassandra on the head in greeting as he seated Blanche next to her. He claimed the chair on the other side of his wife, his gaze on Chloë.

"Greetings, Chloë," he said rather formally. "You are looking well."

Chloë beamed at her father. "I am well," she agreed, looking to her mother for any indication as to her father's mood. Her mother was as emotionless as always and, uncertain, she returned her focus to her father. "Are you well also, Father?"

Anton nodded, accepting a pewter cup from a serving wench. He drank deeply of the contents and smacked his lips before returning his focus to Chloë. This time, he fixed on Keir as well.

"St. Héver," he greeted. "The last time I saw you, you were covered in mail and gore. Now that you are clean and presentable, I see what has my daughter so smitten."

Shocked, Chloë looked to Keir for his reaction, but Keir remained steady. "What is that, my lord?"

Anton cocked an eyebrow as he drank deeply again. "You resemble a hero from legend with your handsome looks and big muscles," he turned to his wife. "You were correct when you said his attractiveness is a fine complement to Chloë's beauty. They make a handsome pair."

Blanche waited to speak until her own cup was filled with ruby red wine. "This is his brother, Sir Kurtis," she indicated the big man sitting on the other side of Cassandra. "He is Northumberland's commander."

Anton gave Kurtis a scrutinizing look before focusing on the food now being placed before him. "How long have you served de Vesci, Sir Kurtis?" he asked.

Kurtis prepared himself for a second round of interrogation. Unlike his brother, the de Gelds did not know him. He was sure they would want to know every little thing about him before agreeing to turn their daughter over to him.

"Six years, my lord."

"And before that?"

"I served the king in Wales, my lord."

Anton continued to drink, delving into his food when a steaming plate of meat was put in front of him. He had had a long talk with his wife about their daughters' collective futures and although he knew, eventually, he would do as the womenfolk wanted, he still had to make a reasonable show of concern as the father of the potential brides. He pretended to be interested in his food when, in fact, he was thinking of questions to ask the prospective bridegrooms.

"Although my wife has had the opportunity to interrogate you, I find that I must satisfy myself," Anton said as he pulled juicy meat off the bone. "Keir, I have known of you for many years. I know you met with some hardship a few years ago when Pendragon was burned and your family killed. I understand that your young son still has not been found."

It was a very touchy subject, something that Blanche had tactfully refrained from. As Chloë looked stricken at her father's question, even Blanche cast her husband a long glance. Keir, however, remained cool.

"He has not, my lord."

"Do you continue to search for him or have you simply consigned the matter to God?"

Keir fought to keep his emotions down at the extremely delicate subject. "I am always searching for him, my lord," he replied steadily.

"He is my son. I will search for him until the day I die."

Anton nodded. "But you will be taking on a new wife and, presumably, new children," he pointed out. "What of the children you have with my daughter? Will they be your heirs or will you hold out for your missing son?"

"Father!" Chloë shrieked in protest, shooting to her feet. "That is not a suitable question. It has nothing to do with our marriage!"

As Keir tried to shush her softly and pull her back down into her chair, Anton went on the defensive.

"It is a reasonable question, Chloë," he insisted. "I must know if this man will take care of you and your children or if he will view you as a replacement for the family he lost. Will he view you as a substitute for the wife that was murdered and will he see her when he looks at you? It seems that a man who has known such heartache would have emotional issues he may not be able to overcome. You would suffer, child."

By now, even Blanche had hushed her husband. Anton was naturally submissive to his wife but he believed he had a legitimate question. Chloë stared at her father in horror before bursting into tears.

"You are hateful," she sobbed. "I cannot believe you would be so cruel to Keir when he has done nothing to deserve it!"

She was trying to pull away from the table but Keir had her, gently trying to coax her to regain her seat. Chloë wept and struggled to pull away, not wanting to create a scene but terribly upset with her father. Keir had his big arm around her torso, blocking her from leaving completely. As Chloë wept softly into her hand, Keir looked at Anton.

"I must put myself in your position when understanding the sincerity of your question, my lord," he said evenly, although he was growing upset simply because Chloë was so upset. "I understand that you want the best possible match for your daughter and I respect that. But you must understand that I love Chloë very much and do not consider her a replacement for the wife lost. The past cannot be undone and I do not wish for things that cannot be. It is my hope to regain my son someday and I will never stop looking for the boy, but any children Chloë and I have will be mine, body and soul, and I will love them and provide for them to the very best of my abilities. They will want for nothing."

"That may be," Anton continued. The fact was that he truly believed he was acting in his daughter's best interest as he formulated questions that were meant to be probing but only made him look foolish. "However, I am deeply concerned at the amount of grieving you did for your first wife."

"Why?"

"Because it suggests that perhaps my daughter cannot compete with a dead woman's memory," he pointed out. "Tell me, St. Héver, if your dead wife was to walk into the room this very moment, who would you choose? Her or my daughter?"

It was a bluntly malicious question, one that was not lost on Keir. He did not want to start off his marriage to Chloë with a distinct distaste for her father, but it was an unnecessary question that was meant to trick him. No good could come of it and he knew it.

"Chloë," he replied with a hint of disgust in his tone. "Satisfied?"

Anton digested his statement, nodding as he came to terms with the man and his ability to remain calm under ridiculous scrutiny. His blue-eyed gaze moved to his stricken daughter, standing next to Keir with her back to the table. Keir had his enormous arms around her, preventing her from going anywhere.

"Chloë," Anton said in a low voice. "Sit down."

"Nay," Chloë snapped. "I will not sit and listen to your cruelty."

"Do you want to marry this man?"

"Aye."

"Then sit down. I will not tell you again."

Chloë wiped her eyes, struggling for composure. Without a word, she gently removed Keir's arms from her torso and bent down to kiss his cheek. It was a surprising show of affection in full view of her parents, something under normal circumstances the modest woman would have never done. Silently and without a hind glance, she walked from the table.

Across the table, Cassandra watched her sister wander away. She closed her eyes tightly, with great sorrow, before turning to her father.

"You hurt her," she hissed. "How could you be so cruel to Keir?"

Anton would not back down. "It is my duty as a father to make sure the man Chloë selected is suitable," he pointed out heatedly. "You will not question me."

Beside him, Blanche rose from her chair. Before leaving the table, she turned to her husband. "I will speak with her," she said softly but with undeniable firmness. "You will now give Sir Keir and Sir Kurtis permission to wed our daughters."

Anton looked up at his wife, his mouth hanging open. "But…!"

"You will do this," Blanche cut him off.

"But I am not finished!"

"You have done enough. Give your permission now."

Anton was gearing up for an epic protest but the words died on his lips. It never did any good to argue with Blanche because she always got what she wanted in the end. As Blanche left the table, Anton looked to the two brother knights, now gazing back at him with varied degrees of hope and apprehension. His lips flattened into a thin line of resignation.

"You heard the woman," he said with some irony. "You have my permission."

Cassandra squealed with delight, throwing her arms around Kurtis and hugging him tightly as Keir smiled faintly and lifted his cup to Anton. Anton returned the gesture purely out courtesy and not because he was genuinely happy about it. He never even got the chance to pick away at Kurtis. He drained his cup and demanded more alcohol as Keir drained his chalice, rose from the table, and went off in search of Chloë and her mother. Even if Blanche wanted to speak with Chloë privately, still, he wanted to be the one to give her the good news.

CHAPTER THIRTEEN

THE HOUR WAS very late but Keir couldn't sleep. On the battlements of Aysgarth, he leaned back against the cold stone of the southeast tower, gazing out over the moonlit Yorkshire landscape and thinking on the course his life was about to take.

One month ago, he was consigned to a dull existence, still hurting for the family he had lost and resigned to the fact that he would grow old and bitter alone. But with the event of the siege of Exelby and the introduction of the youngest daughter of Anton de Geld, he was looking at such joy and possibilities that he could hardly comprehend it all. When he lay down to sleep, his mind was working madly over Chloë, their coming wedding and their life together. He couldn't sleep no matter how hard he tried. Chloë filled his mind from top to bottom.

So he came to the battlements to clear his thoughts. As he stood there and gazed over the silver land, he kept reliving Anton's question to him... *If your dead wife was to walk into this room, who would choose?* He had given Anton the answer he sought, an off the cuff reply that he hadn't thought hard on. But now that he'd had time to think on it, he kept coming around to the same answer and he felt guilty for it.

He and Madeleine had been pledged very young, so she was not someone he had chosen for himself. It was purely by chance that he liked her, eventually coming to love the small woman with the long dark hair and quirky sense of humor. She could make him laugh. But with Chloë, there was such an overwhelming emotional and physical attraction to the woman that he couldn't seem to breathe when she was around. It was as if she filled up every part of him with her luscious beauty and sweet manner. She made him feel special, as if he was important in her eyes, and all he wanted to do was love and protect her. Were Madeleine and Chloë to stand side by side and he was forced to choose, as much as he respected and loved Madeleine, he knew in his heart that he would have to choose Chloë. She was very quickly becoming his all for living. And that realization made him feel increasingly guilty.

Pushing himself off the stone wall, he moved to the parapet and rested his elbows upon it, leaning against the wall as he gazed over the front of the wall. There were soldiers with big dogs and torches patrolling the exterior of the castle, the road and the woods just to the south. He could see the torches moving through the dark trees, phantom floating balls of light in the blackness.

His mind began to wander to the impending wedding; when he had informed Chloë of her father's permission earlier in the evening, all the woman did was squeal. Keir's ears still hurt but it brought a grin to his face to remember her happiness. Chloë's mother already had plans for sending out announcements and the location of the weddings. She, too, mentioned the church in Leaming but Keir wasn't going to argue with the woman at the moment but he fully intended to before she sent out any invitations. At that moment, he simply wanted to enjoy the thrill of Chloë becoming his wife.

"What are you doing up here?"

The soft female voice came from behind him and as he turned, Chloë suddenly appeared beside him. He had been so swept up in his reflections that he hadn't heard her approach. Surprised, but very pleased, he grinned at her.

"I am making sure the castle is safe while you are sleeping," he told her. "At least, I thought you were sleeping. Why are you not in bed like a good girl?"

Wrapped in a dark blue cloak against the cool night, she smiled up at him as she wound her hands around his left arm, snuggling against him.

"I could not sleep," she admitted. "Every time I close my eyes, all I can think of is you and our wedding. I never knew I could be so excited. I feel as if I am walking on clouds."

He chuckled softly. "I feel the same," he agreed. "That is why you find me here. I could not sleep, either."

"May I join you in your insomnia, then?"

"Absolutely."

She leaned her head affectionately against his arm and he kissed the top of her head, eventually putting his arm around her and pulling her close. Together, they gazed off across the moonlit night.

"I never thought I would be happy ever again," he murmured. "But I find I am so joyful that I am actually eager for the future. I have never felt that way before."

She smiled up at him, her porcelain face framed by the dark blue cloak. "Nor have I," she said. "I will confess that I imagine what our children will look like. Perhaps we will have six girls who look just like me."

He laughed softly as she giggled. "I could only be so blessed," he replied, brushing a stray lock of red hair from her cheek. "I cannot imagine a house full of little Chloës but I am sure it would be a loud and beautiful place. I would have men from here to the Holy Land beating down my door."

She continued giggling. "Or, we could just as easily have six boys in your image."

He grunted. "I could field my own army with a powerful group like that. It would make me the envy of all men."

She watched his expression, her smile fading as she thought on sons of Keir St. Héver. "Was your son just like you?" she asked softly.

He looked down at her, seriousness in his gaze. After a moment's reflection, he nodded. "Just like me," he replied. "Merritt was a big lad with very blond hair. He had a little wooden sword that I had given him and he used to carry it around constantly. He would try to fight me and the other knights with it."

She could see the pain in his eyes as he spoke even though his expression remained somewhat warm. She reached up and gently stroked his cheek.

"He is out there, somewhere," she encouraged. "I will help you search for him. We will not stop until we find him."

The warmth returned to his eyes and he kissed her on the forehead. "That is sweet of you," he said. "Truth be told, I am not sure where else to look. I spent a year wandering the north of England looking for any sign of him but there was none. I have paid people for information, thrashed and threatened them to tell me what they knew, but nothing I was able to glean came to fruition. I try not to grow discouraged but it is difficult."

Chloë sighed faintly, rubbing his cheek with her soft palm. "Someone, somewhere, knows something about him," she assured him. "We will find that person and we will bring Merritt home."

Keir hugged her tightly, thinking on his blond-haired son and the sadness the memories provoked. It was difficult not to become disheartened at all of the failure he had met with in the search for his little boy. He'd spent so much time focused on finding him alive that when the dark fingers of depression grabbed at him, it was increasingly difficult to fight them off.

"He has probably forgotten about me," he muttered, letting his disenchantment show through. "He was so young when he disappeared. He probably does not even remember who I am."

She could hear the despair in his voice and she shifted so her arms were wrapped around his torso. She gazed into his handsome face.

"He will remember the man who gave him a wooden sword," she assured him softly. "I am very much looking forward to meeting Me-Me and I have little doubt that someday, we will find him."

He tried to be positive along with her. "It is my hope," he said sincerely. "Speaking of Me-Me, did you receive any more visits from our little ghost girl during the time we did not speak? I assumed you would tell me if you did."

She shook her head. "Oddly enough, she has not come back and I am worried about her."

"Worried? Why?"

Chloë shrugged. "I suppose because I feel so sorry for her, this little ghost girl who is looking for her little brother. She is all alone and I feel very badly for her."

Keir fell silent a moment. "I have a confession," he murmured. "There were times when you were not in your chamber and I went in, calling to Frances and seeing if she would come to me."

Chloë looked at him, not surprised by his admission. As a caring father, she expected nothing less. "And?"

He shook his head. "She never appeared."

He seemed sad about it. Chloë hugged him gently. "Not to worry," she whispered. "We will all be together again someday. I have faith in you, Keir. You are not a man who knows failure."

He was touched by her words, by her respect for him. She made him feel strong again and he hugged her tightly, rocking her sweetly in the moonlight and thinking on the future for all of them, his brother and Cassandra included. Thoughts of Merritt drifted from his mind as he began to think on his somber brother and how much Chloë's sister had brought the man out of his shell.

"Is Cassandra awake also?" he asked softly.

Chloë's thoughts shifted from Merritt to her sister. "She is not in her chamber so I would assume so."

Keir thought on all of the greater implications of that statement and of his brother, so quiet and serious, yet with a decidedly lusty streak in him. While Kurtis had accused Michael of his rutting ways, it was a fact that Kurtis liked it hard, fast and frequent. He wondered how Cassandra would deal with that hot blooded aspect of her new husband but he didn't say anything to Chloë about it. If Cassandra wanted her sister to know, she would tell her.

"I thought she was the sister who had accompanied you to Pendragon so you would not be unchaperoned and fall victim to men's wiles," he teased. "Now you tell me she is not in her bed? I find that shocking."

Chloë giggled as she gazed up at him. "If she is only half as joyful as I am, then I am sure she and Kurtis are being sleepless together."

Keir grinned, kissing the end of her nose and cupping her face with a great hand, stroking her velvety cheek with his thumb.

"We will spend many nights like this together, I assure you," he promised, bending down to kiss her soft mouth. "I do not intend to ever let you out of my sight, not even for a moment."

Chloë responded to his kiss, delivering a heated one of her own. Keir's body language changed dramatically at her lusty response as he pushed against her, his hands coming up to hold her head still as his mouth feasted on her warm lips. Seconds before, he had been affectionate but proper. Now he was a man in love, his physical needs gaining the better of his self-control now that he knew Chloë would be his wife. There was no reason to restrain himself in the least, so he devoured her tender lips, his tongue tasting her mouth before moving on to her cheeks and neck.

In his grasp, Chloë gasped softly in awakening passion. Keir feasted on the flesh of her neck before returning to her mouth and kissing her so hard that Chloë had to tear her mouth away or suffocate. As she gasped for air, he began to come to his senses and realize he was ravaging her for all to see. She was his now, legally, and his self-restraint was suffering. He stopped kissing her and put an arm around her, pulling her towards the southeast tower.

"Come," he said softly.

Chloë was still trying to catch her breath. "Where are we going?"

"Where Kurtis and Cassandra have gone."

She looked queerly at him as he grinned, taking her down the narrow spiral stairs to the bailey below. It was cold and dark in the bailey, being patrolled by soldiers and torches, as Keir put his arm around her shoulders and pulled her towards the keep.

"Where are you taking me?" Chloë could see the keep looming head.

"I am taking my betrothed back to her chamber," he told her, noting her look of disappointment. He grinned. "Not to worry, love. I will not leave you alone."

She fought off a smile as they entered the keep. The great hall was directly in front of them, the spiral stairs that led to the upper floors to the left. There were still people in the great hall, drinking and talking, and Keir peered inside, keeping his gaze on Coverdale and Anton at the table as he motioned Chloë up the stairs. She slipped up the stairs, racing to the third floor as quietly as she could. As she hit the landing, Keir suddenly appeared behind her and together, they silently made their way into Chloë's borrowed chamber and quietly bolted the door.

Chloë was giggling as she removed her cloak. "If my father knew you were here with me, he would have something to say about it."

Keir cocked an eyebrow, spying a pitcher of wine in the corner and moving for it. "I am your betrothed now and, by God and the law, already your husband. Your father cannot do anything about it."

Chloë's grin turned somewhat shy as she put her cloak away. "Do you have lascivious intentions then, my lord?"

He laughed softly. "The first moment I saw you, I had lascivious intentions."

She gasped in feigned outrage. "How can you say such a thing? We were battling one another when first we met."

He went to her, wrapping his arms around her. "Do you remember when you ran from me at first? I chased you and you ended up tripping. I fell atop you. Do you recall?"

She did, sort of. "I believe so. Why?"

He gave her a seductive expression, pulling her closer. "I remember feeling soft flesh beneath me, even through the layers of armor."

She blushed furiously. "You did not."

"I did. Soft, warm, delicious female flesh."

She giggled again and tried to pull away but he would not hear of it. He pulled her close, nuzzling her neck, running his hands through all of that miraculous hair. He adored her hair. He bent down to kiss her, gently at first, but as his passion roared, he picked her up and held her fiercely against him. Chloë wrapped her arms around his neck and held on tightly as he carried her over to the bed.

The bed was massive, four posters with a great curtain around it, and it sat back in the corner in the shadows. A low fire burned in the hearth, flames licking at the fireback and sending undulating golden light into the room. Keir laid Chloë upon the bed, his mouth fused to hers, trying not to jab her with the armor still on his body. Keeping his mouth on hers, he began to remove the cold steel pieces.

Chloë's arms were around his neck as he kissed her and she could feel him moving about unstrapping pieces of armor. She could hear things falling to the floor. When he was down to his mail coat, he pulled his mouth away from hers and silently stood up, bending over and deftly removing it. The big mailed garment was very heavy and he tossed it aside, listening to it make a big commotion as it fell on the floor. Clad only in a damp tunic, breeches and big boots, he returned his attention to Chloë.

She was sitting up on the bed now, watching him practically disrobe before her. Without a word, he sat down beside her on the bed, his eyes drifting over the dark bronze damask surcoat that so deliciously emphasized her shapely torso. White cleavage daringly peaked out from the neckline of the surcoat and Keir's gaze was lustily drawn to it. One arm went around her shoulders as the other went to her torso, and he pulled her close again, his mouth on her neck as the hand on her torso began to gently stroke her belly.

"You are so incredibly beautiful," he murmured, kissing her sweet flesh. "I do not know what I have done in life to warrant such a prize as you, but rest assured that I will never take you for granted and I will always treat you with the greatest respect."

Chloë's eyes were closed as he nuzzled her neck, the hand on her belly moving gently to her ribcage. She was so overwhelmed with his hot breath on her skin and his delicate touch that she threw her arms around his neck, falling back onto the bed and pulling him with her.

Keir gladly lay down, his enormous body half-covering her own.

His seeking lips found her mouth and he resumed kissing her with the greatest of passion. The hand on her belly moved to the underswell of her breast and she gasped softly as she felt his hand against her bosom, pausing a moment with wide eyes to look at him. Keir gazed back at her, steadily, before dipping low to gently kiss her cheek. As he nuzzled her soft skin, his hand moved up and fully enclosed her right breast against the palm. He squeezed gently, fondling her, and Chloë groaned softly when she realized how good it felt.

Keir heard her groan and his kisses resumed with force. He couldn't seem to kiss her enough, taste her enough, and the hand on her breast grew bolder. Fingers slipped along the neckline, trying to pull it away somehow, but the bodice fit snuggly against her body. As his passion grew and their kisses grew more heated, Keir didn't have the patience to properly disrobe her. He took hold of the top of her bodice and ripped it in half in one swift, clean motion.

Chloë gasped with shock as her bodice fell away and her pure white flesh was exposed. Before she could make any manner of protest, Keir's mouth was on her soft white cleavage and his palm was against her naked breast. A pink nipple, soft and taunting, rubbed against his hand and, with a growl, his hot mouth descended upon it, suckling furiously.

Chloë cried out softly as his hot, wet mouth pulled her nipple into a hard little pellet. He had somehow managed to wedge himself in between her legs, his big body overwhelming her, and Chloë knew that she could not stop him. Her passion had run away with her also and everything he was doing to her was new and wonderful and wicked. She craved it.

Keir paused long enough to rip his tunic off before collapsing back against her, his mouth on her breasts. Chloë held his head against her bosom as if nursing a starving child, feeling each suckle send bolts of dangerous excitement shooting through her body.

Keir was in haze of lust and attraction. Her flesh was sweet and delicious and he nursed hungrily at her breasts, first one and then the other, before getting a grip on the tear he had started in her surcoat and giving a big tug, ripping the entire thing in half. Her shift was torn too, the edges of it clinging to the damp flesh of her breasts, wet with his saliva. Keir ripped at the shift until it was in tatters, peeling it off of Chloë's body until she was completely nude beneath him.

He paused a moment to admire her naked body, the voluptuous lines of her breasts and hips, and he'd never been so wildly aroused in his entire life. He fell back atop her, his mouth on her breasts and belly, somehow managing to remove his boots and breeches in the process. He didn't even remember doing it but the next thing he realized, he was naked, too, his hot manly flesh completely covering her soft, feminine curves. From where he was, he could smell the delicious musky scent of her woman's center and something inside him snapped; grabbing her buttocks with both hands, his mouth descended on the sweet pink folds and he feasted.

Chloë shrieked softly as Keir put his entire face between her legs, his tongue forging into virgin territory. Shocked, embarrassed, words of protest died on her lips when she very quickly realized how marvelous it felt. He was stroking her strongly, grunting softly with every stroke of his tongue as if devouring the most delicious thing God had ever created. Overwhelmed, Chloë panted and wept softly, becoming acquainted with Keir on a level she could have never imagined. It was all so new and shocking but in the same breath, she had never known anything so wonderful existed.

Keir lapped and suckled her tender pink folds and her body jerked involuntarily as he repeatedly pleasured her woman's center, that taut bud of pleasure that would take her to a new level of ecstasy. Chloë could feel heat building in her loins, something that promised complete and utter pleasure should she only submit, but she truly had no idea what would bring her such release. All she knew was that Keir was doing wondrous and wicked things to her body and she was fully submissive to his desires. She didn't care that the man, her betrothed, was taking shocking liberties with her. All that mattered was the feelings he was creating within her. She was a willing captive.

Something was happening deep in her loins; she could feel something pulsating and warm starting. Keir gently insert a finger in to her virginal passage and Chloë was so wet that there was no pain or tightness at all; in fact, she groaned softly and brought her knees up, reacting to his touch, opening her legs wide for the primal ritual of mating, instinctive to men and women since the beginning of time. Realizing how ready she was for him, Keir could no longer refrain from claiming her. He had to feel her around him, her warm and wet tightness that would pleasure him like no one else ever had.

Lifting himself up, Keir's lips found Chloë's once again as he carefully guided his manhood into her tender, virginal walls. Thrusting gently with his hips, he seated himself halfway on the first thrust and then completely on the second. Beneath him, Chloë cried out softly at the sensation of his enormous member inside her, the realization of their first coupling, so distracted by his sweet kisses and heated body that all she could do was encourage him as he thrust into her. It seemed like the most natural of things, his body buried deep within her as it was always meant to be.

She was so highly aroused by Keir's tongue and decadent attentions that by the third or fourth thrust, she gasped sharply at the thrill of her first climax. Keir could feel her wet heat throbbing around him, pulling at him, milking him for his seed and it was the most supreme struggle of his life not to answer. He would, but not now.

At this moment, he simply wanted to savor the event of their first coupling. It was more than he had ever dreamed, her heated, wet body responding to his as he'd never known a woman to respond in his entire life. He wanted to experience her, just a little, before succumbing to his lust.

His thrusts were measured and deep as he held Chloë's pelvis against his, his mouth on her lips. His fingers were in the crack of her buttocks and he could feel all of the moisture from her body running onto her flesh, dampening the linens beneath them. It was coupling beyond his wildest dreams and as he continued making love to her, he could feel another climax wash over her and still another. Chloë was gasping beneath him as if she couldn't breathe, her body stiffening as wave after wave of rapture coursed through her.

Finally, Keir could feel his own climax approach and he accepted it, thrusting into her with one hard, final thrust, releasing himself, filling her womb with his hot seed and mingling her body with his. Even after he released himself, he continued to grind his pelvis against her and continued to feel her ripple with climaxes. He'd lost count after five. His hands, his mouth, were all over her flesh, her breasts and belly, arms and head. As he lay on top of her, still joined to her body, he knew without a doubt that it had been the most miraculous experience of his entire life. Nothing he had ever sampled had come close, not ever.

"I love you, Chloë," he mewed as he kissed her ear. "Until the end of my life, I will love you and only you. You are my angel, sweetheart. You are my life."

Exhausted, overwhelmed, Chloë opened her mouth to respond but ended up bursting into tears. Concerned, Keir lifted his head to look at her but she covered her face with her hands. Deeply worried, he pulled her tightly against him and held her close.

"What is wrong?" he whispered. "Did I hurt you?"

She wept softly, wrapping her arms around his neck as he pulled her closer. "Nay," she sobbed. "You did not hurt me. But I never knew... like this, I never knew it was like this. I feel... I feel like everything has all come down upon me all at once and I am frightened."

He held her close, her soft body against. "What are you frightened of?"

She sniffled, trying to compose herself. "I... I am not sure," she sniffed again, pulling her face from the crook of his neck and gazing up at him. "I think I am afraid of losing this. Of losing you. What if I wake up and this was all a dream? I would want to die."

He smiled faintly at her, kissing the end of her nose. "You will never lose me," he assured her. "I will always be with you, Chloë, no matter what. Put your mind at ease, sweetheart."

She was trying to. She wiped at her watery eyes and he kissed her forehead, the tip of her nose, smiling gently at her until she smiled in return. Then he pulled the curtains closed around the bed so they were safely shut in and snuggled down into the bed with her. With Chloë cuddled safely in his arms, Keir drifted off into the best sleep of his life.

CHAPTER FOURTEEN

S OFT KNOCKING ON the chamber door roused Keir from a deep sleep. Blinking his eyes, he oriented himself, realized where he was, and then looked down to see Chloë curled up against him, warm and cozy.

Warm, fluid feelings rushed over him as he gazed down at her, remember their night of passion. He didn't think it was possible to love something as much as he was coming to love her. She was sleeping quite soundly and a second round of knocking on the door didn't rouse her. Keir gently shook her awake.

Chloë groaned and tried to ignore him but he shook her again, kissing her on the cheek. "Wake up, love," he whispered. "Someone is knocking at your door and I do not think it would be wise for me to answer it."

Chloë yawned and blinked the sleep from her eyes, smiling sleepily when she realized Keir was beside her.

"Good morning, sweetheart," she snuggled up against him and closed her eyes. "Did you sleep well?"

He grinned at her half-awake antics as he wrapped his arms around her and sat up, taking her with him. The pounding on the door was growing louder and Chloë popped an eye open as Keir pulled back the curtains.

"Ask who it is," he whispered to her.

Chloë frowned at the intrusion, rubbing her eyes. "Who in the world would be knocking at my door at this hour?" she grumped.

"Ask, you silly wench," Keir grinned.

Chloë was sleepy and unhappy. She rubbed her eyes again. "Who is it?" she called.

"Kurtis, my lady," came the muffled reply. "I am looking for Keir. Perhaps you might know where he is?"

Keir was immediately up, grabbing his leather breeches as he approached the door. Chloë remained in the bed, wide-eyed, as Keir pulled on his breeches and went to the chamber panel, throwing the old iron bolt. Carefully, he opened the door so that only his eye was apparent. If there were more people in the landing beyond, he didn't want anyone else to see him.

Kurtis was alone. He didn't seem shocked or surprised to see his brother in Chloë's room. In fact, he had expected it, which was why he had come straight to her chamber.

"You are needed downstairs," he told him. "A messenger has come."

Keir opened the door wider. "A messenger?" he repeated. "From whom?"

Kurtis looked as if he had been woken up, too at this ungodly early hour. He did not look happy, rather slovenly dressed for the usually letter-perfect knight.

"A rider bearing Edward's banner rode in about a half hour ago," he lowered his voice. "There is a missive addressed to Coverdale but it concerns you. You had better come."

Keir didn't like the sound of that at all, mostly because he couldn't imagine what the king wanted from him. That association had ended nine years ago. He gave his brother a disbelieving expression.

"Are you serious?" he said, surprised. "What on earth could Edward want with me?"

"The only way to know is to come downstairs and find out."

Keir cocked an eyebrow as he nodded pensively, fighting down ominous feelings. He eyed his brother. "Where were you last evening?"

Kurtis gave him a knowing expression. "Doing the same thing you have been doing," he told him, "but at least I had the good sense to return to my own bed. That is where they came looking for you and you, my brother, were nowhere to be found. It did not take a great intellect to figure out where you were."

Keir grunted, conceding the point, and scratched his scalp. "Do her parents know?"

"They are asleep as far as I know. I doubt anyone other than me has figured this out, mostly because you and I think alike and I have been doing the same thing."

Keir grinned. "I will meet you downstairs."

He shut the door in Kurtis' face and locked it, making his way back over to the bed. Chloë was sitting up with the bed linens pulled up around her, more awake by this time. She looked sweet, cozy and inviting. Keir smiled at her as he reached down for his tunic.

"I have been summoned," he told her quietly. "Go back to sleep and I will see you at the morning meal."

She was watching him with big, bottomless eyes as he pulled the tunic over his head. "Did the king really send you a missive?"

He could hear the fear in her voice and he leaned over, kissing her on the mouth before he began pulling on his boots. The great mail coat was next.

"I do not know," he said honestly. "But I will find out and report back to you right away, General."

He was trying to make light of it but Chloë was not amused. Clutching the bedcovers to her breast, she crept over to the edge of the bed where he was straightening up the mail coat that hung heavily on his big body.

"Do you think he will call you to London?" she asked with uncertainty.

He shrugged as he popped on the pieces of armor he wore last night. "I must admit, I am curious to know why he has sent a missive mentioning my name," he said. "I served Edward in Wales many years ago but I have not had any contact with him since."

She was watching him more closely now as he deftly donned his armor. Since there was nothing more she could press him on regarding the missive awaiting him, she focused on something she had never seen before – a knight donning his armor. Keir was a very big man in his natural state but compounded by the armor, he was positively surreal.

"What do you call those pieces of shield on your arms?" she asked softly.

He glanced at her as he tightened the straps. "These are called a vambrace," he showed her the armor on the lower part of his arm. "Have you never seen these before?"

She shrugged her soft white shoulders. "My father does not wear armor," she said. "We had two knights at Exelby but I was never around them enough to ask them what they wore. I have never seen a knight dress before."

He winked at her. "Well and good that you have not," he muttered. "Were that the case, I would be forced to kill someone."

She giggled, pointing to his mail coat. "Your mail looks very heavy."

He nodded. "It is," he agreed. "In fact, it almost weighs as much as you do. It is built to withstand a great deal."

"I have seen you wear more pieces of armor on your body," she said as she watched him secure the vambrace on his right arm. "Why do you only wear pieces of it at times and then all of it other times?"

He looked at her as he shook his arm to settle the vambrace in to the correct position. "When I am outside of this fortress or any place exposed, I wear every piece of armor I own," he replied. "I have a breast plate, back plate, greaves, and any number of other pieces. But when I am inside the fortress, I dress down slightly. I am not expecting an attack from within but one must always be prepared for the unex-pected."

She watched him finish with the coat and tug on his boots. "Have you ever been badly injured?"

He looked at her, finished dressing. "Nay," he replied honestly. "I have been hit on more than one occasion, but never seriously."

Before she could ply him with more questions, he bent over and scooped her up from the bed, covers and all, and carried her with him to the door. Chloë wrapped her arms around his neck, her forehead against his cheek.

"Now," he said softly, kissing her forehead. "I will go downstairs and find out what the king has to say and you will go back to sleep. The sun is just starting to appear."

She gazed up at him, her face so sweet in the dim light of the room. "Keir?"

"Aye, love?"

"Please…," she faltered. "Please come back to me when you are finished. I do not want the next time I see you to be in the great hall with everyone else around us. I want you to return to me before the sun rises when it is just the two of us."

He looked at her, a faint smile on his lips, as he leaned over and kissed her sweetly on the mouth. "You tempt me beyond reason, lady," he murmured. "If I return before sunrise, then we more than likely will not make it to the great hall at all. Your parents will come looking for you and should they find me here, we might be in for more trouble than we know."

She held him around the neck as he kissed and nuzzled her cheek. "Please," she begged softly, closing her eyes at his blissful attentions. "I cannot stand you away from me, not even for an hour. I will be counting the minutes until you come back to me."

He kissed her ear, her cheek, her mouth. "As will I," he agreed, gently setting her to her feet. "I will return as soon as I know what the king would have of me."

"Promise?"

"Of course I do."

She smiled, seemingly satisfied. "Go then," she urged. "Hurry back."

He took her hand and kissed it as he put his fingers on the latch. "I will."

"Keir?"

"Aye, sweet?"

"I love you very much."

His heart was softened by her words, her very presence. He cupped her face between his two enormous hands and kissed her gently.

"I love you, too."

With that, he opened the door, made sure there was no one in the landing outside, before slipping out into the dark stairwell. Chloë shut the door behind him and bolted it, missing the man already.

❦

"THIS IS UGLY, Keir," Coverdale sounded exhausted. He looked exhausted, half-dressed as he met with his senior soldiers in his lavish solar. "We have a new Welsh prince rebelling against the king and Edward has requested support. This new prince is cunning and powerful, and he has already sacked Caernarfon."

Keir stared at the man, shocked. "Caernarfon?" he repeated incredulously. "That place is a mighty and impenetrable bastion. That is pure madness to think the Welsh could overrun it."

Coverdale lifted an eyebrow, turning for his great oak desk which held the missive sent by the king.

"I would agree with you, but Edward would not lie," he said pointedly. He picked up the missive again and looked at the carefully scribed letters. "Caernarfon, Hawarden, Denbeigh and Ruthin have also fallen under Welsh control and the English garrison commanders killed. Edward is riding to battle again and he asks that you ride with him."

Keir was stunned. He stood in the center of the solar, surrounded by his brother, Lucan, and other Coverdale knights, all of them as shocked as he was. His mind was whirling with the news and he held out his hand to Coverdale, who was still holding the missive.

"Did he ask for me by name?" he asked.

"He did.

"May I read the missive, my lord?"

Byron handed it over. Keir could read and write, unlike most knights, and he quickly read every word of the beautifully written missive that looked more like a piece of art than a communiqué. It had Edward's stamp all over it. Then he read it again, more slowly, absorbing the contents and attempting to wrap his mind around the words.

"Madog ap Llewelyn, cousin to Llewelyn the Last, has declared himself the lawful Prince of Wales and has wrought much havoc throughout northern Wales," he muttered, his eyes riveted to the vellum as he read it word for word. "The king has sent missives to all the great northern lords requesting men and material to gather at Beeston Castle in Chester. Remembering my meritorious service at the Battle of Irfon Bridge, the king orders me to take command of the Army from the North under the Earl of Lincoln's supervision and move west into Wales by the first of October."

"Are you serious?" Kurtis repeated, his normally calm voice laced with disbelief. "You already fought a hard-won battle against Llewelyn the Last, Keir. You ambushed the man and defeated him. You have done your duty."

Keir snorted ironically. "It appears that I am ordered to do my duty again," he said with more control than he felt. "Madog has overrun five castles and all indications are that he is moving for Harlech and Conwy Castles next. When the Army of the North moves, it will be for Harlech."

For a moment, no one spoke. Kurtis was shocked into silence and Keir remained fixed on the vellum. Everyone was waiting for him to say more, but there was no more to be said. The contents of the missive had been revealed.

Coverdale sighed heavily, moving for the wine. It was early in the morning to be drinking but he found he needed it.

"I will supply you with five hundred men, Keir," he said quietly, turning to look at the knight who was still looking at the vellum. "Staring at that missive will not change the contents. You must ride to Chester immediately because men will be arriving and looking for direction, including Henry de Lacy, the Earl of Lincoln. You must be there to lead them."

Keir stared at the vellum a moment longer before handing it back to

Coverdale. He was thinking so many things at that moment – although it was a great honor to be called back to service by the king, Keir wanted no part of it. He wanted to marry Chloë and return to Pendragon to live a nice, quiet life with his new wife. He didn't want to return to Wales and back into the heart of the nasty fighting that had gripped the country for so long. He'd never heard of Madog ap Llewelyn, but he had a feeling the man was going to be the bane of his existence from now on. Already, the man had disrupted his plans of a wonderful and happy life.

"Kurtis," he said, his voice raw and somewhat weak with resignation. "Is it possible that Northumberland has received the call for support for Wales?"

Kurtis knew what his brother was feeling; God help him, he knew all too well. He, too, had served with Keir in Wales, back when they were young and had a false sense of immortality. Since they had done their duty in Wales, they had happily retired to the north of England to relatively quiet lives. Kurtis had seen action against the Scots but it had been nothing like the vicious wars in Wales. Something about the Welshmen was brutal and animalistic, fighting on a level rarely seen. Kurtis didn't relish getting back into that situation as he nodded to his brother's question.

"More than likely," he replied. "If that is the case, he will more than likely keep me at Alnwick and send other knights with the army. With the Scots border being so close and potentially volatile, he will want me with him."

Keir turned to look at him, silent words passing between the brothers. They both knew the stakes and Kurtis would much rather go and fight with his brother, but the truth was that his liege was old and set in his ways, and he depended upon Kurtis a great deal. He would not let him go to Wales, not even to fight for the king. Kurtis began to feel some desperation as he gazed into his brother's eyes. They would be separated and Keir would go to battle without him.

"Perhaps we should just tell Edward that you are not to be found," he said, grasping at the last straws of hope. "Pembury can go in your stead. Let Michael fight off the Welsh this time."

Keir opened his mouth to reply but Coverdale cut him off. "Keir will be marrying a niece of the king," he reminded them. "If Edward finds out that Keir shirked a direct order, the consequences could be critical. I forbid you to even consider such a thing."

Keir was much calmer than he should have been. His gaze lingered on his brother, on the other knights in the room, all the while having difficulty believing that any of this was real. To be ordered back to Wales to quell a rebellion that was already massive and deadly in size was not a light undertaking. It was as important and serious as it could possibly be, the worst news he could have imagined to hear. Perhaps it was a big joke meant to rattle him. He simply couldn't believe what was happening, not now when he was finally happy again and his life was in order. It was God's cruel joke.

As Keir wrestled with his immediate future, Coverdale watched him closely for any signs of an explosion. He couldn't believe the man was taking the news so calmly but sought to capitalize on the Keir's seemingly numb demeanor.

"The men will be ready to leave at dawn on the morrow," he told Keir. "Take this day to get your affairs in order. At daybreak tomorrow, you will ride for Chester."

Keir turned to him. "Summon a priest," he said quietly. "If this is to be my last day with Chloë, then I intend to marry her this day."

Coverdale nodded. "I will send for one immediately. Is there anything else?"

Keir struggled to collect his thoughts. "Aye," he added. "Send for Pembury. I have need of him."

"Of course."

There wasn't much more to say after that. Keir has his orders, as horrible as they were, and he quit the solar in silence, waving off Kurtis when the man tried to follow. All he could think of was how Chloë was going to accept the news. Keir had a thousand preparations to make before he departed Aysgarth but the only thing he could think of at the moment was Chloë. He wanted to hold her, to make love to her, to swear he would return to her when the madness in Wales was over.

As he mounted the stairs to the upper levels of the keep, he realized he was scared to death that he would not return to her. He couldn't stomach the thought of not growing old with her, of not seeing any children they might have. He couldn't stand the thought of going back on his promise to her. Perhaps she would lose him, after all.

When he reached her chamber door in the dark, shadowed hallway, he realized that his palms were sweating. It was a struggle to remain calm. Softly, he knocked on the door and in little time, Chloë answered.

Seeing her smiling face was something of a shock, one that almost put tears in his eyes, but he fought the extreme emotions surging in his chest and smiled in return. He slipped into the room and she bolted the door behind him.

"Well?" she demanded, turning to him. Dressed in a soft white dressing gown, she looked radiant and beautiful. "What did the missive say?"

He continued to smile, holding out his arms to her. "Unlatch my armor and I will tell you," he tried to sound as casual as he could. "By the way, I was thinking as I was walking up the stairs about our wedding date. We have not set one, you know."

Successfully diverted, Chloë nodded as she unfastened the straps on the forearm protection. "My mother is sending out announcements today," she said. "In fact, the riders should have already left, as it was her intention to begin sending them out at sunrise. Mother was preparing missives last night with the help of Coverdale's scribe. There should already be several going out this morning and, I am sure, one directly to Ingilby."

He lifted an eyebrow at her. "Why him?"

Chloë shrugged, unfastening the other piece of armor. "Mother feels that if he knows I am betrothed, he will leave me alone and seek a target elsewhere."

Keir grunted. "Absolutely not," he grumbled. "Sending him a missive is asking for trouble. She may as well go to him personally and laugh in his face. He will see it as a direct insult."

The pieces of armor came off in her hands and she deposited them into his big palm. "I do not see how," she argued gently. "If he knows I am married, then why continue to pursue me? He will know I am out of his reach."

Keir just shook his head, displeased with Lady de Geld's intentions. "This is not a wise decision."

She watched him bend over to remove his mail coat. "Should I tell her what you have said?"

He peeled the mail coat off and stood up. "Nay," he said. "I am going to find your mother myself and see if the missive has gone out yet. If it has not, it never will. If it has, then I will send someone out to retrieve the messenger. It was foolish and arrogant of her to send a wedding announcement to a man who very nearly razed her castle because of an unrequited love. I fear he will only be a threat to you in the future."

Chloë could see he was upset about it and she made her way to him, timidly, as he laid the mail coat over a chair.

"I am not worried, sweetheart," she said softly. "You will protect me."

He looked at her, sharply, as if she had just struck him. All he could think of was that he could not protect her if he was in Wales. She was smiling up at him and he felt his control slipping. He couldn't look at her and not feel the horrific pangs of grief slash at him like claws.

After a moment, he reached out and pulled her against him, holding her so tightly against his chest that she grunted when he tightened his grip. His cheek was against the top of her head, feeling the soft texture against his skin. He sighed faintly, deeply distressed at what he must tell her. The time had come.

"I want you to listen to what I am about to tell you very carefully, sweetheart," he demanded. "It is important."

Chloë held him tightly, burrowed against his chest and belly. "Of course."

He paused a moment as he collected his thoughts. "Do you remember when I told your mother of my history as a knight, that I mentioned my service for the king in Wales?"

She nodded, rubbing her luscious hair against his cheek as she did so. "I do. Is that what was contained in the missive? Did the king send something to that regard?"

"In a manner of speaking," he caressed her back gently with one big hand. "He remembers my victory against the Welsh prince. It was a great victory although I think it was skill coupled with a good deal of luck. It seems that there is another uprising in Wales at this time and the king has requested my assistance with it."

"Your assistance?" her head came off his chest, the big brown eyes gazing up at him. "What does he want from you?"

He held her head between his hands, his thumbs on her cheeks. "He wants me to go to Wales and help him quell the uprising. It seems that I am the only man in all of England who knows how to suppress a rebelling Welsh prince."

She looked at him for a moment, digesting the information, before shaking her head. "You cannot go," she said flatly. "We are getting married soon and we are going to live peacefully at Pendragon. You have already done your duty for the king. He will have to find someone else to help him quash the Welsh."

He almost laughed. She said it firmly, as if she was issuing a command to both him and the king. He stroked her cheeks with his thumbs.

"I wish it was that simple," he said sincerely. "He has issued an order and I must go."

The brown eyes grew cloudy when she realized there was no choice in the matter, and she pulled away from his caressing hands.

"You cannot," she countered sternly. "You and I are to be married soon."

"Aye, we are," he agreed. "We will be married today before I leave."

Her eyebrows flew up. "Leave?" she repeated, growing increasingly agitated. "You are not leaving."

He sighed faintly, seeing that an explosion of epic proportions was brewing.

"Sweetheart, I must," he said gently. "I do not have a choice. The king has placed me in charge of the armies gathering in the north. I am to lead the armies into Wales and support the king's efforts against Madog ap Llewelyn as he tries to usurp the king in Wales."

Her mouth popped open. "Who is this Madog?" she snapped. "I have never heard of him. And you cannot go because we are to be married."

He shook his head, exasperated because she did not seem to understand what he was telling her. Everything revolved around their marriage, around what she wanted for her perfect life. He wanted it, too, but the reality was harsh and brutal.

"Chloë, my sweet love, listen to me, please," he went to her, grasping her by the arms and holding her firmly when she tried to pull away. "We will be married today and I will send you back to Pendragon with Pembury. You will stay there, well protected, until I return from Wales."

"Nay," she said angrily, the tears starting to come. "You cannot go, Keir. You swore you would never leave me, not ever."

He pulled her into an embrace even as she struggled. "Of course I will never leave you," he kissed her head, her angry red cheek. He tried to look her in the eye but she was still fighting him. "I will always be in your heart, your soul, in everything about you. A man cannot love something as much as I love you and not be a part of the very air you breathe."

The tears were falling now, fast and furious. She gripped him, sobbing loudly as she collapsed against his chest. Keir held her tightly, so very sorry she was so upset. His heart ached for the both of them.

"You are going to battle," she wept.

He kissed her hair, her forehead. "Aye," he whispered.

Her sobs were loud and unrestrained. "I may never see you again."

He couldn't lie to her. He could feel tears stinging his eyes. "Aye, you will," he said confidently. "I will return to you, I swear it, even if it is in the caress of a breeze or the visit of a sparrow who sits on your windowsill. Even if my body does not return, my heart and soul will always find you, Chloë. You have them with you even now. That will never change."

She wept loudly, devastated at the news. Keir held her, rocking her gently as she expended her grief. After several long and painful moments, he swept her into his arms and carried her to her bed. Laying her down on the overstuffed mattress, he lay down beside her and gathered her into his arms.

Chloë sobbed until there was nothing left. Wrapped in his enormous arms, she clutched his tunic, her face buried in his neck. Keir had one arm around her body while the other was up around her shoulders, a great hand in her hair, caressing her head, soothing her.

"Please," she whispered, begging. "Please do not go."

He hissed her forehead tenderly. "I must," he replied.

Her sobs renewed with vigor for a time, eventually fading off into sniffles and hiccups. Eventually, she fell still and Keir knew she had fallen asleep. He could hear her deep, steady breathing. He lay there with her for a while, simply to feel her close to him, before very carefully disengaging himself and rising from the bed. She was so emotionally exhausted that she didn't stir in the least.

Pulling the coverlet over her, Keir silently gathered his mail and slipped from the room. With Chloë sleeping, he could focus on what he needed to accomplish before tomorrow's departure. The first thing he intended to do was stop Lady de Geld from sending any sort of missive to Ingilby. Without Keir around to protect Chloë, he was very concerned. Better not to rattle the man's cage and leave well enough alone.

After a shave and a clean change of clothes, Keir went in search of Lady de Geld and found the woman in Coverdale's solar. She was there with her husband as well as Lord Coverdale. Keir didn't like the mood of the room when he entered it and liked it even less when Anton began to speak. He knew of the missive from the king and had something to say about it.

By then, stopping a wedding announcement to Ingilby was the very least of Keir's worries.

CHAPTER FIFTEEN

"**N**AY!" Chloë was screaming at her father. "You promised, Father. *You promised!*"

Anton held his position in a very unpopular battle. His wife and both daughters were against him, but he had to hold fast. He knew best in this instance. The womenfolk in his family were thinking with their emotions, as women often do, and he was thinking clearly where they were not. Truth be told, however, it was a struggle to hold his ground. He did not like to see his wife and daughters so unhappy when it was directed at him.

"I made the promise before I knew the man was going off to war," he told his daughter steadily. "You will marry this man today and be a widow tomorrow? I think not. I know you do not agree with me, Chloë, but you must understand I am doing this for your own good. If St. Héver perishes in Wales, as his widow, you will be relegated to the average offers for your hand. As an unwed maiden, your price is premium."

"*Nay!*" Chloë screamed again, smacking her hands on the desk in Coverdale's solar. "I will not hear of this. You promised Keir and me that we could be married and we will."

Anton was becoming increasingly upset over her disrespectful tone. Chloë wasn't usually a screamer, which was something else of a shock to him. However, Cassandra was livid. The blond sister had a bold mouth and was not afraid to voice her opinion in the face of what she considered sheer stupidity.

"And me?" she spat. "Kurtis is not going to war but will you make me wait as well for some foolish, contrived reason?"

"You will not speak to me in that tone," Anton warned her.

"Or what?" Cassandra snapped. "Will you prove that I am right and you are not a man of your word? How dare you go back on your word to Keir and Chloë. The man is going off to war and all you can think of is keeping your daughter's price high for the next potential husband?"

"Enough!" Anton roared. "Leave this solar, Cassandra. This matter does not concern you."

Cassandra wasn't finished nor would she allow her father to cast her aside. She moved towards the man, teeth bared, and lowered her voice.

"Think very hard about what you are doing," she seethed. "If you go back on your promise to Keir and Chloë, men will know this. They will know this because I will tell them and your oath will be no better than sand through fingers to any man who holds bond with you. Keir is a well-respected and honored knight, and I am ashamed that you would rescind your word to him. It is a vile, treacherous act against your own flesh and blood."

Anton reached out and slapped her across the face but, to her credit, Cassandra didn't flinch or cry. She took the blow, her blue eyes drilling holes through her father before turning and quitting the room. Chloë watched her sister go with big eyes, turning to her father with a new round of venom.

"You *struck* her?" she gasped. "Why would you do such a thing? She only speaks the truth."

Anton jabbed a finger at her. "Do not believe for one minute I will not beat you as well for your insolence. You insult my integrity."

"That is because you have none if you go back on your word to Keir!"

"I will not hear this!" Anton bellowed. "If you cannot abide by my wishes, I will marry you to the next man who bids for your hand and forget all about you, you ungrateful wench. My castle is in ruins because of you and now you seek to question my authority on the matter of your marriage? You are mine to broker as I please, daughter, and I will not marry you to a man who is riding off to his death in battle. You are more valuable as an unwed maiden than you are as a widow."

Chloë was so upset she could hardly breathe. She gazed steadily at her father, hating the man more than she could express. He had always been rather shallow and careless, but nothing like this. He was turning into something dark and deceitful right before her eyes and she hated him for it.

"I will commit myself to a convent before I allow you to broker me like a prize mare," she hissed. "I will be Keir's wife and no one else's."

"You will do what I tell you."

"Is that all I am to you? A bargaining tool?"

"You are my daughter and I will mold your future as I see fit."

Chloë was beginning to tremble, her emotions overwhelming her. "And if Keir returns from Wales? What then?"

"Then you shall marry him," Blanche looked up from her needle-work, which she had patiently been working throughout the entire violent argument between her husband and daughters. She glanced at Anton as if daring him to contradict her. "If Keir returns from Wales, well and good. You shall marry him. But if he does not return, your father only wants you to have the best opportunities. Your selection of husbands as a widow will not be nearly as prestigious as your selection as a maiden. Although I do not agree with your father's tactics, I understand his reasoning. In the end, he is only thinking of you, Chloë."

Chloë looked at her mother, wishing she had more support from the woman. But something stuck in her mind, something both of her parents had said – *an unwed maiden*. After last night, Chloë was no longer a maiden and that little fact was verging on the tip of her tongue. She wasn't ashamed of it in the least. Perhaps if she told them, they would have to allow her to marry Keir. It was her secret weapon, one that could easily be used against her, but she had to take the chance.

"I will not command as high a price as you think," she said deliberately, turning baleful eyes to her father. "I am no longer a maiden,

Father. There is no value in used goods. You must marry me to Keir now because I belong to him, body and soul. I am his forever and you cannot separate us."

Anton's eyes bugged with shock, with outrage. "He stole your innocence?"

"Nay!" Chloë shouted back. "I gave it to him willingly because I love him and because you promised him that we could be wed. I gave my innocence to the man intended to be my husband. Now you would seek to take that away from us both!"

She was screaming by the time she finished, so much so that Blanche stood up and went to her, putting her hands on her daughter to calm her. Chloë was struggling against tears but it wasn't working; little sobs kept bubbling out and she wiped at her eyes, her nose. Blanche, never one to be particularly comforting, put a soothing hand to her daughter's red cheek.

"Anton," she said in a low, firm voice. "Perhaps we should reconsider. You did give your word to Chloë and Sir Keir."

Anton began to stomp around, throwing the cup in his hand that was half-full of wine. "I will not hear this," he shouted. "Now Chloë is compromised, the most beautiful woman in the whole north of England, and she is cheapened like a whore by a knight who could not resist her flesh. Who would want to marry her now that St. Héver has marked her?"

"I would rather be a whore than a liar," Chloë screamed at him, the tears beginning to fall. "You have always been weak and foolish, Father, but this goes beyond what I even thought you were capable of. You cannot keep me from Keir!"

He jabbed a finger at her. "One more word from you and you will never marry this man, not even if he returns from Wales, and I will sell you off to the brothels in London if you cannot show more respect and common sense."

The door to the solar suddenly flew open, slamming back so hard that the iron hinges bent and one of them actually popped out of the wall. Keir charged through, his handsome face taut with rage. He went straight to Chloë, who collapsed into loud sobs when she saw him. He threw his arms around her, holding her tightly, trying to focus on comforting her and not snapping Anton de Geld's neck. He had been lingering outside of the solar, listening to every word spoken until he could stand it no longer. His ice blue gaze was steady over the top of Chloë's dark red head.

"If you ever speak to her in that manner again, I will kill you," he growled. "She is not a whore and she is not cheapened. She is a wise, gifted and beautiful woman whom I am deeply in love with and if there is any shame in this matter, it is yours and yours alone for breaking your bond. Chloë has done nothing wrong."

Anton was pale and trembling as he stood near the hearth, the anger in his veins pumping but not foolish enough to lash back at St. Héver. The man was twice his size and many times more deadly. As his mouth worked, struggling for a reply that wouldn't send St. Héver's sword into his gut, Kurtis suddenly charged in to the room and moved straight for him. Cassandra, her cheek still red from her father's slap, bolted after Kurtis, holding on to the man and struggling to restrain him.

"Nay, Kurtis," she begged. "Please… he was angry. He did not mean it."

Anton could read his death in the eyes of the men before him. He scurried away to the hearth and grabbed the nearest implement he could find, which happened to be a big copper shovel used to remove ash. He wielded it against Kurtis as the man came close, but Kurtis lashed out a big hand and knocked the shovel halfway across the room. As Anton backed up against the wall, Kurtis thrust a finger in to the man's face.

"Only because she has asked me not to kill you, I will not," he growled. "But I will tell you this; I do not care if you are the father of my wife. If you ever touch her again in anger, I will rip your head from your body. Is this in any way unclear?"

Before Anton could reply, the room filled up with knights and Lord Coverdale. They had heard the shouting in the solar and seen the reaction of the St. Héver brothers, and Byron was quick to gather muscle and race into the solar to save Anton from being cut to pieces. Coverdale knew what Keir was capable of and he would not see the man hanged for murder. He could see Keir with Chloë in his arms but the more immediate problem seemed to be Kurtis. He went to the man, putting himself between Anton and the knight.

"Kurtis," he pointed to the door. "Get out of here. Take Lady Cassandra with you. The priest should be here shortly so you will go and wait in the chapel. Do as I say."

With Cassandra tugging and Lucan shoving, they managed to remove Kurtis from the solar. It was like trying to drag a stubborn bull but they managed it. Keir watched them pull his brother from the room, focusing on Coverdale as the man came over to him. Chloë was still sobbing softly in his arms and Coverdale was not unsympathetic. He eyed the woman with some pity before looking to Keir, sighing heavily.

"I think it would be best if you left also," he said quietly. "Your presence will only inflame the situation."

Keir looked at his liege before turning his attention to Anton, still backed up against the wall. "I asked you this earlier when you informed me that due to my orders from the king, you had no intention of allowing me to marry Chloë before I left for Wales," his voice was hoarse with emotion. "I will ask you again – what will it take for you to allow us to be wed today? I will give you all that I have, everything that I own, if you will allow this."

Chloë lifted her head, looking up at him with surprise. "You... you offered to give him your...?"

Keir nodded, shushing her softly as he returned his attention to Anton. "Well, my lord? You will gain the Lordship of Sedberg, a rich fiefdom that will supply you with income. I will give it all to you if you will allow me to marry Chloë before I leave on the morrow."

Anton was shaken, furious, indecisive. He knew one thing for certain, however, and that was the fact that he would not be bullied into changing his mind. Now it was the principle of the matter. He had made a decision and he was going to stick with it, no matter how unpopular it was. It wasn't even a matter anymore of doing what was best for Chloë. Now it was a matter of standing up for his ability to make a decision regarding his family, right or wrong.

"You cannot buy her," he told him. "I told you earlier today that I cannot allow my daughter to wed a man who is going to battle. If you die, her marriage prospects will be seriously limited. Is that what you want, Sir Keir? To limit my daughter from having a rich and comfortable life simply because you selfishly want to marry the woman before you go into battle? It would seem to me that if you truly love her as you say you do, you could understand my concern."

Keir could see the man was twisting the situation to make it seem as if he had not gone back on his word. He was trying to rationalize a truly bad choice. Keir had had the same argument with Anton earlier that day.

"I do not intend to die," he pointed out. "Moreover, if I do, Chloë will inherit my Lordship of Sedberg. If that is what you are truly worried about, that fact alone will make her attractive to a potential husband."

Anton waved him off. "She will inherit more from her mother when she dies," he brushed him off. "Sedberg is not worth much, and certainly not enough to make her appealing to a potential husband enough so that he will overlook the fact that she has already been married."

Keir looked at Chloë, who was now calming in his embrace. He smiled faintly at her.

"Nay," he argued. "Her beauty is enough for any man to overlook what might be considered a flaw or less than attractive. Chloë herself in the prize, not what she inherits or how much money she has. I would take her with only the clothes on her back and be deliriously happy for it."

Chloë smiled weakly at him and he winked at her. It was a warm moment between them, something that lifted both their spirits, only to be doused again when Anton spoke.

"Be that as it may, I have made my decision," he said, coming away from the wall where Kurtis had cornered him. "I will say nothing of the fact that you have taken my daughter's innocence because it cannot be regained. She was a willing participant and it is done. However, I still feel strongly that you not marry before you leave for Wales. I have explained my reasons and my decision on that is final."

"But she is already compromised. She is already my wife in the eyes of God if not in the eyes of the law. I have claimed her and she is mine."

Anton would not be swayed. "It does not matter. I would not make my daughter so willing a widow. Let us see if you return from Wales. Let us see if I was wrong."

Keir was still looking at Chloë, the smile fading from his face as he turned to Anton. "And if I return from Wales, will you still deny us?"

Before Anton could reply, Blanche spoke. "Nay, we will not," she said in her firm, resolute tone. "Chloë will remain pledged to you during such time as you are in Wales. If you return, you will be permitted to wed her. Consider it your incentive for keeping yourself alive in the midst of the Welsh rebellion. You have my word that Chloë will remain yours until, and if, you return. Is this acceptable?"

It wasn't what Keir had wanted but it was the best that could be done under the circumstances. It was enough. After a moment, he nodded his head.

"It is," he agreed. "But I will add one more provision. She goes to Pendragon and remains there until my return, under my protection."

"Agreed."

It was done. With nothing left to argue and nothing left to say, Keir's attention returned to Chloë. He could already see the horrible longing in her eyes and it shook him.

"Then with your permission, I would like to spend my last few remaining hours with Chloë before I leave on the morrow," he said quietly.

Anton opened his mouth to respond but Blanche cut the man off with a sharp hand as if to block whatever was intended to come out of his mouth. He'd said enough, creating chaos with his unpopular decision, and Blanche was now in charge.

"You may," Blanche waved the pair off. "Go now and say what needs to be said. There is no way of knowing how long you two will be apart."

Keir didn't have to be told twice. He grasped Chloë by the hand and quit the solar in a hurry, putting as much distance as he could between Anton and himself. He couldn't stand looking at the man any longer, knowing he was keeping him from Chloë.

Chloë clung to his hand as he took her into the entry hall. She was still extremely upset, struggling to keep her emotions in check as he silently led her to the spiral staircase that ascended into the upper floors of the keep. All around them, the structure was alive with soldiers and servants, people going about their busy day, but Keir and Chloë remained quiet and somber, locked in their own little world, wondering what the future held now that everything was so uncertain.

On the third level they came to Chloë's chamber and Keir opened the door, ushering her inside and following her in. He closed the door softly behind her, throwing the bolt, before turning to look at her. It was God's honest truth that he didn't know what to say to her. He was perhaps more devastated than she was.

"I am so sorry," Chloë spoke first, her lower lip quivering. "I had no idea that my father would do such a thing. I do not know what to say to you other than I am deeply sorry."

He went to her, shushing her softly as he pulled her into his arms. He held her close, listening to her weep softly against him.

"It is not your fault," he whispered. "You cannot control what the man does."

"But it is so unfair," she sobbed. "I do not understand why he would do such a thing."

Keir didn't, either. "In his own mind, perhaps he believes he is truly doing what he feels is best for you."

She pulled her face from his shoulder, gazing up at him with big, wet eyes. "You are going to return to me," she insisted. "You are going to return and we shall be married and have a dozen children."

He smiled faintly. "Six girls just like you and six boys just like me?"

She grinned when she thought on their previous conversation about such things. "Exactly," she agreed, her tears fading. "I cannot wait to see your expression when presented with our first son."

His expression grew intense. "It will be the best day of my life."

She smiled at his vow but as he watched, her smile faded and her expression grew cloudy again. He could see the tears returning.

"I will wait for you at Pendragon for as long as it takes for you to return to me," she murmured, her lip beginning to quiver again. "But… but if God is not merciful and all turns against us, what… what should I do if you do not come back?"

He sighed heavily and pulled her over to the bed, sitting her gently on to the mattress. He sat beside her, taking both of her hands in his. He kissed her fingers thoughtfully, gently, formulating his reply. He took her question very seriously and was impressed that she had the fortitude to ask it. He was, in fact, trying to figure out how to bring up the subject and she had saved him the trouble.

"I want you to do what makes you happy," he explained. "What do you want to do?"

Tears were streaming down her face and she pulled one hand from his grip to wipe at her cheeks. "I do not know," she whispered. "I only want to be with you. I want to be where your memory is strongest, where I can feel your presence. If I leave Pendragon, I am afraid I would lose that forever."

He sighed, stroking the side of her head with a big hand. "I do not like the idea of you wasting away in an old castle, pining over a lost love. I do not think you would be happy there. It would only bring you sadness."

She appeared genuinely torn. "Then what would you have me do?"

He leaned forward and kissed her forehead. "You may stay at Pendragon as long as you wish," he told her softly. "But when the time is right, it would make me happy if you went to live with Kurtis and Cassandra. My brother would take good care of you and would make sure you married a man worthy of you."

Chloë wiped at her nose, nodding as she digested his instructions. "Do you think he will mind?"

"Of course not. You are family and he will be ferociously protective over you. I trust my brother as much as I trust myself when it comes to you, Chloë. Kurtis' word is as good as mine."

She nodded reluctantly. "Very well," she agreed. "If that is what you want."

"It is."

She just sat there, staring at her hands as they were encased in his enormous ones. Keir could see the fog of gloom hovering around her like a cloak and he pulled her into his embrace to comfort her. They had so little time left together and he didn't want to spend it in tears and doom. Rocking her gently as she clung to him, he eventually lay back on the bed and took her down with him.

In the bright mid-morning of the new day, Keir kissed her tenderly, tasting her sweet lips, memorizing them for the lonely times to come. Chloë wrapped her arms around his neck, responding to his kisses, and Keir's arousal took flight.

All of the emotion, anxiety and grief they were feeling came spilling out as Keir began to undress her, kissing exposed flesh as he peeled off layers of her surcoat and shift. Chloë couldn't stop the tears, thinking this might be the very last time she touched the man, and she wept silently as he nursed at her breasts and rained heated kisses along her belly.

Her hands were in his hair as he again put his face between her legs, his tongue on his favorite target, and Chloë moved beyond the initial embarrassment and gave in to his wicked mouth. The man's touch was magic, and although lovemaking was still extremely new to her, something about Keir washed away her inhibitions. She gave herself over to him willingly.

Keir took a very long time with her, gently, tasting every inch of her body, flipping her over onto her stomach and feasting on the back of her thighs and her rounded buttocks. His mouth moved to her shoulder, her neck, while his hands snaked underneath her and fondled her soft breasts. Her thick mane of hair was long down her back and he gathered it up, holding it like a rope, pulling on it and biting her neck until she groaned. He covered her with his big body, memorizing the feel of her soft flesh against his, tucking it away deep so he could think of it on nights when his longing for her threatened to consume him. He knew that time would come. He wanted to remember this moment for the rest of his life.

Rolling her onto her back, he pinned her arms above her head as he mounted her, his stiff arousal pushing into her slick body, savoring ever thrust, every withdrawal. He found himself wishing for a son, a lad that was a part of him and a part of her, with his strength and her magnificent looks. Chloë was his wife regardless of her father's actions and he felt more married to her, more a part of her, than he had ever felt with Madeleine. It was no insult against Madeleine, of course; he simply felt deeper and more for Chloë than he ever imagined he could feel for anyone.

As his thrusts deepened, he could feel Chloë climax around him, her soft cries of pleasure filling his ear. Before he released himself deep within her, she had climaxed at least twice more and then a fourth time when he spilled himself. She was exhausted and panting by the time he finished and he lay on top of her, his mouth on her neck, his body still embedded in her. In little time, he was aroused again and he took her twice more before noon, never wanting the day to end but knowing that it must.

As he lay against her towards noon, still buried deep in her sweet body, it was Keir who shed silent tears into her dark red hair, deeply pained at the thought of leaving her. When Chloë fell into an exhausted sleep, he lay there with his hand on her breast, watching her sleep, allowing his tears to fall freely. He couldn't help it.

He prayed this would not be the last moment they would spend together. He very nearly couldn't live with the thought. Already, it was killing him.

CHAPTER SIXTEEN

TWO HOURS BEFORE dawn on the next day, Michael of Pembury arrived from Pendragon. When he rode into Aysgarth's bailey, it was already full of men mobilizing for the march into Wales, including Keir. Kurtis was also with his brother, helping him organize the man and provisions, and Lucan was suited up and prepared to go with Keir into Wales.

It made for a busy scene, the ward of the castle filled nearly to the brim with men, horses and wagons. Michael knew, from the missive he had received from Coverdale, what was happening. As soon as he arrived, he went straight to Keir.

Keir saw the big knight coming through the sea of torches and men. He was speaking to Kurtis, seeing Michael approach and wondering how Kurtis was going to react to the appearance of his arch rival for Cassandra's attentions. Even though the competition was over, still, Keir wondered if there would be bad blood. He watched Michael's body language as the man came upon them.

"Keir," Michael greeted. His bright blue gaze moved to Kurtis and, after a tense moment, he bobbed his head at the man. "Kurt."

"You are just in time," Keir said to him, diverting Michael's attention before he and Kurtis could glare daggers at each other. "I am to depart at dawn and I wanted to make sure I spoke to you before I left."

Michael nodded. "As I wanted to speak with you," he replied. "I would ask to go with you, Keir. If Kurtis is not accompanying you, then I would ask to."

Keir shook his head. "Although I will sorely miss you, you have a more important task."

"What?"

"Escorting Chloë back to Pendragon and guarding her until I return."

Michael wasn't particularly happy with that order. "De Velt can return with her," he said. "I am more valuable at your right hand, Keir. You need me in battle."

Keir could see this wasn't an argument he was going to win in just a few sentences. Leaving his brother with a few softly muttered orders, he pulled Michael along with him as he moved to an area with more privacy.

"Michael, I appreciate your request," he said steadily, "and I would be lying if I said I will not miss your strength. But I have spent the past day and night arguing, at odds with, or in just plain contention with everyone at Aysgarth and I would sincerely appreciate it if you could simply abide by my wishes without an argument. I do not know how long I will be in Wales and it would ease my mind considerably knowing that Chloë was under your protection. She is the most important thing in the world to me and if I cannot be there to protect her, then I would only trust you."

Michael still wasn't happy but he understood somewhat. He pursed his lips angrily but refrained from arguing as Keir had requested. Still, he couldn't help getting the last few licks into the losing end of the battle.

"What do you mean you have been at odds with everyone?" he wanted to know.

They reached the steps leading into the keep and Keir paused, looking over the mass of men and animals in the bailey. A faint haze of smoke hung over the grounds from the heavily burning torches being used to illuminate the area.

"Chloë and I are betrothed," he finally said. "However, when her father found out about my orders from the king, he refused to allow us to be wed before I leave for Wales. In his opinion, an unmarried daughter is worth more to a prospective groom than the widow of a knight. If I return from Wales, all well and good, and we shall be married, but if I do not, then he feels she has a better chance of attracting a prestigious husband if she has never been wed. When I have not been arguing with the man, I have been comforting Chloë. It has been chaotic and painful to say the least."

Michael was beginning to feel bad about badgering Keir when the man had apparently suffered through a turbulent time.

"Where is Lady Chloë now?" he asked, with less force.

Keir looked to the keep. "Asleep, I hope," he said. "She has been nearly hysterical since yesterday morning. She needs to rest."

Michael's gaze moved to the bailey, seeing Kurtis in the distance. "And Cassandra?"

Keir looked pointedly at him. "She and my brother were married at Vespers yesterday," he replied. "Remove her from your mind, Michael. She and Kurtis are husband and wife, and very shortly leaving for Northumberland. Is that clear?"

Michael wasn't particularly shocked but he was disappointed. "It is, my lord."

"I do not want to hear of any more trouble between you and my brother. If that happens, my wrath will be swift."

"There will be no trouble, my lord."

"Do you swear on your oath?"

"I do."

Keir eyed him as if he didn't believe him but he accepted his vow. He didn't want to out-right insult the man.

"Chloë has asked to stay at Pendragon while I am away and Cover-dale has agreed," he thought it best to focus on the subject at hand. "I do not have to tell you to treat her with all due respect until I return. Guard her with your life."

Michael regarded him for a moment. "And what if you do not return?"

Keir drew in a long, pensive breath. "My instructions to her are to do what makes her happy," he said quietly. "If she wants to stay at

Pendragon forever, so be it. But I do not want her wasting her life. I have told her that if I do not return from Wales, it will make me happy if she would go and live with Kurtis and Cassandra at Alnwick. If it comes to that, I would ask that you escort her to Northumberland."

Michael nodded. "Of course, my lord."

"She means everything in the world to me and I love her deeply. Take care of her, Michael. I am depending on you."

"I will protect her with my life, Keir. You need not worry about her in the least."

Keir didn't reply to that. It seemed like such a final thing to say, as if he was already gone. But the fact remained that he wasn't gone yet and he wanted to see Chloë before he left. Leaving Michael standing on the steps to the keep, he entered the cool, quiet keep and made his way up to the third level.

Chloë's chamber was unlocked because he had already been in and out of it a few times that night simply to check on her. Keir was a master of multi-tasking, preparing an army for departure and all of the details related to that while at the same time, making sure to check on his betrothed to ensure she was comfortable and sleeping. Truth was, he just wanted to see her, greedily sneaking in a glimpse or a touch here and there when he could. The memories would have to last for the separation to come.

The third floor landing was dark and cold. As he reached out for the door latch, the panel suddenly opened and Cassandra appeared. She nearly ran in to Keir, gasping with fright when he narrowly avoided smashing her.

"Good heavens," she gasped. "Forgive me, Keir, I did not see you until it was nearly too late."

He smiled at his new sister. "No harm done," he looked into the dark room beyond. "What are you doing here?"

Cassandra glanced into the dark room also. "A servant fetched me about an hour ago," she said. "Chloë has been ill."

Keir was suddenly very concerned. "Ill?" he repeated, pushing in to the room. "What is wrong?"

Cassandra grabbed him by the arm as he moved past her. "Wait," she cautioned. "Do not go in yet. She has been weeping uncontrollably and vomiting for the past hour. The closer your departure looms, the more ill she becomes. It is nerves, I am sure, and she is distraught to the point where she is making herself ill."

Keir stared at her a moment before sighing heavily, a look of pain rippling across his face. He patted the hand on his forearm gently.

"Let me speak with her," he said. "Let me see what comfort I can give her."

Cassandra nodded, gripping his arm one last time. There was genuine concern and sadness in her features.

"Keir," she whispered. "I want to say... I want to say that I am sorry for how my father has treated you. You are a good man and you have made my sister very happy. I shall pray for your safe return."

He smiled faintly and patted her cheek before moving into the room and quietly closing the door. He could hear faint sobs from where he stood and he moved towards the bed, the curtains partially pulled back. Coming upon the mattress, he could see Chloë in the dim light, wrapped up in the bed linens, her face turned away from him and her arm over her forehead. She was sobbing intermittently and he stood there a moment, his heart breaking to see her so upset.

Carefully, he bent over the bed and kissed her softly on the cheek. "Greetings, love," he whispered, kissing her again. "It is time to rise and shine."

Startled, Chloë turned to him with big eyes. "I... I thought you were down in the bailey. I could hear you shouting."

He grinned. "That is Kurtis," he told her, sitting on the edge of the bed. "He sounds just like me."

She forced a smile because he was grinning. But then she sat up and threw her arms around his neck, breaking down into tears.

"Please," she begged. "Please do not go to Wales. Let us run far, far away where the king can never catch you or punish you. Let us run far away from these wars."

He hugged her tightly. "Sweetheart, as much as I am tempted to do exactly that, I cannot," he told her. "My honor is at stake and so is the honor of our children. I cannot burden them with the terrible legacy of a coward for a father. It would do them, and you, a great injustice."

She wasn't in the mood to agree with him. "At least you would be alive," she wept. "I would rather have you alive and dishonored than honorably dead."

He sat back and held her face in between his big hands. His ice blue eyes glimmered warmly at her, his expression gentle and sweet.

"I will be riding from this bailey in one hour," he told her calmly. "It is my wish that you compose yourself, get dressed, and see me off. You are a strong and remarkable woman, Chloë, and I realize that you are pushed beyond your endurance right now. I am deeply sorry for that. But I want my last glimpse of you to be as I know you to be, a strong and beautiful woman, not a quivering wreck. That is not the woman I know and love."

She gazed into his eyes, fighting the tears, the nausea, coming to understand that it would comfort him to know she wasn't a hysterical mess as he went about his duty. She knew that he was having as difficult a time as she was, only he was too strong to show it.

Crying and begging would not change things. It would not stop the man from doing his sworn duty for king and country. She'd known that all along but she still had to make a stab at it. Realizing nothing could change his mind, she nodded unsteadily.

"You are correct," she wiped at her eyes. "I am sorry to show such weakness. I am sorry if I brought you shame."

He frowned at her. "You did nothing of the sort," he scolded gently. "I would be joining you in your tears except that it is unseemly for a man of my station to weep like a woman. But I assure you it is only by the grace of God that I am able to remain strong. I need you to be strong for me, sweetheart. I am depending on it."

Chloë struggled to get a grip on her composure, forcing herself to focus. He needed her strength and she would give it to him. She had cried enough; now was the time to show Keir what she was truly made of.

"I will not disappoint you," she said, wiping at her eyes one last time and squaring her shoulders. "Can you tell me when you estimate you will reach Chester? It will bring me comfort knowing where you are, and when."

He nodded, rising from the bed and reaching out his hands to her. She placed her small, warm hands in his big palms and he carefully pulled her out of bed.

"We should reach Chester in three days if the weather remains good," he told her as she went to the wardrobe to search for a clean shift. "Once we arrive, I have three weeks before I must leave for Wales."

She turned to him, her face alive with hope. "Three weeks?" she repeated. "Could... could I come with you to Chester? I promise I will not be any trouble."

He smiled at her. "I wish you could, truly. But I will be in a war encampment surrounded by thousands of men. It would not be safe or comfortable for you. I hope you understand my reasons when I tell you that you cannot come."

Disappointed, Chloë let the subject drop and turned back to the wardrobe. "The missive from the king said something about Harlech," she said as she pulled out a soft yellow shift. "Is that where you are going?"

He nodded. "My orders are to ride for Harlech Castle by the first of October," he watched her pull out her shoes. "Moving a few thousand men and dozens of wagons, that should take about a week. We will be traveling through the heart of Wales, which will make the trip itself dangerous. I do not know how big the rebellion is but if they have already taken five castles, then it must be enormous."

Surprisingly, she wasn't harried by his chatter of big rebellions and dangerous travel. She listened carefully, absorbing the information.

"Who is this Welsh prince wreaking such havoc?" she asked. "Do you know of him?"

He shook his head. "Nay. There are dozens of Welshmen that proclaim to be the next Prince of Wales, but this man seems to have rallied a good many Welsh to his cause. I am curious to know more about him."

She was thoughtful as she pulled out a lovely golden surcoat. "How long were you fighting in Wales the first time you went?"

He didn't want to tell her the truth but he knew he could not lie to the woman. "Nearly two years," he replied honestly. "But take heart that I survived all that time against Welsh archers and rebels who were lurking at every turn. It is my intention to survive this time also."

She turned to look at him, her pale face regaining some color. "I know," she smiled weakly. "I will be watching the road every day for your return. Will you write to me?"

He nodded. "Of course I will, as often as I can," he went to her, standing before the woman and inspecting her ethereal beauty in the weak light of the room. "I do not want you to become distressed if I do not send missives regularly or if there are large gaps of time in between communications. Such is the nature of war. You will have to have faith at all times that I am alive and well, and yearning every day to return to you. Understood?"

"Understood."

He reached out, cupping her face in his hands and staring hard into her big brown eyes. He could have stared at her forever.

"There is such longing already in my heart for you that I cannot begin to describe it," he confided. "I will miss you with every breath I take. But I swear to you, with God as my witness, that I will do everything in my power to return to you, Chloë. You must have faith in that. You must have faith in *us*."

Chloë struggled not to tear up as she gazed at him. "I do," she whispered. "I love you, Keir."

He smiled tenderly. "And I love you," he murmured. "It is that love that keeps me strong."

He touched his forehead to hers, closing his eyes at the feel and warmth of the woman. He loved her so much that he could hardly express it. With a lingering kiss to her soft mouth, he let her go.

"Get dressed and come down to the bailey to see me off," he told her softly.

Chloë nodded, the lump in her throat preventing her from speaking. Keir winked at her as he quit the room and she hurried to dress as he had asked. All the while, she kept her focus on their conversation, on his promise to return to her. She had to focus on it, to live on it, otherwise she would surely crumble.

Keir had told her to get dressed and to meet him in the bailey, and that was exactly what she would do. Then she would bid farewell to the only man she had ever loved.

She wondered if it was possible to die from a broken heart.

CHAPTER SEVENTEEN

I NGILBY READ THE missive with increasing agitation. In the great hall of Ripley Castle, those around him watched and waiting, seeing his reaction and expecting the explosion to follow. The soldier who had delivered the missive went so far as to take a few steps back and away from the man. He didn't like the color of his face.

But Ingilby didn't explode. His cheeks turned red and he actually might have frothed at the mouth, but he didn't explode. He read the missive in his hand, twice, before setting it deliberately to the feasting table and rising to his feet. He sighed heavily as he moved away from the table, pacing, his mind whirling with thought and prospect. Dogs scattered out of his way as he moved around the room, kicking aside a dog that didn't move fast enough.

"So he has pledged her," he muttered, wringing at his hands. "Anton de Geld has pledged my goddess to St. Héver, in fact. No wonder the man threatened me. Now it all makes sense."

There wasn't anyone to answer him other than the soldier who had delivered the missive. He had taken the vellum from a rider bearing Coverdale's colors and watched with curiosity as the man handed over the stamped and rolled missive, and then tore off in the direction he had come from as fast as he could. The Ingilby soldier promptly delivered the missive to his liege.

"The messenger from Coverdale did not say anything, m'lord, other than the missive was meant for you," the soldier replied. "He rode off before I could question him."

Ingilby cocked an eyebrow at the man. "Of course he did," he spat. "He is a coward. Coverdale is a coward. They are all cowards!"

He was roaring by the time he finished and everyone in the hall tensed. As Ingilby postured angrily, Alphonse entered the hall, moving quickly towards Ingilby. His mail made a loud jingling noise as he moved, his fine Valencia leather boots thumping across the floor. By the time he came to a halt, he was breathing heavily.

"My lord," he said in his heavy Spanish accent. "Forgive me for being late. I was…."

Ingilby waved him off irritably, pointing with great accusation to the missive lying on the table.

"We have our answer, Alphonse," he said angrily. "Do you know why St. Héver threatened me? Well, do you?"

Alphonse shook his head, wondering if he should know the answer and rather concerned that he did not. "Nay, my lord."

"Because he is to marry Lady Chloë!" Ingilby roared at him. "He is her betrothed. No wonder the man has threatened me!"

Alphonse wasn't sure what he was talking about so he went to the table and collected the vellum that Ingilby was indicating. The man was jabbing both hands at it. Alphonse looked the carefully scribed missive over but had to have Ingilby's majordomo read it to him. He could only read Spanish. When he heard the contents, spilled by the old major-domo in a shaking voice, his eyebrows lifted in surprise.

"My lord," he turned to Ingilby with an elated expression. "This is a perfect happenstance, do you not see?"

Ingilby snarled at him. "What are you talking about?" he demanded. "This is not perfect. This is terrible!"

Alphonse was seeing a glimmer of hope in the situation where Ingilby was not. He shook his head emphatically.

"Nay, my lord," he said insistently. "Do you remember why you sent me to Hellbeck to secure St. Héver's son in the first place? Do you remember what you told me?"

Ingilby wasn't in any mood for riddles. He ground his teeth with frustration. "Of course, I do," he snapped. "I wanted to have the boy so I can use him against St. Héver and Coverdale the next time I…."

His sentence abruptly halted and his face suddenly lit up as if a great and overwhelming thought had just occurred to him. Looking to Alphonse who also had an expression of joy on his face, Ingilby's rage suddenly turned to delight.

"The boy," he breathed. "The boy... if I have his boy, St. Héver would do anything to regain him, would he not?"

Alphonse nodded confidently. "Indeed, my lord."

Ingilby was growing increasingly thrilled. "Perhaps even exchange his new bride for the boy?"

"Any father would, my lord."

Ingilby crowed. He clapped his hands and began trotting around the room, throwing his hands up in the air in a thrilled gesture of joy. When the dogs didn't move fast enough out of his path, he kicked them happily and when the servants didn't move fast enough, he kicked them also. In the great smelly, smoky hall of Ripley Castle with its stale rushes, stale people, and thread-worn banners hanging from the ill-kept gallery, John Ingilby displayed his joy. As he skipped past the major-domo, he suddenly came to a halt and grabbed the man by the neck.

"Send word to St. Héver at Aysgarth," he said. "Tell the man that I have the son he has been looking for. He may have the boy in exchange for Chloë de Geld. Those are the terms. If he refuses, I will kill the boy and dump the body at the gates of Aysgarth."

The majordomo fled. Ingilby felt hopeful, more hopeful than he had felt in a very long time. He turned to Alphonse.

"Where is the boy?" he asked.

"In the vault, my lord," Alphonse replied. "He seems to want to escape so I chained him up."

Ingilby thought on that a moment. "Bring him to me. I would see this child."

Alphonse moved to carry out the man's order. He wasn't concerned that Ingilby would discover that the boy in the vault was not St. Héver's son for one obvious reason – Ingilby had never seen St. Héver's son. The child would deny he was the knight's offspring, but that was to be expected. Once the child was exchanged for the beautiful woman that Ingilby called *the goddess*, Ingilby would marry Lady Chloë immediately and there would be nothing St. Héver could do about it when he discovered he'd been tricked. In fact, Alphonse would ensure that the boy was not turned over to the knight until Lady Chloë was Lady Ingilby and not a moment sooner.

Confident, somewhat relieved, Alphonse descended to the vault of Ripley Castle in search of the little blond boy with the big brown eyes.

CHAPTER EIGHTEEN

CASSANDRA AND CHLOË had always been close, but this went beyond that. Cassandra hadn't left Chloë alone for even a moment since Keir departure the day before when Keir had asked her to stay with her sister as much as possible to make sure the woman was well. He was very worried about her, as Cassandra was. Chloë simply didn't look well, the emotional and physical toll of the past few days' events weighing heavily on her.

Keir's departure hadn't been particularly dramatic or wrought with great sobs, but as Keir and Chloë quietly embraced one another, his forehead against hers as he whispered words of love and comfort only Chloë could hear, the emotions radiating from the pair had been palpable. Kurtis and Cassandra had felt it with great sadness, as had Coverdale and Michael. Even Lady Blanche had seemed touched by it while Anton tried not to watch, fearful that his guilt might get the better of him. He wasn't oblivious to it, but he still believed he was doing what was best for his daughter. If St. Héver perished, it would be easier to marry her off as an unwed maiden.

When Keir had finally pulled away with a gentle kiss to her lips, Chloë had held her anguish admirably. She had even given him a smile and wave as he mounted his charger and moved to the head of the army. She had held the smile until he quit the gates, disappearing from view, but the moment she knew he couldn't see her anymore, the tears came.

Kurtis and Cassandra quickly took her away so the entire castle wouldn't see her breakdown. They had taken her up to her third floor chamber where she collapsed on the bed in muffled sobs. She remained in bed all day and all night, and Cassandra remained with her. She even slept with her sister even though she was a newlywed and her new husband slept alone in the chair near the hearth. At this moment, they were all family, bonded together to tend Chloë during this dark time. It was what Keir wanted.

As the day after Keir's departure dawned bright, the birds singing loudly, Cassandra tried to convince Chloë to get out of bed, but Chloë wouldn't budge. She lay in the bed where she and Keir had shared many wonderful hours, staring at the lancet window with the bright blue sky beyond as if imagining some distant place and time where she and Keir were always together, never apart. Kurtis muttered to Cassandra that at least Chloë wasn't crying, but Cassandra found no comfort in that statement. At least crying was the release of emotion. What Chloë was doing went beyond expending emotion; she was staring off as if the world around her did not exist.

Near the nooning meal, Blanche came to Chloë's room to see how her daughter was faring. Chloë was still lying in bed, staring out of the lancet window, and Blanche tried to speak with her daughter in an attempt to elicit a response. But Chloë barely responded, ignoring her mother for the most part, until Blanche finally gave up. She had a servant collect her sewing and she sat in the corner, working her needlework, watching for any hint of life from her youngest daughter. Already she could see that Chloë was withering away and she began to seriously question her husband's decision.

Chloë remained in a daze for another three days. She barely moved, and only then it was to use the privy. Cassandra tried to force her to eat but Chloë would have none of it. Blanche tried to use tough motherly intervention to coerce her daughter into eating, but it resulted in Chloë in tears so Blanche backed away. In spite of her austere façade, Blanche wasn't truly forceful or firm with her children. She felt the girl's pain but didn't know what to do about it. Finally, on the dawn of the third day, Kurtis intervened. He had to. He didn't want to tell his brother that he had watched the woman he loved waste away to nothing. He seriously feared for her life.

On the fourth day of Keir's departure, the day dawned bright and cool. Blanche hadn't yet made her way up to Chloë's bower for the day and Cassandra had gone to the kitchens to see if she could find something to tempt her sister. Alone with Chloë in the early morning hour, Kurtis summoned his courage and made his way over to the bed.

"Chloë?" he addressed her but she didn't look at him. He tried again. "Chloë, I want you to look at me. Look at me and listen to what I have to say."

Chloë continued to stare at the open window but, after several long seconds, she turned in his direction. The brown eyes were distant and vacant but she was at least looking at him. Kurtis sighed faintly, his jaw ticking just as Keir's did when there was much on his mind.

"Three years ago, I received word at Alnwick Castle that Pendragon had been breached and my brother's family killed," he told her. "I rode day and night until I reached Pendragon only to find a brother who was in much the same state as you are now. He had just come upon the burned body of his wife and daughter, and Pembury and de Velt had chained him to the walls of the vault at Pendragon so he would not kill himself in his grief. Are you listening to me?"

The dazed look in Chloë's eyes faded and, as Kurtis watched, she seemed to become somewhat lucid. It was like watching the sun come out from the clouds, or a candle suddenly lit. He could see the light in her eyes. Her delicate brow furrowed and a pained expression crossed her fine features.

"I am listening," she answered. "He did not tell me that he tried to kill himself."

Kurtis shook his head as he sat on the foot of the bed. "He did not in the literal sense," he clarified. "He threatened to and, taking him as a man of his word, Pembury did the only thing he could do. He did not trust that Keir would not hold true on his threat. In any case, he summoned me and I found a man I did not recognize chained in the bowels of the vault. When Madeleine and Frances died, something in

Keir died also. It remained dead until last week when I saw my brother for the first time in months and he spoke of you. Whatever magic you have over him Chloë, restored the part of his soul that died that day. I could see it in his eyes when he looked at you and hear it in his voice when he spoke your name."

By now, Chloë was gazing at him with a mixture of joy and tears. "I did nothing but love him," she whispered.

"I know," Kurtis replied, reaching out to take her cold, pale hand. "Chloë, please understand that it would kill Keir to see you like this right now. I know you are afraid and I know it pains your heart to be separated from him, but you must have faith that he will return to you. I know my brother better than anyone and I know he will do everything in his power to return safely from Wales. But if he were to see how you are right now... it would shatter him. You do not want to do that to him, do you?"

She shook her head, the tears falling down her pallid cheeks. "Of course not."

"Then you must get hold of yourself and carry on in a manner that would honor Keir," he told her, squeezing her hand. "What you are doing now... wasting away like a weakling... does not honor him at all. You are made of better things than this. Show us all why Keir loves you so much. Show us a strong woman."

Chloë wiped at the tears on her cheeks, thinking on his words. After a moment, she nodded. "I... I did not think on it that way," she said softly. "I was only thinking of my own pain. But you are correct, Kurtis. You are absolutely correct and I beg your forgiveness for being so foolish."

He smiled at her and lifted her hand, kissing her fingers. "There is nothing to forgive," he told her. "But I would like to see you up and dressed. I know Cassandra would also."

She sniffled away the last of her tears, composing herself, the twinkle returning to her eyes. "You are a wise man, Kurtis St. Hѐver," she smiled faintly at him. "I am glad my sister married you."

He returned her grin. "So am I," he said, feeling greatly relieved that he was able to talk some sense into her. In truth, he was surprised she had listened to him. "Perhaps it will give you comfort to understand that Keir will not see any action for at least three weeks. Right now, he has already arrived in Chester and I have little doubt that he is missing you as much as you are missing him. But he is safe, healthy and whole, so keep that in mind. Right now, Keir is just miserable that he is away from you. Do you want me to tell you a secret?"

Her eyes glimmered. "Aye."

Kurtis stroked his chin and looked around as if afraid his brother might pop from the walls and suddenly over hear him.

"He took one of your shifts with him," he confessed. "I saw him pack it – it was very fine, white, and looked as if it had been ripped up. I could see the tattered edges. When I asked him what it was, he said it was your shift."

She looked somewhat surprised. "Why would he take it?"

Kurtis smiled faintly. "Because it is yours," he said simply. "It smells of you and has touched your skin. He will smell it, sleep with it, and keep you close to his heart. It is something of you."

Chloë's smile grew as she thought on the remnant that Keir had taken. She suspected it was the shift that he had torn from her body the first time they had made love, something she had shoved far back into the wardrobe until she could either repair it or dispose of it, but he had apparently gone hunting for a memento of hers to take with him and found it. It made her blush to think of it but in the same breath, it was the sweetest thing she had ever heard.

"I tried to cut some of my hair for him to take, but he would not allow it," she said, trying to veer the subject away from the lustfully destroyed shift. "Have you ever been to Chester, Kurtis?"

He stood up from the bed as she peeled the linens back and swung her legs over the side. "Twice," he told her. "An abominable border town. Full of Welsh."

She giggled softly. "You do not like the Welsh?"

He gave her a pursed-lip expression, one of distaste, looking much like his brother as he did so. "They eat seaweed," he grumbled. "They mix it with leeks and oil and fry it. They believe it makes them strong and live long. What idiots."

Chloë continued to giggle as he moved for the door, realizing the young lady needed to dress and he most certainly did not need to be here. He reached the panel, opening it, casting her a glance before he quit the chamber entirely.

"I will tell your sister that you are better this morning," he said. "She went to the kitchen to find you food that might tempt your appetite."

Chloë was at the wardrobe, opening the doors as she looked at him. "I am better thanks to you," she said sincerely. "You have my gratitude, brother."

Kurtis winked at her and quit the chamber. Chloë's gaze lingered on the shut door for a moment, thinking on the new brother she now had and very thankful for him. Although the pain of missing Keir was still great in her heart, Kurtis had eased it somewhat. As she dug through the wardrobe and pulled forth a lovely yellow linen surcoat and matching shift, she thought that she might write to Keir today. It would make her feel even better to communicate with the man.

Calling for warmed water, Chloë bathed quickly with the rose soap that she and Cassandra had purchased from Kirkby Stephen. She scrubbed her face until it was rosy and brushed her hair until it glimmered. Donning the yellow shift and surcoat, she presented a lovely picture to her sister when the woman appeared a half-hour later with a tray of bread, cheese and fruit.

"Kurtis told me you had arisen from bed but I did not believe it," Cassandra said as she entered the room. "How are you feeling?"

Chloë nodded. "Well enough," she said, moving to take the tray from her sister. "Your husband did much to convince me that it was not prudent to remain in bed."

Cassandra grinned as her sister plopped on the bed and began picking at the cheese. "He is very persuasive."

Cheese in mouth, Chloë cast her sister a knowing glance. "I can only imagine, but I will leave you with your secrets."

Cassandra laughed softly and sat on the bed next to her sister. "It is no secret that I love him madly," she said. "Even mother likes him."

Chloë's appetite roared to life as she shoved bread into her mouth and sipped at the warmed wine. "As well she should," she replied. "And father?"

Cassandra shrugged. "It is hard to say," she said. "He spends much time with Lord Byron. I think it is because Byron is the only person who does not chastise him for not allowing you and Keir to marry before Keir left for Wales."

Chloë's movements slowed and her head came up from the tray, her brown-eyed gaze locking with her sister. "I miss him," she whispered.

Cassandra squeezed her sister's arm. "I know you do," she replied softly, but not wanting the mood to sink, she continued the conversation in a positive fashion. "Kurtis must return to Alnwick Castle soon. Although I know you want to return to Pendragon, would you like to come and stay with us at Alnwick for a while? I could certainly use your help in settling in to my new home."

Chloë shrugged, unenthusiastic. "Perhaps," she said. "I will think on it."

"Please do. I would like to have the comfort of my sister in a strange place."

Chloë merely nodded as she continued to down the bread and cheese. Seeing that her sister was struggling with her depression, Cassandra rose from the bed and began to pick up the clutter of the chamber, chattering on about anything that came to mind. She was attempting to distract and comfort Chloë in her own way, but Chloë found the unending talk annoying.

Blanche soon joined her daughters and, upon seeing Chloë out of bed, demanded her youngest daughter accompany her on a walk about the grounds. Having no real choice in the matter, Chloë agreed. Swallowing the last of her meal, she followed her mother from the chamber.

It was a sunny day, breezy, as Blanche, Chloë, Cassandra, and now Kurtis emerged from the dark and cool keep. Blanche took Chloë's hand possessively as she walked, remaining silent and composed, just as she always did while Chloë walked beside her mother and looked at the bailey of Aysgarth with some sadness, as it was the last place she had seen Keir before he had departed to Wales. It was a struggle not to allow despondent feelings overwhelm her as she kept reminding herself of Kurtis' words. *Wallowing like a weakling does not honor Keir.* She most definitely wanted to honor him, whether or not he was able to see it.

The warm sunlight beat down upon them, warmer than usual, as they neared the gatehouse. Chloë and Blanche had to maneuver around a few piles of dung and a big hole that was right in the middle of the path of travel between the gatehouse and the stables, but their walk was uneventful for the most part. Kurtis and Cassandra followed behind them, the newlyweds smitten with each other completely. They whispered and cuddled.

Michael appeared as they neared the gatehouse. His handsome face was relaxed into a smile as he bowed to Chloë and Blanche.

"Ladies," he greeted. "It is a beautiful day today."

Chloë nodded. "Indeed it is," she said, thinking of Cassandra and Kurtis behind her and hoping there would be no awkwardness or hostility. In fact, she thought it would be rather prudent to separate him from her sister, at least until she could ascertain just how Michael and Kurtis were getting along. "Sir Michael, I have a need to speak with you. Will you walk with me?"

Before Michael could respond, Chloë let go of her mother's arm and latched on to Michael's, pulling him away from her family. She practically yanked the man off towards the stable yard, as far away as she could think to take him.

"Do you have specific plans on leaving for Pendragon?" she asked the man.

Michael wasn't oblivious to what she was doing. He went along with her. "Nothing specific, Lady St. Héver," he used the title that was not yet hers, watching her look at him with surprise. "I have been instructed to return you to Pendragon at your pleasure. When would you like to leave?"

She smiled somewhat shyly at him, acknowledging the use of her future title. "I am not sure," she shrugged. "My sister has asked me to go with her to Alnwick for a time, to help her settle in. What do you think about that?"

Michael wriggled his eyebrows thoughtfully. "It is not my decision to make, my lady," he said. "If you wish to go to Alnwick, then I shall go with you. I was instructed to provide your personal protection, always. Where you go, I go, until Keir returns."

She looked at him, somewhat hesitantly. "You do not have to go to Alnwick with me," she said. "Kurtis will provide ample protection."

Michael would not be moved. "He will provide ample protection to his wife," he corrected her. "You would be secondary. Keir ordered me to provide you with my undivided attention and protection, and I shall not shirk nor fail in my duty. If you go to Alnwick, I will go with you."

Chloë came to a halt, craning her neck back to look up at the extremely tall man. "You will understand when I say that I do not believe it would be a good idea for you to go to Alnwick in any case," she said frankly. "With the situation between you and Kurtis, even now we are troubled with keeping the two of you apart. Without Keir here to break up a confrontation, we are understandably wary. To allow you to travel with me to Alnwick, Kurtis' home, would be both unwise and disrespectful to Kurtis."

Michael's good humor seemed to be fading. It was a struggle for him not to get emotional. "I have no issue with Kurtis, my lady," he said somewhat subdued. "He is married to your sister. My pursuit of her has ended."

"What about your animosity towards Kurtis?"

Michael averted his gaze, no longer able to maintain eye contact with her. "He won the contest fairly," he said. "I will not maintain animosity towards him any more than if he beat me in a joust. It was done fairly and it is over. Kurtis is the victor."

Her brow furrowed. "Is that all you viewed this as? A contest and nothing more?"

He met her gaze, then. "What would you have me say, my lady?"

She wasn't going to put words in the man's mouth but she was a little taken aback at his attitude. She shrugged her shoulders. "I would not have you say anything that you did not mean," she replied. "However, it would seem to me that you would have viewed my sister as something more than a contest. That seems rather cold."

Michael was guarded. "You will forgive me, Lady St. Héver, but that is truly none of your affair."

Chloë's eyes snapped to him, with outrage at first, but when she thought on his statement, she realized that he was right. It sincerely wasn't any of her business. After a moment, she simply nodded.

"You are correct," she agreed. "It is not. I apologize. But the fact remains that if I go to Alnwick, you will not accompany me."

"The fact remains that where you go, I go. It is Keir's command and I will not disobey it."

She frowned at him. "But I told you my reasons. I will not have you making my sister or her new husband uneasy."

Michael was firm. "I am a professional, my lady. I believe I can accomplish my tasks without emotion or bias. If Kurtis or your sister is uncomfortable, it will not be my doing."

Her frown grew but she could see that the man would not be moved. He had that same set-jaw appearance that Keir did once a decision was made, firm and unmoving. She scowled a bit, and postured angrily, but she knew there would be no dissuading the man unless she left without his knowledge, and she was sure that would never happen. After the huffing and eye-rolling was finished, she took as firm a stance as he was.

"Then I will not go to Alnwick," she said flatly. "We will leave for Pendragon on the morrow."

Michael was trying not to smile at her antics for she was truly humorous in her tantrum. "Very well, my lady," he agreed smartly. "I shall prepare the escort. We will be ready to leave at dawn."

"I have several trunks," she pointed out. "Do not forget to secure a wagon."

"I will not, my lady."

"And it is possible I will want to shop before we return," she was deliberately trying to be difficult, just to punish the man. "There is a merchant district in West Witton. I may want to go there tomorrow."

"I am not sure Keir would approve, my lady. He is uncomfortable with you outside of the walls of Aysgarth or Pendragon and without the protection that a fortress provides."

She jabbed a finger at him. "*You* will be my protection, will you not? Where I go, you go. You will therefore have to protect me in whatever I wish to do."

Michael resisted the urge to scowl at her. "I do not think Keir would approve."

She lifted a well-shaped eyebrow. "He would let me do whatever I wish and you know it."

It was the truth. Michael pursed his lips at her in defeat. "I will go and prepare the escort, my lady."

"You do that."

He could see she was being petulant, something that didn't entirely displease him. He liked a woman with a little fire in her soul. He wasn't able to maintain his scowl for long and turned away before she could see him break a grin.

Chloë caught sight of the smirk, however, and fought off a smirk of her own. If Michael of Pembury thought he could bully her until Keir returned, then he had just learned an important lesson. Lady Chloë would not be pushed around or denied her wishes.

Chloë considered the battle won.

CHAPTER NINETEEN

A *N ANGEL'S FACE.*

That was all he could see every time he closed his eyes or every time his mind wasn't occupied with men and wars. As Keir settled in to his headquarters in Chester, it was a struggle to think of anything other than his longing for Chloë.

Every hour, every day, saw his longing grow worse until he could hardly breathe. He had told her once that he knew he could love her so much that it would rip his heart and body and soul to pieces to even be away from her for a single minute, and he had been absolutely right. Everything was in tatters and he struggled to keep himself together. He knew it would be hard to be separated from her but he had no idea just how hard.

He was secured at Beeston Castle, a royal castle manned by five hundred royal troops and commanded by Sir Marcus de Lara of the great marcher lordship family, House of de Lara. Marcus was the brother of the current Earl of Trelystan of the Trinity Lordship. He was a very big man with dark hair, cobalt blue eyes, and was brilliant and well-spoken, but rather mean. Men both feared and respected Marcus de Lara.

De Lara was very cooperative with Keir, having received directives from the king to ensure that Keir was well supplied and well housed, and within days of Keir's arrival, men began arriving from all points north.

As de Lara and his men watched the borders, Keir watched for the incoming armies and began arranging them by size, strength and any special skills certain battalions might have. There were archers, foot soldiers, mounted cavalry, miners or diggers, plus a host of valets, cooks and other servants. Men who were ready to plunge into Wales for their king and fight to the death. Keir was a master organizer and as armies trickled into the massive border bastion of Beeston Castle, he was ready and waiting for them.

Even though Beeston housed its own significant force, Keir was able to house the incoming armies efficiently. Beeston had one giant bailey that sloped severely in places due to the fact that the castle was built on the top of a hill, so some men ended up being housed on the slopes. As the days passed and men filtered in, the bailey began to fill up significantly to the point where two larger armies from the north had to set up camp outside of the walls.

After four days of organizing troops and men, Keir finally had a moment to himself away from weary soldiers and brusque garrison commanders. Housed in Beeston's mighty keep in a small and cramped chamber he shared with de Velt, he summoned a young page as he retired to his room.

The little boy that answered the call was a ward of the de Laras, no more than four or five years of age, and he firmly told Keir that his name was Tate. Keir smiled faintly at the serious, dark-eyed lad with the handsome features as he sent him for vellum and ink.

When de Velt entered some time before sunset to prepare for sup, he found Keir hunched over a small table carefully writing out his own missive. Lucan didn't even have to ask what the missive was about or who it was to; he already knew. Keir would not have left something as important or personal as this to an ordinary scribe.

"Be sure to tell her than you cannot sleep at night and are keeping me awake," he pointed out as he casually tossed his helm on his bed. "Tell her I have had to fight you off when you grow lonely for her in your dreams and reach for me."

Keir cast him an intolerant glare. "If you ever love a woman, you will understand."

"I loved my mother."

"It is not the same thing, you idiot."

Lucan smirked as he began removing his heavy mail gloves. "You only saw her a few days ago," he said. "What can you possibly write about?"

Keir just shook his head. "I am going to ask her to come to Beeston."

Lucan froze midway from removing his remaining glove. "Are you serious?"

"I am. I cannot stand being without her."

Lucan resumed removing his glove, tossing it thoughtfully on to the bed. "I thought you told her that it would not be safe for her here," he reminded him. "You told me that you told her that when she asked to come to Chester."

"I did."

"It was the wise response, Keir. It would not be safe for her here. Too many men and too few women make for a disastrous recipe."

"She will be with me, always. She will be safe."

"And when you leave for Wales? What then? Does she come on a battle march with you?"

Keir didn't say anything but his quill slowed. With a heavy sigh, he set it to the table and sat there, staring at the missive. Lucan continued undressing, watching Keir as the man stared at the words he had written. He began to feel some remorse for being blunt, even if it was the truth.

"You go through what every man goes through when separated from the woman he loves," Lucan said quietly. "But the answer is not to bring her to Beeston. That would be a mistake. You cannot take her into Wales and once again, you would be separated from the woman and going through the same anguish you are going through now. Send her a missive and tell her that you love her and long for her, but do not bring her to Beeston. Leave her where she is safe."

Keir scratched his scalp and sat back in the chair, wrought with sorrow and overwhelming love. He was a man torn. He laced his fingers behind his head, leaning back.

"I miss her so much I can taste it," he admitted. "I never imagined I could hurt so badly for anyone."

Lucan pulled off his mail hood. "Do you remember many years ago when we were forced to leave Pendragon because Coverdale had promised support to Mt. Holyoak in Yorkshire?" he looked over at Keir. "We were gone for a little more than a week and I had to listen to you whine daily on how you missed Madeleine and Frances. It got so bad that I wanted to take a dagger to my eardrums just so I would not have to listen to you any longer. Am I going to face that same dilemma again? Must I take a dagger to my own ears or risk going mad?"

Keir gave him a reluctant grin. "If you recall, Madeleine had just given birth to Frances and I was eager to be with my family," he reminded him. "I do not think that is too much to ask from a new father. But with Chloë… it goes beyond that. There is such longing in my heart that it threatens to consume me. I have never known anything like it."

Lucan shook his head and began to peel off his damp under-tunic. "Leave her at Pendragon," he reiterated. "Besides, she will be in good hands with Pembury. That is, if he does not make attempts to woo her from you."

Keir's smile vanished and his relaxed demeanor stiffened. "Why do you say that?" he demanded. "Did he say anything to you?"

Lucan put up his hands. "It was a jest, Keir, I swear it," he assured him, seeing that his attempt at a joke had failed. "Good Christ, man, do you really think he would do anything so outrageous? He respects you too much. And, he fears you even more."

Keir's jaw was ticking as he forced himself to ease, his mind turning to newly horrific thoughts of Michael showing interest in Chloë when he was not around to prevent it. He trusted Chloë implicitly, but Michael was a bit of a wolf. That much was well established. Although he sincerely could not believe Michael would ever do such a thing, still, the unsettling idea gave him one more thing to anguish over. Visions off Michael with Chloë in his arms now haunted him. He glared at Lucan.

"I ought to punch you in the mouth for that suggestion," he growled. "Jest or not, do you think it helps my state of mind?"

Lucan was coming to think his jest was ill-timed and was properly contrite. "Nay."

Keir shook his head with disgust at the man and picked his quill up again. "You have moments of brilliance, Lucan, peppered with moments of complete stupidity," he dipped his quill in the ink. "I am going to write a missive to Chloë and I want for you to arrange for the swiftest messenger at Beeston to deliver it."

Lucan nodded. "Aye, my lord."

"Now, leave me alone," he began to write. "I must concentrate on what I am going to say."

Lucan didn't know when to shut his mouth; he could not resist taunting him. "'Oh, my darling, my sweetest little tasty chick, I cannot breathe for want of you....'"

Keir threw the nearest thing he could find at him, which happened to be the small bag of sand that would be spread upon the vellum after he finished writing to blot up the ink. It was heavy, hitting Lucan in the thigh as the man moved to dodge it. Sand scattered everywhere.

"Shut your mouth," Keir barked. "Another word and I will throw you from the window."

"I will not fit."

"I will make you fit!"

Lucan shut his mouth but he couldn't help the smirk on his lips as he turned away and continued undressing. Keir St. Héver was not a man to hold back his feeling and he suspected the letter to Chloë would be something sickeningly sweet that she would probably sleep with next to her heart. But then he, too, began to think about Pembury and the man's reputation as a rake. He hoped the man wasn't stupid enough to set his sights on Chloë now that Keir was away.

He stretched out on his bed as Keir scratched a missive against the rough vellum, eventually dozing until a sharp rap at the door awoke him. As he bolted up from the bed, Keir was already up and answering the door. Two soldiers stood in the doorway, announcing to Keir words he did not want to hear. A message had arrived from Harlech Castle describing a swift and terrible siege by Welsh rebels. The king was already on his way into Wales and ordered Keir to march to Harlech, whether or not all of the armies they had been expecting from the north of England had joined them. There was no time to waste if Harlech was going to survive.

At dawn the next day, Keir and his army of three thousand, four hundred and thirty two men marched off into the wilds of Wales en route to the siege of Harlech Castle. The missive he had written Chloë went north via messenger.

As Keir rode at the head of his army, loaded down in full armor and an array of weaponry, he prayed it would not be the last message he ever sent her.

CHAPTER TWENTY

CHLOË AND CASSANDRA had been packing for most of the afternoon, carefully rolling garments and securing them snuggly into the trunks they had at their disposal. Since all of their possession from Pendragon had been stored in one big trunk, Cassandra took a big trunk from her mother to take with her to Alnwick.

The afternoon was filled with conversation and packing, and at mid-afternoon, Blanche joined her daughters in Chloë's chamber. Blanche had never packed anything in her life, always having servants to do such mundane things, so she was not of much help with her daughter's preparations. She took her needlework near the window, sat down, and worked steadily while her daughters filled up their trunks.

Cassandra was disappointed that Chloë would not be accompanying her to Alnwick but she understood the woman's reasons. She kept up a steady stream of chatter as they piled things away. Kurtis joined them eventually and she made her husband shove the lid of the trunk closed while she tied it off. It was stuffed to the rim and only his strength saved the day. Then she informed him that she wanted to do some shopping before they reached Alnwick, a suggestion to which Kurtis was rather resistant. The dark clouds began to gather over the happy newlyweds.

"You have enough clothes," he told her. "You are stylish and lovely, and I am very proud of you. You do not need anything more."

Cassandra frowned while over her shoulder, Chloë fought off a grin. She packed a satchel, watching her sister face off against her husband. Truth be told, they had only known each other a couple of weeks and now would come the time for them to truly come to know

KATHRYN LE VEQUE

one another, both the good and the bad. Although Chloë loved her sister very much, the woman liked to spend money. Kurtis was in for a battle.

"Chloë and I must divide the soaps and oils we purchased last week," Cassandra pointed out. "I must have my own things to take with me."

"Like what?"

Cassandra threw up her hands irritably. "I told you," she said. "Soaps and Oils. Since Chloë is going to be in a more remote area, I am insisting she take the majority of the goods because there will be less opportunity to readily purchase such things. That means that I will be left with very little."

Kurtis sighed, scratching his head. "How much will this cost?"

Cassandra's eyes narrowed. "The cost will depend upon what I need," she told him. "And you will not bicker with me over this. You want me to be happy, do you not?"

He wasn't going to fall for her attempt to guilt him. "Of course I do," he said. "But your happiness is not dependent upon the goods you purchase. I will give you an allowance that you may use, but once that is spent, your shopping is finished."

Cassandra's eyebrows flew up in outrage. "I have never heard of anything so stingy!"

"Take it or leave it. It is your choice."

Chloë couldn't help it; she burst into snickers as she closed up her last satchel. "Cassie, for Heaven's Sake, the man is giving you money to spend. Must you have his entire treasury at your disposal?"

Cassandra wasn't happy in the least. Scowling at her husband, she went over to her mother and knelt at the woman's feet.

"Mama?" her tone was considerably sweeter than it had been just moments earlier. "I must have some items and Kurtis does not feel they are at all necessary. Will you please provide me with coinage to ensure I have all I need?"

Blanche didn't look at her eldest and she didn't miss a stitch as she answered. "I am sure whatever he provides you with will be most generous," she replied steadily. "Your father has already provided him with your dowry. He is your husband now and if you want money, you will have to get it from him."

Grossly unhappy, Cassandra returned to packing with a pouty face. Kurtis watched his wife, showing some uncertainty for the first time as he looked to Chloë for reassurance that he wasn't being an ogre. Chloë simply grinned and shook her head.

"Not to worry, Kurtis," she told him. "She will survive."

That didn't help Kurtis' indecision at all. He went to Cassandra as she finished securing a small satchel. "Alnwick has a very large merchant street," he told her. "I know many of the vendors there. Perhaps I can convince them to give us very good prices on the items you need."

Cassandra largely ignored him, sitting down on the bed and struggling not to burst into tears. "All I want to do is purchase some items for my skin and hair," she sniffed. "And perhaps some fabric for a new surcoat. Is that too much to ask?"

Like any husband, her tears undid him. "It is not," he assured her softly. "I will buy you whatever you wish, I swear it."

The tears disappeared and the sun came out from behind the clouds as she turned her bright smile up to him. "Truly?"

Kurtis wasn't a fool. He could see that he had just been grandly manipulated and he cocked a disapproving eyebrow at her.

"Truly," he said begrudgingly.

Cassandra happily hugged him as Chloë snickered softly at her conniving sister. Outside, they could hear alerts from the sentries high on the walls and Chloë, curious, went to the lancet window to see what the commotion was about because Kurtis was being joyfully strangled by her sister and could not see for himself. Aysgarth's great gates were open and there was much activity on the gatehouse. She could see a rider passing beneath the portcullis being swarmed by Coverdale soldiers but it was relatively uninteresting so she turned away from the window and back to the last of her packing.

"What do you see?" Kurtis asked, his mouth partially muffled because Cassandra's arms were around his neck and her face was pressed up against his.

Chloë fiddled around with a few belts on the bed. "I cannot tell," she shrugged. "A rider, I think. The portcullis was up."

Kurtis moved to the window with his wife wrapped up around him. He had his arms around her as he peered from the window while Cassandra peppered his rough cheek with kisses.

"Hmmm," he grunted as his spied the rider. "No colors. I wonder who it is?"

"Kurtis," Chloë said casually from her position over near the bed. "I do not think the oils and soaps will serve me very long at Pendragon. Will you buy me some more, also?"

Kurtis looked over at her. "I will not," he said flatly. "My brother is wealthier than I am. Let him buy them for you."

Chloë bit her lip to keep from giggling. "But that is not fair," she insisted. "Keir would buy them for Cassandra if she asked. Why will you not buy them for me as well?"

Kurtis could see the twinkle in her eye, realizing she was more than likely teasing him. But he could not be sure. He didn't know the woman that well to know for certain. In case she wasn't, he thought it best to leave the room before he was cornered by the both Chloë and Cassandra and ended up in the poor house.

"My lady, I would kill or die for you," he said as he moved towards the chamber door with Cassandra still in his arms. "I would do anything in the world for you. But I will not buy you excess that you do not need."

"How do you know I do not need it?"

"If you do not stop harassing me, I am going to write my brother and ask for permission to spank you."

Chloë burst out into laughter and collected the nearest belt, snapping it at him. "Is that so?" she threatened. "Your brother is far away and unable to help you. I will have Cassandra hold you down while I spank you myself and call it self-defense."

Cassandra started to giggle and Kurtis peeled her hands off him, moving for the door. "You will have to catch me first."

The women squealed as they bolted after him, Chloë leaping over the bed to block his path to the door. But Kurtis was fast and he made it to the door before she did, yanking open the panel and then slamming it shut to prevent them from following. He held the door fast, grinning as they yelled at him from the other side of the door, banging on it and demanding he open it.

"Are you still going to spank me?" he called to them.

"I am going to beat you within an inch of your life and take all of your money!" Chloë yelled. "We shall leave your carcass for the dogs!"

"Then I am not opening the door."

He laughed softly as the women kicked the door and tried to pull it open. Finally, he let it go and raced down the stairs, listening to the women as they yanked the door open and began to pursue. By the time Kurtis hit the first floor of the keep, he was laughing so hard he could hardly run. Chloë barreled down the stairs right behind him, laughing and swinging a heavy copper belt at him. Kurtis broke through the entry door and raced down the wooden steps into the bailey, almost tripping at the bottom in his haste to get away from them.

"I will tell my brother what you are doing and you will be sorry," he threatened as he dodged Chloë's swinging belt. "I will tell him what a mean woman you are."

Chloë laughed and half-heartedly swung the belt at his head. "Give me your money, St. Hévér," she demanded. "Surrender!"

Kurtis dodged Cassandra as she came at him with another belt with heavy tassels on the end. "Never," he announced. "You evil wenches, go away from me."

Chloë and Cassandra were laughing uproariously. Kurtis was so out of breath from laughing that he couldn't go much further. Eventually, he grabbed his wife and pinned her arms, planting a warm and delicious kiss on her mouth. Chloë watched the pair, her laughter fading as it reminded her of Keir to watch the affection between them, and her good mood dampened. Lowering the belt, she struggled against the sadness that threatened to swamp her. As Cassandra and Kurtis lost themselves in sweet kisses and giggles, she turned away only to run head-long into Michael.

He grabbed her by the arms to steady her as she bashed in to him. As Chloë looked up to apologize, the words died in her throat at the expression on Michael's face.

"Michael?" she asked, concerned. "What is wrong? Why do you look so?"

Michael let go of her once she had her balance. "A missive arrived for Keir," he told her. "You had better come."

She cocked her head curiously. "A missive? From who?"

Michael didn't soften the blow. "From Ingilby. Coverdale has the missive and he is in his solar."

Chloë felt as if she had been struck. For a moment, her balance left her and she reached out, grasping Michael so she wouldn't topple over. Her face was a mask of shock.

"Ingilby?" she gasped. "Why on earth would he send Keir a missive?"

Michael could only shake his head, taking her hand as he began to lead her back towards the keep. "I do not know," he said honestly. "But Lord Byron has asked that I bring you. What concerns Keir more than likely concerns you, especially if it is from Ingilby."

Chloë followed him on shaking legs, trying to come to terms with the astonishing happenstance. "This makes no sense. Why would Ingilby do this? And how did he even know that Keir was at Aysgarth?"

"We will soon find out."

Chloë wasn't satisfied with that answer and her mind began whirling with possibilities as the shock began to wear off.

"None of this makes any sense," she said, growing increasingly worried. "He must know that Keir threatened him if he ever tried to contact me again. When Keir saved us from Exelby, Keir told one of Ingilby's soldiers that Ingilby would have to personally answer to him if he ever made another move against me. Do you suppose that Ingilby is threatening Keir in return?"

They were moving swiftly across the bailey, unaware that Kurtis and Cassandra were following. Kurtis had seen the expression on Michael's face and the instant shock on Chloë's, and correctly assumed that something was amiss. His intuition told him to follow.

Chloë was oblivious to Kurtis on her heels as she looked up at Michael, expecting an answer to her question. The big knight was stoic but obviously concerned.

"He would be a fool to do so and bring the threat of Coverdale down around him," Michael replied. "Whatever it is, we shall know soon enough."

There wasn't much Chloë could say to that so she clamped her mouth shut, following Michael into the big, cool keep and into the first floor solar that belonged to Lord Byron. It was lavish and comfortable, and displayed the wealth of the Coverdale dynasty with its fur rugs and silver plate on the hearth. Coverdale's big gray dogs lounged near the fire. By the time Michael pulled Chloë into the room, her legs were shaking so badly that she could hardly stand.

Byron was at his big table, carefully inspecting the seal on a large piece of vellum in his hand. There were four soldiers in the room and an unarmed man Chloë didn't recognize standing in the midst of them. Chloë's eyes fell on the man, tall and dark and swarthy, and already she didn't like the look of him. She didn't even have to ask if the man was from Ingilby; she already knew. He had that smell about him. She made sure to stay close to Michael and his enormous, protective presence.

Byron glanced up when Michael and Chloë entered the room. He waved the missive at her. "My lady," he said. "It would seem that Lord Ingilby has sent a missive for Keir. I have told his messenger that Keir is on the Welsh border and the man has insisted I read the missive to you. I have sent for your father."

Chloë's heart began to beat painfully against her ribs, her mouth gone dry with fear. "You told Ingilby's messenger I was here?" she nearly demanded. "Why did you tell him?"

Coverdale didn't seem concerned. "He cannot hurt you, my lady. There is no need to fear."

Chloë wasn't convinced and was more than uncomfortable that Coverdale had divulged her whereabouts to the messenger, who would undoubtedly return to Ingilby with the news. With Keir away, she felt vulnerable and afraid. She looked to the messenger, his dark and sweaty face, and resisted the urge to lash out at him.

"What could Ingilby possibly have to say to Keir?" she hissed. "What is this madness?"

Alphonse was Ingilby's messenger. He took a long, hard look at the Lady Chloë de Geld and was not disappointed. He'd never truly seen the woman, not in the entire year he had served Ingilby, and he could instantly see what had Ingilby so smitten. He'd never seen a lovelier woman and for a moment, he was actually speechless as he gazed upon her angelic face. She was indeed a goddess.

"Lord Ingilby received the wedding announcement for your nuptials with Sir Keir St. Hévér," he said in his heavy Spanish accent. "Since Sir Keir serves Coverdale, Lord Ingilby has sent a missive of his own to the prospective groom."

By this time, Kurtis had put himself between Michael and Chloë, his big body tense as he sized up Alphonse.

"I am Kurtis St. Hévér, Keir's brother," he told him in a deep and growling tone. "I will make any decisions regarding the Lady Chloë in his stead and at this moment, I would have her removed from the room. Whatever Ingilby has to say, I will hear it first before deeming if it is suitable for Lady Chloë's ears. She does not need to be upset or harassed by a man who only recently burned her home."

Alphonse met Kurtis' challenging gaze. "Hear it, then," he invited. "You may all hear it. It is no secret and I promise you, Sir Kurtis, that Lady Chloë will want to hear this as it pertains to her betrothed."

"'Tis all right, Kurtis," Chloë reassured him. "I will hear whatever must be said. If it pertains to Keir, then I must."

Kurtis didn't like the sound of that at all but he didn't let his thoughts show. He maintained his hostile posture as Coverdale broke the seal on the missive and carefully unrolled it. All eyes turned to Byron expectantly as the man flattened out the vellum, brought forth another taper for more light, and began to read.

Byron read slowly. He read the first few sentences, grunting and shaking his head, until coming to the mid portion of the vellum sheet. Then, his eyes widened and he looked to Alphonse in utter outrage. His mouth worked and sweat popped out on his forehead, but he refrained from speaking, instead returning to the vellum and reading it to the very end. By the time he finished, his rough old hands were quivering.

Meanwhile, Chloë watched the man, slowly dying inside. She was quaking so badly that she eventually had to grasp Michael's arm to keep from falling. Cassandra had come up beside her, grasping her arm and putting a hand on her waist in mute support. Chloë was afraid to look at her sister, afraid she would start weeping if she did. It was easier to remain strong if she did not look at the worried expressions around her. Based on Coverdale's demeanor, she was terrified.

"God's Teeth," Coverdale finally hissed as he laid the vellum to the rough tabletop. He looked at Alphonse in a beseeching manner. "Is this true?"

Alphonse nodded firmly. "It is, my lord."

Coverdale's brown eyes lingered on the Spaniard for a long, volatile moment before returning his gaze to the vellum. He read it again and shook his head when he was finished. His shock, his disgust, was evident.

"If he is lying, I will kill him myself," Byron said sincerely. "I swear by all that is holy, Ingilby will not live to see another day if he is lying about this."

Alphonse maintained his steady stance. "He is not lying, my lord."

With that, Coverdale let out a heavy sigh. He couldn't even look at

Chloë, still staring at the vellum as he spoke.

"My lady," he began slowly. "It would seem that this is something that does indeed concern you. Ingilby is making a proposal to Keir and you are an integral part of that proposal."

Chloë was so tense that her stomach was in knots. She felt like she might vomit. "What proposal, my lord?"

Coverdale sighed again, with great regret, and began to read:

To the honorable knight Sir Keir St. Héver,

Be it known of your impending marriage to the Lady Chloë de Geld is announced. Be it also known that your son, whom was long lost to you, is now in my possession. I will return you your son on the condition that you present to me the Lady Chloë. The terms are non-negotiable and should you refuse, I will kill your son and send his corpse back to you in pieces. Give me Chloë and you will have your son, alive.

You have a fortnight to make your decision.

John Ingilby

For a moment, no one spoke. Everyone seemed frozen with shock. The first two people to openly react were Michael and Kurtis; they lunged at Alphonse, surrounded by Coverdale soldiers, and grabbed the man before he could make a reasonable attempt to defend himself.

Michael had him by the neck, throwing him to the ground as Kurtis pounced. He slammed Alphonse's head onto the floor as Chloë and Cassandra yelped with fright. Cassandra turned her face away, weeping, as her husband began to pound Ingilby's messenger.

"He is lying," Kurtis roared. "God damn you to hell for such lies!"

Anton picked that moment to enter the solar. His blue eyes flew open wide at the fight, watching as Coverdale and Michael tried to pull Kurtis off of Ingilby's messenger. It was a chaotic scene with the women weeping and the men fighting, and Anton slammed the chamber door shut so no one would see what madness was happening inside. It was pure bedlam.

"What goes on here?" he demanded.

Coverdale couldn't answer him. He was bellowing orders to Kurtis, demanding that he release Alphonse. But Kurtis wasn't listening, at least not right away, and pummeled Alphonse with his big fists. Cassandra, scared and upset, realized her husband was out of control and she cried out to him.

"Kurtis!" she wept. "For the love of God, please stop!"

Hearing his wife's sobbing cry broke through Kurtis' fury. He came to an unsteady halt, gazing up at his weeping wife before returning his attention to the dazed man beneath him. He couldn't begin to describe what he was feeling at the moment; fury, grief, and absolute horror. He was feeling everything his brother would have felt had he been there to hear the missive. He allowed Michael and Coverdale to pull him up and he stumbled over to his wife, throwing his arms around her to comfort her. Beside them, Chloë was pale and shaken, weeping softly into her hand. Kurtis threw an arm around her, too, and pulled her into their embrace.

Michael eyed Kurtis and the frightened women as he yanked Alphonse to his feet. The man had a bloodied lip, and was rather dazed, as Michael shoved him onto the nearest chair. He leaned over him menacingly as Byron handed Anton the missive.

"How did Ingilby come by Keir's son?" he growled.

Alphonse wiped at the blood on his lip. "He found him. Now he has him."

Michael shook his head, struggling with his anger. "That is not a proper answer," he snarled. "How did Ingilby come by Keir's son? Tell me now or I turn Kurtis loose on you again. This time, I will not stop him from killing you."

"Kill me and Ingilby kills the boy."

"Nay!" Chloë pulled herself free of Kurtis and Cassandra's embrace, her long red hair catching in the folds of Kurtis' mail. Her expression was pleading. "Please do not hurt him!"

Alphonse turned his attention to her, his dark eyes drifting over her luscious form. "The terms have been conveyed. The child's life is in your hands."

Chloë was desperate, earnest. "I will do whatever Ingilby wishes if he will only send the boy home to Keir unharmed."

A collective gasp went up between Kurtis, Cassandra and, surprisingly, Anton. "You will do no such thing," Anton said firmly, having finished reading the missive that was still in his hand. "Ingilby is a beast. You will not give in to this… this blackmail."

Chloë looked at her father, wiping the tears from her cheeks. "Why not?" she asked softly. "You would not marry me to Keir before he left for Wales, so why are you so resistant to a marriage to Ingilby? Is that not what you ultimately wish? For me to marry well? Ingilby is wildly wealthy and a cousin to Northumberland. Or perhaps you simply do not wish for me to marry anyone. Perhaps you simply want to see me wither away and die."

Anton snapped a finger at her. "Foolishness, Chloë," he hissed, slapping the missive to the table. "You do not know what you are saying. I denied your marriage to Keir because the man can very well perish in Wales and I would not knowingly widow you. You already know this. I am sorry you do not understand that I am doing what I feel is best for you."

"And now?" she was feeling stronger, confronting her father without the devastating emotion that usually accompanied this subject. "Father, if Ingilby truly has Keir's son, then there is no question of what to do. I will go to Ingilby and he will turn the boy over to Keir. That is as it should be."

"Nay," Kurtis was at her side, grasping her arm as if to physically prevent her from giving herself over to Ingilby. "I will ride for Keir immediately. He must make this decision."

She looked at Kurtis, his handsome pale face that resembled his striking brother, and smiled faintly.

"There is no question, Kurtis," she insisted softly. "Keir cannot make this decision. It will tear him apart to have to make such a terrible choice."

A look of extreme pain crossed Kurtis' features. "Chloë, you cannot do this. Keir must know. He must make that determination."

Her voice was soft. "If the question was presented to you, what would you do?"

Kurtis' pale cheeks reddened as he cast a sidelong glance at Alphonse, still in the chair and hearing every word said. He did not want the man reporting their conversation back to Ingilby, in any fashion. They had already said too much in front of him, including the fact that Keir was in Wales.

"Get him out of here," he told Michael. "Throw him in the vault for now. We will deal with him at the appropriate time."

Michael nodded, yanking Alphonse to his feet and thrusting him at the Coverdale guards. Roughly, the man was shuttled from the room and the door slammed behind him, leaving a tense and ugly situation in its wake. Everyone was edgy and uncertain, feeling the pain of the proposal down to their very bones. They all knew the stakes from an emotional standpoint, from Keir's standpoint, and none of them more keenly than Michael. He made his way over to Chloë.

"Kurtis is correct," he said in a low, firm voice. "You cannot make this decision without Keir's blessing. It would not be fair to him."

She looked up at Michael and her composure began to slip. "Listen to what you are saying," she whispered. "Were you not there when Keir lost his wife and daughter? He told me he hit you in the face when you tried to prevent him from seeing their burnt bodies. He has been searching for Merritt for three long years. Do you truly think that if there is a chance Ingilby really has the boy, he would not beg, borrow or steal to have him returned? Merritt is only a child. What he has endured over the past three years must have been truly hellish. He deserves to be with his father and Keir deserves to have the boy returned. It is the only solution."

Kurtis couldn't take it. He let go of Chloë and moved to the nearest chair, collapsing on it and putting his head in his hands.

"Sweet Jesus," he muttered into his hands. "Is this true? Is this really happening?"

Cassandra went to her husband, kneeling down beside him and putting her arms around his shoulders. Torn, upset, she looked between her husband and her sister.

"Perhaps we must ask to see the boy before anything is agreed upon," she suggested. "If Ingilby is lying about the boy, then there is no choice to make."

"How did he know about the boy in the first place?" Michael wondered aloud. "I do not understand how he could even know."

Coverdale, largely silent through the exchange, shook his head and went to sit wearily at his table. "The siege of Pendragon is not a secret in Yorkshire," he said. "It is a sad and bloody tale. Most, if not all, of the northern allies know of it. It is obvious that the man heard about it from someone. But I am very curious as to how the boy came into Ingilby's possession, quite coincidentally I might add. Keir has something that he wants, and now he has something that Keir wants. Very odd."

Chloë's gaze moved between Kurtis, her sister, and Lord Coverdale. Her tears were completely gone and her composure was remarkably strong. It was strange how, when faced with the heart-wrenching proposal, she felt a remarkable amount of peace with the only possible decision. When she should have been hysterical with grief, she was genuinely calm and collected. In her mind, there was no other choice. For Keir to have his son returned, she would gladly make the sacrifice.

"Listen to me, all of you," she said in her sweet, soft voice. "This is not a decision Keir should have to make. It is a decision for me to make. I love Keir more than anything on this earth and because of that, I would do anything for him. I would die for him, and kill for him, and if it is within my power, I would give him back the one thing that he wants perhaps more than anything else. I love him enough to give him his son back. If there is any chance that Ingilby truly has little Merritt, then I must take that chance. If I can do this for him, I will."

Kurtis held her gaze a moment before turning away, clearly wiping at his eyes. Cassandra went to her sister and put her arms around her, holding her close.

"I understand," she murmured, fighting back tears. "You are making a great sacrifice, Chloë. But I completely understand why you would."

"It will destroy him," Kurtis said hoarsely. He looked at Chloë, his eyes watering. "You were not there when he lost Madeleine and Frances. You did not see what the man went through. Chloë, he will go through that again with your loss. I am terrified he will not survive. As much as I hate myself for saying this, he has lived without Merritt for three years. The boy probably does not even remember him. You and my brother can have more children, but he can never find another you. If you do this, if you exchange yourself for Merritt, you will destroy him."

Chloë went to her brother-in-law, putting her hands on his rough cheeks and forcing him to meet her eye. Kurtis was reluctant to gaze into the beautiful brown orbs but found himself mesmerized, unable to pull away.

"Then tell me truthfully," she demanded softly. "You are so sure you can make this decision for your brother. What would you choose if you were Keir?"

Kurtis sighed heavily and tried to look away but Chloë would not let him. She shook him gently.

"Answer me," she whispered. "What would Keir do?"

Kurtis stared at her and his eyes began to overflow. "I do not want to see my brother go through hell again. If you do this, he will not want to live."

"Aye, he will," she whispered. "He will have Merritt to live for."

Kurtis looked miserable. "He will never stop trying to get you back, Chloë, not ever. He will kill Ingilby and anyone else who stands in his way to get you back."

"That is what I am counting on."

"What do you mean?"

"Think on it."

Kurtis could see she was deadly serious and, somehow, he wasn't quite so emotional anymore. The light of realization came to his eyes.

"Then...," he muttered, paused, and started again. "Then you suspect this is not the end between you and my brother?"

She smiled at him. "Of course not," she said. "I know that Keir will come for me. I have no doubt whatsoever, especially if, after Merritt is turned over to Keir, I commit myself to the nunnery at St. Wilfrid in Ripon. I will wait there until Keir comes for me. Who says I shall ever have to spend a day as Ingilby's wife?"

After the full impact of her plans hit him, Kurtis appeared even more distressed. "It is a terrible chance you are taking, Chloë," he insisted. "Ingilby is surely no fool. If he suspects treachery, then your life could be in danger."

Chloë was resolute but not beyond listening to advice. Kurtis seemed sincerely concerned and that forced her to pause.

"Perhaps... perhaps we need to send our own terms to Ingilby, then," she said thoughtfully. "Perhaps we should tell him that I will go to St. Wilfrid for safekeeping until Merritt is delivered to Keir and it is confirmed that he is indeed Keir's son. Once that confirmation is achieved, Ingilby can collect me at St. Wilfrid, only by that time, I will have asked for sanctuary and the protection of the church. They will have to protect me if I fear for my life, at least until Keir can come for me. He will bring his armies and fight off Ingilby."

Kurtis sighed faintly. "It is a well enough plan," he agreed quietly. "But you have neglected to take into consideration that Keir is in Wales. We have no way of knowing how long he will be there. He could return next week or in three years. You may be in for a long wait at St. Wilfrid and Ingilby will not give up in his attempts to acquire you. You may live your days in fear and terror of him."

Chloë seemed to subdue somewhat but her resolution did not fade.

"As long as Keir has Merritt returned to him, I can endure anything. He must have his son back, Kurtis. I can only think of him in this matter and not myself."

"Chloë," Anton spoke from his position near Coverdale's table. "Kurtis is correct. Ingilby will stop at nothing to regain you, especially if he feels you have gone back on your promise. I cannot in good conscience allow you to do this."

Chloë whirled on him, her calm demeanor suddenly stiff with anger. "You would not allow me to marry Keir and I was forced to listen to you. But you will not make this decision for me, Father, not now. I will make this decision for myself and you will not stop me."

Anton tensed. "I most certainly can. I can throw you into the vault and lock you away until you come to your senses."

Chloë would not be bullied. "I wonder what Mother would say to that?" she ventured, watching her father's demeanor change. "I would wager to say that she would agree with me after your disgraceful treatment of Keir. Shall we find out?"

Anton scowled and turned away, waving his hands at his daughter as if to wipe her out of his mind. Frustrated, he wandered over to Coverdale's collection of fine wines and started the process of drowning himself in liquor.

With two daughters and a strong willed wife, he knew his was a losing battle. He'd managed to hold off the marriage of Chloë and Keir, which was surprising in itself considering how his wife felt about it, but in this circumstance, Anton knew he would lose. It was too emotional a subject and for all of Blanche's austere appearance, he knew she would agree with Chloë. Women were too foolish, always thinking with their emotions. He took a long drink of wine, wondering what was to become of his beautiful daughter. It seemed now it was out of his hands.

Kurtis watched the interaction between Chloë and her father, keeping his mouth shut. He was afraid to add to the conversation, unsure of what he was thinking. He hated to think that he agreed with Anton, but he did. Chloë seemed so determined but he knew, as he lived and breathed, that Keir had to know of this. He could not keep this from his brother. No matter what Chloë wishes, Keir would know.

Eventually, Cassandra and Chloë left the solar, quiet conversation between them as they whispered out into the hall and faded away. Coverdale still sat at his table with the missive in front of him while Anton stood near the wine, well into his third chalice. Michael and Kurtis were left staring at each other, former love rivals now united in this new threat. Kurtis discreetly motioned Michael with him as the two of them quit the solar.

Kurtis didn't say a word until they were well clear of the solar. Additionally, he wanted to make sure Chloë and Cassandra were out of earshot before speaking. As they quit the great keep of Aysgarth, Kurtis turned to Michael.

"I am riding for Keir immediately," he told him. "My brother has to know what is transpiring."

Michael nodded. "Agreed, but you should not ride for him. It should be me. You must stay here with your wife. Moreover, someone has to stay here with Chloë and prevent her from doing anything foolish until Keir can be reached. I fear she will not listen to me, but as Keir's brother, she is bound to listen to you."

Kurtis wriggled his eyebrows, emitting a pent-up sigh. "You are more than likely right," he admitted. "Then you should leave right away. There is no time to waste if Keir is only given a fortnight to make his decision."

"He is at Beeston Castle?"

"That is the rally point. I would assume he should be there."

Michael didn't hesitate. As he turned in the direction of the stables, Kurtis reached out and grabbed him. Their eyes met, cornflower blue to pale, icy blue. They had known each other a long time and had faced death together, and they both knew that the hard feelings regarding Cassandra were only temporary. They were still united and still friends.

"You were there when Keir endured Madeleine and Frances'

deaths," he said quietly. "We cannot allow him to go through that again, Michael. You, of all people, know what losing Chloë would do to him."

Michael nodded with some sadness. "I know," he muttered. "But honestly, Kurtis, given the choice, will the man want his son back? Will he sacrifice the woman he loves? Keir will make the decision but it will kill him to do it."

"What decision is that?"

"He will want the boy."

"And I say he will want Chloë."

"There is only one way to know for certain."

Kurtis nodded, letting go of Michael's arm and watching the man head off into the bailey, heading for the knight's quarters and his possessions. He remained on the steps leading into the keep until Michael, on a fully armored charger, rode from the gates and off into the night.

CHAPTER TWENTY-ONE

W ALES IS A *wild place.*

As Keir rode at the head of his army, it was his one predominant thought. He hadn't been here in years, not since the Battle of Irfon Bridge and Llewelyn ap Gruffydd's death. He hadn't truly thought on that event in years but now that he was back in Wales, he found himself reflecting on the battle, the people who had aided in the victory, and the friends he had lost during that campaign. It had been a very long time ago but he still remembered young knights he had served with, men with a passion for king and country, and he missed those who had not survived. It seemed like another lifetime ago.

Glancing over his shoulder, he could see Lucan riding to his right, slightly behind him, his eyes trained on the dramatic green wilds of Wales for any sign of trouble. There were, in fact, about two dozen knights riding directly behind him, all from various northern houses, men he was acquainted with to varying degrees and all very fine warriors. The Earl of Lincoln, Henry de Lacy, had arrived just as Keir was mobilizing the army to leave Beeston and the man rode towards the middle of the army upon one of his wagons because he was completely exhausted from having traveled non-stop all the way from Lincolnshire. Battle marches were difficult for both the young and the old.

Before they had left Beeston, Keir and de Lacy had met privately to discuss the upcoming quest and to render a plan. Keir was to field command the army but the Earl had final say in all commands and control. That didn't particularly bother Keir, but rather took some of the responsibility off of him, which brought some relief. He had enough on his mind and the earl's shared responsibility was welcome.

The army had been moving for three days. They would stop when it became too dark to travel, eat and take what sleep they could, before moving off at the first sign of light again. It had made for grueling days because Keir pushed a swift pace. Harlech was about eighty miles from Chester and Keir tried to push the army at least twenty miles a day, which they had fallen short of twice. The third day, however, they exceeded the goal. By Keir's estimation, they would see Harlech sometime late on the morrow.

He had already sent out scouts, men who would observe the conditions of Harlech Castle and report back to Keir. These men were young, light of weight, and rode swift horses. By night of the third day, they had returned with the news that Harlech was fully under siege by thousands of Welsh and Edward's army was nowhere to be seen. Keir and de Lacy could only surmise that the king was on his way but too far away to converge on Harlech simultaneously with the army from the north. After brief deliberation, de Lacy made the decision to move on Harlech without waiting for the king. Keir didn't particularly agree but he had no choice. They would see battle upon the morrow.

That night, when everyone had retired for, more than likely, their last solid sleep for quite some time, Keir sat down to scribe a missive to Chloë. His tent was dark but for a small taper on his travel table, a dented iron brazier burning peat to stave off some of the Welsh chill, as he carefully scratched out the words that were in his heart. He was increasingly apprehensive for Chloë's fate should he perish in battle and he wanted to send her words of comfort and joy, something she could cling to should he not return. He had already said everything he could say to her but somehow, in writing his feelings, it was different. The words were his, written by his own hand, and she would forever have something that was a physical piece of him.

As he sat and wrote, the torn shift that belonged to Chloë lay bunched up in his lap. Every so often, he would hold it up to his nose, smelling her faint, gentle scent, closing his eyes at the feelings it provoked. He could not begin to describe the loneliness he felt, the longing to feel her in his arms again. It was a physical pain that radiated through his entire body. He clutched the shift in his right hand as he carefully penned the missive with his left.

It was very late when he finally finished, sanding the ink and carefully rolling the vellum to close it with wax and his seal. When he finally slept, it was with Chloë's shift clutched to his face, inhaling her scent as he slept deep and dreamless. But it was only for a few blissful hours and he was up again well before dawn, summoning a messenger to return his missive to Aysgarth and the delicious redheaded woman he had left behind.

As the messenger fled and he began to dress for what would inarguably be a long and brutal day, Keir couldn't help his thoughts from lingering on Chloë.

He said a small prayer to her, hoping she could hear him, hoping she understood just how much he loved her. He wasn't sure he would get another chance to tell her from this day forward and hoped that God, in his infinite mercy, would give him the opportunity. The smell of battle was already in the air.

Unfortunately, the second missive never made it out of his hands. The army was attacked by Welsh rebels before dawn the next day and the entire battalion went into battle mode. The rebels did what damage they could before breaking for Harlech to warn the besiegers of the incoming English army.

Keir had to split his column up to send some men after the rebels while the remaining force swung into high gear and marched at swift speed towards Harlech, preparing to engage the Welsh the moment they arrived. Undoubtedly the rebels attacking the castle would be alerted and ready for them, no matter how hard they tried to prevent it.

The War in Wales was in full swing.

CB

MICHAEL HAD BEEN riding hard from Aysgarth to Beeston, stopping only to rest and water his charger. The animal was a sweating, foaming mess, but that was usual with him. Michael would stop, allow the horse to drink, splash water on the sweaty neck, and then continue on until after nightfall when he would stop for a few hours to allow the horse to rest.

Around noon on the second day, he met up with a rider traveling very fast northward. The man was obviously a messenger because he traveled light and swift, with no armor to speak of, and Michael wouldn't have paid much attention to him except for the pouch the man carried on the haunches of his horse. It was a faded leather pouch but he could see the colors of Edward on it and he raised his hand, stopping the man by blocking his path with his fat black charger. The messenger pulled his excited Spanish Jennet to a halt.

"You, there," Michael boomed. "Where are you coming from?"

"Beeston Castle, my lord," the man replied.

Michael lifted an eyebrow. "Do you know of Keir St. Héver?"

"I bear a missive from him, my lord."

"To whom?"

"The Lady Chloë de Geld, my lord. I am bound for Aysgarth Castle. Please allow me to pass."

Michael waved him off. "Keir is my liege," he told the man. "I mean you no harm. Have the armies from the north gathered yet?"

The messenger nodded. "Mostly," he replied. "They have received orders to move for Harlech Castle immediately."

Michael couldn't help the surprise on his face. "They were not due to leave for Harlech for another three weeks."

"Those plans have changed, my lord," the messenger replied. "When I left, they were already mobilizing."

"How long ago was that?"

"They moved out at dawn yesterday, my lord."

Michael sighed heavily, pondering the information. It was not good news. "Very well," he said. Then he pointed a gloved finger at the man. "Under no circumstances are you to tell the Lady Chloë that Keir has already gone on into Wales. Is that clear?"

"It is, my lord."

"She is the nosy sort. She may bombard you with questions on Keir's condition, but do not tell her he has gone to battle."

"Understood, my lord."

Michael waved the man on. Spurring his charger forward, he could only hope now that he reached Keir before the man arrived at Harlech. As it was, Michael was going to be chasing the English army through the badlands of Wales, something he was not particularly looking forward to doing. A lot could happen to a lone English knight with Welsh rebels about, especially if they were out for blood.

Michael briefly considered turning back, but given the consequences, he was willing to risk his life, mostly because he knew that if the situation was reversed, Keir would do it for him. There would be no question.

He pushed on.

CB

STANDING IN CHLOË'S borrowed chamber at Aysgarth, Kurtis watched his sister-in-law calmly finish packing whatever bags she hadn't already packed for her return to Pendragon. He was agitated, angry and frustrated, a bitter combination that made him pace about.

Kurtis was trying very hard to think like his brother but he was beginning to second guess himself, especially since Chloë seemed so determined to have Keir's son returned to him. He was terrified he was fighting a losing battle, terrified of what Keir would do to him when he found out. The situation was beginning to speed out of control.

"You should never have sent a missive to Ingilby agreeing to his proposal with your provisions," Kurtis fumed. "The proposal was addressed to Keir, not you. It is his right to respond to it."

Chloë didn't rise to his anger. She knew Kurtis was upset and she understood why. But that didn't change facts.

"My mother gave me permission to send it," she told him. "She approved of every word written. I thought we agreed that I would make the decision for Keir."

"You decided," Kurtis shot back. "I never agreed with you. I still do not."

Chloë sighed faintly and returned to the satchel she was securing. "I am sorry you do not understand," she said quietly. "As much as I respect you, Kurtis, I must make my own decision in this matter. I must do what I feel is best for Keir."

Kurtis growled and turned away, pacing the wooden floor like a caged animal. "This is *not* what is best for my brother," he grumbled. "Do you not understand anything of the art of negotiation, Chloë? I would stake my life on the fact that Ingilby will not kill the boy because in doing so, he loses his only bargaining tool. Did you not think of that? What you have done is play right into his hands. You have made a naïve mistake and committed yourself to something you had no right to commit yourself to."

Chloë looked at him, a flicker of uncertainty in her eyes. "But what if he is not bluffing?" she wanted to know. "What right do I have to play with Merritt's life?"

"You do not even know if the boy is Merritt!" Kurtis was starting to shout, pointing fingers at her as he spoke. "You know nothing of these games and neither does your mother. You have behaved stupidly!"

"Kurtis," Cassandra admonished softly. "You are unkind. Chloë is only trying to do what she feels is best."

Kurtis was furious. "She had no right to do it," he snapped. "I told her to wait for Keir. I have even sent Michael after him. If your sister does not trust my judgment better than that, judgment that Northumberland trusts implicitly I might add, then I have no idea what I am doing here. I should be on my way home if your sister is too stubborn and foolish to listen to sage advice."

By this time, Chloë was tearing up, turning back to the bags on the bed and struggling not to weep.

"I do respect your judgment, Kurtis," she said softly. "But I feel strongly that I cannot take the chance that Ingilby will not do as he has threatened. Who will tell Keir that his son was killed because we did not agree to his demands?"

"And who will tell Keir that his betrothed has married another man?" Kurtis shot back. "You are involving yourself in deadly games, Chloë. What if your amazing plan of committing yourself to St. Wilfrid does not work? What if Ingilby captures you and marries you? Do you have any idea what that will do to my brother? He will go mad and your foolish surrender will have been the cause of it. Are you so perfect that you think you know everything?"

He was shouting angrily by the time he was finished. Chloë held her tears as long as she could but his words were hurtful. She was attempting to do what she felt best but Kurtis didn't think much of her thought processes. He was condemning her, perhaps rightfully, perhaps cruelly, but it was condemnation nonetheless. Distraught, she burst into tears and fled the chamber.

Cassandra tried to grasp her sister as the woman moved past her but Chloë slipped her grip, fleeing the room. Furious, Cassandra looked at her husband.

"That was a terrible thing to say to her," she hissed. "How could you be so cruel?"

Kurtis' fury was doused by his wife's anger. Still, he maintained his firm stance. "It is true," he said. "She is young and naïve. She has no idea what she is doing and refuses to listen to anyone else."

With a growl, Cassandra bolted from the chamber and after her sister. Kurtis remained in the room, wondering if he'd been too harsh, when he suddenly heard his wife scream.

CHAPTER TWENTY-TWO

ASSANDRA EMITTED NO ordinary scream; it was long and painful and full of hysteria. Kurtis was seized with panic. Racing from Chloë's bedchamber, he took the steep spiral stairs to the second level far too fast. When he was about halfway down, he could see what had provoked his wife's scream.

Chloë lay at the bottom of the stairs in a heap with Cassandra hunched over her, weeping loudly. When she glanced up and saw her husband, she cried out to him.

"She has fallen down the stairs!" she cried. "Call for the physic!"

Kurtis managed to race down the remainder of the stairs, nearly falling himself in his haste, until he reached the bottom. He ended up plummeting to his knees, nearly toppling over his wife in his urgency to get to Chloë. The first thing he did was put his fingers on her neck.

"She is alive," he hissed with relief as he felt the fast, weak pulse. "What in the hell happened?"

Cassandra was sobbing heavily. "She must have fallen," she wept, then spat vicious at her husband. "Or perhaps she threw herself down the stairs after your terrible words. All I know is that I have found her lying here."

"You did not see her fall?"

"Nay," Cassandra wept. "Chloë, sweetheart, can you hear me? Chloë, wake up!"

Kurtis paled, shouting to anyone who could hear him to find help for Lady Chloë. His heart was thumping with fear as he gazed down at her, pale and still. Gingerly, he reached out to roll her onto her back to gain a better perspective of her injuries. Cassandra was clutching at her sister, preventing him from getting a good look at her. Kurtis eventually had to push his wife aside so he could get a look at her injured sister.

"Chloë?" Kurtis rubbed her soft cheek, seeing that she already had a massive lump forming on her forehead. "Chloë, can you hear me?"

Chloë remained still and silent. Kurtis' panic began to grow by leaps and bounds. She was so pale that her lips were nearly blue. He looked up at his wife, a sobbing mess beside him.

"Go find your mother," he commanded softly, swiftly. "Tell her what has happened. And for Christ's sake, get the physic up here. I am going to return her to her bed."

Cassandra was quivering so badly that she stumbled when she tried to stand up. Kurtis could see how shaken she was and he put a big hand on her head in an effort to console her.

"Calm down, sweetheart," he tried to sound comforting but the truth was that he was just as frightened as she was. "Everything will be alright. Hurry, now. Find your mother."

Cassandra managed to get to her feet on the second try, nodding at her husband and scurrying away. Kurtis watched her as she descended the stairs to the entry level before hoisting Chloë up into his arms. She groaned softly at the movement, in pain, and Kurtis thought she might be conscious, but she did not respond to further attempts to rouse her. Swiftly and steadily, Kurtis mounted the treacherous stairs for the upper levels.

With shaking arms, Kurtis laid her upon her bed, watching for any signs of recovery from her, but as the minutes ticked away and Chloë remained still he began to feel some desperation. There wasn't much more he could do for her until Blanche and Cassandra appeared, followed shortly by the castle surgeon, a tall man with long, spindly fingers.

Time was flying by yet it was moving unbearably slow as Chloë remained unconscious. It was an odd and painful state. While the women hovered anxiously bedside, the surgeon proceeded to examine the limp and bruised form.

The anxiety mounted as Coverdale and Anton appeared, having heard of Chloë's accident from a frantic servant. Soon, the room was crowded with family and friends alike, all waiting with fear and anticipation for the surgeon's assessment.

It was an odd vigil, one of uncertainty and concern. Cassandra stood with her stoic mother, weeping softly as the surgeon went through his paces. He lifted eyelids, checked ears, felt along the neck and shoulders. He listened to Chloë's heart and pressed on her ribs to feel for any broken bones. He inspected the bump on her head and instructed a frightened serving woman to bring him cold water. Then he rolled Chloë onto her side and began feeling down her spine.

As the room watched apprehensively, the surgeon came to a halt when he felt something on her spine that was significant enough to cause him to pause. He ran his finger over it again and although unconscious, Chloë emitted an unearthly moan. The surgeon gently rolled her onto her back again and resumed his inspection of her limbs.

"Why did she groan like that?" Blanche wanted to know. "What is the matter?"

The surgeon was running his hands down her thighs to feel for any broken bones. "I am not certain, my lady," he said in a strangely high-pitched voice. "It could be bruising and nothing more."

Blanche, ever stoic, seemed to show an undue amount of emotion. "But there is something wrong?"

The surgeon nodded, meeting her eye. "Something is out of place on her spine, I can feel it. It is causing her great pain."

Cassandra's eyes widened as she looked between her mother and the surgeon. "Her back is broken?"

As Blanche put her arm around Cassandra's shoulders to quiet the woman, the surgeon shook his head. "I cannot know, my lady, for it is too soon," he said. "Only time will tell us what damage there truly is. At this moment, I am concerned with reducing the swelling on her head and back. As soon as the water arrives, I will make a paste that I will apply to the areas in the hopes of reducing the swelling."

"But there are no broken bones?" Anton spoke up, seemingly genuinely concerned. "She is intact?"

The surgeon shook his head. "Other than her spine, of which I am not certain, I do not feel anything, not even on her skull. Did anyone see her fall?"

Everyone seemed to look to Cassandra, who shook her head. "I did not see it," she said. "I did not even hear it. These walls are so thick and sound does not travel well. All I know is that I was descending the stairs and I saw her at the bottom."

By this time, Kurtis was moving to his wife, reaching out to comfort her, but Cassandra saw him coming and she jerked away from him angrily. She was still furious with him for being cruel to her sister, perhaps even causing the results lying on the bed before them. In any case, Cassandra didn't want him to touch her. It was a harsh and bitter move.

Kurtis put his arms down, watching Cassandra with devastation on his face. He was struggling not to feel guilty about what had happened but try as he might, he could not shake off the sense that somehow this was his fault. He had been yelling at Chloë and she had fled from him, upset, apparently so upset that her carelessness caused her to fall on the steep spiral stairs.

His gaze moved from Cassandra to Chloë, lying pasty upon the coverlet. He had lectured Chloë on how her loss would affect Keir's life. Now, they were facing something unexpected, something terrible and potentially shattering, and he couldn't shake his guilt.

To hell with Ingilby and his proposal; to hell with Chloë and her counter-proposal. All that mattered now was that Chloë was gravely injured and Keir needed to be here, not on some icy hill in Wales fighting rebels in a foolish battle. Kurtis' mind, his grip on his emotions, was slipping. He was feeling panic and distress as he had never felt in his life.

"Is she going to die?" he heard himself ask the surgeon.

The old man was at Chloë's feet as he finished his inspection. "Only time will tell," he repeated. "It depends on a great many things."

Kurtis turned on his heel and quit the chamber without another word. He could hear Coverdale calling after him but he ignored the old man as he made his way out of the keep. He was heading for the stables, already mentally preparing what he was going to say to his brother and hope that Keir didn't run him through.

The situation was out of control and he felt like a failure, like he had contributed to it somehow. All he was supposed to do was watch over Chloë and somehow, somewhere, it had turned horribly wrong. By the time he reached the stables, he was barking at the grooms to prepare his charger. His emotions had the better of him.

He entered the storage room that contained his saddle and pieces of armor for his horse, hefting up the big saddle and turning to bring it out into the tack area. As he spun around, a body was suddenly standing behind him and he nearly plowed into it.

Cassandra was standing there, her face pale and her eyes red-rimmed. When their eyes met, her lower lip trembled.

"I am sorry, Kurtis," she whispered. "Please forgive me. I did not mean to become so angry with you. But Chloë... she is...."

She trailed off as she started to cry again. Kurtis dropped the saddle and pulled her into his arms.

"I am sorry, too," he murmured into her hair, feeling her body shake with sobs. "I should not have become so furious with her. I know she felt she was trying to do what was right for Keir, but... my brother told me to watch over her and she is not allowing me to do that, not in the least. I let my temper get the better of me and I am truly sorry. I did not mean to be so cruel."

Cassandra wept into his shoulder. "Please do not leave me," she begged. "I did not mean to chase you away."

He shook his head, kissing the side of her head as he stood back and cupped her face between his two big hands. "I am not leaving you, sweet," he assured her. "I am riding for Keir. He must know what has happened, in case Chloë...."

He couldn't even finish the sentence, realizing that the mere thought of Chloë passing away brought him such terror as he could not comprehend. His brother would never recover; none of them would. Life would never be the same. He kissed his wife's forehead comfortingly and pulled her into another crushing embrace.

"Everything will be well," he said, more for his benefit than for hers. "Chloë will be fine. I will bring Keir back with me and everything will be well."

Cassandra struggled against her tears, nodding with reassurance as she touched his face and kissed his lips. "I will stay with her," she sniffled. "Tell Keir that I am with her. I will not let anything happen to her until he returns."

Kurtis kissed her gently a couple of times, glad that all was well between them again, before releasing her and reclaiming his saddle. As Cassandra stood by and sniffled, watching him saddle his charger, Kurtis tried to focus on his trip ahead, of what he would tell Keir when he found him. He knew that his brother would be panicked by his mere presence, knowing that he would not have come personally unless there was a very good reason. Or a very bad one.

"Michael has probably already found him by now," he told his wife as he tightened up the cinch on the saddle. "In fact, I should run into Michael returning to Aysgarth as I travel south. I will send Michael back to you in case you need anything."

Cassandra wiped at her nose, watching her husband as he slung his saddlebags over the back of the horse. "What will happen if the king will not release Keir?"

Kurtis sighed faintly. "He will come anyway and deal with the consequences later."

Cassandra didn't say any more. She could tell that Kurtis was edgy, fearful of what was to come for all of them. He was busying himself with the horse, his armor and weapons, but she could tell he was distracted. Truth was they were both distracted. When he seemed finished with everything, she went to him and wound her arms around his neck. He held her tightly, his face buried in her shoulder.

"Be safe," she begged. "I will look for your return every day."

He gave her a squeeze before kissing her sweetly. "I love you."

"And I love you."

He kissed her again, her mouth and her cheek, before releasing her and mounting the charger. Cassandra stood back as the beast danced about, switching its tail and kicking up straw, and Kurtis expertly guided it from the stable. He turned around to wave at her and she waved back, watching him trot across the yard and into the bailey.

As she walked back to the keep, she watched him leave through the gatehouse. Even after he was gone, her gaze lingered on the last place she had seen him, the open portcullis, imagining she could still see her strong and wise husband.

Cassandra prayed for his safety, for Keir's return, and for her sister in general as she mounted the steps to the massive and imposing keep of Aysgarth.

CB

"A MISSIVE HAS arrived from Aysgarth, my lord."

Ingilby had been seated at the richly carved table in his solar, examining a map he had commissioned from a Florin cartographer. It was the map of his lands and surrounding areas, beautifully drawn with a master hand. He looked up from the yellowed vellum, his expression registering some surprise.

"So soon?" his brow furrowed. "I only sent the missive last week. Where is Alphonse?"

The servant started to get nervous. "He did not return, my lord. The missive was carried by the soldiers you sent with him."

Ingilby was up from his seat. "Not *returned?*" he snatched the missive that the servant was extending, tearing open the careful wax seal without even looking at it. "Where is he?"

The servant shook his head. "The soldiers said that Coverdale put him in the vault."

Ingilby froze, his features stretched with outage. "Fools!" he snapped, tearing at the missive as he tried to roll it open. "Coverdale is a fool if he believes I will not seek vengeance for his actions. He had no right to gaol Alphonse!"

The servant remained silent, nearly prostrating himself as he backed out of the solar. He did not want to be near his lord when the man read the missive.

Ingilby paid no attention to the man as he backed out of the room, instead, focusing his furious gaze on the contents of the missive. With Alphonse held captive, he felt it was indicative of the reaction to his proposal. Surely St. Héver and Coverdale were furious, and St. Héver in particular. In truth, Ingilby had expected no less of a violent response. He was positive the contents of the missive were cursing his actions and refusing to negotiate.

Which was why he was genuinely surprised within the first few sentences to see that St. Héver had not responded at all. Although the words were carefully scribed by someone who produced the written word quite often, the words themselves were of a decidedly female voice.

Ingilby lowered himself into his chair, reading the carefully sanded ink with great interest.

My Lord Ingilby –

As Keir St. Héver's betrothed, it is within my right to respond to the terms offered on the missive you sent regarding his son Merritt. You offered to return Merritt to his father if I would become your bride. Be it known that I will agree to your terms on the condition that I be held in protection at St. Wilfrid until the identity of Keir's son is determined. If the boy is confirmed as Keir's son, I will consent as your bride. If the boy is not Keir's son, then I shall marry Keir St. Héver and never hear from you again. These are the terms and they are non-negotiable.

I await your response.

Lady Chloë Louise Isabella de Geld
Princess Blanche of Rochedale

Ingilby was truly stunned by the contents. He had not expected such a reply, not in his wildest dreams. He had fully expected a war of words and, quite possibly, of weaponry, but no explosion was forthcoming. It was neat, simple and firm.

But even as he read the missive, he wondered where St. Héver was and why the man had allowed his betrothed and her mother to respond. He wondered what kind of weak or indecisive man would allow women to speak for him.

It was a puzzling situation indeed, one he intended to clarify when he delivered his response to the missive personally.

CHAPTER TWENTY-THREE

H E COULDN'T REMEMBER when the last time he slept or ate. The days, rainy and muddy and bloody, were running into one another in a macabre collection of scenes and experiences. Keir was so exhausted that he could hardly think anymore, but he had to in order to stay alive. He had to stay clear of the Welsh who were bombarding the English on all sides, preventing them from moving in to aid embattled Harlech.

The Army of the North was caught ten miles outside of Harlech Castle in the little mining town of Bladnau that was surrounded by the Welsh rebels who had known in advance of the English approach. The English were surrounded and the past four days had been purely a matter of survival. De Lacy demanded that Keir push the army to Harlech but Keir reminded him, several times, that their push forward would be in inches and it would take months to reach Harlech at that pace. Their only option was to retreat and regroup but de Lacy would not allow it. For days, Keir had fought a battle of survival and as dawn on the fifth day approached, the Earl of Lincoln finally gave his blessing to retreat. Keir did so without question.

The three thousand man army from Chester backed off, chased off by the Welsh rebels who were much stronger than Keir had ever remembered them to be. Through the rain, lightning storms and knee-deep mud, he pulled his army out and they made their retreat back the way they had come, through a narrow valley surrounded by step mountains known as the Vale of Conwy. It was exhausting and demoralizing work, slogging through a massive rainstorm to reach the small town of Dolwyddelan, which contained a small but strategic castle that was held by the English.

Unfortunately, the garrison wasn't large enough to accommodate the entire army, but the rebels had ceased their onslaught a few miles back, so Keir took that as a positive sign as he directed what men and wagons he could into Dolwyddelan's bailey. Once the provision wagons were secured, men poured into the bailey to try to gain some protection while an entire army of hundreds of men from Harbottle Castle remained outside the walls, exposed to the rebels should they decide to attack again. Keir remained outside with the Harbottle army while Lucan buttoned up Dolwyddelan.

The commander from Harbottle was a seasoned knight who had seen many battles in the name of the king. He wore battered armor and was missing an eye. Experienced and intelligent, he set up a perimeter around his army including massive bonfires that essentially created a circle of fire.

The Welsh would have to be insane or foolish to breach the soaring flames, but none of his men slept much following the establishment of the firewall. Most of them, including Keir and the commander, were standing just this side of the perimeter, watching the surrounding countryside through the flames. Their senses were peaked for an onslaught at any moment but as the night passed, everything remained peaceful. Eventually, they took turns sleeping.

Keir had been up for nearly four days. Four long, exhaustive days. He stayed awake as long as he could before sitting down near the exterior wall of Dolwyddelan, eventually laying down in the cool, wet grass and falling asleep almost immediately. It was a dreamless sleep, deep and exhausted, and he had no idea how long he had been sleeping when shouts from the wall roused him. He was on his feet with his weapon in his hand before he realized he had even moved.

"What is it?" he asked the commander, rubbing sleep from his eyes.

The man with the missing eye was focused on the darkened land-scape beyond the ring of fire. With the brilliant flame as a backdrop, it was difficult to see much beyond the blackness.

"A lone rider, my lord," he told him.

Keir stopped rubbing his eyes and struggled to focus. "A lone rider?" he repeated. "Welsh or English?"

"We cannot tell."

Keir wriggled his eyebrows. "Whoever he is, he is a fool to be riding alone in this land."

The commander grunted in agreement, ordering his archers to raise their weapons as the rider drew closer. They could see him approaching from the valley below now, heading up the road in the dead of night. The half-moon glistened off the man's armor as he drew nearer and the commander lifted his hand to his archers, preparing to give the order to fire. A word from Keir stopped them.

"Hold your fire," he suddenly barked, his pale blue eyes widening. He jockeyed around to get a better view of the rider. "I... I think I know that man."

The commander turned to him. "You know that fool?"

Keir simply lifted an eyebrow at him, preparing to agree, when he realized that the rider was Michael. The man emerged from the darkness, like Lucifer from the cloaking caves of Hades. There was no mistaking Michael's size or his black and white charger. Keir bolted out of the ring of fire, heading for the knight.

"Michael!" he shouted, waving a hand.

Michael caught sight of him and spurred his charger in Keir's direction. The charger, foaming and weary, kicked up clods of earth as it came to a halt within several feet of Keir. Michael dismounted, nearly falling because he was so fatigued. Keir went to him with a mixture of great curiosity and great fear."

"What in the hell are you doing here?" he demanded.

Michael blew out his cheeks, exhausted. "Kurtis sent me," he told him. "Keir, there are problems you must be aware of. There was no choice but to ride into Wales and pray that I found you. I have been following the army for seven days, into Wales and back again. It was only by sheer luck that I found you."

Fear erased whatever curiosity Keir was feeling, gripping his heart with icy fingers. "And so you have," he said. "Is Chloë well? Has something happened to her?"

Michael shook his head. "Chloë is fine," he replied. Then he lifted his hand in a helpless gesture as if unsure of where to start. "We received a missive from Ingilby. It was addressed to you."

Keir's brow furrowed. "A missive from Ingilby?" he repeated, confused. "What in the hell does the man have to say to me?"

Michael struggled to be gentle with him but there was no way to couch such impacting news. He tried to buffer the delivery.

"Let us go into the castle and I will tell you," he indicated the bastion before them. "I have not eaten in a day."

Keir grabbed his arm and refused to let him move. "You will tell me now," he commanded. "What does Ingilby have to say to me?"

Michael sighed heavily. "Keir, it would be better...."

"Tell me now."

Michael looked at him, knowing he had no choice. He removed his helm and scratched at his dark head beneath the hauberk.

"We received the missive from Ingilby just over a week ago, addressed to you," he said, lowering his voice. "Keir, there is no simple way to put this so I will just come out with it. Ingilby claims to have Merritt in his possession and has offered a trade – your son for Chloë. He says he will give you a fortnight to make your decision and if it is the wrong choice, he will send the boy back to you in pieces. Chloë has already decided that she will exchange herself for the boy, thinking that is what you would want. Kurtis is trying to hold her off and sent me to find you."

Keir stared at him for several long, painful moments, still as stone, the ice blue eyes wide with shock. Michael watched him carefully, seeing no discernable reaction to the news. He finally reached out and grasped his arm.

"Keir?" he shook him gently. "Did you hear me? Ingilby claims to have Merritt and he wants Chloë in exchange for the boy."

Keir still didn't reply. Then, as Michael held on to his arm, his knees seemed to buckle and Michael grabbed him so he wouldn't collapse. But Keir steadied himself, feeling more shock and distress than he ever imagined possible. Like a wave, the impact of the news washed over him.

"He has Merritt?" he breathed. "How does he have my son?"

Michael could see how distressed the man was. "I do not know," he said softly. "Let us go and sit somewhere, Keir. We need to discuss this and I must eat something before I collapse."

Keir, his face still taut with shock, simply nodded his head, distracted, moving for the ring of fire and taking Michael inside the blazing safety. He somehow made it over to his possessions, calling for food, and by the time he reached his little corner of the wall, he fell to his knees. He simply couldn't remain upright any longer.

Michael watched him with concern. When the one-eyed commander came to speak with Keir about something, he noted how fragile and shaken the man looked. He looked to Michael questioningly, but Michael simply shook his head. He did not know what to say. The one-eyed commander, sensing that perhaps now was not the best time for any manner of question, discreetly bowed away.

A soldier handed Michael a cup of some kind of liquid and a big hunk of bread. Michael gratefully accepted the food, crouching down beside Keir, who was still on his knees in the wet, thick grass.

"We do not know how Ingilby came across Merritt," he said to Keir as he tore into the bread. "In fact, we do not even know for sure that he has Merritt. He could be lying. But Chloë is so convinced that he has your son that she is willing to do whatever he says so you will regain your son. She knows... she knows how much this means to you."

Keir seemed to snap out of his trance, looking to Michael with a tightness in his expression that Michael had never seen before. It was as if the impact of the news had stripped away all of his strength and what was left was a volatile and emotional shell.

"How much it *means* to me?" he muttered. "God's Blood, if it is true, then I cannot tell you how much it means to me. I have been searching for Merritt for three long years with no sign of the boy. And now...."

"As I said, we do not even know for sure if the boy is really Merritt," Michael interrupted him. "Kurtis feels that you must make the decision. He does not want Chloë doing anything foolish without your knowledge or blessing."

Keir blinked as if suddenly realizing that Chloë was already planning something that would take this decision, this horrible situation, out of his control. He began to shake his head.

"There is no question," he said in a raspy voice. "Chloë will not go to Ingilby, not ever. I will ask for proof that the child Ingilby holds is, in fact, Merritt and then I will negotiate for his release."

"Ingilby threatened to kill the boy if you do not turn Chloë over to him."

Keir's expression grew darker. "If he does, then he shall rue the day, I swear it. I will raze his castle and put the man to a slow and painful death. I will make him wish a thousand times over that he had never tangled with me. You will make sure he understands this."

"Me?"

"You are going to deliver my response."

Michael sighed heavily. "He will probably kill me, Keir. The man is insane."

Keir shook his head. "He will not kill you. You will deliver the missive from a safe position. You will, under no circumstances, enter the grounds of Ripley Castle. And while you are there, you will demand to be shown the boy. You will recognize him, Michael. You know him."

Michael wriggled his eyebrows. "I knew him as a baby but he has grown much since that time," he pointed out. "What if I am not sure?"

"Then speak with the boy. Find out what he knows."

Michael scratched his head, not particularly happy with the directive. Too many variables and too many things could go wrong and he didn't like the fact that the burden had now shifted to his considerable shoulders.

"He was a baby when he was abducted," he reminded him. "What child would recall memories of his infancy?"

"He had Madeleine's eyes. You will know them."

Michael was obviously reluctant. "Perhaps," he said vaguely, not wanting to argue about it because it would not end well for either of them. He decided to shift the subject, the wiser choice at the moment. "Chloë, however, seems to have another plan, one that would aid you in both keeping her and regaining Merritt. It is not an unreasonable plan, surprisingly."

Keir shook his head even as the words left Michael's mouth. "She should not worry over this," he said firmly. "This is an issue for me to decide."

"She felt otherwise. She felt you should not have to make the decision because it would tear you apart. She thought to ease you by making the choice for you."

"*Ease* me?" Keir's voice was full of irony. "She believes it will ease me by turning herself over to Ingilby? That is madness."

He was becoming enraged and Michael held up his hand to steady him.

"She would not, not really," he insisted. "Her plan is to commit herself to the convent at St. Wilfrid until the identity of the boy can be verified. Ingilby will believe she is being held by a neutral party until we determine if the boy is truly Merritt, but it is her intention to seek sanctuary from the Church rather than keep her end of the bargain with Ingilby. The baron cannot touch her if the Church protects her."

Keir stared at the man as if he had lost his mind. "Neither can I!" he threw up his hands. "The Church will not take this lightly, considering she is using them to renege on a bargain. If she agrees to Ingilby's proposal in writing, whether or not she commits herself to the Church like some holy holding cell, by law she will belong to Ingilby. She will be his property and he will have every right to take her."

"Not if you take her first."

"Then I would be stealing what is rightfully his, Michael."

Michael didn't have a swift answer for that. He averted his gaze, chewing on his bread and wondering if the situation was truly so complicated.

"Then you had better send word back to Aysgarth," he muttered. "I am not sure if Kurtis can keep Chloë from doing as she wishes. If she feels she is doing what is best for you, then there will be no stopping her. Only a missive from you will prevent her from doing anything foolish, and even then...."

He trailed off and Keir looked at him, knowing what the man was going to say. He knew it was the truth as well. If Chloë truly thought she was doing what was best for Keir, a direct missive from him might not even be strong enough to stop her. He had no choice. He had to go in person.

"Gather my belongings," he commanded Michael. "I am going to see de Lacy."

Michael struggled to his feet. "What are you going to do?"

Keir was already walking for the gatehouse of Dolwyddelan. "I am returning to Aysgarth to sort out this mess."

"Now?"

"This very moment."

Michael sighed heavily. "Can I at least sleep a few hours? I have not slept in almost two days."

Keir cast him a long look over his shoulder. "Sleep if you wish," he said. "I am returning to Aysgarth with or without you."

Michael pursed his lips irritably as Keir continued on into the darkness, heading for the gates of the castle that were lit by heavily smoking torches against the black night. But he did not pursue. Wisely, he sank back to his buttocks to finish the remainder of his meal, knowing it might be his last for a while with Keir in such a determined mode. Michael was positive they would be on the road back to Aysgarth within the hour.

When morning dawned, Michael awoke to the heavy smell of

smoke around him as cooking fires took flight in the early morning air. It took him a moment to realize he had fallen asleep for several hours and Keir had not returned.

CB

HAZE. PAIN.

Those were the only coherent thoughts in Chloë's mind as she lay in a stupor, hovering on this side of unconsciousness, having no real grasp of time or space, or even where she was.

She faded in and out, dreaming of a goat she used to have as a child. Occasionally, visions of a knight with pale blue eyes would enter her dreams and she would reach for him, only to watch him fade into mist. When Chloë finally became lucid, it was like being born again. From darkness to mist to light, accompanied by pain and shock. A stabbing pain in her back and torso welcomed her back the world.

A gasp arose from her lips and she could hear her sister and mother speaking softly to her. But Chloë had never been any good with pain and the agony was more than she could bear. She howled and panted as Cassandra gripped her hand and whispered in her ear.

"I am here, Chloë," she squeezed her hand tightly. "I am here, sweetheart. Everything will be well again."

As Blanche demanded that the physic give her something, Chloë burst into tears.

"It hurts," she wept. "What… what….?"

"You fell down the stairs," Cassandra told her. "You hurt yourself."

Chloë sobbed loudly, squeezing her sister's hand as she struggled through the pain. "I… I do not…"

"Ease yourself, Chloë," Blanche instructed softly, firmly. "The physic will give you something for the pain."

"Mama?" Chloë heard her mother's voice and the great brown eyes rolled open. "Mama?"

"I am here, child. Breathe deeply."

"Mama, what happened?"

"You tumbled down the stairs and hit your head. Be still now and rest."

Chloë did as she was told, taking a few deep breaths, at least as deep as she could without causing herself excruciating pain. Her gaze was focused on the ceiling and after a few moments, she began to look about.

"Where are we?" she wept.

"Aysgarth Castle," Cassandra replied. "We are at Aysgarth."

Chloë fixed on her sister. "Why are we here?" she asked. "I must return to Pendragon. Where is Keir?"

Cassandra stroked her sister's head. "He is in Wales."

Chloë was confused. "Wales?" she repeated. "What is he doing in Wales?"

Cassandra was puzzled by Chloë's reaction. "He had to go," she said softly. "Do you not remember?"

Chloë had stopped the painful weeping by now but she was shaking and sniffling, looking around the chamber as if she had no idea what was happening.

"Where is Keir?" she repeated. "I want him."

Blanche hovered over her daughter. "He is in Wales, Chloë," she said evenly. "He has gone there with the king."

Chloë looked at her mother as if she truly had no idea what the woman was talking about. Her mind was skittish, foggy, everything coming to her in pieces. She remembered the battle at Exelby and going with Keir to Pendragon. She remembered their declaration of love for one another, but after that, things grew hazy. She gripped her sister's hands tightly, looking fearfully between her mother and sister.

"He is in Wales with the king?" she repeated.

Both Cassandra and Blanche nodded. "The king summoned him," Cassandra said gently.

"But why?"

Cassandra glanced at her mother for support as she spoke. "Well," she said reluctantly. "There was some trouble with the Welsh and...

well, the king needed help. He trusts Keir."

"He went to battle?"

Cassandra nodded sympathetically. "Aye."

Chloë's eyes welled with new tears. "I do not remember any of this," she whispered. "I only know that I love him but... but I do not remember coming to Aysgarth and I do not remember him leaving for Wales."

Cassandra was growing increasingly distraught, realizing that her sister's memory had been damaged by the fall. The lump on her forehead shielded hidden symptoms.

"We came to Aysgarth so that we could seek permission to marry," she told Chloë. "I married Kurtis last week but father would not...."

Thankfully, the physic interrupted her stammering statement with a white willow brew and Cassandra was grateful for the reprieve. In hindsight, she probably should not have told Chloë that her father had denied the marriage to Keir until the man returned from Wales. That would come later, when Chloë was stronger. Or perhaps she would remember on her own. In either case, Chloë's spotty memory was very concerning.

Between Cassandra and Blanche, they managed to lift Chloë up so she could drink the bitter potion. It caused Chloë great pain but she fought it, drinking down the brew with quivering lips before being lowered back to the bed. Her watering eyes overflowed as she lay still upon the mattress, eyes closed, lips shaking.

"I want Keir," she whispered, tears trailing down her temples. "I want him here, with me."

Cassandra stroked her head. "Kurtis went to fetch him," she murmured. "He will be here soon."

"When?" Chloë breathed.

Cassandra looked up at her mother as she replied. "Kurtis left for him four days ago," she told her sister. "He should have already found him by now and I am sure they are on their way back. You must have faith, Chloë. Keir will be here."

"My lady," the physic was trying to get her attention, standing at the base of the bed. "Will you move your toes for me, please?"

Shaken, disoriented, Chloë gazed at the strange man fearfully. "Why?"

"Please do it."

As the man tossed off the coverlet, Chloë wriggled her toes. The physic sighed when he saw the movement, looking to Lady Blanche.

"Praise the saints," he said. "She is able to move her toes. That is a good sign."

Blanche was visibly relieved, displaying perhaps the most emotion her girls had seen in quite some time as she put her hand on Chloë's head in a comforting gesture.

"Thank God," she whispered.

Having no real idea why everyone seemed so relieved, Chloë kept wriggling her toes, eventually moving her legs about. But the movement brought pain in her torso so she stopped moving around. Everything on her body hurt at the moment, from her head to her knees, so she simply stopped moving and closed her eyes, feeling the drag from the physic's powerful potion pull at her.

"Cassie," she whispered. "Please... I want Keir."

Cassandra kissed her cheek. "I promise he will be here soon."

Chloë faded off, into the painless realm of sleep. When Cassandra was sure she was asleep, she looked up at her mother.

"What do we do?" she hissed. "If Keir cannot return, what do we do?"

Blanche lifted a thin eyebrow. "I would stake my life on the fact that the man will return, Cassie," she said. "My bigger concern, however, is Ingilby. We sent him a missive agreeing to his terms. If Chloë does not remember coming to Aysgarth, then I doubt she remembers the missive from Ingilby. I must seek counsel from Lord Coverdale in this matter."

"Not father?"

Blanche waved her off. "The man is too foolish to give sage advice. This was proven by his decision not to allow Chloë to marry Keir before he went to Wales. You stay with your sister while I attend Coverdale."

Cassandra watched her mother as the woman swept from the chamber. Feeling fearful and sad, her gaze moved back to her sister, lying so still and pale upon the coverlet.

The situation with Chloë did not seem to be improving.

CHAPTER TWENTY-FOUR

KEIR WAS STONE-FACED as they cantered along the road that would take them through the small village of Corwin on the Welsh Marches and straight on to the road to Wrexham. From Wrexham, it was a matter of hours to Chester. It was the road that the Army of the North had taken from Chester into Wales and the road that Michael had taken to find Keir. The Marches was a wild place and few roads traversed the mountains region. This one was the road most traveled.

They had been riding hard since mid-morning, when Keir had emerged from the keep of Dolwyddelan with an expression that suggested had had just emerged from an argument with the devil. He had promptly ordered his charger saddled and upon collecting his gear, rode swiftly from the castle.

Michael, riding hard beside him, deduced what had happened. Keir was clearly upset, silently riding as if to put great distance between himself and the Army of the North. Moreover, Lucan had been left behind, which would not have happened unless Keir had been forced to make a decision based upon his emotions and not his orders. Lucan was left behind so he would not get caught up in Keir's disobedience. The man could plead ignorance to Keir having disobeyed a direct command.

So they rode hard, like madmen in flight, thundering along the rocky road and hoping the chargers didn't come up lame from the bad terrain. The weather had cleared from the nasty storm that had blanketed the area for the past several days, so they didn't have to deal with rain or wind. The roads, however, were muddy and difficult to pass.

They continued for the rest of the day, passing through the burgh of Corwin towards sunset and continuing on even after that. They had already paused twice to rest and feed the chargers, big beasts that functioned on great mouthfuls of wet grass, and as the sun set to the west and a blanket of stars came out in the night sky, the horses were growing weary again. Michael's charger was beginning to bleed from the mouth so they reined the horses into an easy trot until they came to the next village.

Llangolen was a fairly large town, one that inhabited the Welsh Marches to the east of the Cambrian Mountains. There was one massive street that ran through it, the Street of the Church, and no less than five taverns lining the avenue. There were probably more that they didn't see because there seemed to be a lot of drunk people walking through the street, disappearing down alleyways or into other taverns.

There was light and music wafting into the dark night, and Keir and Michael dismounted their weary chargers in front of one of the larger taverns. They tethered the beasts and scoped out the area before moving into the tavern, Keir inspecting the room as they walked through the door and Michael covering their back. It was usual when they traveled together that they were on high alert. Trouble was everywhere, especially for men who carried weapons.

Keir went straight to the barkeep and demanded that their horses be tended. The barkeep, a big man with long, thin hair on his balding head, barked at a boy who was working in the kitchen behind him, and the lad bolted from the structure and out into the dark night. As the boy ran off, Keir ordered a meal for himself and Michael.

Michael was already wandering the main room of the tavern in search of a suitable table. It was full of people, drinking and eating and laughing. A blazing fire belched smoke and sparks into the room. Michael found a table near the door where a pair of traveling merchants sat, promptly kicking the men from the table and confiscating it. He tossed the remainder of their meal onto the floor, waving Keir over.

More exhausted than he would admit, Keir removed his gloves, slapping them down to the tabletop as he kicked a chair away from the table and lodged it up against the wall. He sat heavily, pulling off his helm and peeling his hauberk back so he could scratch his scalp.

Serving women began to swarm the table, bringing wine, brown bread and slabs of mutton in gravy. Keir set the helm down next to his gloves and poured himself a healthy measure of wine.

"When did you eat last?" Michael asked as he poured his own wine.

Keir simply shook his head, his handsome face stubbled and weary. "I cannot remember," he admitted. "It seems like years ago."

Michael smiled faintly as Keir drained half his cup in one gulping swallow.

"I heard during my travels that your army took a sound beating north of Harlech," he said. "I cannot imagine that you have had much rest during the past several days."

Keir sighed with exhaustion. "The Welsh were waiting for us," he muttered. "Five days of hell just north of Harlech, struggling to make headway so we could make it to the castle. We were boxed in and never budged, at least not until I convinced de Lacy that we needed to call a retreat. Then, and only then, did the Welsh decide to let us go. That is why you found us at Dolwyddelan, licking our wounds."

"So Harlech is in trouble?"

"From what we know, she has been badly compromised with a very long siege."

"Where is Edward?"

Keir wriggled his eyebrows. "We have sent messengers out, hoping to slip past the Welsh, but I have not heard anything as of yet. The last we knew, Edward was moving up from the south to aid Harlech. It is quite possible that he met the same resistance we did."

Michael took a healthy drink of wine before following Keir's lead into the food. They tore off great hunks of bread as they delved in to the meat.

"How was Chloë when you last saw her?" Keir asked, his mouth full.

Michael's mouth was also full. "She was well and happy," he replied. "However, I will say that she misses you a great deal. After you left, it took her almost four days to get out of bed. She was quite emotional."

Keir sighed faintly, with regret. "She is a very emotional woman," he said. "She put on a brave front the day I left, for my benefit I am sure, so I am not surprised to hear she suffered after I had left. I suspected she would. I suffered, too, although I had no bed to crawl into. I miss her so much that I feel it in my very bones. There is not one minute of one day since we have been apart that I have not longed for her."

Michael shoved bread in his mouth as another serving wench brought a great bowl of boiled carrots to their table.

"I thought that the missive from Ingilby might send her back to bed again, but surprisingly, she was very strong about it," he told Keir. "She seemed very resolute and determined to do what she felt best for you and for Merritt. Kurtis had a devil of a time keeping her at bay."

Keir shook his head, feeling some frustration. "My brother is weak when it comes to women," he said. "He will let Chloë do as she pleases, afraid to upset her if he protests."

"He most definitely protested," Michael countered firmly. "Do not have any doubt for a moment that your brother was not quite upset about Chloë's determination. He was furious."

Keir seemed to be drinking much more than he was eating, already well into his second cup of wine. "Tell me more about the missive," he said. "Who delivered it?"

Michael started in on the carrots. "One of Ingilby's men, who we promptly threw in the vault," he replied. "The missive was read in the presence of Coverdale, Lord de Geld, Chloë, Cassandra, Kurtis and myself. Ingilby was clear in his demands. Chloë made her decision to comply but everyone fought her on it, including her father. But your betrothed would not be convinced. Even now, I am positive your brother is sitting on the woman to prevent her from doing anything foolish until you arrive. He is probably counting the minutes."

"Does Chloë know I am coming?"

"Aye."

Keir sighed heavily again, drained his cup, and poured himself another. Michael watched him take big swallows from his third cup of wine.

"Eat something," he shoved the trencher at him. "You will be useless if you drink too much and we still have many miles to go yet before we are at Aysgarth."

Keir lifted an eyebrow at him but refrained from a snappish retort, knowing he was right. He set the cup down and stabbed his knife into the mutton, bringing it to his mouth.

"It was bad enough being separated from her," he muttered, his mouth full. "Now with this... how in the hell would Ingilby simply come across my son? I am so confused that my brain is threatening to burst in all directions. But I do know one thing; it seems all too damn convenient for my taste."

Michael shrugged. "I asked Ingilby's messenger about that."

"*Asked* him?"

Michael gave him a knowing look. "Well, perhaps a bit more than ask. Kurtis beat him soundly and then I asked."

"What did he say?"

"Very little, I am afraid. He simply said that Ingilby found the boy but would not elaborate. I took him to the vault before your brother could pound him again. A dead man can tell us nothing."

Keir was still chewing on the tough mutton. "So we are led to believe that Ingilby, a man who has ravenously pursued Chloë for two years, finds out she is betrothed to me and now, suddenly, he has my son and wants to use him in a trade? Chloë for the boy? How did he know about Merritt in the first place?"

Michael shook his head. "As I told you before, I do not know," he said. "Ingilby's messenger was not forthcoming with information."

"Is he still in the vault at Aysgarth?"

"Indeed."

"Then I will see this man when I arrive and find out what he knows. He will be very sorry he did not speak with you or Kurtis. It would have been much better for him if he had."

Michael knew that. "He cannot tell us anything if he is dead," he reminded him quietly.

Keir ignored him, sopping up gravy with his bread. "Damn Lady de Geld for sending out those wedding announcements," he mumbled. "This is her fault. What did she think was going to happen when Ingilby found out that Chloë was betrothed? Did she think he was simply going to bow out like a chivalrous man? God's Beard, the man was willing to raze a castle to get to Chloë. How did she think that madman was going to react?"

The wine that Keir had so quickly imbibed was going to his head, making his manner loud and agitated. Michael shoved more carrots in his mouth.

"We shall be at Aysgarth in four days, God willing," he replied. "Hopefully we will have more answers at that time."

Keir continued with his food while Michael slowed down and focused on his drink. As they ate and drank, lost to their own thoughts, the door to the tavern opened to admit a big, older knight and a lovely young woman with long dark hair. Michael's attention was drawn to the young woman as the knight perused the room for a quiet table.

"My, my," Michael murmured. "What have we here?"

Keir glanced up, seeing the big knight before ever noticing the young woman. He perked up.

"That is de Moray," he said. "I have not seen him in quite some time."

"De Moray?" Michael cocked his head thoughtfully. "I have heard that name but I cannot place it. Who is he?"

Keir was already on his feet. "Baron Ashington," he replied. "His seat is Ravendark Castle far to the south in Dorset. They used to call his father The Gorgon. Have you not heard of the de Moray family? The whole clan has built a reputation on the tournament fields. They are related to Baron Lulworth of Chaldon Castle."

Michael nodded at his faint recollections. "I seem to remember my father speaking of The Gorgon when I was young," he said. "I think he said that the man was invincible on the tournament field."

"So is his son," Keir held up a hand to the man and his daughter. "De Moray!"

The big knight turned around and all Michael could see was black eyes set within a tired, weathered face. But the features warmed in recognition of Keir and the man smiled faintly as he collected the young woman next to him and made his way to Keir's table. He was a very big knight with very big hands, evidenced as they rested on the lady's slender shoulder.

"St. Héver," Garran de Moray greeted Keir amiably. "I thought you would be dead or in jail somewhere by now. How is it I find you here on the Welsh borders?"

Keir grinned. "I have just come from Wales," he told him. "There is nasty business afoot there. Edward had need of me."

Garran lifted a dark eyebrow; he was an older man with black hair streaked with gray. "It is the one time I thank God that I am too old to fight any longer," he said. "The king has seen enough of my sorry hide. Now he has younger, stronger men like you to do his fighting for him."

Keir simply smiled, nodding, his attention inevitably turning to the young woman in Garran's grasp. De Moray looked at her as well.

"I do not believe you have met my youngest daughter," he said. "This is the Lady Summer de Moray. Summer, this is my old friend, Keir St. Héver."

The Lady Summer was a slender girl with dark hair and big green eyes. She was quite pretty as she smiled modestly and curtsied crisply.

"My lord," she said. "It is a pleasure to meet you."

Keir smiled in return. "And you, my lady," he replied, indicating Michael to his right. "This is Sir Michael of Pembury."

Lady Summer turned her gaze to Michael and went through her practiced curtsy again. "My lord."

Michael was gallant. "My lady," he greeted. "Your name is quite lovely and quite unique."

Summer presented the very picture of a proper young woman, very graceful and practiced in her speech. "I am named for my grandmother," she replied. "Her name is Summer also."

Michael's interest in the young lady was evident. "Lovely," he said, meaning both her and the name. Keir shot him a rather quelling glance and Michael took the hint. He indicated the table. "Will you both sit? Keir and I were just finishing our meal but we would welcome your company."

Garran pulled out a chair for his daughter, seating her before accepting the chair that Keir handed him over his head. Garran set the chair down next to Summer and plopped his bulk upon it.

"So," he wearily removed his helm. "Where have you been keeping yourself, Keir? The last time I saw you was in Chippenham, about a year ago. Do you recall?"

Keir nodded, returning to his drink. "I do," he replied. "At the tournament they held celebrating the fall harvest."

Garran didn't stand on formalities; he helped himself to the bread and handed some to his daughter.

"You did not compete," he cocked his head thoughtfully. "You were with Coverdale's men."

Keir nodded faintly, thinking on that particular time. "I did not," he agreed. "I had not held a lance or sword in a couple of years and did not want to injure myself or someone else. I attended to give support to my comrades."

Garran's dark eyes appraised Keir, remembering something he had heard at the tournament, whispers from the knights about Keir St. Héver's misfortune with his family and the true reason behind his refusal to compete. Tournaments, if nothing else, were ripe fields for gossip.

"I seem to remembering hearing of the loss of your wife," he said, his deep voice somewhat softer. "I did not have the opportunity to convey my sympathies. I have lost a wife, Keir. I know what it feels like."

Keir didn't want to get sucked into the grief that had so keenly healed since the introduction of Chloë. At the mention of Madeleine, he felt the sorrow, certainly, but not the stabbing pain normally associated with the subject. Now, it seemed more like a dull ache, the remnants of an unpleasant memory. He realized that it did not crush him to speak of it, a shocking realization indeed.

"My thanks," Keir said softly. "As with all things, life goes on. I am betrothed and anticipating marriage once again. I am quite happy for it."

Garran's dark eyebrows lifted. "Congratulations, my friend," he said. "Who is this fortunate young woman?"

Keir smiled. "The Lady Chloë de Geld," he replied. "Her father is Anton de Geld of Exelby Castle. My brother has married her sister."

Garran smiled as well. "May God bless you, my friend," he said. "May you have many fine sons to carry on your name."

"And daughters," Summer piped up, laughing softly when the men snickered at her. "There is nothing wrong with having girls as well."

Garran hugged her gently. "Of course not, sweetling," he glanced playfully at Keir as he spoke to her. "I learned that the hard way."

Summer scowled at her father. "What do you mean by that?"

Garran was laughing at her expense. "As a man with four sons, I was content to demand dowries for other men's daughters," he said. "Then, my last child is a daughter and I find that I am on the wrong end of the marital contract. Why do men demand such high prices for marriage?"

Keir and Michael chuckled as Summer simply shook her head. "It is punishment for all of the one-sided contracts you negotiated for my brothers," she told him. "You will probably have to pay a fortune to be rid of me."

Garran nodded, still looking at Keir and Michael as he spoke. "She is truthful," he made a face. "My daughter is brilliant and opinionated. I will be made poor trying to marry her off because no man wants a wife who is smarter than he is."

Keir laughed, downing more wine, as Michael countered the statement.

"Her beauty is a fine enough prize for any man," he said sincerely. "Any man would be honored to have her."

Summer beamed modestly as Garran looked interested. "And you, Pembury?" he was exaggerating his manner simply to be funny. "Are you speaking for yourself?"

Caught, Michael grinned, glancing at Keir and trying not to look embarrassed.

"I cannot confirm or deny your question," he said, locking eyes with the green-eyed beauty. "I am simply making a statement that no man would dispute."

Garran collected a cup to pour himself some wine. "You and I will speak on this later, Pembury."

Keir snickered into his cup as Michael's gaze lingered on the beautiful young woman, a smile playing on his lips. He wasn't quite sure what to say to the man that wouldn't insult him or his daughter, so he thought it best to keep his mouth shut.

After the sting of losing Cassandra, Michael wasn't so sure he was ready for serious attention towards another woman, no matter how pretty she was. Normally, he saw women as a pursuit, but after the incident with Cassandra, he wasn't so sure any longer. Something inside of him had changed. So he kept silent, drinking his wine as Garran and Keir changed the subject to trivial things. Still, Michael's gaze kept drifting back to Lady Summer.

As the night deepened and the conversation flowed as freely as the wine, the door to the tavern jerked open and a huge gust of wind hurled through. Those near the door pulled their cloaks more tightly about their shoulders to ward off the cold wind. On the heels of the gust came a knight, bulky and heavily armed.

Keir was deep in conversation with Garran but Michael wasn't. He casually glanced up to see who had entered, shock registering on his features when he realized that he recognized the knight. He thumped Keir on the shoulder as he rose to his feet.

"Kurtis!" he shouted.

CHAPTER TWENTY-FIVE

KEIR WAS ON his feet, moving for his brother before he even realized he had stood up. His arms were out, reaching for the man as Kurtis turned in his direction. Before Keir could open his mouth to speak, Kurtis grabbed him.

"You must come with me," he commanded, his voice hoarse with fatigue. "Chloë has had an accident."

Keir must have swayed; he only knew that because Kurtis grabbed him firmly to keep him from falling. Michael was behind Keir, his expression between shock and confusion. It took both Kurtis and Michael to keep Keir on his feet.

"What do you mean?" Michael demanded. "What has happened? How did you find us?"

The questions were coming rapid-fire. Kurtis was looking at his brother as he spoke. He was in battle mode, having ridden for three days straight with little rest. He was exhausted and edgy.

"I happened to be passing through the town and recognized the chargers in the livery," he said. "Praise God that I took this road – I almost took a shorter route through the mountains but the weather was so foul that I did not want to take the chance. De Lara at Beeston told me where you had gone so I hoped to find you, but I could truly only guess which road you had taken."

By this time, Michael had a hand on Kurtis' shoulder because the man appeared ready to collapse himself. Between Keir's swaying and Kurtis' exhaustion, both brothers were about to go down.

"Chloë," Keir grasped at his brother and ended up grabbing him by the neck. "What happened to her?"

Kurtis' ice blue eyes were fixed on his brother. "She fell down a flight of stairs," he told him, not at all gently. "She struck her head. When I left, she was still unconscious. The physic... Keir, the physic believes she might have badly injured herself. You must come back right away."

Keir abruptly yanked away from him, already moving back for the table where his possessions were. He staggered, knocking over another table as he went. He grabbed at his gloves and bags with shaking hands, dropping his bags and struggling to pick them up again. Garran, having heard the entire conversation, reached out to steady him.

"I will get your bags," he said evenly. "Take your helm and gloves. I will have the horses brought to the front. Pull yourself together, my friend. You must remain calm if you are to make it home healthy and whole."

Keir heard him but he lacked the understanding to adequately respond. He was so shaken that he was having a difficult time functioning. As de Moray began barking orders to the barkeep and the servants, Michael grabbed Kurtis and pulled the man over to the table laden with the remnants of the meal. He shoved him down into a chair and then shoved Keir down into another. Both brothers were walking a very brittle and exhausted path, so much so that Michael was seriously worried for both of them. But he was worried for Keir more.

"Chloë was fine when I left," Michael said as Lady Summer poured wine for Kurtis. "What happened? How did she fall?"

Kurtis took a deep breath, gratefully accepting the wine from the pretty young woman. "Truthfully, I do not know," he slurped the wine. "We did not see it happen. All we know is that she fell down the stairs."

Keir was sitting next to his brother, looking pale and sick. "What did the physic say?"

Kurtis looked at his brother, realizing he should probably speak more kindly to the man. He was so upset, however, that it was difficult. Exhaustion had a hand in his inability to control his manner.

"He examined her and said that something was wrong with her

spine," he muttered, his eyes taking on a painful reflection. "God forgive me, Keir. Dear God, please forgive me."

He slumped forward, his face in his hand. Keir's ill expression washed with confusion. "Why? Why do you say that?"

Kurtis was verging on tears, unusual for a man who was perpetually in control of his emotions. "Before... before she fell, we were discussing Ingilby's missive and I was telling her how foolish she was for having sent a reply to the man."

Keir stiffened. "She sent a *reply* to him?"

Kurtis nodded. "Her mother told her to. I did not know about it, Keir, or I swear I would have never allowed it." His head came up and he looked between Keir and Michael. "I would assume Michael already told you of Ingilby's proposal."

Keir nodded. "He told me. He also told me of Chloë's plan." He suddenly sat back in his chair, snorting with the most painful irony imaginable. "So she replied to the man without your knowledge?"

"Aye."

"With her mother's blessing?"

"That is what I was told."

Keir stared at his brother for a long moment before shooting to his feet, kicking the chair out from under him and sending it smashing into the wall.

"Where in the hell were you?" he bellowed, jabbing a finger at his brother. "I left you in charge of her, Kurtis. Where were you when all of this happened?"

"I stayed with her as much as I could, Keir, but even I need to sleep."

"I would have done better had I left Ingilby in charge of her!"

Kurtis knew he deserved the lashing but he still tried to defend himself. "I did my best, Keir. I could not be with the woman all day and all night, never sleeping, watching her every move. Moreover, I cannot control her mother. The woman has the last word in all things."

"I trusted you!"

"Blame her mother if you must blame someone, for I did all I could. I swear I would never knowingly disappoint you."

Keir began throwing things around in his grief, smashing a couple of chairs as the patrons of the inn began to scatter. Garran pulled his daughter out of the way as Keir put his fist through the wooden shutters that had been closed over the large front window. Wood exploded in all directions.

Keir stood in the window frame as splinters rained down on him, hanging against the window, half in and half out of the tavern. It was beginning to rain again, light droplets pelting his face. After the initial explosion, he was suddenly still, feeling every raindrop like the thousands of knives of anguish piercing his heart.

"My sweet God," he breathed. "What has she done? Chloë, what have you done?"

Kurtis was on his feet, standing behind his brother. "She thought she was sparing you from making a heart wrenching decision," he offered, not sure if it would be well-met given his brother's state of mind. "She did not believe it was fair to expect you to make the choice between her and your son, so she thought to make it for you. She thought she was doing what was best for you."

Keir had heard the same thing from Michael. With a heavy sigh, he pulled himself out of the window frame and turned to his brother.

"I would choose Chloë," he said hoarsely. "I know that sounds terrible, as if I am a terrible father for choosing a woman over my son, but the truth is that I do not even know if the boy that Ingilby has is mine. I very seriously doubt it because the timing of his proposal is too neat, too convenient. Therefore, I will choose Chloë until I know more about this mysterious child that Ingilby claims is my son. I will not believe it until I see the child's face."

"And then?"

Keir cocked an eyebrow. "And then I keep Chloë by my side while I negotiate for my son. If Ingilby will not negotiate, then I will do what I must in order to regain my son, up to and including razing Ripley

Castle. Make no mistake, I will have my son and my vengeance as well, and Ingilby will rot in hell for having tangled with me."

Kurtis knew that. But he was also concerned with his relationship with Northumberland and if, at some point, he might be fighting against his brother should Ingilby call on Northumberland for assistance. But he kept his mouth shut, not wanting to cloud the issue. At the moment, he was far more concerned with his brother's mental state.

Without a word, he reached out and gently pulled his brother away from the window.

"Let us eat and rest for a few minutes before we return," he said. "I could use something to eat, to be truthful. I have been riding for three days."

Keir shook his head. "We must leave now. I must return to Aysgarth immediately."

Kurtis sighed wearily. "My horse is spent, Keir," he told him. "I would wager that your horse is as well. Let the animals rest a bit before we drive them into the ground."

Keir hesitated. "But I must...."

Kurtis cut him off. "You will not go anywhere if you kill your horse. Come along now, sit down and let us eat something while we can. An hour will not make a difference."

Keir reluctantly allowed his brother to push him back into his chair, an undamaged one. As Kurtis, Michael and Garran regained their seats, Lady Summer dared to speak.

"Sir Kurtis," she began respectfully. "I know you do not know me, but I am Sir Garran's daughter. My name is Summer."

Kurtis looked at the woman and Garran as if just noticing them for the first time. He smiled weakly at Garran.

"De Moray, you old ox," he muttered. "I have not seen you in some time."

Garran smiled timidly. "I thought the Scots would have hung you by now, St. Héver. You tend to stir them up on the borders, or so I hear."

Kurtis actually laughed. "I do indeed," he agreed, his gaze moving back to Summer. "It is an honor to meet you, my lady. Forgive me for being rude when I first entered the room."

Summer smiled at him. "There is nothing to forgive," she said. "You were busy with other things. However, if you would not consider it too forward, I would like to ask a question."

"Of course, my lady."

She cleared her throat softly, glancing at her father somewhat nervously.

"I heard you say that the Lady Chloë has injured herself," she said. "Forgive me for asking, but I know something of healing arts. I was wondering what her symptoms were."

The smile faded from Kurtis' expression as Garran spoke. "She is a miraculous healer," he assured the men at the table. "There is no one finer in all of Dorset than my daughter. She has vast knowledge of healing."

Kurtis looked at the woman, somewhat hesitant to discuss Chloë's condition. "No offense intended, my lady," he said, "but you seem rather young to have acquired such accomplished skill."

Summer was not offended. "I learned from my mother, who was a very gifted healer, from a very young age. I have been healing since I was ten years of age."

"Believe her," Garran confirmed. "She has a skill that few can emulate. My dear wife, God rest her soul, passed along her talents to our only daughter and Summer has learned well. I would not make such claims if I did not implicitly believe in her skill."

Kurtis's dubious gaze moved between the lady and her father. He trusted de Moray and knew the man would not lie to him. After a moment, he looked at his brother.

"Do I have your permission to discuss Chloë's state?" he asked.

Keir was back to drinking, which only seemed to aggravate his brittle manner. He looked at Lady Summer, at Garran, before replying.

"Go ahead."

Kurtis returned his attention to Summer. "She tumbled down a flight of stairs," he told her. "When we found her, she was unconscious at the bottom. She has a massive bump on her forehead and when the physic examined her, he said she had some kind of injury to her spine. He felt a lump, he said. Beyond that, I do not know any more."

Summer listened carefully. "She was still unconscious the last time you saw her?"

"Aye."

"How long was it since her fall?"

Kurtis shrugged. "An hour, perhaps less."

"And the lump on her head," Summer persisted. "Where was it, exactly?"

Kurtis tried to remember that beautiful, battered face. "Here, I think," he put his hand up to the right side of his forehead. "It was right in front, about the size of a walnut."

"I see," she said thoughtfully. "And her spine; what did the physic say about it?"

Kurtis thought hard to that harrowing moment, realizing it was difficult to remember because he'd had so much more on his mind.

"He said he could feel something out of place on her spine that was causing her great pain," he replied. "He said that it could be bruising and nothing more."

Summer thought on that, realizing that Keir was watching her. She knew it could be any number of things and did not want to give the man false hope, but on the other hand, he looked desperately as if he needed something to cling to. She smiled weakly at him.

"The physic could be correct," she said. "It could be a bruise and nothing more. Furthermore, your brother was only aware of her unconscious state for an hour or so, which could mean nothing at all. She could have easily awoken after he left. There is every reason to believe that she will recover but, of course, I do not know for sure since I have not seen her."

Keir's gaze lingered on her a moment before sighing heavily and returning to his wine.

"Perhaps," he muttered.

Summer could see how distraught he was. She didn't even know the man but she could see that the situation was tearing him apart. She looked at her father.

"Dada," she said. "Perhaps we should return with them to see if I can help the lady. I would be most honored to lend my assistance."

Garran lifted his eyebrows thoughtfully, perhaps reluctantly. "There is no finer healer in the land than you," he looked at Keir. "We would be honored to accompany you home, Keir."

Keir was feeling numb, disoriented. It was difficult for him to think much less make a decision. He knew that Garran meant the offer kindly and he didn't much care one way or the other if they accompanied him back to Aysgarth. He simply wanted to get to Chloë, as fast as possible.

"You are not traveling the borders of Wales for your health," he said. "Surely you have another destination in mind."

Garran shrugged. "We are heading home from visiting my new grandson in Manchester," he replied. "We are in no hurry to return home."

Keir considered the request. "If you wish to come, I am grateful," he said. "But we will ride hard and fast. I will not have time to wait for women or stragglers."

Garran actually grinned. "You have not seen my daughter ride," he said. "She has a leggy warmblood that will outpace the chargers. You will be fortunate to keep up with *her*."

Keir merely nodded, losing himself in more wine and dark thoughts. By the time Kurtis had finished with his meal and the horses had been properly fed and watered, he was quite drunk and quite emotional. Kurtis and Michael were concerned for him but once he mounted his charger, he seemed to come around. He was focused and at least pretending to be lucid.

Garran and Summer joined the knights, Garran with a big hairy charger and Summer astride a long legged horse the color of mud. In the dead of night, the five of them took to the road north, one that would take them through Wrexham, skirt Chester and Manchester, and then head north through York. It was easily a three day ride, one that was too long for Keir even if it took three minutes. His desperation to get to Chloë knew no limits.

They rode hard day and night, through weather that was mercifully mild. By the time they reached familiar lands, Keir was more panicked than he had ever been. He refused to stop, continuing on even when Garran's charger took on a decided limp. All he could see or feel was Chloë, drawing closer to her by the moment, feeling such anguish in his heart that he could not contain it. It was bleeding out of him like blood pouring from a wound.

About an hour out of Aysgarth, the tears came. Tears were still streaming down his face when he entered the bailey of Aysgarth, the familiar haven of Coverdale's empire.

He was sobbing by the time he entered the keep.

CHAPTER TWENTY-SIX

CHLOË WAS VAGUELY aware of movement. Someone was holding her hand and she could hear soft whispers. Someone was speaking to her, gently and lovingly, and for the longest time she thought she was dreaming. Mist covered her mind, making thought and focus cloudy. Emerging from a deep sleep, she realized that someone was kissing her hand.

Keir. She seriously thought she must have been dreaming when she opened her eyes and saw Keir kneeling beside her bed, sobbing softly as he held her hand to his mouth. His eyes were closed, tears all over his face and her fingers. Chloë lay there, watching him, not at all sure that he was real. There was only one way to find out.

"Keir?" she whispered.

His eyes flew open and he looked at her, his ice blue eyes wide with shock. He opened his mouth to say something sweet and meaningful, but the words wouldn't come. Instead, he collapsed against her, his face in the crook of her neck as he wept.

"Chloë, sweetheart," he sobbed softly. "Please… please do not die. I cannot live without you. You are my life."

His warmth and firmness against her told Chloë that he was not a figment of her imagination. She lifted her weak arms, wrapping around his armored bulk as he laid his head against her shoulder and sobbed.

"Who told you such nonsense?" she whispered into his dirty, damp hair. "I am not going to die. I would never leave you."

Keir sobbed for another moment or two before abruptly pulling away, wiping quickly at his face as if ashamed of his outburst. He touched her face, her hair, not trusting himself to speak for a moment.

All he could do was touch her and reassure himself that she was alive.

"I could not stay away," his lips were quivering as he spoke. "Neither God nor king could keep me away from you at this time. I... I feel like my entire life is fragmenting, the pieces of the grace I have known with you now transforming into horrid, mortal grief. I survived Madeleine's death only by sheer necessity but with you, I could not survive. I would not want to. If you die, I die. I will not be without you."

Weakly, Chloë put her hand against his bearded cheek and he kissed her palm eagerly, reverently, tears from his face dampening her flesh. She shushed him softly.

"And I will not be without you," she murmured. "I have no intention of dying, Keir."

"Promise?"

"I do."

"I love you, sweetheart."

"And I love you."

Keir kissed her hand, her cheek, caressing her fingers and struggling to compose himself. He began to realize that he had charged into the room without regard for anyone else in the chamber, as his sole focus had been on Chloë. He had been blind to all else. Now, he was coming to realize there were others in the room, watching his breakdown.

He wiped at his eyes, taking a moment to look around. Cassandra was standing a few feet away, sniffling softly in her husband's arms, as Blanche and an older man Keir did not recognize stood near the foot of the bed. He focused on Blanche because he knew she would tell him the truth.

"How is she?" he half-demanded, half-asked.

Blanche, ever-present sewing in her hand, moved in Keir's direction. Her expression was surprisingly gentle having witnessed one of the more touching things she had ever seen in her life. She would not have imagined a man like Keir St. Héver to have such emotion in him, but in retrospect, the man knew what it felt like to grieve. He had done it before. Blanche felt a good deal of pity for the man.

"She has taken a bad fall," she replied. "The physic does not believe there is any permanent damage, but the truth is that her memory has been poor since the fall and she cannot stand. The physic believes that time will heal these issues."

Keir's attention jerked back to Chloë, his eyes wide. "You cannot stand?"

Chloë gripped his hands tightly. "My legs are a bit weak," she admitted. "It is difficult to walk."

He almost dissolved into tears again. "Have you tried? What I mean is, how *much* have you tried? Perhaps it is only a matter of regaining your strength."

She touched his cheek when she saw his eyes watering again. "Mother is not entirely correct," she said. "I can stand somewhat, but not for very long. It is walking that is the difficulty. My legs feel very weak."

He closed his eyes, tears running down his cheeks again. He pressed his mouth against her hands, absorbing the news, struggling not to succumb to the grief.

"It is of no matter," he whispered, forcing bravery. "I am here now and I will help you. We will walk and walk until your legs are no longer weak. And if you cannot regain your... well, it is of no matter. I am here now and I will never leave you again. I consider it a privilege to carry my beautiful bride in my arms for the rest of my life. It is of no consequence, Chloë. Either way, I am here and will never leave your side, not ever."

She smiled at him, touching his face again while he kissed her hands, her cheeks, eagerly. As they lost themselves in reacquaintance after days of separation, Michael timidly entered the room.

He had been standing in the doorway with Lady Summer and Garran, watching the tender scene. It had been difficult to watch it and not feel a great deal of sorrow for the pair, and for Keir in particular. The man had known much sorrow in his life. He came up behind Keir quietly.

"Keir?" he cleared his throat softly. "Lady Summer has come all this way to see to Chloë. Will you allow this?"

Keir was holding Chloë's hands to his mouth, smiling at her as he whispered words no one else in the room but Chloë could hear. He heard Michael's softly uttered question and turned to the man.

"Of course," he said. His voice was hoarse from weeping as he wiped the last of the moisture from his eyes and stood up. He looked over to Garran and his lovely daughter. "Please, come in. I did not mean to be rude."

Garran and Summer stepped into the chamber, Summer passing a lingering smile at Michael as they did so. In fact, Michael and Summer had ridden together most of the trip north and Michael had been respectful but obviously attentive to the woman.

Usually, he could be quite aggressive when he wanted something, but not this time. Whether it was because of the woman's enormous father or because he felt a genuine and sincere respect for her, Michael could not be sure. All he knew was that she was sweet and gentle, and he responded in kind. When she smiled at him, Michael broadly smiled back.

Summer reached the bed, gazing down at the very pale, very beautiful young woman with an enormous mane of dark red hair. She smiled timidly as Keir rolled through introductions.

"Lady Chloë de Geld, this is my old friend, Sir Garran de Moray and his daughter, the Lady Summer," Keir looked down at Chloë. "Lady Summer is a miraculous healer. When she heard of your accident, she asked permission to examine you. Perhaps she can help you."

"That is not necessary," the old physic at the foot of the bed found his voice. "I have tended the lady since her fall. She does not need another physic."

Keir's expression turned to stone. "I will say who tends Lady Chloë and who does not," he growled. "Keep your mouth shut or I will throw you from this keep."

The old man looked stricken but did not argue, looking to Blanche for support but being met by an emotionless expression. He backed away as Summer came to the edge of the bed.

"Greetings, my lady," she said to Chloë. "I understand you have done battle with a staircase."

Chloë grinned; she could already tell she liked the woman simply by her manner and the tone of her voice. She was young, perhaps her own age or even younger, with long black hair and soft green eyes. She was also very pretty. Chloë felt much more comfortable with her than with the gruff old physic from Aysgarth.

"So I am told," Chloë said. "Truthfully, I do not remember much. It seems to be coming back to me in pieces."

Summer went to remove her cloak. Keir extended his hands to politely help her, but Michael was suddenly there, all but snatching it out of Keir's hand. He was insistent that he alone help the lady, in any fashion. Keir stepped away, without a fight, when he saw Michael's challenging expression. He had to suppress a grin.

Summer didn't notice any of the male posturing going on behind her as she sat on the edge of the bed, visually examining the greenish lump on Chloë's forehead. She then removed her leather gloves and lifted her hands.

"May I examine you, my lady?"

Chloë nodded. "Be careful of my head," she said. "It is still rather tender."

Summer's warm, delicate fingers moved around the bump. "I have no doubt," she said sincerely. "You took a hard knock. And you say your memory has been poor?"

Chloë nodded faintly, feeling the woman's soothing hands on her head.

"At times," she said quietly. "My memory over the past several days has been vague. I did not remember that Keir had gone to Wales but last night, suddenly, I remembered that he had gone. I remembered the battle of Exelby, and of meeting Keir and traveling to Pendragon, yet I still do not remember much about coming to Aysgarth but it is coming back to me bit by bit."

Summer felt Chloë's forehead for a moment longer before, satisfied, removing her hands.

"I do not feel any damage other than the lump," she said. "I do not feel any cracks in your skull. I would guess that your memory should fully return. Does your neck pain you?"

Chloë nodded again. "A little."

Summer drew in a thoughtful breath. "That is to be expected but if there was any serious damage, you would be getting worse, not better." Her gaze moved down Chloë's body to her legs. "You say you have weakness in your legs?"

Chloë struggled to prop herself up on her elbows. Keir saw what she was doing and knelt beside the bed to help her. Chloë smiled gratefully at him as he propped her up.

"Aye," she replied. "It is exhausting to stand and difficult to walk."

"Is there pain?"

"A little. Mostly in my back and hips."

Summer thought on that a moment before standing from the bed. She turned to Keir.

"My lord," she said. "I would like to more closely examine Lady Chloë but I will not do it with an audience. Will you please clear the room so I may preserve the lady's modesty?"

Keir nodded sharply, snapping his fingers at Michael and Kurtis, who were already herding Cassandra and Blanche from the room. The women protested but did as they were asked. Keir focused on the old physic, who didn't seem to think the orders to clear the room pertained to him, and snapped his fingers sharply at the man, pointing for the door.

In a huff, the old man swept from the chamber. When everyone had cleared the room save Keir, he turned to Lady Summer.

"May I stay?" he asked politely.

"Please," she replied.

Keir shut the door quietly, ignoring the collection congregated in the landing outside. A host of curious and insulted faces were looking at him but he shut the door to block them out. He returned to the enormous bed just as Summer pulled back the coverlet.

"Stand up, my lady," she commanded softly. "Let us see what you can do."

Chloë looked a little fearful but dutifully began to move. Slowly, she swung her legs over the side of the bed but Summer put out a hand to Keir when he moved in to assist her.

"Nay, my lord," she told him. "I want to see what the lady can do on her own. Only then will we know the true extent of her injuries."

Keir nodded reluctantly, crossing his big arms over his chest with his hands tucked into his armpits as he fought the urge to help Chloë. It was difficult for him to watch her struggle and not move in to assist.

Chloë was pale and exhausted by the time she swung her legs over the side of the bed. She was also trembling; both Keir and Summer could see it. It took Chloë three tries to finally stand on her feet, unassisted, and even then she could not maintain her balance for more than a few seconds. She fell backwards on the bed before struggling to her feet a second time. It was very hard to watch.

Summer was gentle with her. "Can you take a step, my lady?"

Shaken and struggling against tears, Chloë nodded. She was staring at her feet, her face down so that they would not see the tears in her eyes. She took one halting step, and then a second. By the time she took her third, she was sobbing softly and Keir looked at Summer.

"Please," he begged quietly. "Let me help her. Can you not see how it pains her?"

Summer held out a quieting hand to silence him as she focused on Chloë. "Where is the pain, my lady?" she asked steadily.

Chloë was trying very hard not to break down. "My... my back," she whispered tightly. "The pain runs from my back down my hips and legs."

"Do you feel any numbness?"

Chloë shook her head, the unbrushed red hair settling around her shoulders. "Nay," she gasped as she took a fourth and fifth step. "No numbness. I can feel everything."

"So it is the pain that makes it difficult to walk, not the lack of feeling?"

Chloë nodded, biting off more sobs. Yet, she still continued to walk, very laboriously and haltingly. Summer watched her take another few steps before looking at Keir and motioning for him to go to her. He did, swiftly, and scooped Chloë up into his enormous arms. She wrapped her arms around his neck and wept quietly into his shoulder.

Summer watched the pair, thinking a great many things at that moment. She could feel the love and devotion radiating from them like a great palpable thing. But more than that, Summer was thinking on Chloë's symptoms and the causes. She had seen such things before and was fairly confident in her assessment.

"Sir Keir," she indicated the bed. "Please put her back to bed."

Keir, pale and watery-eyed, did as he was told. He lowered Chloë down to the mattress, smoothing her hair comfortingly as she wiped the moisture off her face and looked to him for reassurance. The both of them turned to Summer expectantly.

Summer approached the bed. "My lady, will you be so kind as to lay upon your stomach?"

Chloë appeared both fearful and confused. "My stomach?

"Aye," Summer replied. "Do you need help to accomplish this?"

Chloë shook her head hesitantly. "I think I can do it myself. I will try."

She shifted around stiffly but didn't make much progress. Summer eventually moved to the other side of the bed and between her and Keir, they managed to put Chloë onto her belly. The shift she wore was of fine linen, soft, and Summer immediately put her hands on Chloë's lower back and began to feel around.

Keir watched her with a mixture of fear and anticipation. "What are you doing?" he asked.

Summer was focused on Chloë's back. "I am trying to feel her spine to see where the swelling is, and how much of it there is."

Keir accepted the reply, kneeling beside Chloë and putting a great hand on her head. He stroked it tenderly, smiling at her when she looked at him.

"Not to worry, sweetheart," he kissed her forehead. "Is she hurting you?"

Chloë smiled in return, weakly. "Nay," she replied. "She is much more gentle than the old man."

Keir's smile faded somewhat. "He touched you?"

Chloë could see from his expression where he was leading and she softly reassured him. "He had to examine me, Keir. How else was he to know how injured I am?"

Keir understood but he didn't like the idea of any man, even a physic, putting his hands on Chloë. Seeing his cloudy expression, Chloë touched his face with the hand resting near her head. Keir kissed her hand, her forehead again, before returning his attention to Summer's activities.

The dark-haired lady was engrossed in the lower part of Chloë's spine. She caught Keir's attention when she realized that he was watching her.

"I am going to lift her shift so that I can see her injury more clearly," she told him. "You will look away, my lord."

Keir didn't have the strength to argue with her and he didn't feel it was any of her business to know that not only had he seen that part of Chloë's anatomy, but he had done wicked things to it. He simply refocused on Chloë's face as Summer lifted the shift.

When her patient was naked and exposed from the waist down, Summer paid very close attention to the lower spine. She ran her fingers over it and visually inspected the area. She could see green bruising from the lady's waist to the tailbone. There were also bruises on the lady's buttocks and a big black and green bruise on her right thigh. After more poking and prodding, she gently lowered the shift.

"Well," Summer said thoughtfully. "It would seem to me that the physic was correct – you indeed injured your back when you fell. But I believe it will heal in time. The fact that you suffer no numbness tells me that there is no great damage, only bruising. It is my opinion that a good deal of rest, coupled with daily walks, will help you recover completely. As for your head, that too is something time will heal. I do not suspect you will have any permanent damage from your staircase adventure."

Keir looked at her as if he was afraid to believe her. "Are you sure?"

"Positive. She will recover."

Keir closed his eyes with relief and gratefulness. He held Chloë's hand to his lips, eyes still closed as if praying.

"Thank you, my lady," he said softly. "You have no idea how much relief you have given me. I cannot adequately express my gratitude."

Summer smiled as she stood up from the bed and pulled the coverlet over Chloë.

"You already have," she told him. "It is my pleasure to help an old friend of my father's."

Chloë turned slightly as Summer came within her line of sight. "Thank you," she said sincerely. "I feel much better having you examine me."

Summer's smile broadened as she gazed down at her patient. "You are most welcome," she said, sighing after a moment and brushing the stray hair from her eyes. "If you do not mind, now that I have accomplished my task, I would be very grateful for something to eat. We have been on the road for days and…."

Keir was already on his feet. "Forgive me, my lady," he said as he moved for the door. "I should have been more thoughtful. You have proved yourself incredibly durable and selfless in accompanying me from the borders and all I have done is think of my own problems."

Chloë was in the process of shifting to her back. "Have you not taken care of this woman, Keir?" she demanded, although there was jest to it. "How unchivalrous. I suppose you made her ride like the wind just to keep up with you, too."

Keir was at the door, lifting a blond eyebrow at her. "It was I who was riding like the wind to keep up with *her*," he pointed out. "You should see this leggy gelding she rides. I swear the horse has wings."

Chloë giggled softly, looking up at Summer. "He is usually much more thoughtful. I apologize if he put you to any hardship on your ride here."

Summer helped Chloë shift onto her back. "He was considerate and kind," Summer assured her, putting two pillows under Chloë's knees to take the strain off the lower back. "Moreover, he had more important things on his mind."

Chloë cocked a doubting eyebrow. "Somehow, I think you are being kind. I know how the man is when he becomes singularly focused. He is blind to all else."

By this time, Keir had opened the door. He rolled his eyes at Chloë.

"You ungrateful woman," he muttered, finding Cassandra on the landing outside of the door. He addressed her. "Your sister is going to recover and when she does, I will spank her soundly for her insults. But for now, we would like some food, if you please."

Cassandra half-grinned, poking her head inside the chamber. "Chloë?" she couldn't see her sister from the angle of the bed. "Who are you insulting?"

Chloë grinned up at Summer as she spoke. "Keir," she said. "He has been rude and thoughtless to the woman who has assured me that I will heal."

Cassandra laughed softly, glancing at Keir as she moved for the stairs. Blanche, Kurtis, Michael and Garran were still in the small hallway, with varied degrees of curiosity and anxiety on their faces. Keir opened the door wide to admit them entrance.

"Lady Summer has declared that Chloë will heal and I choose to believe her," he announced. "For now, she requires much rest and daily walks, and I require food, sleep and a priest."

As Blanche went straight to her daughter, Kurtis looked at Keir curiously. "A priest?" he asked.

Keir nodded wearily, finally allowing himself to feel his exhaustion. Now that they had arrived at Aysgarth and he was assured that Chloë wasn't on death's door, he permitted himself the luxury of exhaustion. He hunted for the nearest chair, realizing he was at the point of collapse.

"Aye," he muttered. "I will not leave this place without marrying Chloë. Summon a priest."

Blanche heard him. She turned away from her daughter to gaze steadily at the big, blond knight, now slouched with his hands wiping wearily at his face.

"Sir Keir," she began somewhat hesitantly, an odd manner for the usually confident woman. "There have been some... issues since you left. I was told that you were to be informed. Perhaps we should retire to the solar to...."

Keir looked at her, the ice blue eyes blazing. "I know of these issues," he didn't give her a chance to finish. "I know that Ingilby sent a missive addressed to me to which you inappropriately discovered the contents of, and I furthermore know that you quite presumptively responded to the missive. It was not your right, Lady de Geld, in any fashion, and I take issue with you for having sanctioned the action. Was your husband a part of this?"

He was standing up and growling at her by the time he was finished. Blanche was not intimidated but she did have a healthy respect for the man. She tended to respect men who stood up to her, not cower at her feet like her weak-willed husband. Blanche held up her hand to calm the man.

"Since you left for Wales and the controversy that surround my husband's decision not to allow you and Chloë to wed, he has left all subsequent decision making to me," she said, somewhat softly. "In answer to your question, he was not a part of the response to Ingilby."

"So it was you who took charge of something that was not your right?"

She was subdued. The woman didn't seem at all like the austere, self-assured women he had come to be acquainted with as Chloë's mother. She was quieter somehow, perhaps even timid to a certain extent. Perhaps all of the events over the past few weeks had caught up to her and even she was showing signs of weakness.

"Believe me when I say that it was not my choice," she replied quietly. "Chloë read the missive and believed it was in your best interest for her to make the decision. She did not want you to go through the hell of having to choose between her and your son. She is my daughter, Sir Keir – I agreed to help her because it meant so much to her. She was determined to do it with or without my help and, like you, I cannot refuse her."

Keir cooled somewhat, knowing that what the woman said was more than likely true. He sighed heavily after a moment, with some regret, before moving in the direction of the bed. Blanche reached out to stop him.

"Where are you going?" she asked softly.

"To speak with Chloë about it," he replied.

Blanche shook her head. "She does not remember any of it," she whispered. "She does not remember the missive or agreeing to Ingilby's terms. She does not even remember the part about the boy. I have not mentioned anything to her for fear of upsetting her. We have not yet heard from Ingilby, so I see no need to upset her until we absolutely must."

Keir stared at her a moment before sighing again, this time with great emotion. He ran his hand across his cropped hair, pensive and agitated. After several moments of indecisiveness, he looked at Blanche.

"I will marry her before I leave Aysgarth," he declared. "Ingilby be damned."

Blanche's dark eyes were intense. "But what of your son?"

Keir shook his head. "Ingilby does not have my son," he replied firmly. "I would stake my life on it. He is simply trying to gain Chloë by other means, another in a long list of tricks he has used to try and obtain her for his own."

Blanche watched his face, his expression, to see just how serious he was about his statement, but he seemed resolute.

"What if you are wrong?" she wanted to know. "What if he really does have your boy and the child suffers because of your decision? How do you think that will affect your relationship with my daughter? You will grow to hate her."

Keir looked at her as if startled by the statement. "How can you think that?" he hissed. "I would never hate Chloë for a decision I made. Furthermore, I could never hate her under any circumstances. Have I not proved that my love for your daughter transcends all else? She is all to me, Lady Blanche. I am not sure how much clearer I can make that."

Blanche backed off, but it was hesitantly done. She didn't want to see Keir make a rash decision that Chloë would suffer for in the end. For a man who had been searching for his lost son for three years, to deny the possibility that the child was finally found alive did not seem logical. But, then again, men in love were not logical creatures.

"We have already extended an offer to Ingilby," she finally muttered. "What would you have me do?"

Keir's features hardened. "I will marry Chloë immediately and you will send a missive to Ingilby rescinding your offer. Have a marriage contract written up, witnessed and signed, and we shall be done with this madness once and for all."

Blanche nodded, quitting the room without another word. Keir watched her go, as did Kurtis, before the brothers turned to each other.

Kurtis lifted his eyebrows at him. "What do you want me to do, Keir?"

Keir began to unlatch the armor that had been a part of his body for nearly two weeks. "As I said before," he repeated. "Summon a priest. Tell him he is to perform a marriage mass."

Kurtis nodded and quit the room, taking Garran with him, as Keir began to wearily remove his armor. Summer was still next to the bed, speaking softly with Chloë, and a glance over his shoulder showed that Michael was standing in the shadows of the room, watching Summer as she interacted with Chloë.

Keir didn't care if Michael remained, mostly because he knew he couldn't remove him, anyway, so long as Lady Summer remained. Michael was on the woman's scent and there would be no dissuading him.

When all of the armor came off, the hauberk and mail coat ended up in a heap in the corner. Keir lugged his weary, dirty body over to the bed where Chloë lay with her knees propped up to take the pressure off her back. He was more exhausted with every step he took. As the women chatted quietly and Michael hovered in the shadows, Keir threw his dirty, beaten body onto the bed next to Chloë.

Chloë yelped, startled when his significant weight jostled her, looking over to see that the man was on his belly, his face buried in the mattress next to her head. He was absolutely filthy and smelled strongly of dirt and body odor, but it really didn't matter. He was alive and breathing, healthy and whole as when he had left her, and Chloë was content. She reached out to touch his dirty, sweaty head in a sweet and comforting gesture, feeling the satisfaction of finally having him with her again.

However, it was fairly bold for the man to lie down next to her, considering they were not married. She hoped that Lady Summer didn't think too poorly of them, but on the other hand, she didn't much care. They were married body, heart and soul if not by law. Yet that too would soon be rectified.

As Chloë leaned over to ask Keir if he wanted a pillow for his head, he suddenly let out a great snore that set both her and Summer to giggling. The man had fallen instantly, and deeply asleep, and Chloë merely looked at Summer and shrugged.

"Poor dear," she whispered. "He has had a trying day."

Summer smiled, shaking her head as she looked at Keir. "He will sleep for days now that his mind has been eased on your condition." She looked back to Chloë. "Are you comfortable, my lady?"

Chloë nodded. "My back feels much better with the pillows under my legs," she said. "I am so glad you came. You have eased all of our minds considerably."

Summer's smile brightened. "I am glad to help," she murmured. "And now that you are tended, I think that I would like to eat and perhaps sleep just as Sir Keir is doing."

It was Michael's cue to move. He had been waiting for just this opportunity, a chance to speak with Summer again and to be of service. From the shadows, he suddenly pushed himself off the wall and made his way towards her.

"It would be my pleasure to escort you, my lady," he said.

Summer smiled up at the big knight. She was not oblivious to the fact that he had been very solicitous towards her since nearly the moment they met, but she wasn't going to make an easy target for him. She was intelligent and beautiful, and knew her worth. Although Michael was exceedingly handsome and would inherit a barony, as he had boastfully told her, she didn't want to make herself seem too eager to fall at his feet.

"Dare I trust him, Lady Chloë?" she asked, her gaze on Michael. "He seems quite bold."

Chloë giggled as Michael's face fell. "He is trustworthy," she assured the woman. "I would tell you if he was not."

Summer could see Michael's expression brightening again. She reached out and slipped her hand into the crook of his right arm.

"Very well, Sir Michael," she said. "I will permit you to escort me."

Thrilled, Michael escorted her from the chamber, leaving Chloë alone with the exhausted and snoring Keir.

When the chamber door shut softly and the room was abruptly still, Chloë continued to stroke Keir's head tenderly. She had slept so much over the past several days that she was no longer tired, content to watch Keir sleep beside her and listening to his snoring as if it were the sweetest music.

It occurred to her as she gently stroked his head that she might, in fact, be dreaming. She'd had some very vivid dreams over the past few days, so she wouldn't have been surprised if she awoke to find the bed next to her empty.

She wiled away the rest of the afternoon listening to the reassuring snoring of Keir at her side.

CHAPTER TWENTY-SEVEN

INGILBY HAD NEVER been to Aysgarth before. In fact, he'd never even been near it. Although the castle wasn't particularly far from his own residence, it was set in an area not too well traveled and nestled within the lush forests and valleys of Yorkshire.

Ingilby had planned the trip carefully. The culmination of two years of effort was within his grasp in the form of Chloë de Geld and he wanted to make sure that nothing was left to chance. He had chosen his escort carefully and brought along every weapon in his considerable arsenal. The man had come prepared.

The goddess was finally within his grasp.

The rain from the past several days had eased, leaving a wet landscape and bright blue sky in its wake. The roads were uneven and mucky, more so as they neared the rocky terrain of Aysgarth. A gentle wind blew in from the west as they approached the soaring-walled fortress.

Aysgarth sat like the jewel of a crown amongst a scattering of rocky peaks, beckoning with her great gray-stoned walls. The party from Ripon announced themselves to scouts who had been sent out from the fortress. Ingilby wasn't shy about spreading his name, a name that Kurtis received from of the sentries as he packed up his charger for his return to Alnwick. That name sent him running for his brother.

Keir had been asleep all night and into the morning. Chloë, feeling better than she had in days, had risen with the help of her sister as the two of them tried to be very quiet. They soon came to realize that they could whisper in nearly normal speaking tones and Keir slept right through it. He was no longer snoring like an old bear, now flat on his back and spread out all over the bed. He had practically pushed Chloë off at several points during the night.

Keir's breathing was deep and steady and, at one point when Chloë and Cassandra were chatting as Cassandra helped her sister bathe, he groggily pulled a pillow over his head to block out the noise they were making. That set the women to giggling.

The hot water of the bath helped Chloë's back tremendously. Keir slept through the servants lugging the tub into the room, through the water splashing, through Cassandra helping her sister scrape off weeks of dirt and wash her abundant mane of hair. The scent of lilacs filled the air from the soaps and oils the women were using. He slept through Chloë being dried off, the tub being lugged out, and through the general commotion it created. Through it all, he slept. But he did not sleep through his brother.

"Keir!" Kurtis burst into the chamber without knocking.

Keir's head shot up as both Chloë and Cassandra startled. The women were perched in front of the hearth, using the heat to dry Chloë's hair. Cassandra dropped the comb in her hand and it bounced across the floor.

"Kurtis!" she yelped. "Are you mad to burst in here like that?"

Kurtis didn't even acknowledge his wife, going straight to his brother instead. Keir was already sitting up, wiping his hands over his face to shake off fifteen hours of sleep.

"Get up," Kurtis snapped softly. "You must come with me now."

Keir rubbed the sleep from his eyes, although he was alert. "What is the matter?"

Kurtis didn't even look at the women. His expression was intense. "Not here," he hissed. "Get dressed and come with me."

Keir almost questioned his brother again but thought better of it. From the man's expression, it was serious indeed. Kurtis was not the excitable type but he was most certainly excited at this moment, and not in a good way. Keir stood up from the bed, looking around for his tunic.

"By the window," Chloë said helpfully, suspecting what he was looking for. "I had it washed for you."

Keir smiled at her, appreciatively, as he moved to the drying frame by the window that held his tunic. Chloë watched him closely as he pulled the dark blue linen over his head.

"Where are you going?" she asked, hoping Keir would tell her what Kurtis would not.

He smoothed the tunic over his broad chest, looking for his boots and struggling to shake off the grogginess.

"My brother has need of me," he said evenly. "I will not be gone long."

"May I come?"

Keir looked at her. "How do you feel?"

She shrugged. "Better than I have in days," she said. "I am sure it has everything to do with your return."

He smiled in response. "How is your back?"

"It hurts, but the warm bath helped. May I at least walk with you wherever you are going?"

Keir found his boots and sat on the edge of the bed to pull them on. "Nay," he said, pulling on the first boot. "You will remain here and rest. I will return for you shortly and we shall go for a walk."

Chloë didn't argue but she did gaze at him with big, sad eyes. "Promise?"

"Of course I do." Keir yanked the other boot on and stood up, moving to Chloë to kiss her swiftly on the lips. "You will stay right here and rest for now."

She nodded seriously. "Aye, Keir."

He kissed her again, winking at her as he made his way to the door. "That is my good girl."

He followed Kurtis from the room and the door shut behind them. Out in the landing, Keir grabbed his brother's arm as they moved for the stairs.

"Now," he hissed, "what is so important that you would drag me from a dead sleep?"

Kurtis' jaw was set. "Ingilby has arrived."

Keir's brow furrowed in disbelief, then lifted in flagrant surprise. He almost stumbled on the stairs in his shock.

"Ingilby?" he repeated, incredulous. "*Here?*"

Kurtis grabbed his brother to keep him from tumbling down the steep stairs. "Aye," he said ominously. "I was packing my charger for my return to Alnwick when the sentries took up the call. Ingilby announced himself in a big way and I told the sentries to deny him entrance until Lord Byron gave the word. Then I came for you."

Keir's eyes were wide with astonishment. But just as quickly, the fire of fury began to burn, so hot that Kurtis could see the sweat popping out on his brother's brow. Keir's pace down the narrow stairs quickened.

"He is here to claim his prize," he growled. "He is here in response to the missive Chloë and her mother sent."

"What will you do?"

Keir's jaw was ticking so furiously that Kurtis was sure his brother was about to break his jaw. It was a struggle for Keir to keep calm, knowing why the man had come.

"Did you send for the priest as I asked?" Keir queried through clenched teeth.

Kurtis nodded. "I did," he replied. "The man arrived a couple of hours ago. I did not want to wake you so I put him in the knight's quarters for rest and food until you awoke."

They had hit the entry level and could hear voices in Lord Byron's solar off to the left. Keir grabbed his brother by both arms.

"Go get that priest and bring him to me," he hissed. "I will marry Chloë this instant and there is nothing that Ingilby can do about it. She is mine, body and soul, and I will kill the man if he presses his suit."

Kurtis's expression was serious. "It may come to that."

Keir's jaw began ticking again as he pushed past his brother. "I know," he muttered.

Keir entered Byron's solar as Kurtis quit the keep. It was warm, almost overly, in Coverdale's solar as Byron, Anton and Blanche huddled in a small group near Coverdale's massive table, quite clearly in conference until they saw Keir. At the sight of the massive knight, Coverdale pushed his way through Anton and Blanche, making his way towards the knight.

"Keir," he said, some trepidation in his voice. "I am glad you are here. There has been a...."

Keir put his hand up to silence his liege, struggling not to become furious with the mere sight of Blanche.

"I know that Ingilby has arrived," he said flatly, his gaze moving pointedly to Blanche. He couldn't help it. "I also know the man has no claim. He must be turned away immediately."

Blanche responded, attempting not to appear too intimidated. "Chloë and I sent him a proposal, Sir Keir," she said evenly. "It is a legal offer."

Keir shook his head strongly. "It is not," he countered firmly. "Ingilby's missive was sent to me and by rights, only I am allowed to read it and negotiate any terms. You and your daughter took matters into your own hands, matters you had no right to negotiate, therefore making your offer null and void. Surely you realize that."

"He believes he is here to negotiate in good faith," Anton said weakly, trying to support his wife's actions. "The sentries said he has brought at least two hundred men with him."

Keir's brow furrowed at the man's weak stance. "And you are afraid of two hundred men?" he asked, incredulous. "I have fought two hundred men myself and have emerged without a scratch. We have almost a thousand men housed here at Aysgarth. What on earth are you afraid of?"

Anton backed down. He was uncertain in his dealings with Keir, a much stronger personality, and had no desire to butt heads with him. When Anton looked away, Keir turned back to Coverdale and Blanche.

"I will go to the gate and explain to Ingilby what has happened," he told them in a tone that left no room for dispute. "My lady, you will attend me when I do this and recant your offer so he understands. As we speak, my brother is escorting a priest to Chloë's bower and I will marry her before the hour is out. We will be done with this once and for all."

Coverdale and Blanche passed concerned glances but said nothing. Keir stood there a moment, glaring at the both of them as if daring them to contradict him, but no one dared to speak on the subject. Finally, Coverdale put a hand on Keir's shoulder.

"We should make preparations for all possibilities," he said seriously. "Ingilby will undoubtedly not take kindly to this. Moreover, I doubt anyone has had the opportunity to tell you that we are holding one of his men in the vault. He will more than like be demanding the man's release."

Keir eyed him curiously. "Why are you holding him?"

"Because he delivered Ingilby's missive regarding the exchange of Chloë for Merritt. Kurtis was so incensed that he nearly killed the man before Michael was able to remove him to the vault."

Keir stared at Coverdale a moment, eventually scratching his head in thought. "I do not want anything of Ingilby here after this day," he grumbled. "Turn his man back over to him and let us be done with this. I do not want to give Ingilby any excuses to return to you, me or Aysgarth. Let us rid ourselves of him once and for all."

Coverdale agreed. As he and Keir swung into action, Blanche and Anton regrouped around Coverdale's enormous table, softly speaking of the course their future was about to take.

❦

"WHAT ARE YOU looking at?"

Cassandra heard her sister's soft question, turning away from the lancet window that overlooked the bailey of Aysgarth. She had been mostly looking for her husband but had instead spied a small army amassing outside the gatehouse.

"I am not sure," she replied. "There seems to be a great many men outside of the gatehouse. I wonder who it could be?"

Chloë was seated near the hearth, where she had been ever since emerging from her bath. It felt better to sit up, as her back had been warmed and greatly eased by the bath. In fact, she felt brave enough to stand up and slowly make her way towards her sister.

Cassandra turned around when she heard the shuffling, concerned as she saw her sister slowly making her way to the window. She rushed to help her but Chloë waved her off.

"I can do this on my own," she insisted, huffing through the pain radiating down her back and legs. "I must learn."

Cassandra pulled her eager hands back but they hovered around her sister just in case the woman faltered as she made her way to the window. When Chloë reached the long lancet window, she gripped the wall for support and inhaled heavily of the cool breeze.

"Everything smells so wonderful," she sighed, smiling as she took another deep breath. "The world is right and new this morning."

Cassandra watched her sister, suspecting why everything seemed so marvelous this day. "It does," she fought off a grin," and I am sure that Keir's appearance has nothing to do with it."

Chloë looked at her sister, giggling. "Of course not," she teased. "Why should it?"

Cassandra laughed softly, her gaze finding the gatehouse and the collection of men outside of the walls. "It should not, I agree," she said, her smile fading. "But I would still like to know why all of those men are collecting outside of the gatehouse. I wonder if they came with Keir?"

Chloë saw the large group of men as well, soldiers that were armed and two provision wagons from what she could see. "He would not have left them outside of the walls," she replied. "He will return soon and I am sure he will tell us."

Just as she spoke, there was a soft knock on the chamber door. Cassandra made haste to open the panel to reveal the small figure of

Lady Summer.

"Good morn to you," Summer said to Cassandra. "I came to see how your sister is faring."

"Lady Summer," Chloë was partly blocked by the bed from where she stood near the window. "I am over here and I am faring very well."

Summer came into the room as Cassandra wriggled her eyebrows. "She is very well because Keir has returned," she smirked. "The man can work miracles by his mere presence, apparently."

Summer grinned as she and Cassandra made their way over to the window where Chloë was standing. Summer looked the woman up and down; clad in a lusciously soft blue shift with her amazing red hair freshly washed and cascading down her back, she looked like an entirely different woman. There was color back in her cheeks and lips, and she looked positively radiant.

"Well," Summer put her hands on her hips as she inspected her. "I see that you did not require my attention at all. Apparently the only medicine you needed was Keir."

Chloë laughed softly. "That is not true," she insisted. "Your diagnosis worked wonders. I feel so much better today."

"Good," Summer returned her smile. "How is your back?"

"Stiff but manageable. I sat in a warm bath and it helped a great deal."

"Have you gone for a walk yet this morning?"

"Not yet."

"Then perhaps you can show me this beast of a castle. A walk in the morning air would do you good."

Chloë lifted an eyebrow, glancing outside to the busy bailey and the army gathering beyond the closed gates.

"I am not sure we should," she said. "Keir said he would return for me and we would walk."

Summer looked out of the window as well because the other ladies were. All she could see were horses, men and animals.

"It would be best to walk while you are feeling up to it," she suggested. "I fear if you lay back down to wait for Sir Keir, you may stiffen up and it would be painful. Perhaps we shall take a very short walk now to keep your muscles loose and you may take a longer walk with Sir Keir when he returns."

Chloë didn't see anything wrong with that and neither did Cassandra. Donning a heavy blue brocade surcoat with magnificent gold trim and gold tassels to secure it around her slender waist, Chloë held out her feet while Cassandra put her hose and shoes on. She still couldn't bend over. With her glorious hair long and flowing down her back, she held on to Summer and Cassandra as she quit the chamber.

It was very slow going down the treacherous stairs and Chloë took her time, holding on to Cassandra and Summer as she took one step at a time. When she reached the bottom, she felt as if she had accomplished something, as if those damnable stairs could not beat her again.

Taking the next flight of wider stairs down to the entry level, she was feeling happy and energetic. Too many days of depression and injury were fading away, being replaced by genuine joy and recovery.

"Where would you like to go?" Chloë asked Summer. "There is a stable block off to the left. There are some fine horses if you like that sort of thing."

Summer nodded. "I do," she said. "It will also give me a chance to check on my own horse. I have not seen him since yesterday."

Slowly, they began to move for the entry, past the solar where Anton sat around Coverdale's enormous table. He was tucked back against the wall by the door and did not see his daughters pass. The entry door was open and the ladies stepped through, out into the cool morning sunshine.

The bailey was very busy as they slowly made their way down the stairs. The ground of the ward was soft and moist, but not terribly so, and Chloë was able to keep her footing as they made their way to the stable yard. Several horses were out and being tended, including Kurtis' big gray charger. Summer and Cassandra had a tight grip on Chloë as they made their way to the stalls.

"My father has fits when I ride my horse," Summer said. "He is a tremendously large animal but as tame as a kitten. I have raised him since birth."

Chloë was concentrating on not slipping in any horse droppings as she walked. "You must like horses a great deal."

"I do," Summer admitted. "It all started when I was very young with a white pony my father gave me and my love of horses has only grown from there. I have even raised a few to race, but my father thinks it is unseemly for a woman to race horses, so he races them under his name. The horses have won him a good deal of money."

Chloë and Cassandra looked at her. "Racing horses?" Chloë repeated. "An impressive hobby. Your talents and interests do not seem to be usual, Lady Summer."

Summer grinned, somewhat embarrassed. "I realize that," she said softly. "But I am who I am. No one can change that. Being the youngest of five children, and with four older brothers, I have been exposed to manly pursuits more than most. I suppose their influence greatly shaped my views of the world."

Chloë grinned at her. "I like that," she said. "Will you teach me what you know about good horses? Perhaps I will want to race them, too."

Summer giggled as Cassandra shook her head. "Keir would never allow it," she insisted.

Chloë cast her sister a long look. "If you do not believe I can bend Keir to my will in any fashion, then you are mistaken. If I wish it, he will move heaven and earth to grant it."

Cassandra made a face at her, prevented from replying when a female dog and her litter of three very small puppies crossed their path. The women fell victim to the cute puppies and soon happy little tails were wagging in their hands. As Chloë and Summer cooed over a pair of cream colored puppies, Garran suddenly emerged from the stalls.

"I thought I heard your voice," he said to his daughter as he approached. "What are you doing here?"

Summer had her hands full with a happy licking pup. "I am walking with Lady Chloë," she told her father. "We are taking a short walk to help her back."

Garran knew what was happening at the front gates; every man at Aysgarth knew, and he was very concerned that the ladies were out of the keep, unaware. He hadn't expected to see them. He went to his daughter, opening up his enormously wide wingspan and waving his arms in the direction of the keep.

"Go back inside," he told them. "It is not well for you to be out here right now."

Three innocent and ignorant faces looked back at him. "Why not?" Summer asked.

Garran lifted his eyebrows at her. "No questions," he barked softly. "Turn around and go back inside. Make all haste."

He was waving his arms in the direction of the keep, as if trying to herd animals, so the women put the puppies down and turned for the keep. Chloë was still moving slowly and stiffly, and Summer and Cassandra gripped her from both sides as they walked her back across the stable yard. Garran followed close behind to make sure they did as they were told. His daughter, often, did not.

Clouds were staring to gather overhead, big puffy gray and white clouds intermingled with the brilliant blue sky. The cool breeze was kicking up as they crossed from the stable yard into the bailey, now thickly gathered with soldiers and their frightening equipment.

Curious, and slightly apprehensive, the women picked up the pace as much as they were able to make their way back into the keep. Just as they neared the stairs, Keir emerged from the lower level of Aysgarth with another man. He had the tall, dark stranger by the arm as two soldiers followed behind him, heavily laden with weapons.

Chloë paused on the bottom step when she saw Keir, her heart leaping in all directions at the sight of him. He looked so strong and tall and proud. She smiled and called to him.

"Keir!" she waved an arm.

Keir came to a halt at the sound of her voice, his gaze scanning the compound until it came to rest on Chloë. She was either coming out of or heading into the keep; he could not be sure. But he did know that he was furious and greatly concerned to find her outside. He let go of Alphonse, the man he was releasing back to Ingilby, and took a couple of steps in Chloë's direction.

"Go back inside this instant," he commanded. "I told you to stay to your room."

Chloë's face fell and her cheeks flushed a bright red. "I... I am sorry," she offered, terrified at the look on his face. "I was walking... that is, Lady Summer and Cassandra are walking with me. My back feels much better... I was not attempting to deliberately disobey you."

Keir's jaw flexed furiously and it was a struggle to keep his temper down with her. "Chloë, I am sorry if I am sharp with you," he said with strained patience. "But I told you to stay in your room and rest. Had I wanted you to come outside, I would have told you to. Go inside this instant. I will talk to you later."

He seemed so harsh and impatient. Chloë wasn't used to him speaking to her in such a fashion. Crushed, she lowered her gaze and moved to do his bidding. But she didn't move fast enough.

Alphonse, standing alone with two sentries a couple of feet behind him, had only seen Chloë de Geld once, on the day he delivered the missive. He'd been hearing tale of her for two long years but had only seen her the one time. After she had heard what was in the missive, Alphonse didn't expect to see her again. He was stunned to hear the big blond knight utter her name. He realized his luck immediately. If Alphonse was one thing in life, and one thing only, he was an opportunist. And at the moment, he saw a great opportunity.

He had spent days in Aysgarth's dark and horrid bottle dungeon, a place crawling with damp and moss and furry creatures that nibbled his feet when he slept. He was angry and edgy from his treatment. He also knew that a stroke of grand luck had presented itself with the appearance of Chloë de Geld, the woman on whom so many lives hinged, including his own. Alphonse knew that his reward would be great should he present her to Ingilby. For him, the opportunity must not be wasted. He had to take the chance.

He threw an elbow back into the nearest sentry, smashing the man in the nose. As the man dropped his weapon and fell back, Alphonse swooped down and picked up the sentry's fallen sword. He turned it on the second sentry as the man brought his blade up and stabbed the sentry in the neck. With the second guard down, he turned for Chloë.

Keir was already rushing at him but he swung the sword at the man, catching him across his unprotected chest. A bloody gash slashed through Keir's tunic but he was undeterred as he swiped his arms at Alphonse, who barely managed to evade him. Keir's momentum took him in one direction as Alphonse raced in the other, heading directly for Chloë.

The women had seen what had happened and shrieked with fear as the dark and dirty prisoner ran towards them. Garran, standing behind the women, was unarmed but threw himself forward to protect them. He tried to push them up the stairs, away from the escaped prisoner, but Alphonse was fast. He plowed his sword into Garran's gut, barely stopping to pause as he pulled the blade free and ran at the hysterical women.

Meanwhile, Keir had gained his footing and his momentum, racing after Alphonse but being stopped by Garran. Gored, the man collapsed forward and blocked Keir's path. Keir was forced to leap over his wounded friend, slowing his movement.

The three women were trying to make their way up the stairs but Chloë could not move very fast. Cassandra and Summer had her by the arms, dragging her, as Alphonse mounted the stairs behind her and in a brutal move, grabbed her long and luscious hair and yanked her backwards.

Chloë screamed as she fell back, right into Alphonse's waiting arms. The sword came up to her neck just as Keir mounted the steps.

"Come no closer," Alphonse barked, the blade lodged against

Chloë's slender white throat. "Another step and I will kill her."

Keir didn't outwardly react. The knightly training took over, the professional persona, and he remained cool and calm. He stood a few steps below Alphonse, his ice blue eyes riveted to the dark Spaniard. He didn't dare look at Chloë, terrified that he would see pain and horror in her eyes and he would be unable to control himself.

"Drop the sword," he rumbled. "You will not make it from this place alive if you do not."

Alphonse didn't budge. He held the blade against Chloë's neck, feeling her panicked breathing against him. His left hand was wound up in her incredible mane of hair, holding her fast.

"You will permit me and the lady safe passage or she will not make it from this place alive, either," he told him. "Safe passage is the price for her life."

Keir lifted an eyebrow at him, seeing movement at the top of the stairs in his peripheral vision but making no move to focus on it. He didn't want to tip his hand to Alphonse that something might be going on behind him.

"I was in the process of escorting you to your liege," he said evenly. "You already had safe passage. Taking the lady hostage was unnecessary and a mistake that will cost you your life."

Alphonse smiled thinly, tightening his grip on Chloë. "You cannot threaten me, St. Hével," he said in a low voice. "You will back away now. Do it or the lady will suffer."

Keir took a slow step back and then another, his eyes on Alphonse. They never wavered. He could hear Chloë weeping softly with fear but he never took his eyes off the enemy. He could see movement behind Alphonse, drawing closer, but he kept his gaze fixed. Oblivious, Alphonse pulled Chloë down the steps with him.

Chloë yelped when he twisted her torso due to his grip on her hair, the pain in her back radiating. Alphonse pulled her to the bottom of the stairs and she struggled to get her footing, crying out when he jerked her roughly and caused more pain. Keir backed away, seeing the figure moving down the stairs towards Alphonse in his periphery. He was starting to feel some hope until Alphonse caught sight of the figure as well.

Quickly, he whirled to see Michael bearing down on him with sword drawn. Alphonse was forced to release Chloë as a substantially larger man attacked him and, very quickly, he was in a fight for his life.

Chloë screamed as Alphonse stepped on her in his quest to escape Michael's flying sword. Keir bolted into action, racing to her and pulling her out of the way as Michael and Alphonse engaged in a brutal sword battle. But Keir wasn't particularly concerned about that. He was only concerned with Chloë and swept her into his arms, carrying her up the stairs to the keep as the deadly sounds of a sword fight played out behind him.

He entered the cool, dark keep and the sounds of the battle faded, being replaced by Chloë's soft sobs. Only then, when he was sure she was out of danger, did he slow his pace and speak.

"Are you alright?" he asked, his voice trembling. "Did he hurt you?"

Chloë wept softly, her hands on his face, kissing his cheek as her tears wetted his face.

"Nay," she murmured. "He did not hurt me overly. I am well enough. But your chest…."

She was reaching out to get a look at the gash across his torso but he stopped her, kissing her hands. "It is not as bad as it looks," he assured her. "Come now, let's get you away from this chaos."

Chloë's last vision of the ward was of Garran bleeding on the ground and Michael in mortal combat. It was seared into her brain.

"But we cannot simply leave them," she was pointing to the keep entry. "You must go and help them."

Before Keir could reply, they came across Cassandra and Summer, standing in the solar door near the stairs. Both women were weeping and, upon seeing Chloë, their weeping resumed in chorus. Keir set Chloë on her feet when the woman tried to reach for her sister. As Chloë and Cassandra threw their arms around each other, Summer grasped at Keir's arm.

"My father," she was trying very hard not to sob. "He is injured. I must...."

Keir nodded quickly, cutting her off before she could finish her sentence.

"I shall go to him now," he assured her, heading back for the keep entry. "You will all go inside the solar now and bolt the door. Do not open it for anyone but me, Michael or Kurtis. Is that clear?"

"But...!"

"*Go.* That is not a request."

Shaken but understanding what he was telling her, Summer and Cassandra helped Chloë into the solar and slammed the heavy oak door. As Keir bolted out of the keep, he could hear the heavy iron latch being thrown.

Outside was much as he had left it. Michael and Alphonse were still hacking at each other, only Michael obviously had the upper hand. Alphonse's hands were bloodied where Michael's sword had nicked him, causing blood to splatter on his tunic. They were cornered over by the wall that separated the stable yards from the rest of the bailey, the sounds of their fight echoing off the old stone.

Keir's focus was riveted to the pair for a moment before he looked around to assess the rest of the damage. A few soldiers were over helping the pair of escorts that Alphonse had injured while still more were bent over Garran, who was lying supine on the ground. Keir went for his old friend immediately.

Garran was in a bad way. He was bleeding profusely, his hands over the gushing torrent from his gut, about three inches above his pelvis. His face was devoid of color as his dark eyes met with Keir.

"I am afraid that my time has come, Keir," he said softly. "It appears that I will not live to see my daughter wed."

Keir wouldn't give into the grief. He couldn't. He moved to picked Garran up by the shoulders as he motioned a few other men to help him.

"You are not dead yet," he said flatly. "Your daughter is a miracle worker. She will tend you and you will heal."

Garran grunted in pain as four men picked him up and headed for the stairs to the keep.

"Not this time," he grunted. "Already, I can no longer feel my legs. It is my time."

Keir opened his mouth to reply just as Kurtis, followed by a slender man in dirty ecclesiastical robes, emerged from the stable yards. Kurtis looked at Garran, at Michael and his opponent over by the wall, and scowled with confusion. He raced over to his brother.

"What in the hell is going on?" he demanded. "What happened to...?"

Keir cut him off. "Go and help Michael dispatch that fool," he barked. "When you are finished, come and find me. We have business to attend to." He looked over at the rather shocked young man in the brown drape. "You, priest! Come with me."

Kurtis moved in Michael's direction as the priest leapt to do Keir's bidding. Between Keir and the three soldiers, they managed to get Garran up the stairs and into the keep. Keir was already bellowing for the women to open the solar door as he entered the stone structure so by the time they reached it, the panel was wide open.

Inside the stuffy room, Cassandra and Coverdale were clearing off Coverdale's enormous oak desk while Anton, startled by the chaos, was pressed back against the wall in stunned silence. He just stood there as Keir and several soldiers lay Garran upon the big desk. Summer rushed to her father's side.

Blood was already staining the desk beneath his big body and dripping to the floor as Summer pulled away the tunic and cut through the top of the hose. She was surprisingly calm, having dried her tears to focus on her task. She wasn't hysterical by nature, and that innate calm took over her demeanor. She could see that her father was cleanly gored in a very vital area and if she didn't gain control of the bleeding quickly, all would be lost. She began rattling off orders.

"I need my medicament bag," she said evenly, although her voice was trembling. "I also need rags, or linens, anything to stop this bleeding. Please, I need it quickly."

Coverdale fled. They could hear him hissing at his servants as men moved swiftly to do his bidding. As Summer and Cassandra struggled to stop the life from draining out of Garran, Keir grasped Chloë by the arm.

"Come with me," he ordered softly. Chloë looked at his face, seeing he was in command mode, but before she could open her mouth, Keir motioned to the thin man in the dirty robes hovering near the door. "You, Priest – you will marry us immediately."

The young man with bad skin and a bald head came away from the wall, rather confused and fearful. "A-as you say, my lord," he agreed. "But I do not have any of my...."

Keir cut him off. "Do it now. That is not a request."

The priest looked between Keir and Chloë with big, startled eyes. "*Now*?"

"Now. This very second. Can I be any plainer about it?"

The priest could see that that no one was in the mood for questions or propriety. In fact, he was a little disoriented at the swift falling of events, having been summoned by a big knight yesterday only to end up at Aysgarth where confusing things were taking place – sword battles in the bailey and a big man laying upon the table in the solar, bleeding to death. Aye, odd forces were at work here. Perhaps it was best he do as he was told and be done with it.

"Do we have the lady's parents present?"

Both Chloë and Keir looked over to their left where Anton was still pressed fearfully against the wall. Chloë pointed.

"That is my father," she said.

The priest waved Anton over. "You are required, my lord."

As Anton forced himself to move around the big desk, he ended up slipping in the blood that was pooling at the base. Recovering his balance, he appeared at Chloë's side with the wide-eyed look of a hunted deer. Keir kept waiting for the man to recover his tongue and protest the wedding, but so far, Anton hadn't made a noise. He remained silent, which was well and good. Keir couldn't guarantee that he wouldn't snap the man's neck if he as much as uttered a negative word.

"Where is Mother?" Chloë asked.

Anton muttered unsteadily. "She went upstairs to rest. Shall we send for her?"

"Nay," Keir barked, his eyes on the priest. "There is no time."

Spurred onward by the demanding groom, the priest made the sign of the cross over Keir and Chloë. "On your knees," he told them.

Keir helped Chloë kneel before he sank to his knees beside her. As the door flew open behind them and several servants race in with the items Summer had requested, the priest looked to Chloë.

"Your name, lady?"

"Chloë Louise Isabella."

The priest then turned to Keir, his silent question obvious. Keir responded in a strong voice. "Keir Kenneth Antony."

The priest nodded swiftly, licked his nervous lips, and launched in to the wedding mass, speaking very quickly.

"Keir Kenneth Antony, wilt though have this woman to be thy wedded wife, wilt thee love her, and honor her, keep her and guard her, in health and in sickness, as a husband should a wife, and forsaking all others on account of her, keep thee only unto her, so long as ye both shall live?"

Keir looked at Chloë, the impact of the moment not lost on him. With all of the terror and chaos that had gone on over the past few minutes, he was starting to realize this was the moment he had been waiting for. Chloë was finally to be his. His ice blue eyes regained some of their warmth as his expression softened.

"With all my heart, I shall," he murmured.

As Chloë smiled sweetly, the priest turned to her. "Chloë Louise Isabella, wilt though have this man to be thy wedded husband, wilt thee love him, and honor him, keep him and guard him, in health and in sickness, as a wife should a husband, and forsaking all others on account of him, keep thee only unto him, so long as ye both shall live?"

Chloë's eyes were swimming with tears by this time. "I will," she murmured. "Of course I will."

The priest nodded before looking to Anton. The man was standing stiffly next to Chloë, looking somewhat pale.

"Do you give this woman in marriage, my lord?" the priest asked.

Anton didn't even look at Chloë or Keir. He simply nodded, once, and the priest continued. "At this time the woman is given by her father," he said, looking to Keir. "You will repeat after me: I, Keir Kenneth Antony, take thee Chloë Louise Isabella to be my wedded wife, to have and to hold from this day forward, for better, for worse, for richer, for poorer, in sickness, and in health, till death do us part, if the holy church will ordain it, and thereto I plight thee my troth."

Keir had a smile on his lips as he looked at Chloë and repeated the words. "I, Keir, take thee Chloë to be my wedded wife, to have and to hold from this day forward, for better, for worse, for richer, for poorer, in sickness, and in health, till death do us part, if the holy church will ordain it, and thereto I plight thee my troth."

He sounded so soft and sweet as he said it and Chloë smiled, tears running down her face. She couldn't take her eyes off him as she repeated her own vows, her voice tight with emotion, watching him kiss her hand as she finished. Finally, the priest raised his hand over their heads and made the sign of the cross once again in blessing.

"Eternal God, Creator and Preserver of all mankind, Giver of all spiritual grace, the Author of everlasting life; Send thy blessing upon these thy servants, this man and this woman, whom we bless in thy Name; that as Isaac and Rebecca lived faithfully together, so these persons may surely perform and keep the vows and covenants betwixt them made, whereof this Ring given and received is a token and pledge, and may ever hereafter remain in perfect love and peace together, and live according to thy laws; through our Lord."

"Amen," Keir whispered.

His eyes closed briefly before turning to his new wife and kissing her sweetly on the lips. There was a great deal of emotion between the two of them, deeper and richer now with the reality that they were truly husband and wife. So much had happened for them to reach this point, and now, it was finally finished. Chloë giggled through her tears as he kissed her again and wrapped his arms around her, hugging her tightly and trying not to move her around too much, knowing her sore back had surely been aggravated by Alphonse's abduction attempt. But he had her in his arms and, God willing, they would never be apart again.

Chloë had her arms wrapped around Keir's neck, holding him, as she heard sniffles behind her. She turned in his arms to see Cassandra standing next to Anton, wiping at her eyes. The woman had paused in assisting Summer to listen to the last few strains of her sister's wedding ceremony and when she saw that both Chloë and Keir were looking at her, she tried to laugh off her weeping demeanor.

"I am so happy for you both," she said, though she was mostly looking at Chloë. "I suppose it is not exactly the wedding ceremony you had in mind, but it is good enough."

Chloë grinned as Keir helped her to her feet, and she embraced her sister warmly. "I could have been married in a stable as long as it was to Keir," she said. "We are man and wife and I care not where it has happened, only that it has. I have never been happier in my life."

As they hugged again, they eventually turned to Anton, who was still standing next to Cassandra. He still appeared pale and drawn, but the startled look had faded from his expression. In fact, he looked rather serious as he gazed at Chloë.

"You are a married woman now, Chloë," he said. "I… I hope you understand that I have always done what I thought was best for you and your sister. If that was not a popular choice, then I would at least hope… well, I suppose it does not matter now. I told you that you could marry Keir if he returned from Wales, and I stayed true to my word."

Chloë's smile faded as she gazed at her father. Something had changed between them over the past few weeks, perhaps a trust that would never be regained. All she knew was that she felt differently about him now. She wondered if it was something that time would heal.

"Perhaps you should find Mother and tell her what has happened," she suggested quietly.

Anton merely turned for the door, heading out into the corridor beyond. He was behaving strangely, perhaps resigned to his daughters' futures, oddly removed from everything. But Chloë didn't particularly care and neither did Cassandra. They hugged again until there was a commotion over on the desk where Summer was trying to save her father's life, and Cassandra rushed to help.

Chloë remained with Keir, watching the activity. Now that the shock of their swift marriage was settling, she began to think of what the future would bring for them all. She turned to Keir.

"What now?" she asked softly.

Keir's jaw ticked faintly, indicative of his emotion as he watched Garran fight for his life. "I will go and tell Ingilby that you and I are married," he said. "I want you to retreat up to your chamber and remain there until I come for you."

Chloë looked at him seriously. "Why is he here, Keir?" she wanted to know. "What was happening down in the bailey? Who was that man who grabbed me?"

Keir looked at her, remembering that her memory was still spotty to recent events and that she didn't recall the missive from Ingilby regarding Merritt and her subsequent response. Blanche had refrained from telling Chloë anything for fear of upsetting her and Keir, too, was unsure how much to tell her. They had hoped they wouldn't have to, hoping her memory would make a full return. She had been through a lot over the past few weeks, today included. Still, it wasn't fair to her to not know everything since so much of it centered around her. Better to be prepared.

"Come with me," he said softly.

Keir took Chloë's hand and led her out of the solar just as Michael and Kurtis entered from the bailey. Chloë's eyes widened at the sight of Michael; he was dirty, exhausted, and had a big cut above his left eye. Kurtis spoke first.

"We... well, well may have a problem," he looked at his brother. "Michael... he took his opponent and...."

"Is Garran dead?" Michael demanded, cutting Kurtis off.

Keir eyed the big knight. "I do not know," he said honestly. "Summer is with him inside the...."

Michael blew past him, heading into the solar where there was much activity around Garran spread out over the big oak table. The priest who had so recently married Keir and Chloë was standing at the head of the table, giving Garran last rites. Keir, Chloë and Kurtis watched Michael go with some concern before Keir returned his attention to his brother.

"What happened out there?" he asked. "Where is the prisoner?"

Kurtis sighed heavily. "Michael gored him," he said. "Then he carried the wounded man up to the wall walk and threw him over the side, directly down onto Ingilby's party. They are screaming for blood, Keir. They are furious."

Keir's brow furrowed. "He *threw* the man from the parapet?"

Kurtis nodded, his gaze finding the open solar door and seeing all of the activity inside as they tried to save Garran's life.

"Vengeance for Summer," Kurtis muttered. "I have never seen Michael so enraged. What he did, he did for her and for no other reason than that. Remind me never to get the man angry again."

Keir grunted, wiping wearily at his eyes as he thought on his next course of action. The situation was going from bad to worse.

"I will speak with Ingilby now," he said, moving past Kurtis. "You will take my wife upstairs and confine her to her room. Stay with her. Under no circumstances is she to leave the room."

"Wife?" Kurtis repeated, his surprise registering.

"Wife," Keir replied flatly. "The priest just married us."

He started to move again but Kurtis stopped him. "Wait," he said.

"Keir, Ingilby has the boy at the gate. He is threatening to kill the child immediately unless Chloë is brought out to him."

Chloë's brow furrowed. "Child? What child?"

Kurtis was looking at his brother as Keir looked furious and sickened. Giving his brother a long look, he turned to Chloë and forced himself to relax.

"Sweetheart," he grasped her arms gently, "I want you to listen to me very carefully and with great calm. What I am about to tell you is important and I need your level head. Can you do this?"

Chloë nodded solemnly but Keir suspected she really didn't mean it. Nonetheless, he continued because there wasn't much time.

"Do you remember when I went to Wales?" he asked.

Chloë was listening intently. "I do."

"How much of that do you remember?" when he could see she had no idea what he meant, he tried to explain. "Do you remember what happened after I left?"

Chloë's brow furrowed as she thought very hard. "I remember that you went to Wales because the king asked it of you," she said hesitantly, as if it might be a trick question. "I... I am not sure what more you could mean."

"Do you remember that Ingilby sent a missive to Aysgarth addressed to me?"

She cocked her head. "He sent *you* a missive?"

"Aye."

"While you were in Wales?"

"Aye."

Chloë's big brown eyes were intense with thought as she struggled to recollect. "Nay," she finally said. "I am sorry, but I do not remember a missive. Why?"

His big fingers caressed her arms as he spoke. "Ingilby sent a missive, addressed to me, that in essence said he had found my son and wanted to exchange the boy for you," he watched her features glaze with shock. "You felt that such a decision would destroy me so you sought to make the decision yourself. You sent Ingilby a missive stating that if the boy was indeed Merritt, you would consent to be his bride."

Her eyes widened. "I *did*?"

"You did. You truly do not remember any of this?"

She shook her head, with great astonishment, and he could see the tears coming. "I do not remember anything," she sniffled. "Does he truly have Merritt"

Keir kissed her on the forehead and gave her a hug, comforting her. "I do not know," he said, realizing that it was a struggle for him to keep a calm head about such an emotional subject. If the boy really was Merritt, he wasn't entirely sure how he would react. He'd never really given it much thought because he was convinced Ingilby was lying. "I am going to speak to Ingilby now to tell him that you and I are legally wed. I will negotiate for the boy if it is indeed Merritt."

Chloë was starting to weep. "If it is him, we must get him back. I cannot believe that Ingilby found him."

Keir cocked an eyebrow. "Nor can I," he said with some suspicion. "In fact, it is my belief that he does not have Merritt at all and that it is another trick to try and obtain you."

Chloë wiped at her eyes, struggling for control. "I want to go with you when you speak with him."

"Absolutely not."

She grabbed him. "Keir, it is me he wants. If I sent him this missive as you say I did, then perhaps he needs to hear from my own lips that I...."

Keir cut her off, turning her for the stairs that led to the upper floors. "Nay, Chloë," he said firmly. "Do not argue with me. Go upstairs and lock yourself in"

She winced when he pushed her a little too forcefully and aggravated her injured back. Keir saw her flinch and he stopped pushing, returning to the comforting husband when he realized that he'd been a bit too harsh.

"I am sorry, sweetheart," he kissed her forehead, rubbing at her back gently. "I did not mean to hurt you, but you will do as you are told. Please. I do not have time to argue with you."

Chloë opened her mouth but her reply was cut off by the sight of her mother, emerging from the upper floors. Blanche's intense gaze fell on Chloë and Keir.

"I will go with you, Keir," Blanche had obviously heard a good deal of their conversation. "Since I sanctioned Chloë's missive, it is only right that I stand with you in this."

Keir eyed the woman as she came off the stairs and went straight to her daughter, carefully pulling her into an embrace.

"Although I appreciate your offer, Lady de Geld, you will understand when I say that I will face Ingilby alone, as Chloë's husband."

Blanche kissed Chloë on the temple and let her go. "Ridiculous," she said evenly. "I am responsible for this situation. Let us go now to resolve it."

By her tone, there was no way Keir was going to keep her from attending him. He just knew it. He grunted with frustration, looking to his wife, who looked rather apologetic for her mother's forcefulness. Without another word to Blanche, he took Chloë by the hand and directed her towards the stairs once more.

"To your chamber," he commanded softly, turning to look at his brother. "Go with her for now, but monitor the situation from the window. Watch me; I may have need of you."

Kurtis nodded sharply, moving to take Chloë by the arm to carefully help her up the stairs. Keir watched Chloë until she disappeared from view, turning for the keep entry only to realize that Blanche was watching him. She was just staring at him, the dark eyes calculating. After a moment, she turned away from him.

"I am satisfied that my daughter has married you," she said, as close to an approval as she could come. "Now, let us get rid of this nemesis once and for all, shall we?"

"Do you really think we can?"

Blanche eyed him coolly. "I think *you* can."

Cocking an eyebrow at the woman, Keir let her take the lead and followed her from the keep.

CHAPTER TWENTY-EIGHT

K EIR HAD NEVER actually seen Ingilby, so when the gate of Aysgarth was opened, leaving the big fang-toothed portcullis as a barrier, Keir wasn't sure who to address. There were a dozen men standing at the gate, all of them in armor, now angrily posturing. In his bloodied tunic and without his armor, Keir came to a halt about ten feet from the portcullis. Blanche stood slightly behind him, partially obscured by the shadows of the gatehouse.

"I would speak with Ingilby," Keir announced in a booming voice.

The men shuffled on the outside of the portcullis, grumbling, shouting to each other, and in the midst of it emerged a tall man in fine clothing. He had blond hair, graying at the temples, rather cultivated-looking, and he focused his blue eyes on Keir immediately. In fact, he even smiled.

"You must be St. Héver," he said.

Keir remained cool. "I am," he replied. "And you are Ingilby."

Ingilby nodded faintly, his gaze studying Keir very closely. "Finally, I am permitted a glimpse of the man who has come between Lady Chloë and me, and now I see why. She must think you quite hand-some."

Keir thought the comment rather ridiculous given the circum-stance, pausing for effect before answering. "So now you have seen me. Is that why you have come? To see if I was more handsome that you are?"

Ingilby, too, stood well back from the portcullis for safety's sake just as Keir was, so in essence, they ended up speaking very loudly to each other, and there were two armies within ear-shot. When Ingilby was finished studying the enormous warrior standing in the shadow of the gatehouse, he crossed his arms expectantly.

"Not entirely," he said. "What happened to Alphonse?"

Keir was factual. "As I was bringing him out of the vault with the intention of turning him over to you, unharmed, he felt the need to injure two men and gore another before taking a hostage. He was properly dealt with."

Ingilby, remarkably, remained cool, which was in stark contrast to the rage he had been in not minutes earlier. The death of Alphonse had him infuriated but the appearance of St. Héver, strangely, calmed him. At least, now he had a look at the man who was standing between him and Chloë de Geld. There was an odd satisfaction in that awareness.

"He was murdered," Ingilby said simply.

"He was punished."

"We could debate this all day."

"Indeed we could, but I am sure that is not your preference. You came to Aysgarth for another reason."

Ingilby dipped his head. "Indeed I did," he replied, an almost conversational mood settling. "I have come to accept the terms of Chloë de Geld's missive. I would like my bride brought to me and I am sure you would like your son delivered to you, so let us move past these trivialities and conduct business."

Keir remained business-like. "Correct me if I am wrong, but the missive that Lady Chloë replied to was, in fact, addressed to me."

"It was."

"She had neither the right nor permission to respond in my stead, making her offer null and void."

Ingilby lost some of his composure. "She has offered terms and I have accepted."

Keir's jaw began to tick but he remained in control. "I would see the boy before we go any further."

"And I would see Lady Chloë."

"The boy first."

"Lady Chloë *first*."

Keir shrugged. "I fear we are at an impasse already, for I will not move forward with anything until I see the boy you allege to be my son."

Ingilby was beginning to lose his cool. He'd come too far and did not take kindly to St. Hével's obstacles. With a grunt of frustration, he motioned sharply to the men around him and Keir could see more shuffling going on. There were voices, men moving about, and in the midst of it he began to hear a soft, frightened voice.

A man suddenly appeared from back in the crowd carrying a child over his shoulder and as he drew closer, Keir could see that the little figure was bound and there was a sack over his head. The soft sounds of fear were coming from the child and Keir felt his composure slip as the child was dumped roughly on the ground.

"Here he is," Ingilby said, rather smugly. "Now, you will produce the Lady Chloë."

Keir crossed his enormous arms, trying not to look too concerned for the softly weeping figure on the ground.

"Remove his hood."

Ingilby didn't reply. He just looked at Keir. After a moment, he moved over to the child, now seated on his buttocks, and kicked the child in the leg. The child screamed and fell onto his side, weeping hysterically.

"Bring me Lady Chloë or I will beat your son to death right before your eyes," Ingilby snapped. "I am finished negotiating. Bring her to me or he dies!"

Keir remained stiff and unmoving, although inside, he was ripe with fury. Before he could respond, Ingilby kicked the boy again and other men joined in, kicking the child as he screamed for mercy. Keir watched with horror for a few long, painful seconds before breaking from his stance and rushing back into the bailey. He began to shout for archers and within seconds, soldiers on the battlements were making tight their bows.

Ingilby and his men heard the call for arms and broke off from the injured boy, running for their lives as the soldiers on the battlements let their arrows fly.

Keir saw that Ingilby's men were scattering. He bellowed for the portcullis to be lifted and as Ingilby's men dispersed and arrows rained down, Keir rolled under the small gap between the portcullis and the ground and scrambled to his feet, dodging a hail of arrows to reach the small boy wallowing several feet away. He heaved the child up around the torso and made a break for the portcullis, which had now paused with about a two–foot gap between the iron teeth and the ground below. It was enough space for one person to slide through at a time.

Keir tossed the child under the portcullis and prepared to follow when an arrow suddenly struck him in the back, followed by a second one in the shoulder near his neck. Keir went down as several of Ingilby's men, with shields slung over their heads, now rushed at Keir from their haven of safety behind several trees. Keir was too injured to fight them off but he struggled to crawl through the portcullis gap as Blanche, having remained silent throughout his exchange with Ingilby, grabbed the man by a hand and labored to pull him under.

The old woman was yelling for help, surprising for the usually austere lady, but these cries were from the heart and soldiers from the gatehouse joined her as they all attempted to pull Keir underneath the portcullis. The majority of his body was outside of the portcullis, unfortunately, and Ingilby's men had a better grip on him as a bizarre tug-of-war ensued.

As the brutal struggle progressed, someone inside of Aysgarth shouted for the archers to cease their fire and more men joined in the battle to pull Keir to safety while Ingilby himself had Keir by a leg, yanking with all his might to pull him in the opposite direction. A couple of Aysgarth archers positioned themselves inside the gatehouse and aimed at Ingilby's men through the portcullis, striking down two of them. Blanche and the other soldiers managed to pull Keir about halfway inside the gatehouse, but someone from Ingilby's side was smart enough to lash a rope around Keir's left ankle.

Before those inside Aysgarth realized what had happened, Keir was suddenly yanked out of their grip and went skidding across the dirt and mud, bouncing down the slight incline and out of their line of sight. Horrified, Blanche and the others rushed to the portcullis to see what had become of Keir, and they could see that someone had tied the other end of the rope to a horse which was now running off with Keir in tow. The last they saw of him, he was being pulled off across the road, plowing through an expanse of grass, before disappearing into a cluster of trees.

Blanche screamed until she could scream no more.

CHAPTER TWENTY-NINE

THERE WAS AN abundance of sorrow within the walls of Aysgarth as morning dawned, an ambience not even the bright rays of a new day could erase. It promised to be a brilliant and beautiful day, but the entire castle had a cloud of doom hanging over it that could not be erased. The walls themselves were reeking with sadness as servants and soldiers alike began to move about their tasks, preparing for the new day.

In the solar of Aysgarth, Garran was still on the enormous oak table, bundled up with woolen blankets as he remained in merciful unconsciousness. Summer had been able to stop the bleeding of her father and repair the wound, but it was unknown if he would survive it. He remained still, barely breathing, as Summer remained vigilant at his side. Her wait was a lonely one because everyone else was occupied with the aftermath of Keir's abduction. So she sat alone, in a strange castle, waiting to see if her father would live or die.

Michael had spent most of the night at Summer's side, but as dawn approached, he had an army to assemble. He and Kurtis were up before dawn, in full battle armor, their breath hanging heavy in the moist, foggy air as they bellowed orders to the troops. Coverdale was with them, supervising, watching the assembly of his great army. The bailey and stables were already busy, moving with a purpose, preparing to pull out as soon as the sun crested the horizon. Today was to be a very big day.

Up in Chloë's bower, it was remarkably quiet because Chloë was finally asleep. She had spent the past several hours in hysteria until Blanche, who was also still deeply upset by what she had witnessed, sent word to Summer for a sleeping draught. Summer had come personally to tend to Chloë, who had worked herself up so much that she was physically ill. Poor Summer, stretched so thin between her father's injury and Chloë's hysterics, gave Chloë a dose of a poppy seed potion that put her right to sleep.

Cassandra crawled into bed with her sister and held her, so very terrified of what was to come. Ingilby now had Keir, and Kurtis was going after him. They were summoning a mighty army to accomplish this, and she was terrified for her husband and for Keir. The entire situation was horrifying.

Loaded to the sky with war machines and implements meant to kill, the army finally pulled out mid-morning, a thousand-man strong and heading for Ripley Castle, about a day's travel from Aysgarth. Kurtis and Michael had ridden at the head of the army along with Coverdale, who had brought his personal entourage, oddly including his wife, quite simply because it was her time to visit him and he didn't want to leave her behind.

Kurtis didn't even say anything to Coverdale about the fact that the man's fourteen year old wife was being brought along on a battle march. He had enough on his mind, the least of which was the fact that he was going to battle against a Northumberland ally. All he could think about was his brother and of what he was going to do to Ingilby when he cornered him. Kurtis' emotions on the subject went beyond rage and into the realm of madness. Ingilby was going to pay, ally or no.

Chloë slept through Kurtis' farewells and the army's departure. The poppy potion did its job well and she slept dreamlessly for a while until visions of Keir began filling her head. His smile and his laughter were the first things she saw and heard, and then the dreams grew more vivid and she could feel his touch or smell his hair. She had no idea how long she dreamt of him because she began to realize that her eyes were open and she was staring at the back of Cassandra's head. The two of them were lying on Chloë's bed and she could hear Cassandra snoring softly. But for that, all was still and quiet.

Chloë lifted her head slightly, seeing that there was no one else in the room. The sun was out but she had no concept of what time of day it was. The events from earlier came flooding back and her eyes misted over with tears when she remembered what her mother had told her about Keir's abduction. He had been wounded trying to save the little boy Ingilby had called Merritt, and then spirited away by Ingilby as he had tried to return to safety.

Wounded. Chloë's entire body ached with grief for Keir's injury and disappearance. The not knowing was the worst part. Was he dead? Alive? She simply didn't know. No one did. All of it was her fault, she knew that. Had she not sent Ingilby a missive agreeing to be his bride, none of this would have happened. She had caused this. Her guilt consumed her.

After the initial avalanche of grief, she began to think very clearly on the situation, as if her initial burst of sorrow had expunged itself and now she felt nothing but resolve. It was all very, very clear to her what she must do, and something she felt no fear of as she reasoned her way through it. Ingilby had come for her but had taken Keir instead – therefore, surely the man would free Keir if she were to exchange herself for his freedom. There was no other choice. It was the only answer.

So she climbed out of bed, no longer the hysterical woman but the determined wife, resolved to free the man she loved. Only a calm head would save Keir and she knew that. Perhaps somehow, in some way, she had grown just a little in the time she had known him. He had helped her mature with his wisdom and calm manner. He had done so much for her and now she had to do something for him. Crying in bed wasn't going to solve the problem. She had to save him.

Silently, she went to the wardrobe crammed with her things and removed a heavy dark blue traveling coat and matching cloak. Swiftly, she changed into the garment and donned heavy hose and leather boots that belonged to her sister. Her thick hair was brushed and braided, a single heavy braid hanging over one shoulder. As she finished with her hair, she caught sight of a slender dagger tucked up with a few scarves and belts. Sliding it into her sash, she finished securing the cloak. Now she was ready to travel, knowing where she had to go and what she had to do. With a lingering look at her sleeping sister, she slipped from the chamber.

Chloë was very conscious about the voices she could hear throughout the keep. She didn't want to run into anyone, afraid they would try to stop her if they figured out what she was up to. Thankfully, Kurtis and Michael weren't around, because they were the nosy sort and would have badgered her into confessing her plans. She only had to deal with her mother and father, and perhaps even Lord Coverdale, but she didn't see any of them.

As she slipped silently towards the keep entry, she passed by the solar and was shocked when she came face to face with Summer, sitting vigilantly by her father's side. Their eyes met and Chloë came to a halt.

"Greetings," she said from the doorway, hesitantly, hoping Summer wouldn't ask her where she was going. Her gaze trailed to Garran and she saw an opportunity to take the focus away from her. "How is your father?"

Summer rose from her chair, looking to her father as she made her way over to Chloë. "His condition is unchanged," she said, trying not to sound too despondent. "He sleeps, but I suppose that is a good thing. Only time will tell if he will indeed survive."

Chloë looked at Garran, lying pale and still upon the desk. It began to occur to her that his injury was her fault as well. Everything was her fault, indirectly though it was. Her guilt grew.

"I am so sorry," she whispered. "I will pray for his recovery."

Summer looked at her, forcing a smile. "Thank you," she said softly, her gaze turning intense as she scrutinized Chloë. "How are you feeling?"

Chloë nodded. "Much better," she said. "I... I was just going for a walk to clear my head a bit."

"Do you feel up to it?"

"I do."

Summer's smile faded. "Michael and Kurtis left a couple of hours ago to rescue Keir," she said softly. "They will bring him back, Chloë. You must have faith."

Chloë struggled not to tear up. "I do."

Summer regarded her as if trying to determine for herself how Chloë truly felt. It was hard to know, for she looked stronger at this moment than she had since Summer had known her. "Are you sure your back feels well enough?"

Chloë nodded. "It does," she said. "It feels much better than it did yesterday. There is still a bit of pain in my hips, but not nearly as bad as it was."

Summer's smile turned genuine. "That is good to hear," she said. "We need some good news around here."

Chloë smiled weakly before reaching out to grasp Summer's hand. "If I have not told you again how much I appreciate all you've done, then please allow me to say so," she said sincerely. "You have done so much for all of us. I do not know how we can ever repay you."

Summer was modest. "I am happy to help where I am needed," she said, a bit of a twinkle in her eye. "Besides, I believe I have already received the greatest compensation I could ever have."

"What is that?"

"A husband."

Chloë's smile brightened. "Michael has pledged for you?"

Summer nodded. "He has declared his love and his desire to marry me. I am sure my father would agree."

Chloë hugged her tightly. "I am so happy for you both, truly," she said. "Michael is a good man. He will make a good husband."

Summer laughed softly. "He will have to," she said. "Otherwise, I have four brothers who will make him wish he was."

Chloë giggled, thinking of Michael against four enraged brothers of the lovely Lady Summer. But as she opened her mouth to reply, she caught sight of a young boy seated over by the hearth. He had been tucked out of her line of sight until this moment, shifting out of the shadow and into the light as he reached for a bit of bread. Summer saw Chloë's surprise, then her interest, and motioned to the child.

"This is young Aust," she introduced him. "This is the young man Keir rescued. Aust, this is the Lady Chloë. Will you please greet her?"

The child, blond haired with big brown eyes, looked at Chloë with some terror. As Chloë moved towards the lad, she could see that one entire side of his face was bruised and one eye was nearly swollen shut. He was sitting on some feather-stuffed cushions with a blanket over his legs, the remnants of a meal on the floor next to him. He genuinely looked terrified and Chloë smiled faintly at the boy Keir had saved. The child was the last act of self-sacrifice Keir had performed and the thought made her teary-eyed, but she fought it.

"Greetings, Aust," she said softly.

The boy swallowed the food in his mouth, struggling not to cry himself. He didn't do well with new people, especially after that band of brutal men had thrashed him. Everyone scared him now.

"G-greetings," he whispered.

"How old are you?"

"I... I am not sure," he sniffled, wiping the tears from the eye that wasn't sore.

Chloë's heart softened for the frightened young boy and she knelt down a few feet away from him, as not to further scare him.

"You are a very big boy," she said gently. "You must have seen at least five or six summers."

He shrugged, calming a little bit with the lady's gentle manner. "I... I think so," he said. "I... I have a dog."

Chloë smiled. "A dog?" she said with glee. "What is his name?"

"Dog."

She giggled. "That is a good name for him," she said, trying to figure out if she could see Keir in the little features. She decided to probe him a little, wondering if Summer hadn't already done the same. "Where are your mother and father?"

That set the child off sniffling again and he wiped furiously at his good eye. "I do not know," he said. "Some men... they took me away from them."

"Do you know where they live?"

"In a town. There is a church there."

Chloë sighed faintly, glancing over her shoulder at Summer to see that the dark-haired woman was gazing at the child with some sympathy. She returned her focus to the boy.

"Do you have brothers or sisters?" she asked.

"No," the boy shook his head. "Just me and Dog."

Chloë wasn't sure what more to say or ask, watching the child as he wiped tears off his cheeks. "I am sorry that you were hurt," she said softly, sincerely. "I promise that no one will hurt you from now on. We will protect you."

The little boy's lower lip trembled. He was so very frightened. "I want to go home."

"Can you tell us where your home is?"

"There's a church there."

He said it as if it was an anomaly when the truth was that nearly every town, large or small, had a church. The child had no idea where he lived. Chloë smiled bravely at him and stood up, making her way over to Summer.

"He said that his name is Aust?" she whispered.

"That is what he told me," Summer replied.

"Is he badly hurt?"

Summer shook her head. "He is badly bruised, but nothing is broken," she murmured. "His body will heal, but I do not know if his spirit will heal. The boy has been terrified and brutalized."

Chloë glanced at the lad with some sorrow. "Poor child," she whispered. "I am not at all sure he looks like Keir. Did Keir even get a look at him?"

Summer shrugged. "I do not know," she replied. "Your mother was there when everything happened. Perhaps she knows."

Chloë didn't want to ask her mother because she didn't particularly want to see her at the moment. Blanche would only ask questions and perhaps even prevent her from leaving the keep. So Chloë merely shook her head again as she inched her way towards the door.

"Whether or not he is Keir's son, we will keep him here until everything can be straightened out," she said. "For now, I have much to think about on my walk."

Summer nodded. "Not too long," she told her, watching her make her way to the solar door. "You do not want to strain your back."

Chloë waved her off as she quit the room and headed for the keep entry. It was sunny outside if not a bit cool as she made her way down the stairs to the bailey, remembering the last time she saw this yard was the day before when the prisoner had so roughly captured her. She looked around, seeing how empty it was with only a few soldiers maintaining vigil, so she wrapped the blue cloak around herself tightly and headed to the stable block.

The stables were empty as well with the chargers removed. There were a few horses and Chloë scurried into the dark, smelly stable in search of a good mount. She knew where Ripon was because she had traveled there a few times with her father, and she knew it was at least a half day's ride on a swift horse. If the army was two hours ahead of her, that didn't give her much time. She would have to ride very fast in order to make it to Ripley Castle before they did. She was genuinely afraid of what would happen if they laid siege and Keir was caught inside. Ingilby would not take kindly to the attempts to regain him. She had to get there before they did.

There was a big, brown leggy gelding that looked as if it was very swift. She seemed to remember Keir saying something about the leggy beast that Summer rode. Perhaps this was her horse, so perhaps he was used to women. There was only one way to find out.

Speaking softly to the horse, Chloë advanced on the animal in its stall, hoping it would accept her enough to allow her to ride it. When the animal seemed open to her advances, she swung into action.

She had a man to save and time was running out.

CHAPTER THIRTY

INGILBY COULD HARDLY believe what he was seeing. In the great hall of Ripley Castle, it was a vision so startling that he literally had to rub his eyes to see, in fact, if it was an apparition. But the vision remained, a stunning beauty resplendent in dark blue with her luscious red hair plaited and draped.

Shocked beyond measure, he had to take a deep breath before speaking, otherwise he surely would have gasped.

"My men told me you had arrived and I nearly slit their throats because I thought they were lying," he said as he entered the big, smoky hall. "I can see that they were indeed telling the truth. The goddess has arrived on my doorstep."

Exhausted, sick with fear and loathing, Chloë faced Ingilby as he came to within a few feet of her. She'd had absolutely no trouble gaining entry to Ripley but now as she was actually face to face with Ingilby, her courage took a hit. That evil, hateful man was standing in front of her and she struggled to maintain her bravery and her anger.

"I came because we have business," she said as firmly as she could. "You are holding Keir St. Héver and I want him released."

Ingilby came to a halt, a myriad of thoughts playing across his features. "St. Héver?" he repeated as if baffled by the request. "You... you did not come because I accepted the terms of your offer? The offer that would exchange St. Héver's son for you?"

"This has nothing to do with that offer. I am here to secure St. Héver's release."

"Last I saw of the man, a horse was running off with him."

Chloë hardened. "Do not toy with me," she snarled. "You took him from Aysgarth. I also heard that he was injured. Where is he?"

Ingilby gazed at her a moment before lifting an eyebrow. He pretended to appear pensive. "If you are speaking of a man who threatened and belittled me, then perhaps I do know where he is."

"Tell me now."

Ingilby's movements turned sharp and almost agitated. "Very well," he replied. "He is in the vault where he belongs. He threatened me and I have every right to protect myself."

Chloë stared at him. During her ride to Ripley Castle, she'd had ample time to think. She knew what Ingilby wanted and she was willing to play the game, all the way to the bitter end. Life without Keir was no life at all and she was willing to do anything she could to win the man's release, up to and including sacrificing herself. Once, he had risked everything to save her. It was time for her to return the favor.

"You will release him," she instructed, leaving no room for doubt that she meant every word. "If you want me as you say you do, then you will do what I say. Release the man or suffer the consequences."

Ingilby's eyebrows lifted. "Pray, lady, you are in no position to make demands, for I have you now where I want you and you will never leave this place."

Chloë was beginning to shake, from both fatigue and emotion. She threw a finger in Ingilby's direction.

"Listen to me and listen well," she said. "There is an army from Aysgarth not an hour behind me. They intend to lay siege to Ripley in order to gain Keir's release and from the size of the army, I have no doubt they will tear this place to pieces. I came because I fear that Keir will not fare well if Aysgarth lays siege so it is my intention to offer myself up in exchange for his freedom. Take me and release him. That is all I ask."

Ingilby stared at her, his brow eventually furrowing as he snapped orders to the men around him, sending them on the run. He suddenly looked very tense.

"An army?" he repeated. "If this is true, you have betrayed them by telling me."

"I am telling you because I do not want any harm to come to anyone," Chloë replied, her guard slipping. "You have been attempting for the better part of two years to obtain me. You laid siege to Exelby, my home, a few weeks ago in order to gain your wants and many men were killed in the process. I do not want to see that again, least of all to Keir. Release him and I shall stay with you of my own free will. Refuse me and I will kill myself in front of you. Is that clear enough?"

Ingilby regarded her, mulling over her offer. He couldn't tell how serious she was. "You truly rode all the way here from Aysgarth, alone, to make me this offer?"

"Of course I did. It was not a difficult ride and the weather held. I followed the army's path, rode around them by sticking to the trees once I found them, and then rode on ahead of them as fast as I could."

He regarded her carefully. "You did not think your scheme through completely. I can hold you and still hold St. Hévér. I have you both now. Did you ever think of that?"

Chloë didn't hesitate. She reached into the sash around her waist and pulled forth the jeweled dirk. The blade gleamed wickedly in the weak light as she brought it to bear on her creamy skin, just below her throat, and pushed. It wasn't hard enough to penetrate deep, but bright red blood streamed and she gasped with pain.

"Release Keir from the vault this moment or I shove it in all the way and there is nothing you can do about it," she hissed. "Do you wish to see my death?"

Ingilby lost some of his confidence and threw out a hand. "Of course not," he said. "God's Beard, do not damage that beautiful breast. If you truly want him released, I will do it. But you will swear to stay with me, Chloë. You have made offers before that were not in good faith."

"I swear I will stay here at Ripley. I told you I would."

"What is St. Hévér to you that you would give up your life for him?"

"He is my husband and I love him with all my heart," Chloë was starting to look very pale as a fairly substantial river of blood streamed down her chest and stained the top of her surcoat. "Let him go right now or you will bury me this night, I swear it."

Ingilby thought she might have been bluffing, but from her expression, he could tell that she was deadly serious. There might have even been a little madness there, but he could not be sure. All he knew was that he finally had the goddess in his grasp and he didn't want to lose her to something as mundane as a suicide. So he snapped at his men and they began to scramble on his order.

"Very well," he held out his hands to Chloë, surrendering, so she wouldn't plunge the blade any deeper. "I accept your terms. I will release him, so do not do anything foolish. Stay calm."

Relieved that the terms were finally accepted, Chloë struggled not to come apart. Still, she kept the dirk in position. She had no intention of lowering it.

"I was told he was injured," she said, turning so that she backed up against the wall near the hearth, fearful that someone might try to come up behind her and disarm her before she could secure Keir's release. "What have you done for him?"

Ingilby watched her carefully. "He was struck by arrows," he replied. "The physic removed them. Other than that, I cannot say what has been done for him. He is a prisoner."

Chloë was becoming incensed. "You did not tend him at all?"

"I do not know what has been done for him, but I do know that his is alive." His blue eyes glittered wickedly. "If I were you, I would not worry over him so much. As long as he is your husband, I cannot marry you, so it would be an easy thing to murder the man and call it an accident. You may want to keep your concern to yourself until he is free and clear of Ripley."

Chloë's blood ran cold at the threat. "If you do that, I will kill myself and you will not have either of us. If your threats are sincere, know that mine are as well."

More of his self-assurance slipped. For lack of a reply that might force her to do exactly as she threatened, he backed off and moved to the big, heavy banqueting table that was planted in the center of the room. He sat heavily, all the while keeping his eyes trained on her as if fearful she would do something truly foolish. He would never get over it if he had her so close but watched her slip away. He could hardly believe two long years had come to this point.

It was an odd standoff for quite some time, Chloë with the dirk to her chest and Ingilby watching her like a hawk. She was exceedingly weary and more than once, the dirk drooped, but she did not drop it completely. She was deadly serious and determined to see Keir released... or die trying.

Time dragged on. It could have been minutes or hours for as well as Chloë's fatigued mind was gauging it. But then came commotion as men shuffled about just out of her line of sight. Some were shouting, orders it sounded like, and Chloë tried not to become too distracted by the noise. She was sure they were preparing for Aysgarth's army and it began to occur to her that Kurtis and Michael might not leave even with Keir's release. She suspected that would not bode well for her if that was the case. At some point, her sore back began to ache and she was having difficulty holding the dirk aloft. Just when she thought she could hold out no longer, men entered through the keep entry.

Startled, Chloë kept her back up against the wall, the dirk pressed to her chest, as several soldiers entered the great hall. They had something between then and it took her a moment to realize it was a body. They dumped it on the floor and it was then that Chloë realized it was Keir. Shock and euphoria bolted through her.

Keir was on his knees where he had been dropped, somewhere over by the end of the banqueting table. He was battered, bloodied and bruised, and his left arm had limited mobility because of the arrow injury to the top of his left shoulder. The arrow that had penetrated his back had thankfully missed anything vital, but the physic had wrapped it up tightly to keep the wound from bleeding.

More than the arrow wounds, being dragged by a spooked horse had afforded him a wide variety of bumps, cuts and bruises, and his left ankle had been sprained as a result of the pulling, but he had miraculously emerged without any serious injury. Considering the speed at which the horse had pulled, he was still amazed he hadn't been gravely injured. Even so, he could hardly walk and it was difficult to stand. But he was alive and thankful for it.

Groggy, injured, he hadn't resisted when Ingilby's men threw him in the vault upon reaching Ripley Castle, and he didn't resist still as they dragged him from the vault and up to the great hall, dumping him rudely onto the cold stone floor. He was fairly certain he was in for another go-around with Ingilby until a figure in dark blue near the hearth caught his attention. His muddled eyes didn't fully grasp the features half-shrouded by the shadows, but the voice that suddenly echoed through the hall brought him, struggling, to his feet.

"Keir!" Chloë cried.

Keir nearly fell over as he tried to stand, but his battered body and bad ankle made that nearly impossible. Moreover, Ingilby's men had hold of him, preventing him from rushing to Chloë's side. His heart was in his throat as he gazed at her, struggling to see her clearly in the dimness.

"Chloë?" he said it as if he could hardly believe it. Surely his mind was playing tricks on him! "Sweetheart… my God, what are you doing here? Are you well?"

Chloë broke down in sobs, the dirk still at her chest. She came away from the wall, moving toward the table, but staying out of range of the men who could still grab her and take the dirk away from her. As she came into the weak light, Keir could see the blade against her chest and the blood streaming from it. He nearly came apart.

"Sweet Jesus," he groaned. "Chloë, what happened? What…?"

"You should thank her, St. Héver, truly," Ingilby cut him off. "She came here to offer herself in exchange for your freedom. I have accepted her offer."

Keir's pale features went absolutely ashen as he gazed at his wife.

His mind wasn't as sharp as it usually was but he nonetheless understood well the implications. Ingilby would have done less damage had he taken a blade and cut off his arms and legs. It would have hurt less than the knowledge, the horrific knowledge, of Chloë's offer.

"Nay," he breathed, his eyes beginning to fill with tears. "Chloë, you cannot do this. Please, sweetheart, do you hear me? *You will not do this.*"

Ingilby watched Chloë fall against the side of the table, weeping so heavily that she lost her balance. But the blade remained fixed on her chest, digging into her white flesh.

"Your wife tells me that she will kill herself right before my eyes if I do not let you go," he told Keir, sounding quite detached. "She is very determined. I fear she means it."

Keir just stared at Chloë, feeling sobs of terror bubbling up in his throat. It was a struggle to fight them off, but he couldn't fight off the tears. He was shattered.

"Oh...Chloë," he whispered, his lower lip trembling. "No, sweetheart, please no. All will be well. You will not do this. I forbid it."

Chloë was half-on, half-off the table, bracing herself with her left hand so she wouldn't collapse completely. She wanted so badly to run to Keir but she was afraid the soldiers would capture her and take away the knife. Then she would be powerless. *She had to free him!*

"You would do it for me," she wept. "If I were captive, you would sacrifice yourself for me without a second thought. Because I love you, I cannot think of myself. I can only think of you. If my life can buy your freedom, then I will do it willingly."

Keir blinked and fat tears splattered onto his cheeks. "Chloë, please," he whispered. "Take the dirk away from your chest, sweetheart. I cannot stomach what I am seeing."

Chloë shook her head, so hard that her hair whipped about her face and pulled through the blood streaming down her chest, leaving streaks across her neck. She looked at Ingilby, still sitting quite calmly at the table.

"Let him go now," she demanded, her lips trembling. "I have made my offer and you have accepted. There is no reason to keep him here any longer."

Ingilby had to agree; the longer St. Héver and Chloë looked at each other, the more the intensity of their emotions resonated. Ingilby wasn't particularly comfortable with that. The sooner he removed St. Héver, the sooner he could begin his quest to finally conquer Chloë. Casually, he glanced over at the soldiers holding St. Héver and snapped his fingers.

"Release him."

The soldiers hauled Keir to his feet, who suddenly began fighting back. Injured, weak, he still took out three men before several others rushed in and fought to subdue him. Chloë, seeing what was happening, began screaming.

"Keir, *no!*" she cried. "Stop fighting, please stop fighting!"

Keir pretended not to hear her. He had his big fists balled, pummeling those who were attempting to subdue him. The sounds of broadswords being unsheathed filled the air and Chloë screamed loudly.

"Kill him and I will kill myself right now!" she shrieked. "I will do it, I swear!"

With that, she took the dirk and dragged it across one wrist, and bright red blood began to spill. Horrified, Ingilby rushed over to Keir, shoving his men aside who were preparing to gut the man.

"Enough!" he roared. "Put your weapons away. Can you not see that she means it?"

Keir stopped fighting when he heard the shout. Turning in Chloë's direction, all he could see was her blood spilling on the floor.

"My God," he whimpered. "Chloë...."

"Remove him," Ingilby barked. "Dump him outside of the gate. Get him out of my sight and, for Pity's Sake, get him out of her sight. *Get him out!*"

The last sight Keir had of Chloë was of her sinking to the floor as blood gushed from her left wrist. He began yelling for her, struggling viciously against the men who were dragging him out of the hall, but he was simply overpowered. The pulled him out of the keep and dragged him all the way to the gatehouse, where they threw him out on the road beyond the portcullis.

Keir didn't remember much of being released from Ripley, only that it had been the most painful thing he had ever experienced in his life. Once, he had come across the burning bodies of his wife and daughter. He thought that had been the worst moment of his life.

It wasn't.

CHAPTER THIRTY-ONE

T HE SIEGE OF Ripley Castle was truly something to behold.

After advance Aysgarth scouts found a beaten and somewhat hysterical Keir outside of the castle walls trying to find a way to get back in, Kurtis and Michael had listened to a harrowing story about Chloë and her sacrifice for Keir's freedom.

It had been an ugly scene. Keir had initially raged at his brother for not preventing Chloë from doing such a thing, but he realized, when his emotions began to settle, that it wasn't Kurtis's failure. It was no one's fault. Chloë was always trying to do what she felt best for Keir, whether or not it was a good idea, and Keir could only love her more because of her foolishly noble intentions. He had visions of her bleeding to death in front of him and it took a solid half-hour before Kurtis and Michael could calm the man to the point where he wasn't roaring with rage.

It brought both Kurtis and Michael back to that horrible time when Keir had lost Madeleine and Frances, the madman who was incoherent and shattered. The man before them was dazed, injured and weak, but all he could speak of was regaining his wife. They knew very well that he meant it; the first time he'd lost those dearest to him, he could do nothing about it. This time, he could. He was hell-bent on retrieving Chloë or die trying, and with that in mind, Kurtis sent two men back to Aysgarth for Keir's armor and weapons. If the man was to have a fighting chance, he needed to be prepared.

With Keir having calmed sufficiently to the point of passing out because his body simply gave out, Kurtis and Michael unleashed Armageddon on Ripley Castle, using two big mangonels they had brought from Aysgarth to launch all manner of flaming projectiles over the big walls.

Michael, who had served Aysgarth for many years, followed Keir's usual mode when laying siege to a fortified structure by sending ignited phosphates over the walls which, upon landing, would explode fiery balls in all directions. That was the first wave. The second wave was big, earthenware pots of a smelly, flammable oil that they would collect in big quantities near coal deposits, and it was this oil that they would ignite and launch over the walls. It was worse than the phosphates. The oil would spray and ignite anything in its path, man and beast included.

The gate of Ripley Castle was the focus of great battering rams they had cut from a nearby forest, and Kurtis set dozens of men on this task as archers rained arrows down upon them. Coverdale had shields for the men on the battering rams, however, great long things smelted from flexible metal that was lightweight enough that the men could position it above them and not be crushed.

Ripley's gate, unfortunately, wasn't up to the task of such vigorous tactics and two hours into the siege, the gate was beginning to show signs of weakness. Recognizing this, Kurtis had Michael remain in command of bombarding the walls as he focused personally on the gate. He was positive it was the weak link and he set more men to ramming it in an attempt to crumble it completely.

As darkness approached and great torches were lit all around to provide light for Aysgarth's army, Coverdale, who had spent nearly all of the battle to the rear of the army with his wife and entourage, took it upon himself to personally assess the bombardment. Approaching the gate where Kurtis and about a hundred men were methodically cracking away at the wood and iron, the man took an arrow to the neck.

Falling off his horse, he slowly bled out as Kurtis and a few other soldiers worked furiously to stop the copious amounts of blood. In the end, Baron Coverdale, Lord Byron de Tiegh, died with his sightless eyes wide open to the heavens and not in his bed as he had often hoped. Kurtis remained with the man's body for a few moments, lingering when everyone else returned to the siege, gazing with sorrow at the dead man and praying that this wouldn't be the first costly death in a siege that had the potential to see many.

ॐ

CHLOË BEGAN TO gradually come aware of the distant sounds of men yelling. It was faint, like the buzz of a fly, soft but unmistakable and, if she thought about it, annoying. Stirring slightly, she sneezed and lifted her hand to itch her nose, half-asleep, until she ended up hitting herself in the face with the ungainly bandage on her left forearm. Startled by the linen wrapping, she peered at it in confusion. More than that, she looked around a chamber that she did not recognize. Dark stone walls, an expensive rug, and a very nice bed. It wasn't hers. She could smell cold and rot and wisps of smoke. Then, it all started coming back to her.

She was at Ripley Castle. Feeling a wave of fear wash over her, she tried to sit up but her back was paining her greatly so she just lay there, trying to get a handle on her anxiety, wondering where Ingilby was. She couldn't imagine he'd be very far from her. But then her thoughts turned to Keir and her last vision of him as Ingilby's men dragged him from the great hall. There had been a good deal of screaming going on, mostly from her, but through it all she could see Keir's expression as he faded from her sight. It had been such a terrified expression. Tears filled her eyes and rolled down her temples as she gazed at the ceiling and thought of Keir.

Trying to rise a second time, she managed to get on her feet. Her back was paining her greatly, no doubt from the strenuous events from the past couple of days, but it was manageable. More than that, she felt extremely weak and her left arm throbbed terribly. It was an effort to move about. She noticed that she still had her boots on and her heavy surcoat; the only thing that seemed to be missing was her cloak. She was thankful that Ingilby hadn't made some attempt to undress her while she was unconscious. Stiffly, she moved to the only window in the room and was immediately faced with bedlam.

The long lancet window afforded her a partial view of the bailey, the walls, and the countryside beyond, and she could see armies on both sides of the wall. There were several fires in the bailey, mostly structure fires, and on the opposite side of the wall she could see an enormous army and parts of a great siege engine as they engaged the thing, slinging burning projectiles over the wall. As she watched, shocked, she thought they might have even slung a body of some kind, in flames, over the wall. She thought it might have been a horse.

Horrified, Chloë could see that her suspicions had been right. Aysgarth's army laid siege regardless of who was in, or out, of the walls of Ripley. She had no way of knowing if Keir truly made it out of Ripley alive. She had lost consciousness before she had her answer and it was quite possible they simply threw him back in the vault or killed him. She realized that she had to know. Seized with anxiety, with the desire to know the truth, she stumbled towards the chamber door.

It wasn't locked, which was surprising. Slinking down the dark, spiral stairs and gripping the wall to keep her balance, she had no idea where she was or where she was going. All she knew was that she had to find out what happened to Keir. Moving quietly but not particularly quickly due to her stiff back and weak body, she ended up in a dark corridor that dumped her out into a small, circular room.

The noise from the battle outside was louder here, drifting in through the windows. The smell of smoke was heavy. She noticed a small table off to her right, shoved up against the wall. It was cluttered with all kinds of things and, quietly, she stepped out of the corridor and moved to the table to see what was spread out all over it. As she approached, she could immediately see blades, broadswords, battle axes, pieces of leather and armor, the remains of a meal, and other clutter.

Just as she reached out to finger one of the broadswords that was more squat than long, she heard voices and saw movement off to her left, through the door into another room, and she scurried back into the corridor from where she had come. Grabbing the sword, she hid in the shadows, trying to see what was going on, and from what she could gather they were bringing injured men in from the battle outside. She could hear them shouting for a physic and the groans of the wounded. The blade in her hands was heavy but she was determined to find someone, anyone, and threaten them unless they told her what happened to Keir. It was the best plan her exhausted mind could come up with.

She moved closer to the sounds in the other room, staying close to the wall until she could peer through the doorway. She could see the great hall beyond and men on the floor being tended by servants. There was blood and pain everywhere and she swallowed hard at the sight, trying very hard not to be disgusted.

As Chloë stood in the doorway, she tried to single out someone who might be in charge of the mess, someone who could tell her what had become of Keir. She was sure that Ingilby and his men were outside in the battle, but as she thought on it, she was equally sure that no servant could tell her what she needed to know. They were usually ignorant of such things. She had to find someone who would know. She had to find a soldier.

Keeping very quiet, she looked around for another way to the keep entry that wouldn't take her through the great hall, but there didn't seem to be any other form of passage. With a deep breath for courage, she lifted the sword, realized it was heavier than she had anticipated, but by that time a few in the great hall had already seen her so she charged out and skittered over to the keep entry. She left a few shocked expressions in her wake, men watching a wispy woman with glorious red hair running through the hall. They had no idea who, or what, she was.

The entry to the keep was open, as there was a constant stream of wounded being brought into the hall. Chloë stepped outside, seeing flames everywhere and men running about. It was a battlefield and as she stood in the open doorway, two more flaming projectiles came sailing over the wall, one of them bursting about thirty feet away from her and spraying burning oil everywhere. Resisting the urge to run back inside and hide, she took the few steps down to the bailey, as Ripley's keep was a low-lying structure, she ended up standing in mud and blood. It was a disgusting mix and she focused more on finding a patch of ground that wasn't filled with bloodily fluids than on finding someone who could tell her where Keir was. Just as she found a patch that was relatively dry, she noticed a great deal of commotion at the gatehouse.

The gatehouse wasn't so much a true gatehouse as it was simply a big stone arch that housed a portcullis and enormous oak gate that was currently burning. Great pieces of it were falling to the ground, clipping the men who were trying to reinforce it. As Chloë watched, somewhat transfixed, an enormous piece fell off and revealed the portcullis beyond, nearly in full. She could see the army though the big iron grate.

Many men and at least three great battering rams came into view. It was difficult to make out any features from the angle of the sun and the direction of the shadows, but she could see dozens of men trying to bring down the gate and portcullis. In fact, the burning gate had softened the iron portcullis sufficiently that several of the enemy soldiers were grasping it with ropes sheathed in leather, pulling at a corner of it and trying to bend back the teeth. Those inside Ripley began hacking at the leather-covered ropes, only to be struck down by arrows shot through the portcullis.

"I had no idea you were well enough to fight."

The voice came from behind and Chloë startled with fear, lifting her sword before she even saw the face of the man. In truth, she didn't need to see him. She knew that voice. And she knew she was in for a fight.

Ingilby stood a few feet away in his battle armor, looking rather weary but unharmed. The armor was newer and well-made, and somewhat pristine. In his hand he held an enormous broadsword with a leather hilt, a glorious weapon built for battle. His expression was even but Chloë was terrified as she faced off against him.

"Where is Keir?" she demanded. "What did you do with him?"

Ingilby cocked an eyebrow. "You wanted him released. I released him."

"Released him *where*?"

Ingilby gestured to the crumbling gate and the battle now going on through the portcullis. "Outside," he said. "I should have thrown him over the wall like he did Alphonse, but alas, I did not. Perhaps I am the more civilized between Keir and I. Perhaps that is something you should keep in mind."

Chloë's expression darkened. "How do I know that you did not throw him over the wall?" she asked. "I would see him, otherwise our bargain is at an end."

Ingilby looked confused. "What do you mean?"

Chloë began to shake as she held up the heavy blade. She wasn't in any condition to be holding something so heavy. It was difficult to keep it steady.

"My proposition to you was me in exchange for Keir's freedom," she said. "If he is not truly free or if, in fact, you have killed him, then we have no bargain."

Ingilby's even expression fled and his eyes narrowed. "And then what?" he wanted to know. "Do you propose to walk out of here? I can tell you, quite irrevocably, that you will not leave this place. I will keep you here and you will belong to me regardless of Keir St. Héver's health or welfare."

"Then you did kill him!"

Ingilby's patience was evaporating quickly. "Foolish wench," he rumbled. "Look at this place; look at that gate. St. Héver is leading the attack. He wants you back, but he shall not have you. You belong to me now and I have waited long enough."

With that, he smacked the sword in her hands onto the ground, reaching out to grab her around the wrist in one smooth motion. Startled, Chloë began to scream and pound on him as he began to drag her back towards the keep. Her sounds were those of fear and panic, an innate response, having no idea that just outside the weakened portcullis, someone had heard her cries.

☙

KEIR AWOKE SOMETIME before sunset when his brother came back into the tent that was positioned far back from the fighting. He had been passed out on a woolen pallet sleeping a sleep of such exhaustion that not even the sounds of battle could penetrate. But he startled himself awake when Kurtis entered the tent and called his name, and he lifted his head in time to see a soldier bearing Keir's armor entering the tent, and still another man behind that man carrying Keir's weapons.

Keir staggered up from his pallet, struggling to clear the cobwebs from his mind as he shifted into battle mode. It was a natural state to him, like eating or breathing, and as Kurtis drank heavily of watered ale and shoved a few piece of bread in his mouth, Keir began dressing. He ignored his twisted ankle, the bumps and bruises, as he began to transform into the efficient killing machine. Nothing on earth was more important than what he was about to face, no battle he had ever fought of higher value. As he strapped on his greaves, his breastplate, and had Kurtis help him with his back plate, his mind briefly wandered to the battle in Wales and how he had been ordered to command the king's armies. Not even those battles were of higher consequence than the one he faced right now, a siege at a relatively small castle with relatively unimportant people inside her. All except one.

Chloë. Her name flashed before his eyes, somehow breezed through his ears and ended up in his chest like a great sharp dagger to cut out his heart. He must have somehow whispered her name because his brother, finished with the last strap on Keir's backplate, came around front and looked at him.

"What did you say?" he asked.

Keir looked at him, thinking about what he might have said, and shook his head. "Nothing," he muttered, moving to strap on his broadsword. "What is the status of the siege? Have you made any headway?"

Kurtis nodded, noting the transformation of his brother from wounded prisoner to powerful knight with satisfaction. "The gate is demolished and we are gaining headway with the portcullis," he said, leading Keir out of the tent into the sunset beyond. "We have been bombarding them since we arrived with flammable projectiles. Michael has made excellent work out of the phosphates and oil."

Keir plopped his helm on his head, glancing up at the great plumes of greasy black smoke that were escaping from Ripley's bailey.

"He usually does," he said. Then he flicked a wrist at the walled fortress. "What about ladders upon the walls? I see none."

"That is because we have nearly finished almost two dozen of them," Kurtis indicated the open field back behind their camp and the trees beyond that formed a dark green line in the distance. "See the men out there in the field? They are nearly finished. I wanted to wait until we had all twenty of them built before charging the walls. I did not want to do it in pieces because a solid, big attack will be more effective. Meanwhile, we have been attacking the gate and have managed to seriously damage it."

Keir was following his brother across the road to the main gate of Ripley, noticing that the main cluster of fighting seemed to be within that confined space. Some of his men had ropes around the softened portcullis, pulling it back and away, dislodging it, while those inside of Ripley tried to fight them off. Kurtis came to a halt before they headed towards the chaos of the gate.

"There is something you should know," he said to his brother. "While you were unconscious, we lost Coverdale."

Keir stared at him a moment before sighing heavily, looking particularly distressed. "What happened?"

Kurtis shrugged helplessly. "He was riding up from his position to the rear to see how the battle was progressing and took an arrow to the throat," he said. "I tried to stop the bleeding but there was just too much damage."

Keir's features were lined with sorrow. "Where is he now?"

"I took him back to his wife. She is too young to handle the grief, you know, but regardless, she is now your commander and in charge of the entire Coverdale barony, I might add. You may want to pay her a visit to express your condolences since you are in charge of her armies."

Keir just shook his head. "I will pay her a visit after I retrieve Chloë. Until then, this battle and this army belong to me."

"She does not understand why we are here and wants to return to Aysgarth with her husband's body."

"I will pretend that I did not hear that."

He started to move but Kurtis grasped him by the arm. "All well and good," he muttered, "and I do not fault you. However, there is something more; be advised that the men do not know what has happened to Coverdale. The few that saw him fall I have sworn to silence. I fear the knowledge of his death might kill their morale."

Keir's pale eyes were intense. "Let the men see me tall and strong, fighting this battle, and it will matter for not. I am the true leader of this army and have been for several years. Coverdale was never much of a factor, although he was a decent man. I will mourn him."

With that, Keir charged towards the gatehouse. Kurtis watched the man walk away for a moment, sensing his resolve and determination, before catching up with him. In truth, it had been some time since they had fought side by side and in an odd way he was looking forward to it. Together, they joined the fight at the portcullis as Aysgarth's army gained headway.

The iron grate was twisting nicely as several Aysgarth men retrieved big pieces of wood from the crumbling gate and began using them as a fulcrum to further twist the iron. Keir charged right up to the front of the battle lines, using his broadsword to hack at those on the opposite side of the portcullis who were trying to prevent Aysgarth soldiers from breaking through. He was moving much like an energized man and not one who had been beaten and bruised. He moved like Keir St. Héver had always moved; with power, skill and courage.

In fact, Keir was up against the portcullis defending those who were trying to pry open the iron. Kurtis was behind him, assisting but also supervising the men who had put the ropes aside and were now trying to dislocate the portcullis off its track so they could slip into the breach. Michael had joined them from his post supervising the wall, mostly because he was bored and wanted in on the action. When he saw Keir over next to the portcullis hacking off hands or fingers that came too close to his blade, he made his way over to the man and happily hacked away with him.

Keir and Michael were fighting like old, as they had fought a hundred times before. Keir turned to say something to Michael over the sounds of the chaos but noticed that Michael was looking off into the bailey of Ripley, made clear through the open grates. Keir couldn't see much because of all the men in his way, but Michael could see over their heads because of his height, and what he saw distressed him greatly. He was about to say something to Keir when a woman's scream pierced the air.

Keir heard the scream. He didn't have to be told who had emitted it because he seemed to know. He could feel it, down to his very bones. The expression on Michael's face only confirmed it. More screams came and Keir began pulling at the portcullis like a madman, bellowing at his soldiers to clear a path for him to enter. The soldiers with the fulcrum yanked and pulled and twisted, heeding the man's bellows, watching as Keir tried to shove himself through a narrowed entry point and nearly had his head cut off in the process. Ingilby's men weren't so inclined to let the man in.

But Michael was there, using his long arms to fend off the enemy through the open grates of the portcullis and, eventually, Keir was able to get through with Kurtis right behind him. Michael threw his great strength into widening the breach and, eventually, it widened enough to let two men pass through at a time. Soon, Aysgarth men were pouring into the bailey, killing anything that moved.

Keir and Kurtis were running for the keep.

Cℬ

CHLOË WAS IN a world of panic as Ingilby tried to drag her across the hall and towards the stairs that led up into the keep. She smacked at his hands, dug her feet in, and eventually threw herself on the ground so he could not easily force her to do his bidding. Ingilby was a reasonably big man, certainly bigger and stronger than Chloë was, and he used that strength to his advantage. The more she resisted, the harsher he became.

Chloë's back was paining her tremendously as she tried to fight him off. She could only surmise he was intending to take her to a bedchamber somewhere and rape her, so she fought with all her might, having no idea what she would do once she broke free. There was really nowhere to go in a fortress under siege, but she would not make the conquest easy for him. As far as she was concerned, they had no bargain because she had no guarantee that Keir had been released alive. Until that factor could be proved, she would resist Ingilby with everything she possessed.

At one point, they passed close to the banqueting table and she grabbed hold with one hand, then with both hands when Ingilby let her go as he tried to break her hold on the table. The big, heavy table groaned as Ingilby pulled and Chloë held tight, grinding across the stone floor as Ingilby dragged both the table and Chloë along. But eventually, he grew weary of the ridiculousness and smacked her hands, causing her to gasp in pain and release the table. Then, he had her. But not for long.

Chloë threw herself onto the floor and kicked him squarely in the face as he reached down for her. Then she scrambled underneath the table as he swiped at her. She crawled on hands and knees, dodging Ingilby's hands, until he manage to get hold of the ends of her long hair. As she screamed, he pulled on her hair, dragging her out from underneath the table. She ended up on her back with a bench half over her, and he let go of her hair. Slipping his hands underneath her arms, he pulled her up to her feet.

"Enough foolishness," he snapped, throwing both arms around her body and nearly carrying her towards the stairs. "I have had all I can take of you, Chloë de Geld. I have pursued you for two long years and it is finally time for me to reap my reward."

Chloë was kicking and twisting, trying to release his hold on her. "I do not belong to you yet," she snarled. "We had a bargain and unless you can provide me with proof that Keir is alive and free, I shall not make this easy for you. Not one bit!"

With that, she chomped down on the hand that was gripping her forearm and Ingilby howled. It was enough of a lapse to force him to release her at least partially, and as Chloë tumbled to the ground near the round room that led to the stairs, the front door of the keep slammed back on its hinges and men began pouring in. Ingilby was reaching down for Chloë when a dirk sailed past his chin, nicking him before crashing into the stone wall beyond.

Startled, Ingilby turned towards the source of the flying dirk. Torn between reclaiming his weapon or reclaiming his captive, he opted for the woman. Surely men with swords would think twice before striking him if he held her in a compromising position. It was a confident decision that was about to cost him.

Keir and Kurtis were rushing towards him, broadswords at the ready. Chloë, scrambling to get away from Ingilby, looked up to see her husband in full battle armor running at her. Struck with shock and relief at a sight she never truly thought she would ever see again, she screamed.

"Keir!"

Keir was almost on top of her, straining against wounds and injury to save her from Ingilby, who was closer to his wife than he was. As he feared, Ingilby grabbed hold of Chloë's foot and yanked her towards him just as Keir reached her. Throwing his arms around his wife's upper torso, he yanked hard and prayed he didn't break any bones in the process. Chloë yelped at the shock of the jolt but it was enough for her boot to slip free. Keir pulled her right out of her shoe, leaving

Ingilby only holding her boot as Kurtis descended on the man and shoved a broadsword into his gut.

Ingilby let out a blood-curdling scream as he sank to the stone, his hands over the wound that was pouring blood down his leg and onto the floor. Without any sympathy whatsoever, Kurtis kicked him over onto his back and gored him again.

"That," he snarled, "is for abducting my brother, you worthless bastard. I hope your death pains you all the way to hell."

Wrapped up in Keir's arms, Chloë was gasping hysterically. Her fear, her surprise, was overwhelming her and she was close to hyperventilating. She couldn't feel much of Keir other than his armor and the bulk of his body, but when he started kissing her face furiously, the fear began to fade and the elation took hold. Hysterical gasping turned into pants of joy.

"Are you well, sweetheart?" Keir's voice was trembling as he stopped kissing her long enough to try and get a look at her left arm. "Is your wrist doing well? Did someone tend it?"

Chloë's happy gasps began to turn teary as she touched Keir's face, feeling his warmth, seeing for herself that he was indeed alive and well. There was such jubilation in her heart that she could scarcely describe it.

"I am well," she insisted, more concerned for him than she was for herself. "Are *you* well? They said that they tied a horse to you and pulled you out...."

He cut her off with a trembling, brutal kiss. "Not to worry," he whispered, bumping her with the raised visor of his helm as he kissed her again. "I am well, Chloë. I am perfectly well. All that matters is you and how you are feeling. I was terrified that I would be too late for… for whatever Ingilby was planning. Was I too late, sweet?"

There was such happiness and relief enveloping them, like a warm fog that bound them, flowed through them, and eased them. It was comfort on an immeasurable level, relief now that the madness was finally over. Chloë had her arms tightly around his armored neck as if to never let him go.

"He never touched me," she assured him softly. "But I believe that was what he was planning when you and Kurtis came to my rescue. Thank God you came when you did."

As if suddenly remembering Kurtis, they turned to look at the man as he stood a few feet away over Ingilby's supine form. Chloë looked at the body on the floor for a couple of seconds before looking away; she didn't want to see anymore. It was a gruesome sight. Keir, however, lingered on the body a few moments before addressing his brother.

"Is he dead?" he asked.

Kurtis was looking down at Ingilby as he spoke. "He is," he said, turning to look at his brother and Chloë. "For the fact that he abducted you and for the fact that he can no longer be a threat to your wife, I am happy to end his life. The last time, when there was a threat to Madeleine, I could do nothing for you, Keir. That has haunted me in ways you cannot imagine. But this time... to protect my younger brother in every way that I can, I am happy to do this. While I had breath in my body, you were not going to lose Chloë as you did Maddie. I told you I would never see you go through that hell again and I meant it."

Keir could see the anguish in Kurtis' eyes. "You never told me how you felt," he said softly.

Kurtis turned away from Ingilby, moving to where Keir and Chloë were all wrapped up in each other. His gaze lingered on the pair, so deeply happy and so deeply in love. "Did I have to?" he murmured. "We are brothers. Your pain is my pain."

"I can never thank you enough."

"You would have done the same for me."

Leaning over, Kurtis kissed Chloë on the cheek and made his way out of the great hall, which was now secured by Aysgarth troops. Chloë watched the man go with tears in her eyes.

"It was not just for you," she whispered. "What he did... he saved me, too."

Keir watched her pale face as she spoke, still coming to grips with the fact that she was safe and whole, and their nightmare was over. He could hardly believe it. Carefully, he lifted her into his arms and began to carry her out of the keep.

"My brother has always been dear to me," he said quietly. "Perhaps today… he is just a little more dear."

Chloë held him tightly around the neck, her head coming to rest on his shoulder. "Can we go home now?"

"Of course, sweetheart."

"I mean to Pendragon."

"So do I."

As the siege of Ripley wound down and men began to pick up the pieces, Keir took his wife outside into the deepening evening.

CHAPTER THIRTY-TWO

Two weeks later
Pendragon Castle

"HE SEEMS TO want to participate, but I am not sure he knows how," Keir was standing with Michael in the bailey of Pendragon as dusky shades of sunset loomed overhead. "I have given him chores, which he accomplishes easily, but he still seems very fearful of us."

Michael lifted his eyebrows at Aust as he emerged from the stables with a heavy bucket in one hand. "Summer seems to think it will take a good deal of time for him to become comfortable with us," he said. "Ingilby and his men beat the boy badly. He trusts no one."

Keir watched the lad lug the water bucket to a horse that was tethered outside of the stable. "I have spent so much time looking at that little face," he muttered. "I can say for certain that he is not Merritt, but then there are days when I look at him and he seems familiar. I am only being wishful, I am sure. What do you think?"

Michael was somewhat hesitant. "Like you, sometimes I think I see something familiar," he replied. "What does Chloë say?"

"Since the boy cannot remember who or where he comes from, that we must keep him and raise him as our own."

Michael grunted. "She has a point."

"But somewhere, this child's parents are missing him. I should be doing everything in my power to return him home but I do not even know where to start. He cannot tell us where he comes from. I could be searching for years."

Michael sighed faintly. "A dilemma, to be certain," he agreed.

"What did Kurtis say before he left?"

"The same thing Chloë said."

"Then perhaps the boy has found a new family."

As Michael and Keir debated the fate of the young lad, inside the keep, Chloë and Summer were up in the master's bower of Pendragon going through the last of Madeleine's possessions.

Upon returning to the castle, Keir had asked Chloë to go through his dead wife's belongings to see if there was anything she wished to have. The rest would be stored or discarded. Although there was still sorrow at Madeleine's passing, for both Keir and Chloë, they were both ready to move forward with their new life together and part of that was removing Madeleine's possessions from the master bower and packing them away. It was the signal of a new beginning, especially for Keir. He was happier than he had ever been. He knew Madeleine would have approved.

For the past two weeks, the situation had been calm and wonderful. Ingilby was no longer a threat, Cassandra and Kurtis had returned to Northumberland, and Sir Garran, although still very weak and recovering, had given permission for Michael and Summer to marry. They did, in an intimate little ceremony at Aysgarth, before returning to Pendragon with Chloë and Keir.

Chloë had dutifully asked her parents to accompany them as well, but Blanche and Anton opted to remain at Aysgarth with the very new and very timid Lady de Tiegh. Perhaps they thought the young woman needed their guidance as she assumed the Aysgarth barony, or perhaps they didn't feel comfortable living in their daughter's new home after all of the grief Anton had caused Keir and Chloë. Whatever the case, they had remained behind, along with Garran because he could not travel. Although Michael and Summer were currently at Pendragon, they would soon be returning to Aysgarth where Michael would take charge of her armies.

Chloë was glad that Summer and Michael had come with them to Pendragon. She missed Cassandra dreadfully and Summer was a lovely substitute. The pair had accompanied Keir and Chloë back to their new home mostly because Summer insisted on helping the newlyweds settle in, but they all knew it truly wasn't necessary. Summer and Chloë had formed a bond and the women simply wanted to be together. Keir and Michael didn't complain; like old times, they were together, traveling, living, laughing and loving. Life was good once more.

Therefore, on this rather mild spring day in the early evening, everyone at Pendragon had something to do. As Keir and Michael completed tasks down in the bailey with little Aust, Summer and Chloë worked in the keep. Chloë treated the packing of Madeleine's belonging with great care and compassion, carefully going through the items one at a time, and making note of each. There were several chests to go through and a giant wardrobe, and most of the garments still had a faint musty scent of smoke.

At one point in that late afternoon, Summer came across a chest that contained nothing but baby clothes, so Chloë and Summer sat on the floor and pulled out every little piece, admiring them as well as inspecting them for durability. After all, someday they hoped to have their own children and Chloë was sure that Madeleine would not have minded if they used the clothing. Everything had been carefully and lovingly stitched.

"There is certainly a good deal of clothing," Summer commented as she folded a neat little pile of tunics. "There is enough here for several children all at the same time."

Chloë giggled. "Keir mentioned that it took a long time for Madeleine to become pregnant with Frances," she said. "Perhaps she passed the time by sewing infant clothing and hoping for a child to put them on."

"She must have sewed for years."

"At the very least."

Summer smiled as she held up a dressing gown that was exquisitely embroidered. "But the results are beautiful," she said, lowering the gown to fold it. She sobered as she worked. "Michael told me what happened to Madeleine and Frances. What a horrible thing."

Chloë's smile faded. "Horrible indeed," she agreed softly. "Keir has been through much tragedy in his life. It is a memory I hope to erase."

"Did it happen in this room?"

"Nay," Chloë said softly. "The room across the hall. That is where the children slept."

Summer nodded sadly, putting the neatly folded gown into another pile. As she did so, she caught something out of the corner of her eye and glanced up. Chloë began to say something to her when she noticed that Summer was staring off into the corner of the room, looking rather strange. Reflexively, Chloë turned in the same direction.

A little girl stood in the shadows of the room. It was difficult to see her for the most part, but the portion of her body that was out of the shadow and into the weak sunlight was non-existent, while the other portion in the shadow was pale and shady, like a fog with some definition. Her facial features were clear, the jaw strong and square, the dark circled eyes. She just stood there, staring.

Shocked, Chloë's breathing began to quicken, realizing she was looking at the little lost ghost girl once again. She hadn't seen her in so long she'd forgotten about her, but here she was once again. More than that, Chloë realized that she was appearing in a different room, not the children's room across the hall as she had before. Perhaps speaking of her had caused her to appear; whatever the case, Chloë wasn't fearful in the least. She very much wanted to help the child find peace. The fact that she remained where she had died spoke volumes of a restless death.

As Summer shifted beside her, perhaps to run away, Chloë put her hand on the woman's arm and held her fast.

"Frances?" Chloë said softly. "Sweetheart, is it you? Please do not be afraid. We will not hurt you."

The ghostly little girl faded somewhat before returning, with more definition than before. She seemed to move, undulating, a few inches towards them. Now she was completely in the shadows of the dim room and difficult to make out.

"Me-Me," she said.

The voice was odd, raspy, with an almost echo-type of quality. It was startling and eerie. Next to Chloë, Summer gasped, but Chloë squeezed her arm tightly to quiet her.

"Do you want Me-Me, sweetheart?" Chloë asked softly. "I do not know where he is. Can… can you help me find him?"

The little girl didn't move for a moment, nor did she speak. She simply stood there, fading in and out, eventually becoming more of a mist than a discernible figure. Chloë could sense that she was leaving them and she let go of Summer, rising to her knees as she moved towards the phantom child.

"Please, Frances," she murmured. "If you know where Me-Me is, please help me find him. Can you tell me?"

The little girl remained in the shadows, the mist rising and falling. It was like watching a figure underwater, the lines of her body distorted. She started to move towards the massive wardrobe.

"Me-Me," she said again.

Chloë was on her knees, following the phantom. "Frances, please tell me where he is. I want to help find Me-Me."

By this time, the ghostly girl was near the wardrobe, the massive thing that had contained all of Madeleine's possession, untouched since that horrible day. The phantom paused as she came upon it, her black eyes intense. Chloë wasn't sure if she was focusing on her, or even if she was actually looking at her. Then, the gray mist stopped undulating. It seemed to become very clear as it stood in front of the wardrobe. As Chloë and Summer watched, spell-bound, the small figure disappeared into the wardrobe doors.

"With thee," her spooky little voice faded off, "I now sleep…."

The room was very still and silent as Chloë and Summer continued to stare at the wardrobe, stunned by what they had just witnessed. Chloë didn't even look at Summer; she was still fixated on the wardrobe. Shooting to her feet, she raced to the heavy oak furniture, well made and of excellent quality, and threw open the doors.

She gasped as she was hit by the smell of Frances, the same scent she had smelled before when the spirit of the child had passed through her in those weeks past. It was sweet and earthy. Seized with the desire to seek what the phantom girl was trying so hard to communicate, she began tossing out the stacks of clothing she and Summer had already gone through. Shifts and fine silks ended up in a pile on the floor as Chloë madly ripped them clear of the wardrobe. She had no idea why she was doing it, only that something was telling her to. She was nearly frantic with the knowledge. There had to be a reason why Frances' little spirit was wandering around, looking for her Me-Me. Perhaps there was a clue here, something they'd missed as they....

The last garment she ripped out of the wardrobe was snagged on the bottom panel of the cabinet. When Chloë yanked hard, part of the panel pulled up. Untangling the snag, Chloë tossed the garment on the ground and pulled up on the floor panel of the wardrobe. As the plank came up, she saw that there was a hidden compartment in the base of the wardrobe. It wasn't very big, perhaps the length and width of the wardrobe and about a foot and a half deep.

As the panel came free and she could see the entire compartment, she let out a shriek and her hands flew to her mouth. Shock and grief hit her like a smack to the face and she burst into tears. She was horrified, unable to look away, as a sad and heartbreaking vision lay before her.

Lying inside the compartment was the decomposed body of a small child.

☙

MICHAEL WAS VERY close to sending word to Kurtis to return to Pendragon but he fought the urge, waiting and watching as the tragedy played itself out. The situation was heartbreaking.

Kneeling beside the massive wardrobe, he alternated between inspecting the decomposed corpse of Merritt St. Héver and watching Keir deal with his grief. Wrapped up in Chloë's arms with his head buried against her pale bosom, he seemed to be doing a remarkable job of holding himself together. Certainly, Keir's initial response had been one of pain and dismay. But once those emotions blew through him in the initial explosion, he seemed to grow oddly calm, as if finally, he had the answer he had been seeking all of these years. At least now he knew. As a father, he was comforted by that. But also as a father, the death of his son had him deeply grieving.

"Madeleine must have hidden him here," Michael was trying to put the pieces of the puzzle together because Keir didn't seem capable of deductive reasoning at the moment. "'Tis the only answer that makes sense. When Lord Stain breached Pendragon, she must have known it was only a matter of time before the keep was compromised, so she tried to hide the children. Merritt fit well in the heavy wardrobe in this secret compartment, but there wasn't enough room for Frances. Madeleine and Frances were then forced to take their chances and perished before they could release Merritt from his hiding place."

Keir sat with Chloë in his lap, his head against her chest as she wrapped her arms fiercely around him. He should have been hysterical with sorrow, but instead, he was strangely calm. It was as if he wasn't quite sure what to feel. His left cheek was against the swell of Chloë's chest as he spoke.

"There is no knowing the how or why of it," he murmured. "It took us over a week to return to Pendragon once we were informed of Lord Stain's siege, and when we arrived, Madeleine and Frances had not been dead that long. I do not understand how we could not have heard Merritt's cries. Surely he was still alive when we arrived. Why did we not hear him?"

"Because it is possible he was already dead," Summer spoke softly from her position a few feet away from the bed where Keir and Chloë sat. "The compartment he is in is very tight and sturdy. He was packed very tightly into it. It's possible he was too weak to cry out for help once you arrived and simply passed away from suffocation or hunger. It is difficult to know. I am sure he simply went to sleep and never woke up."

She meant to comfort Keir with those last words. Chloë gazed up at her friend with big, sad eyes reflecting her appreciation, as Keir kept his gaze on the open wardrobe.

"Perhaps," he said softly. "But I do not understand why... a body that is rotting will give a strong scent. I never smelled anything."

"He is sealed up very tightly," Michael said. "Moreover, Madeleine must have piled all of her possessions on top of the compartment to further hide the boy, and then sealed the doors up. After we buried Madeleine and Frances, you never used this room or the children's' room until Chloë and Cassandra came. These rooms have been virtually sealed up for three years, Keir."

"But I searched for Merritt up here," Keir insisted, some passion returning to his tone. "I searched what I thought was every inch of this room. I even looked in the wardrobe."

"But you never looked in the hidden compartment."

Keir sighed heavily, at a loss. "I had forgotten about it," he admitted. "My thoughts were so frantic and scattered during that time... it simply never occurred to me, and by the way the compartment is built into the wardrobe, it is well hidden unless you know what you are looking for. It simply... never occurred to me...."

"It is possible that the scent of decomposition had not yet grown strong enough to be detected when you were searching for him in these rooms," Summer said quietly, trying to ease the man's guilty conscience. "Once you shut the room off and never returned, it would not have been strong enough to penetrate the stone and fill the entire keep. Eventually, it simply faded away."

Keir sighed again, with great remorse and sorrow, before setting his wife on her feet and rising from the bed. He went over to the wardrobe, rather hesitantly, where Michael was still standing, and gazed down upon the nearly skeletal remains of his son. He felt such overwhelming sadness that he couldn't begin to describe it. After a moment, he reached down and collected the little body very carefully.

"Merritt," he whispered, looking at the skull contained within the clothes. There was nothing to hold the bones together but a few scrap of mummified skin and the clothing around it, so he essentially ended up holding a pile of bones against his chest. "I am so sorry, lad. I am so sorry I failed you."

Chloë came to stand beside him, her arms going around his waist and her head against his back. She hugged him tightly.

"You did not fail him," she whispered through her tears. "You were a wonderful father. What happened was not your fault and you must not blame yourself."

Michael stepped away from the grieving couple, going to his wife and wrapping his arms around her. This was such a private and painful moment, yet Michael and Summer remained to support Keir and Chloë. Three years of hell and longing had come to a sorrowful close. As Keir and Chloë wept quietly over Merritt's remains, a small figure entered the room.

Michael caught sight of little Aust as the child stood just inside the door. He hadn't realized that the lad followed them into the keep when they bolted as a result of Chloë's screams, but the boy had evidently trailed the knights as far as the upper floor. Still, he would not go into the room where they were convening over something very serious. He remained in the hall, frightened and uncertain.

But he could hear what was going on, the words spoken. Now Aust was standing in the chamber, gazing up at Keir and Chloë as they mourned over the bundle of rags.

"I... I heard you yell," Aust spoke nervously, then cleared his throat and coughed. "I heard you say you found your boy. Did... did you find Merritt?"

Chloë and Keir looked at him, their eyes red and watery. "How do you know of Merritt?" Keir asked.

Aust, the child who was supremely terrified of people, swallowed for courage. "Those men...," he stumbled over his words. "Those bad men... I heard them speak of Merritt and how he was your son. They told me I was Merritt but I told them I was not. Did you find him, then?"

Keir could only nod, looking back to the bundle in his arms, and Chloë spoke in his stead. "We did," she said softly.

Aust was curious, fearful and pensive as he realized that something must be wrong indeed if they were weeping. He couldn't really see what Sir Keir was holding but he suspected it was something very bad. His little mind began to put the pieces of the puzzle together.

"Is… is he dead?" he asked softly.

Chloë nodded, smiling gently at the boy even though she was wiping her eyes. "You should not worry. He is at peace now that we have found him."

Aust thought on that. His brow furrowed as he watched the adults deal with their grief. "I know…," he swallowed hard and tried again. "I know I will never go home. You have all been nice to me but I know I will not go home. I do not know where I live, only that it was a place with a church and I had a pet goat. If you cannot take me home, then I will stay here and be Merritt so you can stop crying."

Surprised by the rather grown-up and very sweet offer, Keir and Chloë looked at Aust with some shock before looking at each other. Keir, in spite of his grief, was deeply touched by the child's words. He gazed at Chloë a moment, seeing her faint smile, perhaps one of some joy and encouragement, before putting Merritt's remains carefully back in the compartment that had been his crypt. Gathering his composure, he went to Aust and took a knee beside the lad.

Pale blue eyes met with curious, intelligent brown. After a moment, he put a big hand on Aust's shoulder.

"Your offer is very generous," he said softly. "I am pleased and touched by it. But it is not necessary."

Aust's brow furrowed and he took a surprising stand. "You saved me from those men who were hurting me," he sounded older than his years. "I know what you did. You got hurt but you still saved me from those men and then they took you instead. Because you saved me, I belong to you."

Keir's expression suggested that he wasn't quite sure how to respond. He looked back over his shoulder at his wife, at Michael and Summer, only to see that they all seemed touched by Aust's attitude. It was a very pure view of a complicated situation. Keir returned his focus to the boy.

"I saved you because it was the right thing to do," he finally said. "It does not mean that you belong to me. It simply means that I helped you when you needed help."

He started to stand up but Aust grabbed him by the sleeves. Before Keir realized it, the little boy was wrapping his arms around his neck and weeping.

"Please," the child wept softly. "God sent me to you because your boy was dead. He wants me to be Merritt. Please do not make me go away."

Keir could feel tears sting his eyes as he hugged the child. He didn't know what else to do. On his knees with a five year old in his arms, he felt Chloë kneel next to him. Her arms went around them both as she kissed her husband on the cheek.

"Perhaps he is right," she whispered, stroking Aust's blond head. "Perhaps God knew we would find Merritt and has sent you another boy to comfort you. Aust will not take Merritt's place in your heart but perhaps stand beside him as a comfort and a tribute. I, for one, would be proud to be called his mother. He is a brave and compassionate child."

Keir could feel his tears return as he held the child, thinking on his selfless words. "My inclination is to return him to his parents," he whispered. "He belongs to someone else. They are missing him as I missed Merritt."

Chloë hugged him. "But he does not know where his parents live," she murmured. "We could spend years and still never find them. In the meantime, he will be living with us unless you plan to turn him over to an orphanage."

"Of course not," Keir breathed. "But I would feel guilty keeping him when his parents are alive, looking for him."

"Then perhaps until such time as we find them, Aust can belong to us."

It seemed like a fair enough solution and, if he were to admit it, it comforted him to have a five year old boy tagging around after him again. Perhaps Aust and Chloë were right. Perhaps he could belong to them, if only until his real parents were found. Now, Keir had a wife and child again and it was a settling, binding peace that embraced him. Finally, he felt a true peace again, stronger than he had ever known.

Merritt St. Héver was buried in the same crypt as his mother and sister in the small chapel at Pendragon, together again with his family in death as he had been in life. Chloë told Keir of Frances' last visit and how the child's phantom was instrumental in locating Merritt's remains, for without her guidance the mystery of Merritt St. Héver's disappearance would have never been solved.

It was a sweet and poignant end for the little girl who had been constantly trying to get rid of the little brother that had followed her around in life, and when the crypt was sealed on his children and dead wife, Keir felt a distinct sense of closure. Now, he could fully move on with his life with a woman he loved more by the hour.

Chloë had also mentioned to Keir what Frances had said the moment she faded off into the wardrobe, words that had no meaning until they'd found the remains. Then, they held a great deal of meaning and it was that epithet that Keir had emblazoned on the top of the crypt. It was a final and lasting tribute to his dead wife and children, an appropriate statement that would bind them for all eternity.

With thee... now I sleep.

C3 THE END 80

Fragments of Grace is the prequel to the best selling series, DRAG-ONBLADE. The series follows the stories of four knights who served during the time of Edward III. Bonus material from DRAGONBLADE, the first book in the series, is included at the end of this novel. The five novels in the series, in order, are:

Fragments of Grace

Dragonblade

Island of Glass

The Savage Curtain

The Fallen One

Please enjoy bonus material from DRAGONBLADE.

CHAPTER ONE

The Month of January
Year of our Lord 1326
Cartingdon Parrish; Northumbria, England

THE TIME OF year dictated that the landscape would be an eternal shade of twilight, no matter what the time of day. Gray colored the sky, the earth and the mood of the people.

The town of Cartingdon was no exception. The people were pale with the limited nutrition of winter, their woolen clothes barely adequate for the freezing temperatures that the north winds brought. More than the grayness of the air and people, there was something else this day that darkened the land. Everyone could feel it and they were edgy.

There were whispers floating about like the many snow crystals in the air. Word had spread through the markets that morning after Matins, moving to the avenue of the Smiths and finally to the street of the Jews, telling everyone of the meeting that would be held at Vespers. The purpose was to discuss the most recent rumor regarding England's king. These were turbulent times in a turbulent land.

The sun hovered on the horizon and the church-bells chimed the onset of Vespers, calling the masses to the meeting. The townsfolk flocked to the stone church that they had built with their own hands. Fanged gargoyles imported from France hung on the eaves, lending ambience to the disquiet. Once the people filled the church, they stood in angry, hissing clusters.

The priests had lit a few large tapers, giving the sanctuary a haunting glow as they prepared for the meeting and subsequent mass. Several aldermen were having an intense discussion near the great altar; their deliberation raged for some time until the tall man in the center of the discussion silenced the group and called forth the crowds that had gathered. What they had to say would affect them all.

The mayor of the town was Balin Cartingdon. He was a farmer of noble descent who had flourished, turning a small sharecropping plot into a vast agricultural plantation. He had been a very young man when he sank his first barley seed into the ground, when the settlement of Cartingdon had been an assembly of huts called Snitter Crag. Twenty-two years later, his barley production was the largest in Northumbria and he had added wool and sheep to his empire. The tiny town had exploded due to his farming and was renamed Cartingdon in his honor.

"Good people," Balin's voice rang above the fickle buzz. "Thank you for coming. We have called this meeting to discuss the needs of our king and country."

"You mean the needs of Mortimer!" someone from the crowd shouted.

As the others agreed angrily, Balin shook his head. "Roger Mortimer is not our king. I speak of young Edward."

The grumbling grew louder. At the rear of the church, a small figure suddenly entered. It was apparent that the form was a woman from the drape of the cloak she wore, a soft green-blue garment that clung to her shapely body. A few of the village folk recognized her, moving out of her way as she pushed through the crowd. By the time she reached the front of the church, she had removed her hood, revealing cascades of golden-brown hair and almond-shaped eyes that were a brilliant shade of hazel. She had the face of an angel, but beneath the sweet façade lay an iron will. In the township of Cartingdon, the first daughter of Mayor Balin was more feared and respected than her father.

"Mortimer rules the country with Queen Isabella." The woman spoke loudly, addressing both her father and the assembly. "If rebellion is in the air and we support it, his hammer will fall on all of us. Everything we have built, and all that we have, will be confiscated. I personally do not want to see everything that my father has worked so hard for taken away in the blink of an eye."

"It is doubtful it will be taken away," Balin said patiently, displeased that his daughter had chosen not to remain silent. He had gone so far as to ask Toby not to attend the meeting, but alas, that was too much to hope for. If there was an opinion to be had, she was usually in the middle of it. "Our liege, Tate Crewys de Lara, also supports the rightful king. We have no choice but to support the crown if those who hold our fate have such loyalties."

"But what of the Queen?" the crowd spoke again. "She has the support of the King of France. He is her brother. What if she calls on him to quell rebellion? What if the French overrun Northumbria and destroy our town?"

"They will kill us all!" another shouted.

The crowd surged unsteadily and Balin held up his hands. "You forget that young Edward has the Scottish king's support," he replied calmly, hoping to soothe the mob. "He will protect us. But we must help our king and that is why we are here today. It is our duty. Every man must decide for himself if he is willing to sacrifice for a greater cause."

"The king is a child," Toby pointed out. "His mother and Roger Mortimer rule on his behalf. Never forget that they did England a tremendous service by deposing young Edward's father, King Edward the Second. He was a vile infection that drained this country of all that was good and righteous. They subsequently rid England of the Despencers, the father and son who vied for the throne, thereby eliminating the last links of Edward's contemptible reign. For the past three years under Isabella and Mortimer, England has known a measure of peace. Do we truly want to feed the beast of rebellion again and perhaps create a tempest that will destroy us all?"

It was a brilliant summation of the recent past of England's monarchy, given by a woman who should have, respectably, known nothing of the matter. The crowd roared as she finished; some in approval, some in disapproval. Toby looked at her father, sorry she had not completely supported his stance, but in the same breath, hoping it would cause him to deliberate the potential consequences. She didn't want to see her people die for a futile cause. There had been too many of them over the past several years.

"Toby," her father had to raise his voice over the commotion of the crowd. "Please go home. You do not help this situation."

Toby was genuinely contrite. "I am sorry to appear as if I oppose you, but I do not believe you have clearly considered this subject. It is greater than you think."

"I am well aware of how critical it is. But these are simple folk; I cannot outline the detailed politics of England's situation. I should not have even outlined them to you, but I did for reasons that no longer seem valid. I should have known you would find a way to contradict me."

"I did not mean to. I simply meant to give you my opinion."

"I know well enough your opinion. I know it, I think, even before you do."

"I am simply asking that you think about what you are saying."

Balin rolled his eyes. "With you around, I can do nothing *but* think. Now be still before the crowd turns against us."

As Toby and her father exchanged opinions, back against the wall something was stirring. Several men stood in a unit, draped in dark cloaks as they listened to the spirited debate. The first man tossed back his hood; he had a face of classic male beauty, a granite jaw and full lips. His hair was dark like a raven's wing, shorn up the back yet long enough in the front so that it swept across eyes the color of storm clouds. He was a striking example of perfection, completely out of place among the worn, colorless peasants. He watched everything around him like a hawk, not missing a movement or a word. It was apparent that he was absorbing everything in his element until he had enough information to make a reasonable judgment.

The man moved forward through the crowd, taking his entourage of five with him. People moved out his way instinctively, not wanting to be trampled by the man who was a head taller than even the tallest man in the church. He approached Balin and Toby and softly cleared his throat.

"Forgive me, my lord," the man's voice was deep and rich. "I realize this is a town meeting exclusively for the residents of Cartingdon but I wonder if I may speak to the throng."

Balin and Toby looked at the man. Balin's reaction was far less than Toby's; the moment their eyes met, she felt a strange buzzing sensation in her head. It was enough to cause her to pull her gaze away, looking to her father to see if he was having the same odd reaction. He seemed unaffected.

"Who would you be, my lord?" Balin asked.

"I am Tate Crewys de Lara."

As if on cue, the group escorting Tate threw back their hoods and cloaks, exposing enough armor and weapons to handle a small battle quite efficiently. Two of the men were enormous; they were knights of the highest order, clad in expensive metal protection. Two shorter, stockier men-at-arms supported them, dressed in leather protection and sporting fine Welsh crossbows. The last member of the entourage was the squire, of lad of fourteen or fifteen years. He was tall, thin, and fair-haired.

"My... my lord de Lara," Balin was clearly shocked. "Although we have corresponded on the occasion of taxation and audits for your lands, this is the first we have met. I am indeed honored, my lord."

Tate heard his words, but his focus was on Toby. Now that he was closer and could see her more clearly, she was indeed worth a second look. "I have spent the majority of my life in London or in France, with the wars, and have hardly spent time in this land for which I hold title," his gaze lingered on Toby. "Harbottle Castle is a garrison I have seen three times in my life."

Balin could see where Tate's focus was and indicated his child. "May I present my eldest daughter, Mistress Elizabetha Aleanora de Tobins Cartingdon. She is the one who has seen to your requests with regard to revenue from the parish."

"Mistress, I thank you for your service."

"My pleasure, my lord."

Tate's gaze was like an immovable object. He tried not to be obvious about it, but the lady was quite lovely. Such beauty was very rare. He did not, however, like the bold nature he had seen come forth from her since their arrival. Were it not for that flaw, he might have considered speaking further with her.

"Please, my lord," Balin put his hands up to quiet the crowd. "Speak to our people. Tell them of England's need."

When Tate looked away from her, Toby felt as if she had been jolted. He had held her in such an odd trance that his sudden departure startled her. Still, she retained enough of her wits to remain attuned to the subject at hand.

"My lord, if I may," she said carefully. "These are simple people with simple lives. Things like war frighten them, not inspire them. I am afraid a thunderous address will only further alarm them."

Tate looked at her. "Mistress... Elizabetha, was it?"

His tone bordered on contempt. Toby struggled to retain her courage. "I have not gone by Elizabetha since my birth. I am known as Toby, my lord."

"Toby? That is a strange name. A man's name."

"It is a nickname, my lord, given to me by my grandsire."

"Why?"

"His family name was de Tobins. My mother gave it to me as a middle name. Everyone called my grandsire Toby and he called me the same."

Tate's reply was to give her one more look, a once-over, and turn back to the crowd. Toby took the opportunity to study the man; the

Lord of Harbottle, the title for the Harbottle Commons lordship he held, was an exceptionally tall man with arms the size of tree branches and enormous hands. Though he wore no armor, merely layers of heavy tunics, breeches and massive boots, Toby could tell by the width of his shoulders that he was, quite simply, a very big man. She backed off, unwilling to provoke Cartingdon's liege, but she didn't leave completely. To do so, if he was going to war-monger, would have been to do a great injustice to the populace of Cartingdon. She felt as if she had to protect them.

Tate saw that she wasn't leaving and he tried not to let it affect him as he addressed the uncertain throng. He wasn't sure why she was so distracting, but she was.

"Good people of Cartingdon, I am Sir Tate Crewys de Lara, Lord of Harbottle. As your liege, it is a privilege to speak with you this day."

The crowd had simmered, but they were still uneasy. Tate continued in an even voice.

"I have listened to your mayor speak on young Edward's behalf," he said. "I am here to tell you that the king is ready, willing and able to assume the mantle left by his father. Those who are not the rightful rulers have assumed his throne. Most of England's nobles understand this and to them I have made my plea. I have spent many years in the service of the young king and I can personally vouch for his abilities. He is wise, thoughtful, and fair as much as his young age will allow. With the proper advisors, the rest will come with time." Tate raked his fingers through his short, dark hair as he collected his thoughts. "I sent word to Mayor Cartingdon days ago requesting men and money for the king's cause. My men and I have been in town for two days, observing the people and countryside. It is by sheer fortune that we are here for the meeting that will decide the aid you will provide Edward the King. I could easily tax you to death or simply take what, by all rights, belongs to me. But I choose not to do so. I would like the support from Cartingdon to be genuine, for the young king and his cause. I believe he will establish a stable monarchy from which we may all benefit.

Therefore, I ask you to please decide favorably upon him. England is Edward, and Edward needs your help."

By the time he finished, the entire church was silent. The townsfolk looked at Balin, Toby, each other, attempting to determine if what their liege said was true. He sounded convincing. Toby, too, was almost convinced of the young king's cause after his speech; she stood slightly behind Tate and to the right, able to see his strong profile. There was something about him that conveyed truth. She looked at the knights standing well behind him; they, too, seemed strong and virtuous. Even the squire seemed honorable. One of the villagers broke the silence.

"I am a ferrier, m'lord," the older man said hesitantly. "I canna provide ye with gold or coin, but I can provide ye with meself. If Edward the Younger is in need, then we must help."

Toby knew the man who spoke. He was kind but not intelligent. She could see most of the other townsmen talking quietly to one another, no doubt discussing their prowess with a sword and crossbow. Some of the men had already seen battle, called into action a few years earlier with the removal of King Edward and the Despencers. There were some men, however, that had left to aid the crown and had not returned.

"What of the opposition, my lord?" Toby could not keep silent; she hated to see men's lives wasted. "Can you please tell them of the opposition they will face?"

Tate looked at her, her beautiful face strong and her expression intense. He didn't sense hostility from her, merely concern.

"The opposition is Queen Isabella and her lover, Roger Mortimer, Earl of March," he said, glancing over the crowd. "Mortimer has a large army at his disposal, as does the queen. The king's troops, however, are loyal to young Edward; that much we have ascertained. The Queen's strength will come from France and her brother, the king's army. But once we have begun our campaign to reclaim the throne, summoning France's troops will take time. It is my belief that we will have enough time to subdue Isabella and Mortimer before support arrives."

"But what of the nobles?" Toby asked.

Tate's gaze fixed on her again; he seemed incapable of staying away for long. "There are many in support of the king."

"Who?"

"Alnwick, Warkworth and York in the north. Arundel in the south."

He had named some of the most powerful nobles in England. Their armed support collectively was staggering. Toby felt her questions had been answered and was reluctant to press him further, although she was still opposed to the general idea of war. Still, any more questions would have made her appear belligerent, which normally would not have concerned her, but she did not want to shame her father. Balin, sensing she had come to the end of her queries, thank the Lord, stepped in.

"I am sure that each man can find it within his conscience to lend what support he can, my lord," he said. "All men interested in committing themselves to the young king's army will assemble at the church tomorrow at noon for further instructions. For my part, I will supply a herd of my finest sheep to sell at market and donate the proceeds."

Toby's jaw dropped. "Father...."

Balin cast his daughter a withering glare. "My daughter, as she is most knowledgeable in the accounting of my livestock, will be glad to show you the prize herd north at Lorbottle."

Toby was speechless. It was the largest herd of sheep they had, nearly ready to be sheared. The money they would bring would be enormous. Astounded, she grappled with the concept as her father called an end to the gathering and the townspeople began to disband. She was so stupefied that she didn't realize when Tate came and stood next to her.

"If it would not take you away from any pressing duties, I would see the sheep this day," he said. "I would also like a full accounting."

Jolted from her thoughts, Toby looked up at him. From the corner of her eye, she could see that her father was about to make a hasty retreat from the church. "Excuse me a moment, my lord."

She raced to her father, cutting off his exit. Balin held up his hands.

"Not a word," he hissed at her. "You have my orders. Follow them."

"Father, do you realize what you have done?" she hissed in return. "To donate five hundred head of sheep, with the price of wool today, will cost us a fortune in lost money. We still have to pay the wages of our farm, our taxes, and eat on top of everything else. We need that money."

"It will not do us any good if England goes to the dogs under Isabella and Mortimer," he said flatly. "We have suffered so much under Edward's rule. Can you not understand that the young king is our best, brightest hope?"

"I understand that you have apparently lost your mind."

"There are many things in this world that I will tolerate and many things that I learn to accept," Tate was standing behind Toby, listening to everything that had been said. "But the one thing I refuse to accept is a daughter's disrespect to her father. You, Mistress Toby, have an appalling lack of manners. I have seen such display from the moment I first entered this church."

Toby was ashamed and defensive at the same time. "If honesty is a sin, then I am indeed guilty, my lord."

"It is not a sin. But your lack of control is."

Toby wisely refrained from an opinionated retort. She wasn't a fool and calmed herself with effort. "May I speak frankly, my lord?"

The corner of Tate's mouth twitched. It was difficult for him not to smile at what was surely to come. "By all means."

Toby took a deep breath, hoping he wasn't about to slap her for her insolence. "My father became prosperous by hard work and good luck, but only by harder work and even more good fortune have we maintained it. My mother used to maintain the business when I was very small, but that duty passed to me several years ago after she became ill. Since that time, we have seen our prosperity grow many times over. Were it not for me, however, my father would have given everything away and we would be living in poverty. He is generous beyond compare and does not know when to stop."

"And you believe that donating to the king's cause is an example of how your father does not know when to stop?"

"Not necessarily. But we were counting on that harvest of wool to pay wages to our farmhands for the next year. Many people depend on us for their livelihood."

Tate cocked his head thoughtfully. "Then your opposition is not against the king himself."

"Of course not." For the first time, Toby's tone softened. "I simply cannot believe that the king would want aid for his cause at the expense of starving out many of his loyal subjects."

"It is that serious?"

"It could be. Winter is not yet over and harvest will not come again until next fall. Our people must have something to live on, my lord."

Tate was quiet a moment; he glanced at the two massive knights who had accompanied him. One man was a giant, with short brown hair and cornflower blue eyes. The second man wasn't as tall but he was enormously wide with white-blond eyebrows. The pair of them gazed back at Tate and he knew either one of them would have gladly taken the lady over their knee at that moment. His focus moved to the squire, the skinny lad who accompanied him everywhere. The boy had a somewhat submissive expression. So far, none of those expressions helped Tate sort through the situation.

After a moment's deliberation, he turned back to Toby. "What would you suggest, mistress? I will leave it to your good judgment."

Toby was surprised at the question. She had expected far more of a battle, ending in her defeat. She thought quickly, hoping to come up with a solution that would placate him and not send her family to the poor house.

"There is a herd of older sheep that we were considering sending to the slaughter simply because their wool has become so tough," she said. "It is only around two hundred head, but the wool could be sheared one last time and sold for market value, and then the herd could be slaughtered for meat. It would bring you nearly as much given the proper market and negotiations."

"Of which you would so kindly provide me."

Toby nodded, feeling a good deal of relief. "It would be my pleasure, my lord."

"I would see the herd."

"You will dine with us first, my lord," Balin insisted. "Toby can take you to the herd at first light."

He wondered what adventures in indigestion he would discover during the course of dining with the opinionated Mistress Toby Cartingdon. If the woman was formidable in the public arena, he could only imagine her stance in a private setting. He was loathe to admit it to himself, but he was more than curious to find out.

ᘐ

"AN INTERESTING MEETING," the blond knight said as they made their way to their chargers, tethered at the livery near the church. Sir Kenneth St. Héver had served under Tate de Lara for many years and had, consequently, experienced many things with him. But the latest experience in the church was a curious one. "An interesting town."

His counterpart, Sir Stephen of Pembury, was the larger, darker knight. He was the more congenial of the two. "What kind of town can it possibly be that allows itself to be run by a female?" he said what they were all thinking. "A strong man could do wonders here."

Tate had notice an inn across the street and, collecting his destrier, began moving in that direction. "It seems to me that she has done wonders without the aid of a man. No matter how distasteful her manner, we are nonetheless fortunate to have received a sizable donation from her father."

Pembury snorted. "She is a beautiful woman. Too bad she has the disposition of a wild boar."

St. Héver glanced at him. "Do you have aspirations for her, then?"

"Me? Never."

"You could marry her and run the town."

"Somehow, I doubt it. She is accustomed to being in charge. Could you not see that?"

St. Héver merely lifted his white-blond eyebrows in agreement. The very thought was appalling, but Tate wasn't paying any attention to their chagrin. He was focused on the tavern and obtaining some much needed food and drink. Leaving the horses, they made their way inside the smelly hovel and found a table in the corner where a round woman brought them ale, bread and cheese. The young squire with them shoved half a loaf in his mouth before the knights had finished pouring their drink.

"Slow down, lad," Tate admonished lightly. "There is more bread to be had. No need to choke yourself."

The youth grinned and slowed to chew. The two men at arms that constantly shadowed the group of four took position against the wall opposite the table. They were the first line of defense against any potential happening, which was a fairly normal occurrence. England, and the world in general, was a dangerous place.

With the squire no longer in danger of choking and the knights settled with their ale, Stephen put his thoughts into focus.

"Did anyone notice if we were followed?"

Tate shook his head. "I do not think so. I've not seen evidence in a couple of days."

Kenneth took a deep drag of his ale. "We lost them in Rothbury," he said. "If nothing else, Mortimer's men are easy to spot. They follow us out in the open."

"He doesn't have to keep them to the shadows because he governs the entire country," Stephen snorted. "What does he have to fear?"

Tate regarded the ale in his cup. "He has to fear a young man on the cusp of adulthood who holds the throne he so dearly wants," he muttered, more to himself than to the others. He glanced up at the knights. "She asked valid questions, you know."

Pembury looked up from his bread. "Who?"

"Mistress Elizabetha."

"What questions do you mean?"

"About the opposition."

"You were truthful in your answer."

Tate lifted a resigned eyebrow. "Aye, but minimally; I did not mention that Isabella and Mortimer hold all of Windsor Castle and her wealth. That is the heart of the kingdom. And if we are to oust them, we must strike at the heart."

"I thought that was what we were doing."

The squire's soft voice entered the conversation. Tate looked at the youth, breadcrumbs on his fuzzy face.

"The more I go to these little towns, the more I realize that a rebellion must encompass far less than armies and knights intent on destroying each other," he explained to the lad. "We must take control of Mortimer and Isabella on a much smaller scale. Balin Cartingdon's outspoken daughter was correct in some aspects."

"Which ones?"

A distant look crossed Tate's face. "By feeding the beast of rebellion, we could destroy everything. Sometimes a larger operation is not the better tactic than a small, precisely planned one."

"Will we go back to London and re-think our strategy?"

The squire's question was posed with curiosity more than anxiety. Tate passed a glance at the knights before answering. "What would you suggest?"

"We still need support. And we need money."

"True enough; which is why my inclination is to stay the eve in Cartingdon, negotiate for the sale of the sheep with Balin's daughter, and then make our way back to London. I worry being gone overlong. Much can change in a short amount of time."

"That is a wise decision," Pembury said. "Without you in London, Mortimer lulls himself into a false sense of security. I never thought it was particularly prudent for us to have left the city in the first place."

Tate looked at his squire, reading the boy's concerned expression.

He downplayed his knight's comment. "It was necessary," he said simply. "But for now, let us eat and enjoy this moment of peace."

The squire went back to eating only when the knights did. A group of minstrels struck up a lively song and soon the entire tavern was bouncing. It was a good moment of relaxation for them to remember; the future, Tate suspected, would hold few.

CHAPTER TWO

"**T**HEY CALL HIM Dragonblade," Ailsa Catherine Cartingdon danced around the table in the large hall of Forestburn Manor, the Cartingdon home. "Have you heard, Toby? Dragonblade!"

Ailsa was ten years of age, a frail girl with golden curls. She had an energetic mind, sharp and inquisitive, but a weak body that kept her in bed a good deal of the time. She was always ill with something. It had started at her birth when her mother suffered a stroke whilst in labor; Ailsa was born blue and Judith Cartingdon had nearly died. Only by God's grace did either of them live through it.

"Aye, you little devil, I have heard it," Toby said. "But you must not say anything to him. Perhaps he does not like the name."

Ailsa stopped her excited dance. "Why not?"

Toby shrugged, putting the last touch on the mulled wine. "It does not sound very flattering."

Ailsa resumed her dance, ending up lying on top of the table. "And do you know what else I have heard?"

"I am afraid to know."

"I have heard that Tate de Lara is the son of King Edward the First. They say that he was saved from his savage Welsh mother by the Marcher lords of de Lara, who then raised him as their own. He is the half-brother of King Edward the Second and was there when the king was murdered. And some say that Queen Isabella asked him to marry her, but he refused, so she took Roger Mortimer as her lover instead."

"Where do you hear such nonsense?" Toby lifted her sister off the table.

"From Rachel Comstock's mother. She knows everything."

Toby made a face. "Rachel Comstock's mother thinks that she is God's blessing to all of Mankind and constantly reminds us of how she was a lady in waiting for King Edward's mother's sister's cousin by marriage. Truth be told, she was probably just the privy attendant."

Ailsa giggled. "She says that Tate should be king, not young Edward."

Toby paused long enough to ponder that. It seemed like such an immense prospect although she had heard the same thing from her father, once, a long time ago. The fact that Tate de Lara was Edward Longshanks' bastard son was generally accepted. He had the height and strength of the Plantagenets but the dark features of the Welsh princes. The more she thought on his royal lineage, the more unsettled she became. The man she would soon be supping with had a royal heritage on both sides that was centuries old.

"Not a word of this at supper, do you hear?" she said to her sister. "You have no idea the seriousness of your words."

Ailsa pouted. Her sister shoved some rushes into her hand, indicating she spread them, to keep her busy.

"But why must I keep silent? I want to know what it is like to live in London and I want to know of King Edward. Do you suppose he will marry some day?"

"I suppose so. He must, as the king."

"Could he marry me?"

Toby put her hands on her hips, smiling at her sister in spite of herself. "No, little chicken, he could not. He needs a woman of royal blood, not a farmer's daughter."

Ailsa was back to pouting. "But father says we have noble blood in us."

Toby spread the last of the fresh rushes before the hearth. "The best we can do is claim relation to the barons of Northumberland. The last baron, Ives de Vesci, was our father's grandsire."

"And mother is descended from a Viking king named Red Thor."

"So Grandsire Toby has told us."

"Do you not believe him?"

Toby just smiled. She had a beautiful smile; it changed her face dramatically. She could get her father to agree to anything when she smiled.

"Help me see to supper, little chicken."

Ailsa forgot about Northumberland and the Viking king. She skipped after her sister, who was more a mother to her than her real one. Judith Cartingdon had been bedridden since Ailsa's birth, unable to walk, barely able to speak. The care of the infant girl had fallen upon twelve-year-old Toby. As a result, the girls were inordinately close.

Supper was mutton, boiled and sauced, marrow pie, a pudding of currants and nuts, and bread made from precious white flour. Ailsa kept trying to steal pieces of bread and Toby would shoo her away. The cook was an elderly woman who had been Toby's wet-nurse years ago. The kitchen of Forestburn was low-ceilinged to keep in the heat and mostly constructed of stone; therefore, on a cold day, it was the very best place to be. But on a day like today, with the added stress of an important visitor, Toby was sweating rivers.

"Suppertime is near," Ailsa could always judge by the rising of the bread. It happened at the same time, every day, without fail. "Do you suppose Dragonblade will be here soon?"

Toby put the last touch on the finished marrow pie and wiped the beads of perspiration on her forehead. "I told you not to call him that," she told her sister. "And, aye, he will be here soon. I must go and change my clothes."

Ailsa followed her to the second floor of the manor. Her father had received license several years ago from the barons of Northumberland to build a fortified house to protect his family and farm. It was a stone structure with battlements, but no protecting walls other than the heavy wooden hedge fence that surrounded the immediate area of the home. There was a great hall, a solar, and the kitchen on the ground floor, while the upper floor held three large rooms and another smaller room used for bathing and dressing. Ailsa and Toby shared a room, their mother had one room, and their father another.

A servant helped Toby strip off her clothes. While Ailsa lay upon the bed and continued her musings about their alleged royal relations, Toby went to the smaller adjoining room and stood inside the great iron tub as the servant poured buckets of warm water over her body to rinse off the sweat. Scraping off the excess water, she then doused herself in rosewater before drying off and dressing in a surcoat of emerald damask, set with a scoop-necked collar of white satin and embroidered in gold thread. Her luscious hair was braided, left to drape over one shoulder. Ailsa got off the bed and danced around her as the servant put the finishing touches on her hair.

"Do you suppose Dragonblade will marry?" she asked.

Toby sighed heavily. "Ailsa, if you call him that one more time...."

Ailsa kissed her cheek and hugged her neck, careful not to ruin the hair. "Sir Tate, I mean. Would it not be fancy if he married you? You could live at Harbottle Castle."

"He will not marry me. He was married, once, so I was told."

"Where is his wife?"

"I heard that she died."

Ailsa looked sad as only a child can. "He must miss her, do you suppose?" From downstairs, they heard the front door bang open, a signal that their father had returned home. Multiple voices indicated guests and Ailsa began to jump up and down. "They are here, they are here!"

"I shall greet them," Toby leapt off the stool with the servant still fussing with her hair. "Go and see to Mother, Ailsa. Make sure she is tended to before you join our guests."

Ailsa protested. Toby took her by the hand and led her to the door of her mother's bower. The old woman, hearing their voices, called out.

"Toby!"

It was a bellow, a barely recognizable word. Toby, knowing by the tone that her mother's mood was not good, bade Ailsa to stay outside. It would not have been healthy for the child to go in. With a breath for courage, she ventured into the dark, musty bower.

It was like a chamber of horrors, a dusty, smelly, cluttered mess. Rats hid beneath the bed, waiting for the scraps of food that the invalid woman would drop. Judith Cartingdon had been a lovely woman once. But ten years of bad health, the inability to walk and the near-inability to speak, had turned her into a caricature of her former self. When Toby came near the bed, Judith picked up her good arm and hit her daughter in the shoulder.

"Where have you been?" she slurred. "I have been calling for you. Why did you not answer me?"

"We have guests for dinner, mother," Toby didn't rub her shoulder; she would not let her mother see that she had hurt her. "I had to see to supper."

Judith slapped her hand on the bed, drool running down the left side her face. "Supper for me, do you hear? Bring it to me now!"

Toby didn't argue with her; she didn't want to be near her mother, much less engaged in a futile conversation with her. She turned around to leave the room when Judith picked up a small pewter bowl and threw it at her, striking her on the top of her left shoulder. It stung deeply, but still, Toby didn't let on. She continued out of the room.

Ailsa was standing by the door, wide-eyed. "Bring her supper," Toby finally took the time, out of her mother's sight, to rub her back. "Make sure all of the plates are removed this time. And do not get too close. Her mood is foul this eve."

"She hit you again?"

Toby didn't answer her; the back-rubbing was enough. Smoothing her dress and saying a silent prayer that the meal downstairs progressed without incident, she descended the stairs into the hall below.

Sparks from the hearth had caught some of the rushes in the hall on fire; consequently, the hall was smokier than usual. Toby entered the room, curtsying to the men whose attention turned to her.

"Good eve, Father," she said. Then she looked at Tate. "My lord."

"Ah, Toby," her father greeted her, his normal chalice of wine in hand. "I was showing Sir Tate our humble farm."

Tate stood near the fire; there had been a slight mist outside and he raked his fingers through his hair to dry it in the heat. His eyes lingered on Toby in her emerald surcoat.

"This farm is anything but humble," he said. "The size and structure is impressive."

"You may thank me for the size and my daughter for the structure," Balin said. "Were it not for Toby, this would still be but a mediocre working farm, struggling to support a village."

More wine and ale were brought to the table. Tate had been accompanied by his entourage of men; the knights stood and drank their ale while the men at arms stood on either side of the front door in a defensive position. The squire sat on a small stool near the hearth, drying his thin body out.

"It is good to see a community that can support itself," Tate said. "There is so much poverty in the north that the peasants resort to stealing and begging to live. I have had a good deal of trouble with it on my lands."

Toby moved to pour herself some mulled wine. "Do you also not think, my lord, that the wars of the crown have created such poverty?"

"They do."

"Yet still you support another uprising."

Tate knew this moment would come; he just did not think it would come so soon. He turned fully to Toby, a radiant vision in the ambient light of the fire. The sight of her caused the harsh response on his tongue to ease. It was difficult to become angry with such beauty.

"I would not consider Edward's right an uprising, mistress," his voice was steady. "Do you deny the rightful king his entitlement?"

"Of course not. But is there not a more peaceful way?"

"If you have any suggestions, you have my full attention."

Toby wasn't a military expert by any means. Her gaze trailed to the two enormous knights standing near the hearth; their expressions were harsh and she did not like the feeling radiating from them. The men at arms were far enough away that they probably had not heard the conversation, but the squire was looking at her as if he had something to say to all of it. She almost wished she hadn't spoken out; too many times she would speak before thinking. This was one of those times.

"It would seem to me that the Queen would willingly relinquish the right to rule to her son," she said. "He is the king, after all. Unless the Earl of March has poisoned her against her own son, what mother would not want to see her child achieve his claim?"

"Power has a strange way of blinding those it serves," Tate said. "The king has attempted negotiating with the Queen. She does not believe him ready to assume the full mantle."

"And you believe that he is, my lord?"

Tate's dark eyes were intense. "I would stake my life on it."

There was something in his sincerity that Toby dare not question. Thankfully, the meal was brought at that moment, precluding the discussion from burgeoning into something uncomfortable. Her father, however, made sure to corner her privately as the guests took their seats.

"If I have ever asked one thing of you, now is the time. Behave tonight, if not for yourself, then for me. Please."

There was heavy alcohol on his breath. That was a usual occurrence, but Toby would have none of it tonight. "If you promise not to get drunk and fly out of control as you do, I shall promise to behave."

Balin's expression turned cold. "Mind yourself, daughter. And do as I ask."

With reluctance, Toby silently agreed and went to take her seat. She ended up seated at Tate's right hand; the knights were across from her, the squire on her right, and her father at the end of the table.

She was mildly uncomfortable seated so close to Tate. His hand was near hers and she put her hand in her lap. He lapsed into a quiet discussion with his knights while Toby silently attended her meal. When the knights laughed at something and she looked up to see what the joke was about, Tate apologized.

"I do not believe I have made formal introductions to you, my lady." He indicated the two armored men across the table. "These are my trusted friends, Sir Stephen of Pembury and Sir Kenneth St. Héver. They have informed me that I have been most rude by way of presentation."

Toby looked at the men, suspecting they said nothing to Tate about his rudeness. More than likely, the laugh had been at her expense. She simply nodded at them as Tate indicated the young man sitting at her right.

"And this is my squire, John of Hainault." The lad looked mortified as all eyes turned to him. His mouth was full of food and it was a struggle for him to chew and not choke. "Careful not to get close to him, else he might bite. He eats everything within arm's length these days."

"He is a growing boy," Balin said. "Though I have no sons, I was a lad once. 'Tis a pleasure to see a young man with a healthy appetite."

Ailsa made her grand entrance at that moment. Not strangely, she singled out the squire and planted herself firmly between the young lad and her father. She had a tendency to like older boys. Her big green eyes were fixed on him, his clothing, his hair, even the way he held his spoon.

"Gentlemen, my youngest child, Mistress Ailsa Cartingdon," Balin said. "I hope you do not mind that I have allowed her to join us."

Tate passed a cursory glance at the child, who had eyes only for his squire. The knights barely looked up from their meal. The squire, however, seemed clearly uncomfortable.

"Hello," Ailsa said to him.

The young man swallowed hard. He cast the girl a quick glance. "Hello."

Ailsa watched with interest as he practically buried his face in his food in an attempt to avoid talking to her. "What is your name?" she asked.

"J-John," the boy replied.

"How old are you, John?"

"Fourteen years."

"Are you a knight yet?"

John glanced at the men seated around him, silently begging for help. Tate took pity on him. "He is not yet, mistress."

Ailsa fixed her attention on Tate. "Are you Sir Tate?"

"Ailsa," Balin hissed at her, shaking his head.

Tate responded. "A natural question to a strange man sitting at her table. Yes, mistress, I am."

"Why do they call you Dragonblade?"

Toby nearly choked; in fact, only a large gulp of wine helped the clot of mutton slide down her throat. "Ailsa, behave yourself."

"But I just want to know."

"Now is *not* the time." Toby turned to Tate. "Forgive her, my lord. She is young and without tact."

"That seems to be a family trait."

Her cheeks burned at his dig as she remembered her vow to behave. "As you say, my lord."

From what he had seen that afternoon, it was not like her to submit so easily. He found himself alternately pleased and strangely disappointed that she had not reacted. He cast both sisters a final look before returning to his food. "Bad manners aside, I will also say that beauty must be a family trait. It is too bad that one characteristic negates the other."

Ailsa's attention had returned to the squire by this time and Toby merely continued to eat. Balin, fearful that Tate would push his daughter to forget her promise to behave, poured himself more wine and changed the focus altogether with talk of the pear orchard he had planted two years ago on the southern edge of town.

Tate listened to the old man talk, largely saying nothing in return. The more Balin drank, the more he talked. Tate eventually discovered that Balin had nothing more vital to say other than discussing agriculture and that his political knowledge was limited to very basic elements.

His argumentative daughter seemed far more intelligent, at least enough to keep Tate's interest. All the while as Balin spoke and drank, Tate was acutely aware of Toby seated next to him, silently eating her pudding. In fact, he was hardly aware of what Balin was saying at all. He kept hearing the soft music of Toby's voice instead, echoes from their earlier conversation.

Dinner was over, but not before Tate was nearly bored out of his mind by Balin's drunken chatter. The knights had eaten their fill and were given a room in the *garçonnaire*, a small two-room house next to the main house. Its sole purpose was to house traveling guests, usually male. With Tate's approval, they retired for the eve and took the stuffed, dozing squire with them. The men-at-arms, who had remained by the door for the duration of the meal, were given some food and moved into the warm kitchens.

Balin, sensing that perhaps their liege wished some time to himself in front of the fire, excused himself and the girls. A word from Tate stopped him.

"I would have a word with Mistress Elizabetha, if I may."

Balin wasn't sure if he should allow his daughter to be alone with him. She had restrained herself admirably throughout the meal, but there was no knowing how long the restraint would last. Balin would hate to wake up in the morning and discover that his liege had confiscated his lands in a fit of anger. Taking the jug of wine still left upon the table and convincing himself he needed it to sustain his courage, he left Toby alone with the great Lord of Harbottle.

Tate was still seated, watching Toby as her gaze moved to everything else in the room but him. He studied her profile, the way her cheeks curved, the soft pout of her lips. He thought perhaps that he should gouge his eyes out because he was growing more enchanted with the woman by the moment. It was purely based on her appearance and he had no time to waste with such foolishness. Thank God they would be leaving on the morrow and he would be done with this stupidity.

"I will only take a moment of your time, mistress," his voice was quiet. "Will you please sit?"

Toby sat down on the bench opposite him. There was something in her manner that suggested she had something better to do than sit with him. He eyed her, sensing her displeasure. An entirely different subject suddenly came to mind. "How old are you?" he asked.

She looked at him, surprised. "I have seen twenty-one years, my lord."

His dark eyebrows lifted. "And you are not yet married?"

She gave him such a look that he nearly burst out laughing. "My father needs me."

"One has nothing to do with the other."

"You will forgive me, but I do not see how that is any of your affair."

"It is not. It was simply a question."

"Is that what you wanted to speak to me about?"

Tate scratched his chin; the more agitated she became, the more humorous he found it. "Not really, but now you have peaked my interest. You are a beautiful woman and your father is wealthy. I cannot imagine that you have not had men falling over themselves to vie for your hand."

She sighed harshly. "I suspect you will not stop asking these questions until you have had a satisfactory answer."

"That is possibly correct."

"Then I will tell you, succinctly. I have not married because there is not a man in England who would want to marry me."

"That is an extremely broad reason. Why would you say that?"

She lifted a well-shaped eyebrow. "Do you find me agreeable? Compliant? Following you about like a stupid sheep?"

"Hardly."

"Nor shall you. Men do not like a woman who knows her own mind."

He couldn't help the smile on the corner of his lips. She saw it and it inflamed her.

"If you are done laughing at me, I shall bid you a good evening and go about my business."

She bolted up, but Tate was quicker and grasped her arms before she could get away. He yanked her harder than he had intended and nearly pulled her across the table. As it was, she ended up inches from his face.

"You are not leaving until I am finished," he found his face strangely warm to have her so near. "And I was not laughing at you, not in the least. I simply find your manner intriguing and your answer honest."

If Tate was warm, Toby was on fire. Her breath was coming in strange little gasps. "You find my manner horrid," she breathed. "You have said so."

"I never said horrid. I believe what I said is that you have an appalling lack of manners."

"Then you have answered your own question as to why I have never married."

"You realize that you have condemned yourself."

"I would rather be myself than pretend to be someone I am not. Woe to any man who cannot accept me as I am."

He stared into her eyes with that strange hypnotic sensation that Toby had experienced once before. She could feel his warm breath on her face. Just as quickly as he grabbed her, he released her. Toby caught herself before she fell, like a fool, on the table. Shaken, she resumed her seat.

Tate collected his own seat. He took a long drink of wine because he needed it. There were too many strange thoughts floating about in his mind regarding the woman across the table. Angry with himself, he focused on his reason for speaking with her.

"I will expect you to show us the herd at dawn," he said. "I have much to do tomorrow and do not want to be held up at Cartingdon."

"Aye, my lord."

"Can you give me an estimate of the worth of the sheep?"

Her brow furrowed as she struggled to focus on his question, not the heat from his stare. "The top of the market would be six silver florens a head. The wool will sell for twice that for a bale. In all, I would estimate you could gain a thousand gold marks for the entire herd when everything is sold. Leeds would be the best market. They have a huge export industry."

It was a pleasing number. Tate gazed at her a few moments longer before nodding his head. "I thank you, mistress. I know you are anxious to get about your duties so that you may retire."

"I will make sure a meal is prepared and sent with you on your journey tomorrow."

"That is kind of you."

She cocked an eyebrow. "Contrary to what you apparently believe of me, I do have moments of kindness and obedience, my lord."

He gave her no indication of what he thought of her comment. Toby begged his leave and stood up, feeling his eyes on her, wondering why it disturbed her so. She was to the door when she heard his voice again, soft yet commanding.

"Hold, mistress."

She stopped. By the time she turned, he was already standing behind her. His steps had been so silent and swift that she had never heard him approach. Toby's breath caught in her throat as he reached for her neck; for a moment, she thought he was going to throttle her and put an end to her atrocious behavior. Given their first meeting, she probably deserved it. But his hands forewent her throat and grasped her shoulders instead, turning her so that she was once again facing away from him. She felt a warm finger brush the upper part of her shoulder, as gently as a butterfly's wing. It was more than an improper touch and she should have scolded him. Instead, she couldn't stop the shudder than ran down her spine.

"What is this?" he asked quietly.

She was still trying to catch her breath, but she craned her neck around and was barely able to see the angry red welt left by her mother's bowl. Two choices raced through her head; either the truth or a plausible lie. She settled for both.

"I was in my mother's room and accidentally bumped my shoulder," she said.

Tate's face was expressionless. "You should be more cautious."

"I know. I am clumsy at times."

He didn't reply, but there was something in his gaze that suggested he did not believe her. Later, when she climbed into bed beside the sleeping Ailsa, visions of Tate Crewys de Lara danced in her head.

Read the rest of **DRAGONBLADE** in eBook, paperback, and audiobook.

ABOUT KATHRYN LE VEQUE

Medieval Just Got Real.

KATHRYN LE VEQUE is a USA TODAY Bestselling author, an Amazon All-Star author, and a #1 bestselling, award-winning, multi-published author in Medieval Historical Romance and Historical Fiction. She has been featured in the NEW YORK TIMES and on USA TODAY's HEA blog. In March 2015, Kathryn was the featured cover story for the March issue of InD'Tale Magazine, the premier Indie author magazine. She was also a quadruple nominee (a record!) for the prestigious RONE awards for 2015.

Kathryn's Medieval Romance novels have been called 'detailed', 'highly romantic', and 'character-rich'. She crafts great adventures of love, battles, passion, and romance in the High Middle Ages. More than that, she writes for both women AND men – an unusual crossover for a romance author – and Kathryn has many male readers who enjoy her stories because of the male perspective, the action, and the adventure.

On October 29, 2015, Amazon launched Kathryn's Kindle Worlds Fan Fiction site WORLD OF DE WOLFE PACK. Please visit Kindle Worlds for Kathryn Le Veque's World of de Wolfe Pack and find many action-packed adventures written by some of the top authors in their genre using Kathryn's characters from the de Wolfe Pack series. As Kindle World's FIRST Historical Romance fan fiction world, Kathryn Le Veque's World of de Wolfe Pack will contain all of the great story-telling you have come to expect.

Kathryn loves to hear from her readers. Please find Kathryn on Facebook at Kathryn Le Veque, Author, or join her on Twitter @kathrynleveque, and don't forget to visit her website at www.kathrynleveque.com.

66947931R00225

Made in the USA
Middletown, DE
16 March 2018